THE
NEXT
WIFE

LIZ LAWLER

THE NEXT WIFE

bookouture

Published by Bookouture in 2020

An imprint of Storyfire Ltd.
Carmelite House
50 Victoria Embankment
London EC4Y 0DZ
www.bookouture.com

ISBN: 978-1-80019-143-3
eBook ISBN: 978-1-80019-142-6

PROLOGUE

What was she thinking?

Did she honestly think he would just let her walk out and live a life without him? That there would be no consequences? No price to pay for destroying *his life*?

She would learn soon enough she was wrong. And be under no illusions about the trouble she was in. There was no hiding place for her, and no escape either. The top of the front door was bolted tightly, too high for her to reach up and unlock it without standing on something, and he'd taken the back door key after locking it and had the key safely hidden in his trouser pocket. He would put it back afterwards, after he'd finished dealing with her. She was somewhere inside this house, and soon, very soon, he would find her. Her perfume would give her away. Lead him where the scent of sweet jasmine and soft lavender grew stronger. He just had to follow his nose. Then he could punish her.

In the kitchen he picked up a heavy mallet, its double-sided, spiked-faced head shiny new. It was well crafted with a generous wooden handle for a good grip. He used one like it often to tenderise tough cuts of meat, to break down tough muscle fibres to a silky softness that melted in the mouth once cooked. This one would only be used once, and then got rid of. He didn't want reminders, or any microscopic cells of her blood finding their way into his food.

At the bottom of the wide staircase he stood still and listened. The house was never silent. Tick… tick… tick… clocks keeping time, passing time, *stealing time* with their endless arrogant ticking. Wooden floors and wooden doors creaked and sighed and moaned with age. But once you were familiar with hearing them – these sounds of aging and time – you could hear the other sounds trying to be unheard. She was being very silent, but the longer he waited the harder it would be for her to stay silent and hidden.

His fingertips brushed against the flock wallpaper as he climbed the stairs. The familiar velvet-like texture comforted him – the laurel leaf design in keeping with the period of the house. She had wanted to change and modernise their home, but he was all for tradition. It was a shame she didn't share the same values, didn't see the role she had been given to cherish when he placed a ring on her finger. She had broken her vows and thought she could be free.

He stilled halfway up the stairs as he heard a soft whimper. The sound was too young to have been made by her. It cut off abruptly. An infant cry – and his grip on the mallet handle was now less sure. How selfish of her to hide with the child. She must know she put them both in danger. He imagined her hand pressed over the small mouth, her eyes desperately urging the child to be still and quiet. Perhaps she thought hiding together might protect her, might ward off her punishment. She was a selfish mother to have taken such a risk. He was in no mood to be lenient, in no mood to take pity.

At the top of the stairs he strengthened his grip on the hammer. Through the landing window behind him sunlight shone across the oak floor, turning the polished floorboards the colour of autumn leaves, their surface pitted and marked with the imperfections of the past. Mothers and fathers and children had walked this floor and their maids and servants swept it clean. This house had served seven generations, if not more, and soon it would only be him left standing – the last of the line.

There were seven closed doors to choose from, three on each side of the corridor and one at the end. The master bedroom was third on the right and it was to this door he went. As he neared it he heard again the sound of whimpering, followed by a shushing noise as she tried to quieten the child. It was too late for that. He breathed in the air around the door and placed his hand against the grain as if to absorb her essence. He stroked the wood's silkiness before reaching for the doorknob, the cool round shape of it familiar in his palm. It turned with the lightest pressure and let him in.

Her yelp moved him further into the room with a sudden step. He looked down to where she hid by the side of their bed, her eyes full of fear. Her legs were tented to hide the child from view, her arms wrapped around her knees, and her hands cradling the small head to shut out the sight of him standing there. Sitting like that on the floor she reminded him of a drawing he'd seen by a German artist of a woman cradling a dead child, and he remembered learning about the artist's husband, that he too was a doctor.

As he raised the mallet from his side, her eyes pleaded with him, but any notion to change his mind passed as he noticed the suitcases on their bed, packed with everything she was taking.

He tried to smile for her, but his face was full of sadness at what she had brought them to. She would get her wish to leave him. He was granting her that, just not in the way she had hoped. She would be leaving behind her suitcases. Leaving behind clothing and shoes, trinkets and adornments, all the things she felt necessary for her new life which she wouldn't need any longer.

And when that too was all gone, every physical reminder swept away, he would be left with only the memory of her – a scent of sweet jasmine and of soft lavender – that would become part of the air he breathed. Become part of the house forever.

CHAPTER ONE

Martha King shivered as she looked through her binoculars at the face of the man getting out of the car. She shivered not from the cold air blasting under the collar of her coat, but from seeing that face again. No matter how many times she had seen him over the last two weeks, the shock didn't seem to lessen. It was uncanny how his features hadn't seemed to change, how he didn't seem to age. The house he was entering seemed to have stood timelessly too. The front door, the same dark green; the heavy curtains, with the same curved swags. Nothing altered. Nothing changed, except the height of the hedges grown above the stone wall wrapping the property nice and neat, private and safe from prying eyes.

And the woman, of course. She was a change.

Martha thought the house would lay empty forever, would never have a light on inside or a car on its driveway again. Watching and waiting and for it then to happen had tested her sanity and given her a false hope that the lights on inside the house were from before. And then cruel reality reminded her it was the present. Her memories were fading on so many other things, like paper drawings bleached from the sun – she had difficulty seeing them clearly. Yet here, they were painfully vivid. She had been kindled by those memories when she saw the new couple arrive. Rooted to the spot, stuck in a trance, just seeing, disbelieving; a silence in her ears as her eyes took their fill, before a sound intruded. Her laugh, as she was carried over the threshold. The sound of such joy shocked Martha's ears awake, shocked her that such a sound could be allowed after what happened. As if regard for the past was all forgotten.

They'd been ensconced in their new home for over two weeks now, and Martha was there every day watching. Casually passing by, or stopping outside to stand and stare as if looking up at something of interest in the sky. On the odd day when rain was predicted, she took shelter in a spot under a tree in the field behind the house, and used her binoculars. Or she would go in the car, as she had today, parking it down the street to wait out the rain. If anyone noticed her, and so far not a single soul seemed to have, she was ready with her answer – she was a birdwatcher, a lover of nature, and spring was the best time to spot wildlife – and be ready to show her copy of *Collins Complete Guide to British Wildlife* from the library. For now, though, she was invisible. Just an old lady pottering about with her shopping bag containing a thermos, sandwiches, binoculars and library book, minding her own business.

A pattern had emerged over the last few days. Each morning he would step out of the house at seven thirty, wearing a suit and carrying a briefcase, get into his car and drive to the hospital. Martha followed him the first day and found driving behind him in peak-time traffic a challenge. She'd caused a bother to other drivers somehow, with car horns blaring at her for something she had done wrong. Since then she only drove to the house, as the car found its own way there, and watched the comings and goings of his new wife, just like she was doing now.

She was certainly full of energy, this new wife – light and quick as she came out of the front door and bounced on the balls of her feet in her running shoes. She stretched arms and legs, bending and pressing and limbering in her bright blue Lycra for over a minute, and then proceeded off at a pace down the road, her long dark hair up in a ponytail, swinging from side to side across her shoulders. Martha gazed after her and then, realising the house stood empty, she made her way up the drive to peer in through windows she once looked out of.

Her anguished cry trapped the air in her throat, and she had to relax the muscles in her face and purse her lips in order to breathe out. She had expected it to look different, changed from her memories of it, not for it to be exactly the same. The lamps, the paintings, all of the furniture – it was all just as before. He had changed nothing for his new wife.

Martha didn't need to imagine what it felt like to be inside this house. She could feel, as if she was touching it now, the raised threads of the brocade fabric as she smoothed the arms of the small Queen Anne chair. *Her chair*, reserved for her when visiting. A tear in the fabric, where an arm was worn, had been mended with black thread for lack of silver, but was only noticeable if you knew where to look or where to touch.

A heavy sting inside her chest had her quickly fumbling in her coat pockets for the tiny pump bottle. Her memories had brought back to life images and sounds so real that if she knocked on the window they would see her standing there looking in, as clear as she could see them looking out. She could hear music, and her eyes darted to the corner of the room where the piano stood. His graceful hands were moving over the keyboard, playing a melody that once soothed her but now made her shiver.

Raising her tongue she sprayed liquid into her mouth, ignoring the slight burn as she repeated the action. She rested her forehead against the windowpane, waiting for the sharp stinging in her chest to ease. It would settle in a moment and then she would be on her way.

Her eyes closed to shut out the ghosts in the drawing room. How could he bring his new wife here and not change a thing? Had he no care to change it? Was he happy to have his new wife touch the same things, see the same things? Maybe he got a kick out of watching her walk around the house touching things, unsuspecting; felt pleasure at her not knowing? Martha suspected he did. He would not have changed. A leopard cannot change its spots. No more than this man can change his ways.

Adrift in the memory of it all, she lost time and stayed still, standing with eyes closed and memories open. She was startled out of her trance as something touched her shoulder, and she swung around too fast. The woman neatly saved her from falling, and Martha gratefully kept a grip of the hands holding her upright, trying to catch her breath and offer her gratitude. 'Oh, my dear, you gave me a fright, but thank you for catching me.'

Up close, his wife had startlingly blue eyes, the same turquoise as the hydrangeas Martha chose for the grave.

Her smile was warm and generous, and her voice full of care. 'I'm so sorry. I didn't mean to startle you. Are you here to visit me?'

Martha shook her head. 'No, my dear, I'm not. I thought this was my friend's house till I peered in the window and saw that it isn't. Silly me, I've got my roads mixed up, I think. Hers is the next road along.'

'Do you want to come in and catch your breath, have a glass of water?'

Martha stepped back from the window. 'No, thank you, dear. I'll be on my way as she'll be waiting. You have a lovely home. Have you been here long?'

'No, not long at all,' she replied, smiling again as if unable to contain her happiness for any length of time. 'I'm newly married and I'm getting used to everything being new, including my new name. Which, by the way, is Tess Myers.'

Martha did well to hide her surprise, lowering her eyes and moving her shopping bag to the other hand. 'That's your husband's name then, is it?' she asked.

'Yes. Dr Daniel Myers. That's my husband.'

Martha bade her goodbye, offering thanks again for being saved from a fall, her hands trembling so badly she had a job to get the car keys out of her bag. As soon as she could she got into the car and sat in it shaking, her mind whirring with what she had just learned. He *had* changed something after all, which would allow him to hide in plain sight. He'd changed his name.

CHAPTER TWO

Tess held a wooden meat mallet up to the light, wondering if it would be unhygienic to use it on the steak. She'd found it in a drawer of kitchen tools that she'd not got round to cleaning yet. It might have been there years. The utensils all looked old – the potato masher and rotary egg whisk had green-painted handles. She decided against using it. The steak probably didn't need tenderising as it was a nice dark red with a good trim of fat along its side.

She'd not given much thought to preparing this meal as her mind was buzzing over getting the job. She hadn't expected to hear back so soon, after having the interview only that morning.

The thought of going back to work filled her with relief. She was not cut out to stay at home. There was only so much cleaning her brain could take. Deciding where to start each day, whether to shine old furniture back to new again or clean a cupboard full of tacky Delftware that had been left unused for too long, was not how she wanted to spend her days. She'd prefer to pay for a cleaner, and would when she was back at work. After working for a living for the last decade she wanted to get back out there and do the job she had trained for. Otherwise she'd stagnate in this new place and get lonely.

Apart from the occasional nod she got from the quirky old lady she met a few days ago, she didn't know anyone yet. She had spent the last month getting to know her new home with its far too many rooms. Its grandness made her feel like she was a visiting guest. It would embarrass her to ever say she had a drawing room and a library with a proper rolling library ladder for the wall-to-wall and floor-to-ceiling built-in bookcases. She'd only got as far as dusting the old books, but they'd all seemed very highbrow in blocks of different colour denoting different collections. She still expected to wake up and find she had been living in a dream house.

To be told they were moving somewhere new had come as a complete shock and not how she'd imagined starting married life. She assumed that they would live at his flat in London on the doorstep of St Mary's Hospital where they both worked. But in the blink of an eye her old job was gone, as he'd got a new one in the city of Bath. Two weeks after their honeymoon they moved. She'd been alarmed at the idea of leaving the familiar for somewhere she'd only heard of, resisted being swept up in the vortex of his excitement for living somewhere new.

When they first arrived she had gazed at the house waiting for him to say he was only joking, but when he took a key out of his pocket she was stunned that the house she was looking at was really theirs. They'd driven along a wide road of walled and gated properties and then Daniel slowed the car and drove it through wrought-iron gates that were open. She'd thought he was making a U-turn until he carried on up the driveway and parked by a wide garage. She'd looked to where he was pointing at a pale stone Georgian house rising three floors to chimney stacks atop a grey slate roof. Tall windows in perfect symmetry gave a glimpse into some of the rooms, and in the one above a pillared porch she'd seen a chandelier hanging with a long drop from the ceiling. She'd felt herself floating until the thought of *how did one change the lightbulbs?* helped pin her back to the ground.

Completely thrown, she could only stutter when she asked how many bedrooms it had. He'd laughed and said not enough once children arrived, and she'd been reminded of her guilt for letting him think it could happen soon. On their honeymoon he'd suggested they start trying, that neither of them were getting any younger. He'd been delighted when instead of her swallowing her contraceptive pill she spat it out in the sink before getting into bed. In the night she'd taken another one as he lay sleeping, as while she wanted a family she didn't want one straight away. She wanted to be a wife first and to have time with just him as they'd only been together a few months. As selfish as that seemed, with him nearing forty, it was important to Tess to feel she was wanted for herself alone.

She'd shrieked with laughter when he picked her up and carried her over the threshold of their new home. Where yet another surprise waited.

The house was fully furnished, and looked lived-in. So much so, Tess expected to meet its occupants. He'd set her down on a black-and-white chequered floor next to a tall ebony grandfather clock, and her eyes had taken in the sweep of the wide wooden staircase, backed by a dark red wall. When the clock gave a resounding bong she'd laughed with nerves. The hallway was long and rectangular with three doors either side. Tess slowly wandered along the hall, peering in through the open doors. On the left and from front to back was a drawing room, library and a study. On the right a dining room, a cloakroom and the kitchen. A short passageway next to the stairs led to a back door and a downstairs bathroom. Hanging over the radiator in the bathroom she'd found a heavy cotton skirt in a khaki brown as if left there to dry.

In a daze she'd walked around the rooms gazing at sofas and armchairs, tables and ornaments and lamps and clocks. Many paintings hung on the walls in all the rooms, and in the corner of the drawing room a baby grand piano was hidden under a velvet cover. The kitchen cupboards brimmed with china and silverware and crystal, and pots and pans hung on hooks above an old stove. She'd climbed the stairs to the first and second floors and found all the beds made ready with white linen. She counted them and wondered why on earth would they need seven bedrooms?

It was as if the family who lived there before had upped and left the house and all their possessions behind a hundred years ago – the furniture was old and the white linen threadbare. Daniel had laughed at her bafflement before telling her the contents came with the house, leaving her to imagine how much it all cost, and feeling guilty for not being able to financially contribute. In London she'd only ever rented her flat and had come to this marriage almost empty-handed after spending her savings on the wedding.

Tess returned from her reverie when she heard the front door opening, and waited eagerly to greet her husband. He looked immaculate as he walked into the kitchen. His tall figure moving fluidly towards her gave her butterflies. His black hair, free of any grey and cut short, had a hint of a side-parting, and his naturally pale skin drew attention to his dark eyebrows and sea-green eyes. In a suit cut from cloth that bore a label with only the tailor's name and their location in Mayfair, he looked like someone very much in charge, and very sexy too. She went to kiss him, but stopped at the look he passed.

'What's wrong?' she asked.

He gestured towards her clothing. 'It's still early. Anyone could knock on the front door.'

She laughed lightly. 'Well, it would be no one we know. No one knows where we live yet. And anyway, you like these pink pyjamas. I've only just put them on after getting out of the bath. It's seven o'clock in the evening in case you didn't know.'

He didn't laugh back, but instead raised his eyebrow at her. He removed his suit jacket and hung it carefully over the back of a chair before joining her at the stove. Tess knew her face had gone red. He'd made her feel embarrassed and now she didn't want to tell him her good news. Instead, she mumbled that dinner would soon be ready.

He eyed the two steaks waiting to be cooked, the dish of tinned peas waiting to be popped in a microwave and the frozen chips she was placing in the oven. He waited while she adjusted the oven temperature before giving his unimpressed opinion.

'Is this what we're eating?'

Tess was startled. She'd never heard him being peevish before, and she was mildly shocked by his manner. It wasn't like she was offering him beans on toast. He was getting steak. She turned to tell him he should be grateful for what he was getting, but he was ready for her.

'Look, Tess, I don't want us to get off to a wrong start here, so things need to change.' His tone of voice was careful, as if it were important that she listen to him. 'I'm not saying this to sound unkind, but coming home and finding you dressed like a teenager isn't appropriate. We're not living at my flat anymore. We live in this house now. You should dress for dinner. We have different standards. No doubt we will be entertaining in the future and how you present yourself will be noticed. I don't want you judged as…' He frowned, sighed, screwed his eyes shut, before quietly saying, 'Slovenly.'

Her eyes could not have got any rounder, or her heart thud any harder. Her husband had just told her she was an embarrassment to him. She wanted the ground to open up and swallow her. Standing there in her Asda pyjamas with him in his sophisticated attire was a stinging reminder of how ordinary she was. She had no answer for him. She'd been dressing like this when they were on their own in the evenings from day one. Had he been thinking all the time that she shouldn't be? She felt an unbearable ache in her throat from holding back tears and wanted to hide away fast.

'Look at me, Tess.'

She didn't want to look at him and let him see how wounded she was. Instead she bowed her head and heard him sigh again.

'Look, this shouldn't upset you. You're perfect. I just want to make sure everyone sees that. We just need to work on the small stuff.' He lightly plucked at the material of her top. 'You needn't look for cheap goods anymore. You're top-shelf, Tess.'

Her insides squirmed. He'd made it sound like she was penny-pinching, but she wasn't mean, just mindful that bills came first and buying a bargain was better than being broke.

She stood rigid when his arms went around her, not wanting this hug, and shut her eyes to hide her tears of shame. His fingertips brushed her wet lashes, and she heard him breathe out yet another sigh, lasting longer this time.

'Tess... let's not allow this to be a point of argument between us. Please see that I am only trying to help.'

His voice gentle and his words unrushed made them no easier to hear. He smoothed her hair back from her face, and then gently clasped the nape of her neck.

'Work with me, Tess,' he urged in a soothing tone. 'You'll see I'm right. I promise.'

She kept her eyes closed when he stepped away from her, wondering when she should make her escape. With her appetite gone she just wanted to be alone under the covers of her bed with the lights off to hide her humiliation.

'Tess,' he called out lightly. 'Stop standing there, I've said my piece. Don't let it spoil the whole evening. I've got you a present. So open your eyes like a big girl and come and see it.'

She opened her eyes to see him fetching something out of his briefcase and felt bewildered. *Another perfume.* The third in as many weeks. Was he spoiling her or did he think she stank? *Slovenly.* She couldn't get the word out of her head. He'd have been better off buying her some fancy pyjamas seeing as the ones she wore offended him. Or an invisible cloak to hide her for when she embarrassed him. The pale pink box he handed her was tied with a tiny black bow and with trembling fingers she untied it, wishing she didn't have to do this right now as this scent would remind her of this horrible feeling of lowliness.

He took the perfume from her and trickled a drop on the inside of her wrist. Then, raising her hand near his face, he breathed in the fragrance before pronouncing his judgement.

'Not quite as I imagined. Not quite what I was hoping for.'

Later in bed, a tear in her confidence gaped wide as she wondered if he was referring to her and not the perfume. Was *she* not quite as he imagined, *she* not quite what he'd hoped for?

Sara, her best friend and sole bridesmaid, had jokingly quoted, 'Marry in haste, repent at leisure,' but she hadn't meant it. She thought Tess was the luckiest girl in the world. And so had Tess. She had met a man, enjoyed a whirlwind courtship, and hadn't once thought things were moving too fast. She'd thought him the most elegant-looking man she had ever seen. He was thirty-nine and a successful doctor and had wanted her as his wife. Was he now regretting that?

Her mind wouldn't stop dwelling on the things he'd said. Everything had seemed perfect considering the upheaval they'd just gone through of moving to a new house in a new city, and a new job for him. Had she missed something that might have alerted her? Had he been quieter or different with her? Was he stressed by it all? His new position as a consultant vascular surgeon held more responsibility. He was in charge of a team of doctors and his time was spent training and supervising, whilst carrying out his own clinical duties and managerial roles. He was responsible for running outpatient clinics and coordinating complex theatre lists. The operations he performed were as physically taxing as they were mentally draining. The patients were the sickest in the hospital and went ahead of any other 'urgent' cases. When they went wrong, they went spectacularly wrong. Vascular surgeons had a reputation around the hospital for having the God complex, not surprising considering the pedestal their patients put them on after saving their life.

She looked at the sleeping face on the pillow beside her, making out his features in the dark, wishing she'd not let tonight happen. She'd fallen into the complacency trap and had taken for granted this new beginning. He may have hoped that by living here they'd live differently, be different people, dressing for dinner like in a bygone age? Not that she'd carry on wearing her pyjamas during mealtimes. Tonight, old fears had raised a finger of doubt in her mind, making her feel like a child again. She was not good enough to have been chosen for this grand house. She was letting it down. While he, with his bearing, epitomised the characteristics of someone who should be there.

What if he were to fall out of love with her? She had taken his love for granted until he revealed she wasn't always so pleasing. She could lose him if he found other things about her not to like. A sickness settled in the pit of her stomach at the thought of that. It would destroy her. She could lie there in self-pity for being embarrassed and having her feelings hurt, or she could take heed of his words. Show him she loved him.

Sighing quietly, she wondered at the ways she would have to change, pondering this dismantling of her, and how this new version of her would all come together. In separate pieces or as one whole part? Bits of her old self piled in a heap as the assembling began. What if it didn't fit her properly? What if a missing part couldn't be found to fit? Would the bits and pieces piled in a heap of her old self be put back together again? Or would they be discarded as damaged and tools put down?

CHAPTER THREE

The following day she rose early, determined to show her husband that she had taken on board what he'd said. The slight against her character still stung, but she was moving on from it, mindful of how new they still were, mindful of the gamble they'd taken to love each other after so little time getting to know one another. Whirlwind romances leading to marriage needn't end at the first hurdle, if they were both mindful of avoiding the problem happening again.

Last night needn't have been an issue if she had known from the start he wanted to introduce some changes into their marriage. Then he could have told her in a more teasing manner without any upset being caused. She would lose the habit of throwing on her pyjamas after a bath and get into the custom of dressing more properly until bedtime. And in future be mindful of any undercurrents.

Hopefully, after tonight, he'd have a better opinion of her and wouldn't say anything to spoil this overture she was making. He was lucky she was not spending her day sulking and that she was the forgiving kind. And he was lucky she was resilient and able to get over hurt like that.

This gesture today was her being mindful. She had dinner already planned (no peas or chips on this menu) and the ingredients already prepped for something delicious. She'd been working steadily throughout the morning to get things ready, to have food and the dining room all sorted, leaving her time for some pampering. She'd waxed her legs and treated her hair to a deep condition. Her skin was silky soft from bathing in aromatic oils. Her toes and fingernails were painted a metallic blue, and her favourite jeans, the ones he liked best, were out ready on the bed. She would wear her hair down and wear her most feminine top – a baby blue affair that hung from her shoulders with long flowing sleeves. Her silver summer flip-flops, far too pretty to wear on any beach, which was why she never had, would suit perfectly the look she was aiming for. With everything now decided on she was left at imagining his surprise, and anticipating the reaction she'd get when he walked through the door and got a look at her. Yesterday was the first time she hadn't kissed him goodnight. She'd feigned sleep so as not to have to while she nursed her wounded pride. She'd feel differently tonight dressed up. She'd be confident again.

Making her way back downstairs she heard the doorbell ring. A delivery van was parked on the driveway, and boxes were piled up outside the door. One extremely large one was standing to the side. The delivery man handed her a small screen to sign, before pointing to the large box. 'Looks heavy, but it's not,' he informed her. 'I'll bring it into the hallway if you like?'

Tess thanked him, telling him she'd manage on her own, shocked by the sight of so many boxes with her name on.

A short while later their presence in the hallway was an obstacle to get around. *What had he bought her?* she wondered. It seemed like an awful lot of parcels and boxes if they were 'sorry' gifts. A one-word text message popped up on her phone. *Enjoy.* One word, but it was enough to put a gleeful grin on her face and send her in search of some scissors.

She slid the largest box to the centre of the floor and set about peeling off tape, before running a blade of the scissors through the sellotaped seam of the lid. She raised up the flaps and saw at the top of the box a quality dress bag folded carefully and felt a thrill. She lifted it out and hung it by its hanger over a door. She repeated this action five more times, getting more excited by the minute. He must have spent a fortune on her. Eager to see what was in them she unzipped the first one.

Her face grew comically alarmed at the colour of the dress – a shade of washed-out lavender a granny might wear, and in a style that would also suit one. A *for fuck sake* went off in her head. Had he gone out to find a granny to choose it or had he one in mind that could wear it? She hoped to heaven they were not all the same. By the time she came to the last one she was fizzling with disappointment.

Out of six dresses not one of them was to her taste or what she would wear. Each dress, undoubtedly elegant, with sensible hemlines and modest necks and nipped-in waists, screamed out the same thing. *Not her.* Not now, not ever. They were dresses for an older woman, an old-fashioned woman, an afternoon tea of cucumber sandwiches and Earl Grey type-of-woman. Was this how he saw her, dressed like this? Was this the change he was after?

Despondently, she opened the other parcels. Court shoes in flats and medium heels, in black and navy. Open-toe sandals that only a woman with a crippling foot problem would wear if it came down to a choice of comfort or fashion. They were ugly and brown with wide straps and silver buckles at the sides. Cardigans and jumpers spun from softest wool were spoiled by the drab colours he'd chosen, no doubt picked to go with the plain A-line skirts and pleated trousers. Pure silk blouses with round lace collars had her eyes popping in despair at the thought of finding matching pearls and clip-on earrings. *Where were the designer jeans and hoodies and pretty tops, the modern styles in shops she could never afford?*

Rubbing her face in frustration at the complete let down, she picked up the last package. Feather-light considering its size – comparing it to the last one she had opened, which contained a pair of ladies' leather slippers in a horrible burgundy red – she ripped it open without a care and frustration turned to bewilderment at the sight of exquisite lingerie. The satins and silks and delicate lace slipped through fingers like a waterfall. All in exquisite colours she could love.

She stared around the hallway at her wardrobe of new clothes and saw the conflicting directives. The ugly clothes were for how he wanted others to see her, while the delicate scraps of material in her lap were for his personal viewing only. She could take it as a compliment that he spent such time choosing these clothes, and wondered when he had. From his office at work this morning, or last night after she'd gone to bed? Choosing it all would have taken a while, and again she could take this as a sign he cared, and she might have – regardless of whether she liked them or not – if it didn't feel like she was being controlled. If she gave in to this and accepted them, was she not in danger of losing herself? Or was she reading this all wrong and it was simply a case of poor taste? On someone like Kate Middleton they might look divine. She was a beautiful willowy brunette. On Tess they'd hang past her knees and make her look like a frump. He was asking a lot of her because he cared. All she had to do was not mind having to change.

Early evening, and the sound of his key in the front door set her ready to shock him. The idea had come to her in the last few hours and she'd quickly revised how she would look tonight. She sat in a Queen Anne chair instead of going to greet him, poised and straight-backed, feet flat on the floor and knees pressed together. His eyes opened wide in surprise as he stepped into the room. She now rose from her seat and went to take his briefcase and jacket. Her graciousness marked the occasion of her new attire. A lace-collared blouse, an A-line skirt, finished off with a pair of flat court shoes. She'd styled her hair differently too, in a low bun, giving her the look of a provincial schoolmistress.

'My, you look different,' he eventually said.

She smiled. 'How was your day?'

'Busy,' he said. 'Yours?'

'Busy,' she murmured, beginning to feel like an actress on stage, playing the part of 'The Lady of the House', modelling best behaviour. 'Dinner won't be long,' she said sweetly.

'Better, much better,' he declared, after taking a longer look at her.

She waited for him to burst out laughing and admit to making a bloomer with his choices, but instead he carried on the charade. He stepped over to the mahogany drinks cabinet and picked up a small sherry glass from a silver tray. Holding it by its delicate stem he offered her a drink.

'May I pour you a glass of sherry?'

She feigned a demure look, refusing politely. 'No, thank you.'

He put down the glass and gave her an acknowledging nod as if to say *well done*. He was monitoring her drinking. He didn't deny her a glass of wine in the evening, but was careful not to pour her more, no doubt thinking it wise to drink less when trying to conceive. She felt guilty for this deception – telling lies was not in her nature. She should have told him the morning after that she'd taken the replacement birth-control pill that she wasn't quite ready, but she had chickened out.

He poured himself a neat whisky, taking a sip, before looking at her over the rim of the glass. 'Have you tried on everything?'

She flushed at the intensity of his gaze, at the meaning of his words. A polite enquiry she would normally be able to answer if he was making polite conversation, or wasn't looking at her that way.

'No. Not everything,' she replied, throwing him a slightly indignant look.

His eyes wandered slowly down her body, stopping too long in some places. 'Well, do you want to go and choose something now?'

'I'm not tired,' she replied, almost snappily, and saw his eyes darken.

'Did I say you were?' he asked in a tone that surprised her.

His voice was what had first attracted her. She had heard it across an auditorium when he gave a lecture and it had made her toes curl. When the lecture ended, without thinking, she'd joined a short queue of people waiting to ask him questions. When it got to her turn he waited politely for her to speak and when she didn't a warm amusement entered his eyes and he whispered something no one else could hear. 'I saw you sitting at the back.'

She didn't recognise the voice he was using now and wondered if he spoke this way to others. With slow rises and falls. It sounded a little unpleasant, instilled an uncertainty to her mood. She shook her head, thinking she would tell him she was getting uncomfortable with this play-acting, and ask him to stop messing about and tell her how awful she looked in the clothes.

'Well, do you? Want to go and choose something?'

That tone again. Where was he going with this? Perhaps she should let him carry on and see how far it went. But if he spoke like that again, she was likely to tell him to fuck off. Then he'd be shocked, having never heard her swear before. She found herself nodding.

'Good. I'll join you shortly then. And, Tess…'

She halted as she reached the door.

'Wear something less.'

In the bedroom, wearing black bra, panties and stockings, her dark hair still up in a bun, she waited nervously. Standing close to the bed, she knew she looked awkward. Stiff. Not sexy. Not able to relax. As he entered the room, her nervousness increased as he slowly advanced towards her. She raised her hands to cover herself. He pulled them down by her sides. Turning her to face the bed he held the back of her head and rested his forearm against her upper spine. With that leverage he easily pushed her so she bent over the bed. She heard him behind her, unbuckling his belt, unzipping, getting ready, and decided this should stop. She didn't want to make love this way, her back towards him. She wanted him to hold her lovingly and end this silliness, to turn her to face him so they could kiss. She made to move and felt his vice-like grip on her hips.

'Hey, back up,' she chided. 'What's your rush?'

His answer: fast fingers, fast actions, tearing the gusset of her panties, her yelp ignored when his nails caught delicate parts. Her cry ignored when thighs made to part.

'Stop! You're hurting!' she cried.

No warning, no pausing, he thrust in fast. A second thrust to push in fully took her breath. Holding tightly to her hips, bearing down on her back, he kept still what was his to enjoy. He had the power to do to her whatever he liked. Dragging and burning and shaming her flesh with all his might.

Her mind was slipping, elbows buckling, wrists burning, arms kept straight, hands spread flat on the bed. Muscles straining, on the verge of giving up, when suddenly he pulled her up hard against him, her breasts grabbed to lock her in an embrace. A low groan let her know it was ending. Then his crushing weight lay heavy on top of her, his breath hot against her skin, and *his* skin, slick with sweat, sliding over her. He planted a wet kiss in her ear and asked if she wanted dinner. She gave a shake of her head, keeping her face pressed into the bed.

When he finally moved she covered her nakedness and shivered as if ill with fever. A weakness spread throughout her body and she could barely raise her head to see if he were still there in the room, still in her presence.

Sounds from the kitchen identified where he had gone. A clanking of dishware and ping of metal said he was now serving himself dinner. The lovely dinner she had made him, meant to have been shared across a table illuminated by the candles that never got lit. Then silence, and she guessed he was eating. He'd be hungry after expending all that energy. While she… Her throat closed in upon her at what she thought, at what she felt, at what she couldn't bear have in her mind. *Why? Why* had he just done that to her, as if she were nothing more than a plaything? She felt dirtied and used, and right now she wished she'd never met him.

A short time later she heard piano music drifting up the stairs. He hadn't told her he could play the piano. He was playing Chopin. He had played this piece of music to her in the car during their honeymoon as they drove through Cornish villages and along winding roads, one hand on the wheel and his other clasping hers. She liked it then. Now it just made her utterly sad. That he chose this moment to let her remember something quite special, after what just happened on this bed.

CHAPTER FOUR

Martha had tears in her eyes as she tied the ribbon back around the bundle of condolence cards. She had read them so many times she knew them off by heart. Carefully, she packed them away again in the small wooden box with her other precious possessions. Many of her memories were inside this box, and even though she looked at them sometimes, she wished she could recall where she got them and what they might mean to her. She kneeled down to push the box under the bed where it was kept safe from harm's way and then got back up to sit on it. She stared at the flowery wallpaper. The light blue flowers had been vivid once and she could hear the ghost sounds of giggles after it was put up. She patted the bed as if Ted were there, wishing he was so she could talk to him. He'd advise her on what to do.

She mopped her face with a handkerchief and gave her nose a blow as she heard sounds downstairs in the kitchen. In a moment she'd go down and say hello, once her face was less blotchy and her eyes didn't give her away. Ted, if he were alive, would tell her off for crying and tell her to pack it in. She'd like to tell him she once nearly did, and but for intervention she'd be up there with him now keeping him company. That memory was still vivid in her mind.

She'd been mortified when led away from the railway track. More so, when she saw it would be Father John taking her confession. He'd asked her what it was that changed her mind, no doubt hoping it was divine intervention? She never told him it was the sight of her shopping bag. The ridiculousness of how she would look, standing there at the pearly gates with her Tesco shopping bag in her hands, and hearing God asking her why she thought she would need it. He didn't have a shop up there.

She was grateful for whatever it was that saved her that day. Apart from it being a mortal sin, there was a day of reckoning to be had.

Four weeks on she could safely say he was not a mirage. Right now, this minute, he was no doubt at home in his house, never suspecting he was being watched. She just hoped she had the same courage to one day step out and show herself.

Jim was making tea when she joined him. The layout of the kitchen was practical and minimalistic, with just the essentials for two people. Everything needed was out on the surfaces. Jim, a stickler for having things put back in their rightful places, had labelled the cupboard doors with their contents to make it easier to find things. Simple words like plates and bowls, biscuits and Weetabix had been written in bold black capitals, causing Martha to wonder if in a past life he was a primary schoolteacher, and had forgotten to stop practising these habits.

He seemed to have lived with her forever yet that couldn't be so because while Ted was alive it was only ever the two of them there.

Jim had to have lived in his own house at one time; he'd had a wife once, a memory of a thin moody woman wearing click-clacking heels was crystal clear. He never spoke about his past and Martha, being private herself, was not the sort to pry. She was glad for whatever the reason he chose to be there. He had become a good friend and was easy company and in his fifties he was well house-trained. He kept house better than her.

She could tell by his face he had something to say. He put a mug of tea on the table in front of her and sat down. He cleared his throat a couple of times and pulled at his collar, a clear indication he was finding it hard to begin.

'Martha, you left the lights on this morning when you went out.'

She breathed easier, relieved it wasn't something worse.

He caught hold of her hand and squeezed it gently. 'And you left the tap running upstairs. It's all right,' he assured her as he saw her alarm. 'I've had the floorboards up and it's all drying. A lick of paint on the hall ceiling will see it right again.'

She squeezed his hand back. There was no point telling him she had no memory of it. It would only fret him more. 'Thank you, Jim. I'm sorry to have put you to that trouble. I'll take better care next time.'

'Martha, those things don't matter. But you do. I'm worried about you and you'd be doing me a big favour by having a check-up with a doctor.'

Martha inwardly sighed. That was the only downside to having Jim live there. He saw every little change in her. A mischief twinkled in her old grey eyes.

'What do you expect at eighty-four? I'm an old woman. I'm allowed an off day.'

His eyes showed his fondness and he briefly smiled. 'Tell me what year it is and I'll leave you alone.'

She gazed at him reproachfully. Disliking to be tested like this. 'OK, how about the month and the season?'

She refrained from smirking. She wouldn't be as rude as that. But inside she was feeling gleeful that she could answer him so easily. 'The month is March and the season is spring.'

Jim lowered his head, his eyes avoiding her. Reluctantly, it would seem. He pushed back his chair and got up to walk over to the kitchen window. He rolled up the kitchen blind and then opened the back door. Next he turned on the garden light.

'Can you see the trees, Martha? The apple and pears and the plums? And the blackberry bushes? Can you see them? They're full of fruit, Martha. Summer is nearly over. It's September.'

He sat back down at the table and there was a flush to his face, a worry in his eyes.

'You need to see a doctor. You can't go on like this. Wearing yourself out, day in day out, visiting that house. You can't keep tormenting yourself believing it's *him*! That's not possible, Martha. It's just not possible.'

Her upset was so great Jim had to fetch her spray. When she was recovered he saw her up to bed, leaving her with water, her spray medicine and her bedside light left on.

She heard the stairs creak as he went down them and knew he would sit up awhile worrying about her, believing she had something wrong with her mind because she forgot what month it was. *September.* Was it any wonder she would prefer it to be spring? She eased herself up against the pillows and reached over to open the bedside drawer. The brown envelope was still there and so was her magnifying glass. A moment later she was staring at his face from a newspaper cutting, holding the paper close to the light. The quality of the photograph was grainy, but under magnification she had no doubts. The man in this photograph was the same man she had been watching, the same man who got out of a car a month ago and let himself into that house. Changing his name to something else and removing his moustache did not change that fact. Jim was therefore wrong. It was possible. This man had returned home, he had come back to his roots, to what was familiar and once the home of his victims.

Martha stared at the eyes in the photograph. She had no doubts whatsoever that it was him. And no doubts in believing he could do it again. He had done it before. Coldly, brutally, without compassion. Why not again?

CHAPTER FIVE

Her eyes couldn't take much more of this crying. They were stinging as if they had been bathed in saltwater. She saved all these tears from throughout the night and only let them fall once he was gone. She'd kept one hand out of the water to keep it dry so that she could hold her mobile and talk to Sara while she was in the bath. She trusted Sara with all her heart and had told her most of it now, about the clothes Daniel bought, the surprise of pleasure she got from opening the door to all the deliveries and then the awful disappointment after seeing them, about how ugly they were, about how unworthy and embarrassed she'd felt standing in her Asda pyjamas.

'But that's not the worst of it,' she cried.

'So what is then?' Sara asked.

In fits and starts, between trying to quell her embarrassment and a rise of indignation for mentioning such intimate details, Tess finally got to the events of last night. 'He then asked me if I wanted any dinner! I can't get my head around it, Sara. Why would he behave like that? Why is it all going wrong?'

'Where are you now?'

'I'm sitting in the bath. Have been all the while we've been on the phone. I'm turning into a prune.'

'And Daniel? Where's he?'

Tess gave a short bitter laugh. 'Would you believe playing golf? It's as if nothing happened.'

Sara sighed heavily down the phone. 'You may not want to hear this, but maybe for him nothing has really happened. Nothing bad, that is. The clothes, he can be forgiven for. You can't blame him for trying, even if it does sound like he's trying to dress you like a member of the royal family. He's thinking of his position, possibly, how he imagines you should dress. And the sexy underwear is because he knows the real you.'

'Really, Sara? The real me? When have you ever known me to wear sexy underwear? I like my sports bras, and my knickers covering my bum with more than a piece of string. No, that underwear was for him to use me like a sex object! He... He... ' Her voice cracked and Sara cut in to make her stop talking.

'Hey, calm down, just calm down and stop speaking for a minute. I know you're upset, Tess, but just calm down a bit. Listen to me. I know you think what he did was terrible, but let's be realistic about this. He gets home from work and you're all dressed up like the Queen, and things just got a bit out of hand. He read the signals wrong, as simple as that, and you didn't put a halt to it soon enough. What did you expect to happen, you silly moo? Daniel's not a saint. He just read it wrong! And now you have to put it right again. Explain it to him. Truth is he probably already knows but is embarrassed to talk about it. Do you think you can do that? Do you want to give him a chance to put his side across?'

'I don't know, Sara. I thought he liked how I was. How I am. Comfortable and—'

'Ha!' Sara laughed, before pretending to cough exaggeratedly. 'Sweetie, you take comfortable to a whole other level. I can barely recall a time when I saw you in anything but your fluffy slippers and PJs. Whenever I saw you at work, I'd have to look twice to make sure it's you. Now that's not to say you don't look perfectly gorgeous in them, because you do, but you have to bear in mind most of your dating before you married him was spent shagging in bed. You've got daytime hours now to consider. Just get him to send it all back and go out and buy new stuff.'

'He got me a pair of leather slippers.'

'Send them back.'

'He got me a lavender dress only a very old, very blind granny would wear.'

'Send it back! Though maybe scratch that. Don't send it back. Bin it as a kindness to all the old blind grannies out there!'

'He hurt me.'

'I know he did, Tess. I know you don't forget. I know just how sensitive you are about fitting in.'

Tess stared at her naked breasts, at the faint blue bruises where his fingers gripped too hard. Her hips bore similar marks. Nothing so drastic as to stop her in her tracks if she found them unexpectedly. They were barely tender, and, if covered, not felt at all. It was how she came by them that made her feel them more. She'd had no control over what was done to her and dark memories from her past had flooded back. She'd not told Daniel about that part of her childhood.

She remembered Sara getting a carpet burn on the base of her spine from having sex on the floor. She'd laughed it off, saying good sex came at a price.

'Do you think I'm a prude, Sara?' she now asked her friend.

'No! You're not,' came her emphatic reply. 'And don't you dare start questioning or doubting yourself. You're full of insecurities, but you're not a prude. For you it's all about the love, being loved, but that doesn't mean to say you don't like sex. You just need to feel there is love behind it. That's what he needs to realise.' Sara paused for a few seconds, before speaking again. 'So, are you going to be OK, Tess? I'm wishing now it was another few weeks before I leave.'

Tess closed her eyes as she remembered Sara would be leaving next week. Her dream job of working as a nurse in the Australian outback, flying in little planes to far-reaching places to attend the sick or ferry them to a hospital, was finally happening. She would no longer be working in London as an intensive care nurse, and these long phone calls might not happen or be as possible. Her friend would be on the other side of the world, not in a city where Skype and internet access was immediate but in the middle of nowhere where radio communication or a satellite phone was more often used.

Tess forced some positivity into her voice. 'Don't say that. This is what you've always wanted. And I'll be fine. Just having a little wobble, and you've helped put me right again. So I'll be fine. I am fine! OK?'

'I hope so, you complicated little flower.'

Tess smiled sadly. In the eleven years since they were student nurses together, Sara had used this phrase a thousand times, changing the noun to suit the mood, or at Tess's dithering when ordering food. *You complicated chicken nugget. You complicated McFlurry.* Birthday cards though, every year, never changed – happy birthday *you complicated dear friend.*

'We'll talk again soon,' Sara said. 'Oh and Tess, put a cold flannel on your face before he gets home. I know what your face will look like now. It swelled up like a balloon when we watched *Me Before You.*'

After saying goodbye, Tess climbed out of the bath and looked at her face in the mirror. It was true. Her face looked like she was having an allergic reaction. Her eyelids were so swollen they half covered her eyes, her nostrils were shiny red bulbs. It would take more than a cold flannel to calm it down.

She breathed deeply, more easily now the ache in her chest had gone. She was better for talking it over, and now saw she was probably to blame for some of last night, waiting for him in her stockings and underwear. She had chosen black for God's sake when she could have picked something less obvious. She had all those beautiful colours she could have chosen to wear. She would talk to Daniel and tell him how upset she'd been and then put the whole thing from her mind. She didn't want to be miserable with him. She wanted to get past this, to be loving him again, to be feeling happy again. It was not much to ask for from a new bride.

Mid-afternoon she was coming to the end of her chores. The house was clean, dinner decided on (again no chips or peas on the menu) and she had just put fresh linen on their bed. She opened the bedroom window to air the room as it had an odour to it when warm, like a dusty sweet scent of dried petals. She sniffed the gold-and-ivory curtain material and got a whiff of musty sweetness and wondered when they were last taken down for cleaning. The smell was trapped in the fabric and no doubt in the carpet too. The people who lived there before had probably become used to it, the air smelling normal to them. She imagined the woman as elderly with her scents long standing in vintage-style perfume bottles with atomiser bulbs and tassels. Maybe these curtains had been hanging since the day they were first put up and never been cleaned, instead squirted with sprays of perfume. She would make it a priority over the next week to get rid of these old smells – take down all the curtains and have them cleaned, and find a carpet-cleaning firm to come in and do the carpets. Better she get it done now before starting her new job, than hope letting a gust of wind blow through would make it disappear.

She turned to close the window, feeling there was now too much fresh air as goosebumps rose on her arms, and was surprised when she saw the old lady standing by the gates staring in at the house. Her thin white hair was blowing on top of her head like white candyfloss and Tess worried she'd get cold standing so still. What was she doing there? Was she confused or just lost again? She'd told Tess on that one occasion when they spoke that she was visiting a friend on another street, only she got the streets mixed up which she discovered after looking through Tess's windows. Was she mixed up again? Tess had seen her a few times now when out running. Surely she wasn't still getting confused about where her friend lived, not if she was visiting her often? The adjacent streets weren't that similar and landmarks usually reminded people of the right way to go. The obvious reminder for most was the street name. She was old though, perhaps easily confused. If she didn't leave soon Tess would go outside and help her, maybe walk with her to this friend's house.

The ringing of the landline phone by the bed startled her. It so seldom rang she could be forgiven for forgetting they had one. Maybe Daniel was calling, having tried her mobile first which was downstairs in the kitchen charging and possibly on silent. She felt queasy at the thought of speaking to him, not yet ready to have that talk. She forced herself to pick up the receiver and speak in a calm voice.

'Hello.'

'Hello, is that you, Tess?'

For a moment she was speechless. Her mother-in-law was on the phone. She hadn't spoken to the woman since her wedding day and had only met her on that one occasion.

'Hello,' she said again for want of something to say.

'Is Daniel at home, Tess? Only I'd like to speak to him.'

Tess gaped at the phone, at hearing the abrupt request. The woman clearly had no time for pleasantries, or else her need to speak to Daniel was more urgent.

'Um, no, Mrs Myers, I'm afraid he's not. He's playing golf.'

The woman gave a small sigh. 'No matter. I just wanted to see he was all right. If he's playing golf I'm sure he is.'

'Has something happened?' Tess dared to ask.

'No, dear. I ring him every year on this day just to see how he is.'

Tess wanted to ask why, but before she could utter another word the phone went dead, and she was left shocked by the woman's rudeness. She had hung up without saying goodbye. Tess placed the receiver back in the cradle and sat down on the bed in a quandary. What a strange call. Why had his mother called, and why this day every year? What did September 12 represent? A celebration? An anniversary? It wasn't his birthday. So maybe the death of someone, perhaps a grandparent?

Tess eyed Daniel's large wardrobe and wondered if it held any answers. She walked over to it and opened both doors wide. The contents were the same as when last opened to hang away his ironed shirts. She had no idea what she suddenly expected to see or find. There would be nothing new in it as everything was what she'd unpacked, already seen, put there by her after moving in. His mother's tone was maybe just her way. Tess hardly knew her so there was no way of knowing if she was normally like that or not. Her cryptic reply was weird, though. *I ring him every year on this day just to see how he is.*

There was so much she didn't know about her husband, Tess realised. Their time together had only scratched at the surface of who they were before they met. They hadn't even exhausted topics such as first dates, first loves, first time. They'd each summarised their lives, their growing ups (hers harder than his) almost quickly as if to get to the part that really mattered. Them. In love. Finding each other. It was a forward-moving relationship with no time to look back on what had shaped them to become who they were now. Although, looking back, he knew far more about her than she him. After making love one night, then virtually living together in his flat with barely a month passed since they met one another, she'd opened up to him about her dream of having a large family one day. I want to belong, she'd told him. *I want to belong. That's what I want. I never belonged as a child.*

Her words hadn't scared him, which so soon into the relationship they could have. Instead they had encouraged him to make it happen. He'd proposed to her two months later, and on their wedding day had whispered in her ear just after they made their vows words she would never forget. *You belong now, my love.*

Tess sighed to herself. Remembering his words was what she needed right now. It had been an emotional few days, a rollercoaster few months, and last night was just an unexpected blip. No more than that. She wouldn't even mention it later. Nor about his mother's rudeness. She'd just say his mother called and leave it at that.

CHAPTER SIX

When Tess looked out of the window a short while later she was relieved to see the old lady was gone. If she saw her again she'd start up a conversation to gauge her mental capacity. She may just be a little eccentric and there was nothing wrong with that so long as she was safe, and knew where she was and where she was going. If this was confirmed Tess would rest easy and revert back to occasional nodding again.

Her spirits had lifted a little and she was now less worried about Daniel coming home. She would not make things awkward between them and had already decided to wear some of the new clothes again, a navy dress with a Peter Pan collar that would look OK if she wore her hair up in a high ponytail and her pretty flip-flops. Her legs were still tanned from summer, and her toenails only polished yesterday so there should be nothing he could find fault with. She squashed the negative thought, telling herself he wasn't out to look for faults. He was aiding her to look her best.

He smelled of fresh air when he returned, and had a finger-length width of colour across his high cheekbones. His dark blue golfing top fit snugly, outlining his broad chest, and Tess felt strangely reserved as she gazed at him. Mental images of the previous night's sex flushed her warm and confused her emotions. Like Sara said, she did like sex and she was strongly attracted to him, only not like last night when she was unwilling and he must have known. He seemed to sense her discomfort as he leaned against the kitchen counter, keeping his distance and folding his arms in a relaxed manner.

'Everything OK?' he asked.

'Yes.' She nodded.

'Anything I can do to help with dinner?' he offered.

'No, it's all in hand. Sea trout, salad and potatoes, and fruit salad for dessert. Is that OK?'

'It's more than OK. It sounds like a feast.'

His enthusiasm seemed a little overboard, but she was grateful to him for putting her at ease.

'Well, in that case I'll hop in the shower and change before dinner.' He stepped towards her and kissed her cheek. 'Pretty dress, pretty hair,' he said, and then frowned as he stared at her footwear.

'What?' she lightly challenged, and then afterwards wished she hadn't.

'Not what I would call sensible footwear for the kitchen, Tess. Maybe keep them for the beach. I'll dig you out a pair of shoes while I'm upstairs.' He gave her appearance a further inspection, and as if deciding on something gave a small nod. 'Maybe wear a little less make-up. Your face doesn't need it.' He smiled as if he'd been helpful, before taking his leave from the kitchen.

Tess stared at his retreating back. Her small bubble of confidence was burst. He undid the nice words in those last remarks. Had he meant them to be kind? There were facets to her husband's character she was starting to see more and more. His forceful opinion for one, and the swing from someone she knew to someone unknown was playing with her confidence. The last few days had thrown her off-kilter. A shift in the balance of their relationship had taken place. She felt as if she had been given a smaller voice, one of less importance than his. Had she allowed this to happen by submitting to wearing the clothes he chose? Given him permission to now correct her other choices?

Last week she would have been trailing after him up the stairs, lounging on the bed while he dressed, just to be in his company or to talk. Now, she was standing like a guest in her own home awaiting his return. That wasn't normal. In the space of three days something had changed between them. Since the evening he came home from work and found fault with what she was cooking and wearing he'd been different. It can't have started because of the food and her clothing surely? She needed to get back to how they were before then, get back to behaving naturally, otherwise she saw problems ahead. She poured herself a glass of wine to calm her thoughts. When he came back down those stairs she was going to tell him she was going back to work. This is what they both needed, for him to see her as she was before becoming a wife, a person who had things going on in her life other than what shoes to wear. Because he seemed to have lost sight of that.

She was a trained nurse with eight years' experience, not a wife from the fifties happy to stay home all day and bake cakes and clean house. She took a gulp of wine. She'd tell him good and proper and if he didn't like it he could lump it.

Without a nylon barrier covering her feet the shoes were rubbing the backs of her heels. She had kicked off the flip-flops when he'd returned with the low-heeled courts, and hoped when she took them off later her heels were blistered to make him feel guilty or sorry for acting like a prig. They had eaten dinner in near silence, with him sat one end of the long oval dining table and her the other. He was in a quiet mood with nothing to say despite glancing at her frequently. She could feel her resentment brewing. She'd eaten enough silent meals while growing up, her hearing always tuned and eyes watchful for a change in mood. Her childhood had left her with a built-in antenna for impending unpleasantness, and anxiety from always waiting for it to happen. Something was happening, but what? Was it the change to their lives coming between them? In that case she wanted to go straight back to London.

They were coming to the end of their meal and she, despite two further glasses of wine, had yet to tell him about her job. She cleared her throat.

'Before I forget there are two things I need to tell you. First, your mother called today. She wanted to speak to you, but I said you were playing golf.'

He raised an eyebrow. 'And you're telling me now? Did she say what about?'

Her insides tightened a little. She should have said something sooner. Maybe today's date meant something and was why he was in this mood?

'Sorry, I should have mentioned it earlier, and no, she didn't say what about. We didn't even talk. She asked if you were here and when I said no, she said OK and goodbye.'

'And the second thing?'

'I got a job. I start a week on Monday.'

He stared at her across the table and slowly, without saying a word, rose from his chair and walked out of the room. It was the second time in the space of a few hours she was left gazing after him. This time she got up and followed. He'd gone into the drawing room and was standing next to the drinks cabinet.

'Have you nothing to say?' she asked.

He remained silent, fixing himself a drink, before giving her his attention. A slight impatience flitted across his face, as if this was an effort. 'Why?' he eventually asked, in an off-hand manner.

'What do you mean, why?' she asked in return, vexed by his tone and one-word reply. 'It's what people do. They work. I work. I have a career. I'm sorry if that doesn't suit you or that I can't be at a different hospital to where you work, but I want this job. No one need know we're married, if that's what's bothering you. I haven't yet changed my registration name to my married name so I'll be working under my maiden name. You needn't be concerned that people will know about us.'

'I wasn't, as a matter a fact,' he said back. 'Eventually, some of my colleagues will meet you. It's no secret I'm married. No, Tess, you misunderstood me when I asked why. My why is because I thought we were trying for a family? Though I noticed you guzzling back the wine tonight. You said you wanted a large family and I see no reason to change our plan. So why go out and get a job? We don't need your salary. There is much to do in taking care of a house this size so it can't be for lack of something to do. So again, why get a job?'

She was tempted to blurt out she wasn't ready; he was making her feel so guilty when she knew they weren't even trying yet. But she wasn't ready, nowhere near ready after the last few days.

'Daniel, I've got a brain in my head which I wish to use. And yes, I would like a family, but I don't wish to sit around just waiting for that to happen. It's better that I work and enjoy being a wife, though I must say I'm not enjoying it at this precise moment.'

He raised his glass at her, the gesture ever-so-slightly jeering. 'You don't say.' Then he drank the liquid in one swallow. 'Well, that's not what you led me to believe before we married, is it? You said you wanted a large family. You said you wanted to belong. So what is it, Tess? Do you want a family or not? Or is this about last night? Is that it? Are you sulking, Tess, over a little rough sex and have now changed your mind?'

Her mouth opened in shock. She could feel blood draining from her face. *He had known it was rough?* He had known, and now he was what? Mocking her for minding? Her insides did a somersault. The room closed in as she focused on the man before her. *Where was the man she married? The one she was in love with?*

'I'm going to bed,' she said stiffly, trying to hold on to her dignity. 'I don't understand why you're behaving like this, Daniel, but it's not very nice.'

He laughed as if what she'd said was something funny, and she could only stare at him with hurt confusion. He winked at her and clicked his tongue as if he were letting her in on the joke, or geeing her up like a good little horse.

'It'll be like old times, Tess. You in your scrubs looking cute, and trying to get me inside a storeroom with you and into your hot little hands.'

Her face turned beetroot red, her eyes reproachful. Their passionate kissing and heavy petting – up to this moment – had been remembered in her mind as something to cherish and keep unsaid. They'd already slept together and it was this that had made her daring and behave wantonly, but not in a tarty way, not like how he was making it sound. Sordid.

'What's got into you, Daniel? This isn't you.'

It was as if a switch had been flicked inside him. His expression immediately changed, all pretence of humour gone from it. She couldn't read what was going on in his mind. His eyes had closed shut, his hands pulling at the back of his head to bring it down low, while his upper body rocked slowly in a back-and-forth motion.

Tess didn't know whether to stand and watch, or say something. She felt helpless from seeing him like this, at not knowing what was wrong with him. Was he ill? Depressed? It would make sense of his recent behaviour. Or was there another cause?

His voice was so quiet his first words didn't reach her. She'd missed something he said and now listened hard. His voice sounded defeated, the volume turned low. 'Best ignore me when I'm like this, Tess. Best for both of us. Go on up to bed now and forget what I said… about the job. I won't stop you or spoil it for you. I'm sorry… not just for now… for last night too.'

Tess studied his form. The back of his neck looked vulnerable with his head bowed so low. She felt his turmoil and ached to ease him, from what though, she couldn't fathom. This husband of hers was a complete mystery, she was realising. He never spoke of his family or friends; never spoke to them on the phone as far as she knew. His mother made it sound as if it were a once-a-year phone call, to check up on how he was because today was significant. He was so self-contained, wasn't worried about moving to a new city, moving away from everything familiar. Maybe friends or family didn't mean that much to him?

He'd wrung emotions out of her left, right and centre the last few days. Last night she thought his behaviour was appalling, yet now she wanted to walk across the room and hold him. But something stopped her. Something in his stillness said that it might not be the right thing to do. It might embarrass him. She backed away to allow him to be private, and called out softly instead, 'Goodnight, Daniel. I hope you sleep well.'

CHAPTER SEVEN

Martha had gone up to bed as cranky as hell, and was lying there now agitated at being unable to sleep and feeling guilty about Jim. She'd been feeling down all day, blaming him for it, for seeing his wooden calendar up on the kitchen wall that morning. If he'd left it alone, instead of twiddling with its knobs to get the day's date, she might not have been reminded.

The images came to her easily, crystal clear, as if her mind held only room for them, while other memories from her life were completely gone. She was sure stress was part of the reason why she was forgetting. She had a bizarre thought earlier that none of these images were real but dreamed up by a persuasive mind and had panicked until she remembered Jim's calendar. It was not false memories she was having, but reminders of that time. Today was an anniversary.

She remembered the very first time she met that man, thinking him far too suave and wondering why he'd not already married, but she'd kept such worries to herself knowing her voice would never be heard. She should have spoken out. She should have shouted her reservations right from the start.

She sucked back the cry trying to get free, for if she let it go it would tear her throat apart, and this she couldn't afford to let happen as it would only weaken her. Her strategy was to stay strong all the while he was still breathing and walking free. Only when he was no longer a danger to others would she let go, and, God willing, be able to then join Ted. She swallowed against the ache in her throat and sat up to drink some water.

She heard Jim's tread outside the bedroom door again, and gave a mild huff as it opened and he peered in at her. 'I'm not dead yet,' she informed him with a curt tone. 'So no need to keep checking if I am.'

His expression of mild amusement was telling her he was taking no notice – regardless of her grumbling he was coming in to see her. He sat down on the side of her bed, mindful of where her legs were, placing his hands in his lap, regarding her.

'Why can't you sleep?' he asked. 'It's nearly midnight.'

'Ooh, I'm so scared,' she sang out in a mock-scared voice, waggling fingers at him to look spooky. 'I might change into a bat and fly out the window.'

He softly chuckled. 'You're already a bat, and you fly off the handle when you want.'

Had she a mirror she would have seen her small wrinkled features resemble a wrinkly baby-faced monkey, with her large rheumy eyes luminous and her sparse hair fluffy around her forehead. He shook his head at her mildly, his voice barely telling her off.

'You came home very cold, Martha. Any colder and you would have had hypothermia, then it would have been the hospital for you.' He felt one of her hands. 'You're still chilled. How long were you standing there?'

She pulled the sheet up to her eyes like a naughty child, mumbling an answer that might be true. 'Not too long. His wife saw me out the window.'

'And how long were you standing there before she noticed you?'

Giving consideration to how cold she'd been, she hazarded a guess. 'Maybe an hour, maybe two? Not in the same spot, mind. Don't want someone calling the police on me thinking I'm looking to rob the place.'

'I don't think anyone would mistake you for a robber,' he pronounced dryly. 'Maybe for being batty standing there, maybe getting concerned and then calling the police.'

Her eyes turned mournful. 'It's the twelfth today, Jim.'

He nodded, to show he was aware. 'I know. I realised too late I should have left the calendar on yesterday's date.'

'You forgot, I suppose,' she replied, letting out a small sigh, rubbing a finger against the bridge of her nose to ease an ache. 'Otherwise I'd have been none the wiser. It happened on a day like today. Blustery. Cold. If I'd seen him today who knows what might have happened, if I'd had a knife in my bag?'

She said it quietly, impassively, as if the idea of carrying a knife in her bag was no big deal and Jim's face showed his alarm. His voice was firm. 'Martha, don't ever do that. Never carry a knife in your bag. Regardless of your age, you could get locked up for that, so don't be under any illusion age would save you.'

'Well, it wouldn't matter much if that were to happen, now would it?' she replied gruffly. 'If he was dead, it would be a small price to pay for putting something right. It sickens me that he's free. That woman he married can't be aware of who he is, which is why I'm still going there. I need to let her know about the man she married.'

'It's not him, Martha!' he declared forcefully, letting her hear his frustration. 'Please trust me when I tell you that!'

Martha turned her head away, not listening to him anymore. He was a stubborn man, refusing to believe what she could prove if he just went to that house and saw for himself.

'It is him!' she cried belligerently.

Jim had nothing to say to that. He sat there beside her now in silence, staring off into space in his own thoughts, and his quietness rattled her. Would he stop her going there again? Hide things away from her, like he had done with the car keys? She'd looked for them everywhere, in cupboards and drawers, and in the garden shed in case they'd been hidden in an old flower pot. She saw Jim now looking at her again. She could see a rare glumness in his eyes.

'Don't be getting all huffy on me, Jim. It's me who should be huffy. Hiding the keys like that when you know I have to go out shopping? I can't carry it all!'

'I do the shopping, Martha,' he calmly replied. 'And you stopped driving last year.'

'I did not!' she protested strongly. 'I drove recently. I sat in the car when it was raining.'

'Illegally,' he stated simply. 'You drove illegally. That is why I hide the car keys, why you won't be getting hold of them again. You were damn lucky you didn't get caught. Have you no fear of the law?'

Her answer was arrogant, a little self-righteous. 'The only authority I recognise is God's authority. His laws are what I abide by, not man-made laws. We people didn't create the idea that it's a crime to murder. God did!'

He was staring at her long and hard, his face as serious as she'd ever seen. 'I'm making an appointment for you to see the doctor, Martha. I'll come with you, so you won't be going alone. You could have got ill from standing out in the cold looking at that house again. It makes no sense to you when I tell you it's not him, because your mind is playing horrible tricks on you. It won't allow you to make sense of things, because at the moment everything in your mind has got a bit muddled. Your memories have got confused. And there's no shame in that and it's not your fault, but it can be helped. You can see any of the doctors at the surgery, one you like and can trust.' He sighed heavily. 'Do it for my sake, Martha. See a doctor.'

Martha stared at his tired face and saw concern in his eyes and felt an overwhelming fondness for him. Unflappable Jim, kind Jim, always there for her, poor man. He looked exhausted and yet he was sat on her bed at this time of night. She realised she had been selfish and hoped Jim didn't find her too much, that he wasn't longing to live somewhere else.

'You're a darling man, Jim,' she said to him now. 'Did I ever tell you that?'

'You did, Martha,' he answered, rising slowly from the bed, giving his arms and his long back a good stretch. 'But I appreciate you saying it again.'

'Well, I'm so glad that I did,' she said. 'Because it's true. You have a lot to put up with living with me. I'll go to the doctors and I promise from now on I'll try not to give you more grief.'

His eyebrows nearly disappeared into his hairline, his look saying he was not holding out hope on that happening. 'We'll see,' he commented dryly.

'I promise,' she said earnestly, with a hurt tone in her voice.

'OK, I believe you,' he answered quickly, sounding like he now did.

She looked up at his face, turning soulful eyes on him, holding the look for a few seconds…

'I won't go looking for your car keys anymore.' Then a wicked little grin spread across her face. 'I'll walk there instead.'

CHAPTER EIGHT

They had gone for a week without speaking about that evening, leaving what she'd witnessed shut away. Tess carried the image of her husband standing with head bowed, eyes shut and locked in turmoil and had hoped he'd talk about it at some point, but he hadn't so far. It was as if it hadn't happened. A line had been drawn underneath all of the upsets of last week and a truce of sorts had formed with Daniel bringing only his best behaviour forward.

He smiled at her, talked to her, but the conversations were of inconsequential matters, or about people or events that had no meaning to her. She could have these types of conversations with strangers. She in turn responded by taking care of how she looked and dressed for dinner each evening. She put away her flip-flops and boxed up the many pairs of jeans and tops she would no longer wear, swapping her old clothes on the shelves in her wardrobe for her new ones. She was showing him she cared, but inside she felt alone, as while there was a harmony there was also a void. She felt something shut off in him. And yet the day Sara flew to Australia he sent her flowers with a message on a card. *Thought they might brighten your day*, it said, showing he was aware that this day had been difficult for her. The thoughtful gesture made her feel reconnected to him, until they made love.

The intimacy was missing in the way he kissed her. He kissed her now with his eyes closed. The light presses he traced along the outline of her lips, the soft pressures and teasing that made her shiver with wanting, the soft groans as he pressed more firmly seeking her warmth as if he needed a part of her to be a part of him, absent from them now. Their kisses for each other were like signatures. Instantly recognisable. He kissed her now as if copying a signature not quite his own. She knew she was not wrong to sense something amiss; it showed in those absent caresses and his closed eyes.

Tess wondered if Sara would scoff at such a notion. She was in tune with Tess on many levels, but this was a hard one to explain. He had changed in the way he made love since that show of domination, and she wondered if that night had suppressed his passion or if he felt ashamed? She wished it had never happened as it gave her a squirmy feeling inside when she thought about it, like now. She gave her head a little shake as if to physically dislodge it and forced herself to focus on something else: the chores still to do today and the ones to do before starting her new job.

The trouble with her, she realised, was that she had too much thinking time. From Monday, her new job would put a stop to her obsessive thinking about her relationship. Daniel would have run a mile if he'd known how easily she was made to feel insecure. *You complicated overthinker* Sara would say if she was there.

She would say it, and then tell Tess to file her insecurities away in her imaginary filing cabinet and to leave them there, back with her 'overthinking' childhood. The filing cabinet in Tess's mind stemmed from being an unwanted child. She'd imagined a file with her name on tucked away in a drawer with its front cover stamped all over with the word 'REJECTED' each time prospective parents bypassed her in favour of another child. Tess imagined that file for most of her childhood, which was why she was feeling so damn sensitive and was resorting to overthinking things and wasn't ready yet to get pregnant. She wanted to be wanted for herself.

The last eleven years had seen her grow strong mentally for the simple reason that she hadn't given anyone her heart. She had boyfriends, but not loved them, so hadn't cared whether she was loved back. Now it was the most important thing in her life that she was loved and that she had qualities that could be loved.

Old insecurities were rising that she thought left behind in that file when growing up was all done. She was afraid of being rejected again. She needed to stop thinking this way or she'd find herself on shaky ground with her confidence gone. Daniel hadn't married her just to have babies. He fell in love with her. She needed to remember that before she ruined her future happiness.

As if to concur, the grandfather clock in the hallway gave four loud bongs. She laughed at feeling some relief for having her sensible head back on, and was grateful also for being reminded of the time. She still had jobs to do.

She squirted Pledge on the dressing table and knew she needed to find a cleaner who really liked polishing. It would take a month of Sundays to clean all the silver ornaments and painted ceramics out on display. She hoped all these things did come with the house as Daniel said and that he hadn't offered to buy the contents, because then she wouldn't have to feel guilty for wanting to get rid of most of it.

She wanted to change a few things in this house, especially the colours of the walls. They were all too dark, and probably why there were so many lamps in the rooms. The red wallpaper up the stairwell was overpowering and impractical. The laurel-leaf pattern with its velvety texture was a dust collector which she'd had to vacuum to get clean. She was relieved to be on the last job; the curtains in her bedroom that had been crying out to be cleaned since they moved in. She let the heavy weight of them drop to the floor and was grateful when she heard Daniel home and coming up the stairs. He'd help her put up the spare pair of curtains she had ready.

The seriousness of his face told her something was wrong. Alarmed she came down off the ladder.

'What's the matter?'

His gaze was fixed on the mountain of material lying across the bedroom floor. 'What do you think you're doing?'

'I'm just—'

He cut her off. 'Why have you taken them down?'

She stared at him bewildered. 'Well, why do you think? To get them cleaned. They smell.'

'Well, put them back up again, please!'

She gaped at him. What the heck was wrong with him to ask such a daft thing? He looked paler than normal like something had happened.

'Did you hear me?' he said, when he saw her still standing there, making no move to do it.

She was rooted to the spot, her brain trying to work out why there was a problem. Common sense was telling her to put up the new curtains. Apart from smelling better than the ones taken down, there was no other difference to them as the curtains in every room were identical.

'They'll be back in a few days once they're cleaned, and can go up then. They smell of dead flowers, or can't you smell it?'

He ignored her, and instead bent down to pick up the bundle of curtains from the floor. He placed them carefully on their bed. 'Put them back, please, and don't take them down again,' he replied in a dreary voice.

She blinked hard, keeping her eyes on him. His request was downright odd, and she didn't have a clue why. She heard him breathe in deeply, and then watched how bizarrely calm he became as he smoothed his hand across the material. She had to look away. It was worrying her to see him do that. Was this a mental problem? Did he have a form of OCD, some sort of anxiety disorder if things were rearranged or changed in his absence, which he found difficult to deal with? It would account for this behaviour if he did.

'I'll put them back,' she quickly said, wanting to get him out of the room before he tensed up again. 'Go down and get a drink and I'll get on with it.'

After he left the room, Tess was unable to move a muscle. The situation had lasted no more than a minute, yet her energy was gone, as if she'd climbed a high mountain. His strange behaviour had completely wiped her out. Did he think she'd damage them? They were just an old pair of curtains. She was going to suggest they buy new ones, but was staving off asking him to spend more money as he must have already spent a fortune. A troubling thought crossed her mind. Had their new home cost him too much? It was a millionaire's house so how had he afforded it, unless he was paying for it with an astronomical mortgage? If this was the problem he had every right to be a bit unbalanced.

Concern for him now overrode her qualms about his lack of intimacy towards her. He could be facing financial ruin for all she knew. The last thing on his mind would be his performance as a lover. If the cause was a financial predicament she would help fix it. They could sell this house and go back to London. She would work double shifts for the next year if need be.

By doing nothing, saying nothing, her deepest fear of all was she would lose him. Because something was definitely troubling her husband and she had to put that right.

CHAPTER NINE

He slept deeply the entire night. She knew this because she lay awake all night beside him, listening to his breathing, and taking comfort in knowing he was resting. They'd spent a pleasant weekend with him in his study catching up on paperwork and her occupying herself with cleaning and reading. Both evenings they went to bed early, but she'd slept poorly since Friday night. He made no further reference to the curtains once they were back up and in fact behaved beautifully following that bizarre episode.

After putting them back up she'd gone to find him to see how he was, and was greeted with a nice surprise. He'd nipped out to get their dinner while she was working and had it set out on trays. Fish and chips, a rare treat for them that they hadn't had in a while, with a dollop of tomato sauce for her on the side. Seeing that small added thoughtfulness had swelled her emotions. They'd sat side by side on the sofa with trays on their laps like they used to in London, enjoying simple pleasures and him attentive to what she liked.

He put on an old black-and-white movie and this too nearly made her cry. Not long into their relationship he'd found out she loved them. She'd shared a secret, of how as a child she'd mastered how to unlock this great big metal cabinet and taken black-and-white films from it to watch in secret at night. Then afterwards she'd put them back and relock the cabinet with no one being any the wiser. After telling him the story he'd gone quiet and had asked her why she'd had to do it in secret. She'd told him about her upbringing in a children's home but not about the rules.

He stirred in the bed, turning onto his side, and gave her a sleepy smile. 'Big day for you, Mrs Myers.'

She felt a huge relief. He'd remembered she was starting her job today.

'Miss Morris to you, if you don't mind,' she answered back mock-snootily.

He kissed the tip of her nose. 'OK, Miss Morris. Just so long as Miss Morris doesn't forget she's married. That she's a Mrs and not a Miss. I take it you're driving in with me, then?'

She shook her head. 'No, I'm taking the bus. I don't have to start till ten. They're giving me some induction days so it's more like office hours.'

He stretched fully before climbing out of bed. 'In that case, while I get ready, a cup of coffee made by you would be very nice indeed.'

She smiled at him, not trusting herself to speak. Her beautiful man was back. Overnight the person masquerading as him had gone away, and under the cover of blankets she crossed two fingers for him to stay away.

Lying there under the covers she watched as he walked over to the window to pull back the curtains and then get his dressing gown hanging on the back of the door. He looked back at her and did a hands-on-hips pose, trying to look stern but let down by his amused face.

'Are you going to just lie there?' he quipped. 'That coffee won't get made by itself, you know. Chop chop.'

She grinned at him, and then hoping she wouldn't ruin this moment she said, 'Can I ask you something a bit odd without you getting annoyed with me?'

'You can ask,' he said lightly. 'But if it's to make the coffee instead of you, then the answer is no!'

'It's not.' She smiled. 'The thing I want to ask you is this. You know all this furniture and stuff we have – did you have to pay an awful lot of money for it? Only I'd hate to think buying all of this, as well as the house for us, has put you under any financial pressure?'

She held her breath as he stared at her from across the room, and then felt her heart sing at his beautiful smile.

'You are a funny one to come out with something like that,' he said, sounding very amused. He sighed and shook his head at her, turning it slowly one way and the other, as if not knowing what to do with her. 'If I'm short of a bob or two, Miss Morris, I'll be sure to let you know, OK?'

'OK,' she mumbled sheepishly, waiting for him to be gone from the room before she smiled fully to herself. She felt gloriously full of energy as if she'd slept all night instead of none of it. He had given her a lovely start to the day, and the confidence to believe it was a new beginning. He'd implied they'd got off to a wrong start and said things needed to change. This change he was wanting could come by way of her working. Providing them both with a new outlook. Their lives would still be different than in London, where they were in a world of their own as new lovers, where work and normal things like washing and ironing and putting out bins was not part of it. They could have a new lifestyle here and build a home that people would love to visit. They could entertain new friends and become part of a wider community.

Thinking back to how they were, Tess could see now that the complex part of loving him hadn't presented itself. They hadn't uncovered enough layers to know one another well enough before taking the leap. She loved him as much as she did then, but would like to know more about him, instead of thinking sometimes she knew very little. It was September and she'd met him in February. This time last year they were still strangers and would have remained that way if there had been milk and bread and loo roll in the flat that day.

She'd almost decided not to go to the lecture when she looked out of the window and saw the weather. It was no milk, no bread and running short on loo roll that had her put on her warmest coat. She'd decided to go to the lecture and get provisions on her way home. That all changed when she heard him speak, when he made her toes curl.

The surprise was that neither of them had been aware of the other one working at the same hospital. While both worked in the same theatres, they'd never been in them at the same time. Tess had never assisted him as a scrub nurse during an operation. She'd heard of him, of course, but not once in the two years he was there had she spoken to him.

Their first date was arranged by him after that whisper in her ear. He wanted to meet her just two hours later to go for a walk and talk. They'd braved a quick walk through Hyde Park in the bitter cold and he'd held her hand in his coat pocket to get it warm, but they hadn't talked as her teeth were chattering too much. They made love that same day, almost through the night, and she'd never felt closer to anyone. In the morning he asked how old she was and what was her surname and then from February to May they spent every moment they could together. They ventured out to pubs and bistros, museums and galleries, but cut visits short in their eagerness to get back home to bed. Sara was right about that, they were always in bed, though *shagging* wasn't the word Tess would have used. She would have said, *loving* one another.

In May when he proposed, she imagined months of planning her wedding. He picked July, as why wait longer when they could just get on with being married, as nothing would change how he felt by having it later. So why wait? Tess wondered if his rush to be married had something to do with him getting a new job. That it was already on the cards then, and he hadn't wanted to lose her.

August brought her to this house. It put her at the beginning of a new life. Then September gave her a few surprises. She was no different to other brides, she supposed, she just needed to uncover more layers than most to know her new husband. Some layers she might not always like, but so long as she communicated this he would know. The same way he communicated he wanted different standards. She'd listened and not greeted him in pyjamas again. More layers, more knowing, was what marriage was about. And more tolerance too. Not every day could be lived happily ever after. They had to allow for blue days too.

CHAPTER TEN

Compared to St Mary's in London, with its arches and gold lettering and busy red-brick walls dusted by London traffic, Bath Hospital, despite the busyness of its nature, was an oasis of calm. With cool colours of cream and sand and soft green buildings.

Tess breathed in the fresh air and stared at the wide blue sky, and was glad for the first time that they had moved to this city. She was smiling without realising until an old man in a wheelchair passed by.

'Someone be happy,' he commented.

She grinned. 'Just starting here today.'

He saluted the side of the soft-cloth cap on his head. 'Where's 'ee to, then?' he asked curiously, in a Somerset accent. 'Heart ward?'

'Theatre, where all the operations get done,' she replied, in a solemn teasing way.

'The blood-an'-guts place, then,' he grimaced, before wheeling smartly away. His voice reminded her of Sara's warning that she wouldn't answer if Tess started talking like Pam Ayres. Tess had tried telling her Pam Ayres wasn't from Somerset, but it fell on deaf ears.

It would be funny if it was Sara who picked up an accent and came back speaking like an Aussie. Sara loved letting people know she was a Londoner, usually while travelling on a tube after a night out, usually drunk, and usually for the benefit of some poor tourist. Without warning, she'd call out in the loudest voice ever, 'Get the London Look', the one-time popular thing to say by females after putting on their lipstick, as they posed, hand on hip, practising a catwalk, keeping alive the old Rimmel strapline even though their new slogan 'Live the London Look' was more suited to what she was saying. Sara was expressing a sense of what London gave to her – a boldness – as if dressing in bright colours and having crazy blonde hair wasn't enough to already stand her out as having attitude.

Tess stopped reminiscing and stepped inside the main entrance of the hospital. The dome-shaped atrium with glass ceiling was home to an open-plan café, a shop, and a reception area. This was the hub. From here all wards, offices, and departments could be reached through a maze of endless corridors. She'd walked miles on her tour of the place at her interview.

Activity in the atrium was constant, people passing through the concourse to their various destinations. Some strode purposely, confident of where they were heading. Some took it more leisurely as they had a drip stand to consider, a catheter bag to remember – patients off the wards let out to roam half-dressed with bare legs and bare feet shoved into shoes. Invisible to those sat at the tables, the doctors, the nurses, the carers, having quick breaks, quick teas and breathers – a moment for them to be anonymous.

Tess breathed it all in – the noisiness, the busyness, the vividness – and felt a liveliness fire up inside her. It was a good feeling and confirmed for her she'd made the right decision to go back to work.

On the first floor a network of interlocking corridors all looked similar, but Tess knew where to go – she remembered from her previous visit.

She was approaching the end of the corridor when she saw the closed windowless doors set back a bit. Above them was the name of the department – Main Theatres. Deciding this was a good time to check on her appearance she fetched a compact mirror out of her bag. She checked hair, face and teeth.

She realised she was not alone. Turning her head she saw a man in blue scrubs. He was standing still observing her, and she blushed at being caught out. He had very fair hair and looked young, possibly early twenties. He was enjoying himself from the amused look he was giving. She snapped the compact closed and put it away.

'Whoever he is, he'll think he's a lucky guy,' he declared with a cheeky grin.

She stared at him and gave a small dismissive shake of her head, before turning her back on him – a brush-off to let him know she wasn't interested. Then she proceeded to the doors ahead. A second later he was standing beside her, swiping his ID card. The door buzzed to unlock, and he pulled it open. He looked at her curiously, his eyes smiling, a little flirty as she stayed out in the corridor.

'Were you coming in here, or were you following me? Or do you prefer corridors, I wonder?'

She gave a tiny huff, wondering whether to allow the doors to shut again so that she could present herself without him. Deciding it would be churlish she stepped into the department.

'I'm here to see Stella Malloy,' she replied.

'Well, I'll let her know you're here, then, shall I?' he said with exaggerated kindness in a sing-song sort of voice, as if she were a cranky old lady. 'Shall I tell her your name, or is that something you'd rather not give me?'

Tess's attempt to ignore him was proving difficult. Her clamped lips were holding back a smile. Aside from him being a little flirty he seemed very funny, and he *was* trying to help. And she was aware she could be working with this man today.

'Please, could you tell her Tess Morris is here to see her?'

Saying her maiden name came naturally to her. It wasn't that long ago she was using it all the time, and until she notified the Nursing and Midwifery Council of her married name she was legally obliged to use the name on the NMC register. She'd made Human Resources aware of that so it was all above board, so she hoped Daniel hadn't thought she was joking about her being called Tess Morris.

He led the way through a second set of doors to a reception area, pointing out some seats where she could sit while he disappeared through more closed doors to fetch Stella. Tess smiled politely at the receptionist behind a curved desk, who'd looked at her briefly before focusing her eyes back on a screen. She stayed standing and straightened her jacket, one of the ones Daniel bought, which she'd jazzed up by wearing it with a pair of more flattering trousers than the ones he'd chosen, finding after trying them on they made her slim hips look wider than they were. Something to do with the pleats at the front probably, and the fact she was only five foot three, and not tall and leggy enough for them. A round-neck cream T-shirt beneath the jacket made it look less fussy.

Alerted by the doors opening, she cleared her mind of her personal concerns and waited. The man was back, accompanied by a woman in her late forties, wearing the same colour scrubs and a pink theatre cap.

'Tess, so lovely to see you again,' Stella exclaimed, giving Tess a warm feeling of welcome. 'Did you find your way here OK? It's like a labyrinth out there. It was so much easier to find one's way around when departments and wards were just called by a name and didn't have letters and numbers added to them. I get lost for days when I step out of this department. It's a wonder any patient gets a visitor, their relatives get so lost sometimes.'

Tess lightly laughed. Liking Stella straight away, remembering her being nice at the interview. She liked the woman's soft Irish accent as well, the lilt in her voice.

'The instructions you sent me were perfect, especially the tip on what bus to catch. So thank you.'

'Well, that's good. The number four will get you straight here, whereas some buses will take you all around the houses.'

'I wouldn't mind that on another day,' Tess said. 'To get to know the area better. I still can't get over how much countryside there is around here. It feels very green and airy after London.'

'London?' the man commented curiously, having been standing there silent.

Stella glanced at him. 'Sorry, Cameron, I should have introduced you.'

He stepped forward and extended his hand to Tess. 'Cameron Gould. Lovely to meet you, Tess. I'm new here too, ST1 general surgery. But not new to Bath – I was born here.'

'You're not new anymore, Cameron,' Stella remarked, scrutinising him with a wily amused look on her face. 'You stopped making tea for everyone a while back.'

Tess was surprised. His position meant he must be older than she'd thought. If he was an ST1 he was already a doctor in first year of Speciality Training. Nearer to late twenties. His blond hair and boyish features made him look younger.

'Nice to meet you, Dr Gould.'

'Please, feel free to call me Cameron. And if you'd like a tour of the hospital grounds give me a shout later. I'm in theatre three all day.'

Smiling at them both, he disappeared through the swing doors and Stella glanced at Tess in a knowing way. 'Bless his little cotton socks for trying. I didn't think the poor man was going to leave us.'

Tess felt a slight awkwardness and hoped Stella hadn't thought she'd encouraged Cameron. 'I think he was just being friendly.'

'He was,' Stella replied, before changing the subject. 'Come on, I'll take you through to the changing rooms, get you sorted with your locker and where we keep scrubs and then give you a tour of the place. You're with me all day, so ask as many questions as you want.'

Tess said she would, and kept pace with Stella while her eyes clocked everything she passed. She shivered a little with first-day nerves, telling herself that in a few days everything would seem less new. She would be familiar with these surroundings and be part of this place, just like she had been back in her old job in London. It was only now dawning on her she was never going back there. It had been like her second home for the last eleven years, three as student and eight as qualified. She had gone without any fanfare or a party, with hardly even a goodbye. Which said something about her. She'd been too much of a loner having only one friend. She now had a chance to change that. It would be good for her to make new friends, good for Daniel too so as not to be solely reliant on him for companionship. He had a busy life already without having a clingy wife adding to it. Otherwise he might get bored or feel suffocated. Independent. That would be the new her. An independent woman he was proud of.

CHAPTER ELEVEN

In the female changing room Stella showed her to an empty locker and handed her the keys for it. She pointed out the rack of shelves against a wall packed neatly with laundered blue scrubs in different sizes, and to a large laundry skip against another wall where dirty ones went after use. On a bench in clear polythene was a pair of new theatre shoes waiting for Tess. She was impressed that someone had actually thought ahead to order her new shoes before her first list. She had waited three months for her own theatre shoes at St Mary's. Leaving her to change, Stella said she'd see her back out on the floor when she was ready.

Tess felt like the new kid on the block. Even though this clothing was as familiar to her as the next person here, wearing it made her feel self-conscious, like she was putting on the uniform for the first time. Checking her hair was under her cap, her nails were clean, and her shoes fit, she went back to Stella to begin the tour.

As Tess stepped into an empty operating room she gave a contented sigh. Everything was familiar. When asked what she did for a living, Tess would say she worked in theatre and then have to explain – not that type of theatre, up on a stage. But not unlike it either. In both there was a performance, in both an audience. In both, fine performances were the norm, but sometimes something could go badly wrong. And occasionally you could be lucky enough to be in the audience when pure brilliance is on display with a star performing.

Tess didn't ask any questions as she was shown along an L-shape corridor of theatres. It was a different hospital, but the layout was the same. The same named storerooms, the same labelled shelves with the same supplies to equip a smooth run every time something was needed. In the Recovery Room, where patients were still sleeping, she heard the same phrases she'd heard a thousand times before. Nurses calling encouragements. 'Open your eyes. Squeeze my hand.'

Tess smiled to herself feeling a lot less new.

At one o'clock she took five minutes out to visit the bathroom to cool down a little. Her face felt warm from lots of smiling at new colleagues, whose names she had already forgotten, as in blue scrubs and theatre caps it was hard to distinguish one from the other and put a face to a name. In time she would get to know them, but for now she would make do with using eye contact to start up a conversation.

Stella was easy company and Tess felt genuinely welcomed. She was not only friendly, she was organised.

Tess knew what she would be doing for the rest of the week: a two-day induction course held in the Education Block, starting tomorrow, followed by two days' orientation back in the Theatre Department. So an easy week, really.

'You know we have a band 6 position available?' Stella said, as they stood ready to leave the office, where they had been sat chatting. 'Did you not feel like going for it?'

Tess shrugged her shoulders lightly. 'I think I'll be happy being a band 5.'

'After being a band 6?' Stella sounded surprised.

Tess felt her recently cooled face warm again. She wasn't about to tell Stella that her reason for not going for a more senior position was because she had a husband who thought they were planning for a family, and who might question the wisdom of taking a senior position when she would be stopping work soon. She was wondering if she should tell Stella she was married. It might be better in the long run for her to know now.

The opportunity was interrupted by a knock at the door. A porter wanting to let Stella know a delivery of pizzas had arrived. She suggested Tess could look in some of the unoccupied theatres as most of the morning operation lists were now over so Tess made her way back to the corridor of theatres.

She had yet to see the emergency theatre. An operation had been ongoing for the last three hours. Earlier, she'd seen the circulating nurse come rushing out to fetch something, and had felt a tension in the air. The circulating nurse or 'runner' then fairly flew back to the theatre carrying what was urgently needed.

She was about to step into another theatre when the doors to the emergency theatre opened, and the trolley was wheeled out. She stood back against the corridor wall to allow the patient to pass. A network of wires stuck out from his neck as if the man was part human part machine. The trolley was loaded with medical equipment, short drip stands attached to either side of it, holding swaying bags of fluids and blood, and monitor screens brightly lit up so as to see at all times heart rate, blood pressure, oxygen levels, and ECG trace. It was a critical watch right now to be ready if the machines emitted warning beeps to respond if the blood pressure dropped or the heart rate rose. Or worse still – flatlined.

A huddle of staff followed. Their euphoria and relief was palpable as they talked fast among themselves. She heard the word 'brilliant' said a few times. 'Bloody brilliant' from one. Then some made room for the person joining them so that they could give him a small clap. Wearing a theatre mask and cap low down on his forehead, his face was all but hidden, but Tess didn't need to see it to know it was Daniel. Daniel getting a clap from colleagues for a miracle just performed.

'A leaking triple A,' Stella said quietly in her ear, having now joined her. 'It was nearly too late for him by the time he got here.

His wife put off calling for an ambulance because she thought he had trapped wind. Had the poor man pulling up his knees to his chin to pass it. It's a miracle he's still alive.'

Tess's eyes widened at the thought of that scenario. *Madness! Pulling his knees up to his chest would have increased his intra-abdominal pressure.* A leaking triple A – abdominal aortic aneurysm – was a lethal condition, not many patients survive. Most die suddenly at home and of those that make it into hospital, only half make it through the operation. Like waiting for an overstretched balloon full of water to burst, an overstretched artery would eventually do the same. Unlike water that could escape through a tiny pinprick in a balloon, blood was thicker and clotted as it left the artery, leaving a gelatinous plug in the wall – the only thing stopping them from bleeding out into their abdominal cavity, and exsanguinating. The only hope of survival was at the hands of a skilful vascular surgeon, who could control the artery whilst the abdomen repeatedly filled up with blood. A leaking triple A wasn't just any old vessel bulging out its walls with trapped blood, it was the main artery of the heart. The main high-pressured pipeline feeding blood to the rest of the body.

Tess felt a thrill as she witnessed this moment. She'd never seen a surgeon being clapped before. She was letting her pride go to her head, but just for a moment she wanted to feel a little smug. To feel a little sense of ownership. And hug the secret of knowing those hands touched her.

Stella took hold of her arm and was now propelling her towards him.

'Mr Myers,' she called. 'Well done from all of us. I hear it was a little hairy?'

Tess moved to stand behind Stella as he pulled off his mask and grinned at the woman. 'Stella, it was a bloody nightmare in there at one point. I am mightily relieved, let me tell you. And bloody grateful to this team!'

Another round of applause sounded from the small group, and Daniel waved it off good-naturedly. 'All right, the lot of you; I wasn't alone in there dealing with it. You lot were there too, you know. Give yourselves a clap not me.' One or two back-patted each other.

'Free pizza and cake for the lot of you in the staff room when you get a chance to eat,' Stella announced, which saw most of them quickly disperse, leaving the corridor near empty except for Daniel, Stella and Tess. Stella made the introductions. 'Mr Myers, let me introduce you to a new member of our team. This is Tess Morris, just joining us today. She's a very experienced scrub nurse and cites vascular surgery as one of her special interests, would you believe.'

'My hands have been washed,' he said, as they shook hands. He put his head to one side, a small smile appearing as he looked her straight in the eye, and Tess felt herself tense up. She wondered what Stella would think of him looking at her this way with them only just supposedly meeting. 'Nice to see you here, Tess.'

Tess held her breath as Stella spoke. 'You two know each other?'

Tess shook her head at the same time Daniel nodded his, and she saw disappointment in his eyes as he saw Stella confused.

'I'm sure it will come back to Tess if we give her a minute,' he said, turning to Stella to give a rueful smile. He folded his arms as if to settle and wait for Tess's memory to return.

Tess could feel heat climbing up her neck.

Stella was staring at him wide-eyed, then spoke quickly as Tess turned red. 'You're embarrassing the poor girl, Mr Myers. Of course she'll remember you. It's just the shock of seeing you here, no doubt, that's lost her tongue. I've just realised you both worked at St Mary's. It's no doubt thrown her to suddenly see you down this neck of the woods,' she stated, looking at them for confirmation. 'Having only recently been working together somewhere else?'

'No, we never worked together,' Tess answered truthfully, the only truth to give in this whole damn deception. She should have told Stella this morning she was married to one of the surgeons. It might have made Stella wonder why Tess hadn't mentioned it at her interview, as it wouldn't have lost her this job if she had, but Tess could have brushed that over and made some excuse. In a workforce as big as the NHS it was impossible not to have married couples sometimes work together. So long as you conducted yourselves in a professional manner, and kept personal lives out of it, it wasn't a problem.

She looked at Daniel as she spoke another truth. 'I do remember you at St Mary's, Mr Myers. You were well known, but I never did your lists as I was always paired up with Mr Kumar or Mr Hassan.'

Stella seemed to understand this as she was nodding. 'And that can happen,' she said, sounding pure Irish. 'I looked a right eejit not long ago. I asked this doctor had he been here long and how was he liking it here. The poor man looked at me and said he'd been here two years. The trouble is I never step foot in Day Surgery so I'm not familiar with the faces.'

Tess felt rising panic from the half-truths being told, and breathed in deeply to bank it down. She was sinking in a mire of deception and what excited her five minutes ago, pretending not to know him and finding the play-acting even a little titillating, was now like a bucket of cold water over her head. Working together shouldn't have caused this problem. Being married needn't have been a problem either. It was Tess who had made it one by deliberately not mentioning her married name at the interview in case somehow they connected her to Daniel. With both of them coming from St Mary's it wouldn't have been that difficult to join the dots if she'd said she was called Myers. She didn't want anyone telling him she'd applied for a job. She wanted to tell him herself once she got it. He hadn't said she couldn't work but neither had he encouraged it. *He thought they were trying for a family.*

It was too late to say something now. She had let it go on too long. She had let Stella come to her rescue and provide a reason why

Tess couldn't remember their new surgeon. Their being married was now like a state secret. So who would he now introduce her as to his colleagues, when she met them? Miss Morris? Or Mrs she-forgot-she-was-married Myers?

She could cry, she really could, for going and spoiling what was to be a new day. She had ruined it completely, including her job, by not thinking things through properly. She could already see it happening. She would have no choice but to leave because as much as she wanted to stay, keeping the truth of them a secret would be impossible.

CHAPTER TWELVE

Martha rummaged in her bag, nearly losing her head inside it in her quest to find something.

'What are you looking for?' Jim asked.

'Nothing,' she said, putting the bag down by her feet and sitting up straight again in the seat with a piece of fruit cake in one hand.

'Are you going to eat that now?' Jim asked, his tone suggesting she shouldn't.

'I am. I'm starving. I'd eat my own hand if not for this cake.'

The waiting room had thinned out since Martha and Jim arrived. They had a long wait after getting there too early. Jim's idea, of course, to stop her going off and watching the house. She could sometimes read him like a book. He'd managed to keep her at home for God knows how many days now, because of getting a simple chill, and insisting she see a doctor before she went outside again. She said no to Jim this morning, telling him she wasn't going to the doctor again. But he'd bullied her into coming by reminding her she promised. What she promised she had no idea. She just hoped it was the doctor she liked, having a memory of the woman being a sensible sort. Sensible shoes, she was thinking.

A small boy who'd been running around in circles stopped in front of her, looking at her with his big blue eyes. Martha stared back and couldn't take her eyes off him. He was holding his small thumb up for inspection to show her his plaster. He put his other little hand to the side of his head and patted curls.

'I felled over, and got the baddest, baddest –' he stretched arms wide to show her how bad '– baddest blood. My hair was red,' he announced solemnly.

Martha couldn't take her eyes off him, off his solemn little face. His black hair wasn't bloody now, thank goodness. The blood was all gone. Someone had washed it well and his lovely curls were dry again.

'Martha... Martha!'

Martha peeled her eyes away from the boy's hair. Jim was talking to her, his face was worried.

'Are you OK there?' he asked. 'You seemed in a bit of daydream.'

Martha turned to look at the little boy again but something was different. His light brown hair wasn't black. He wasn't the little boy she saw.

'I'm OK,' she said, wishing the little boy gone.

'Martha King?' a voice called.

Martha looked up at hearing her name and saw a woman of about fifty standing in an open doorway. She stared at the doctor and hoped this visit wouldn't take too long, or that she wasn't going to ask the same questions that Jim asked. Following Jim she reminded herself to remember that it was spring.

Her blood pressure was a little high, her tongue a little dry, but no chest infection, thank God.

'How's your water works?' the doctor asked.

'I spend enough pennies in the day, if that's what you're asking.'

'Any stinging when you pass it?'

'No. And my number twos are fine as well in case you were going to ask that,' Martha said primly, before giving the doctor her own opinion of her health. 'Look, Doctor, I'm as fit as a flea. Ask Jim here. I walk for miles every day. I can't remember the last time I spent a whole day indoors before this. I'm never ill, apart from this brief chill I got, but that's passed and I'm well now.'

The doctor smiled at Martha, and Martha found herself looking at the woman's shoes. Brown leather slip-ons, the leather looked baby-soft; probably Hush Puppies.

'How often do you have to use your spray for the angina?' the doctor asked, on her feet now, examining Martha's neck and palpating the veins.

'Not too often,' Martha told her, ignoring Jim's look. He'd have her wrapped up in cotton wool if he had his way.

The doctor put her stethoscope against Martha's neck and listened. Martha wanted to tell her the heart wasn't there.

The doctor sat back down at her desk, and Jim and Martha stayed quiet while she stared at some things on her monitor screen. After a minute or so she turned in her chair to look at them both. Some of the liveliness had gone from her eyes as she smiled at Martha.

'It sounds like physically you're doing well, though I'd like to get a second opinion on the blood flow in your neck to make sure it's getting through the vessels nice and strong. I'd like to take some blood from you here today, and then arrange to get you seen by a different doctor at the hospital, where we can get a scan of your neck. Would that be all right for you, Martha?'

Martha nodded. Wondering why the doctor was asking. She could walk to the hospital in twenty minutes, she wasn't being asked to go a long way.

'Good, we'll get that sorted for you then,' she said, turning back to the screen, tapping quick fingers across her keyboard. Martha was relieved it was nearly over, except for taking her blood, which shouldn't take long as she had good veins.

'How are you, Jim?' she asked, while typing.

'Good,' he replied. 'Can't complain.'

Martha was surprised he knew her doctor, before thinking she was probably his doctor too.

'He can if you let him,' she butted in, giving Jim a fond look.

The doctor gazed at the two of them as if curious about the relationship. 'How long have you two been living together?'

Jim sat forward in his chair. 'I moved in with Martha after her husband died. That has to be two years now.'

'He has my sympathy,' Martha said. 'Having to put up with a landlady like me.'

'So you're with Martha quite a lot of the time?'

Martha answered for him. 'All the time if I let him. He's taken it upon himself to be minding me, I think,' she informed the doctor, giving her a direct look.

Jim then contradicted the charges against him. 'That's not true, Martha. You look after yourself mostly. You just get a little forgetful sometimes.'

Martha stared at him as if he'd suddenly turned a traitor. How dare he say that in front of her doctor?

'Do you think you're getting forgetful, Martha?' the doctor asked.

Martha damned the man beside her. She'd be stuck in this chair another while now. She thought about the question, considering how to best answer it. Stop all the questions to come.

'I remembered the type of shoes you like wearing, Doctor,' she answered smugly.

The doctor smiled. 'What about day to day? How's your memory then? Today's Monday, do you remember what you did yesterday?'

Martha nodded. 'Stuck at home until I saw you. Banned from going out.'

'OK, what about Saturday?'

Saturday? Martha concentrated. *Saturday, Saturday, Saturday.* She'd done something that day, but what? Was it a trick question? The only place she went to was the house and before that, the cemetery, which she hadn't been to since he moved in with a new wife. The wife? What was she called? She had his new name.

She'd been running in her blue exercise clothes. Jumping on the spot. Looking out of a window? Began with a B? No, not a B? She concentrated hard to hear her say it, and with blessed relief she did. Tess Myers! 'I went to see Tess Myers,' Martha said in a rush.

'That wasn't this Saturday, Martha, it was the Saturday before,' Jim corrected her. 'You've stayed home all week getting better.'

'You seem to have been struggling a little bit, Martha, to remember this,' the doctor now said.

'Well, so would you if you were stuck home a week!' she replied defensively.

'OK,' the woman said calmly, nodding as if she agreed. 'So what happened on the Saturday you can remember?'

Martha's eyes turned worried. 'I saw her at the window. She's new living there in that house. Living where it happened. Living with the man who did it! She's in danger and she doesn't even know it. Jim says it isn't him, but I know it is. Just as I know your face looking at me. Once you know someone you don't forget their face!'

A short silence followed. Jim and her doctor looked at one another, and Martha in a temper now picked up her shopping bag and stood up from her seat.

'Come on, Jim. It'll be Christmas by the time we get out of here. We've taken up enough of the doctor's time.'

'Martha, please sit down,' her doctor asked. 'I'm sorry if this has upset you. Please?'

Martha sat with the shopping bag on her lap. The doctor looked like she was struggling a bit with what to say, reminding her of Jim when he got awkward and cleared his throat to say something. The doctor's eyes were frank. She was looking at Martha very sincerely. Alarming her a little. When she reached to hold one of her hands, Martha knew she was going to hear something bad.

'Martha, it seems to me you are having some difficulty with your memory, something we shouldn't ignore. Having your memory at its best is very important, and can be helped if we know the cause. I'd like to get your memory assessed.'

'But why?' asked Martha in a voice robbed of vitality, leaving it to sound old and shaky. 'I know you. I know where I am.'

The doctor looked at her kindly. 'This is the first time we've met, Martha. Your old doctor, Doctor Gracie, she retired. This is the first time you've seen me.'

CHAPTER THIRTEEN

Tess couldn't have been more surprised or more relieved as Daniel stared at her with sympathy. She'd been on tenterhooks waiting for him to come home, rehearsing her apology over and over. That he should walk in and be instantly understanding of what she was going through made her love him more, vowing never to deceive him again. She felt her eyes water.

'You have got yourself in such a pickle, Miss Morris,' he said softly, holding out his arms to her. 'Come here, you silly thing.'

She properly cried in his arms, wetting the lapels of his suit jacket until he gave her his hankie. She was hiccupping by the time she stopped, and stared up at him as he laughed. But he was laughing with kindness at hearing her annoyance at making the sounds.

'You need some water,' he said, gently untangling her hold on him. Then, handing her a full glass, said dryly, 'It should probably be a drip with all the fluid you've lost.'

This set her off again, only this time she was half laughing between the hiccups.

'Go and have a long soak in the bath, it will make you feel better,' he suggested.

Tess didn't want to leave him. She wanted to stay by his side all night and hide away from the embarrassments. The conversations with Stella wouldn't let up in her head, making her squirm each time she heard them. The sad thing was she'd not only spoiled her own job, she'd probably spoiled some of Daniel's too. She'd seen how he was treated by his colleagues today. He'd only been there a short while yet she saw they genuinely liked him.

'He's a very nice man,' Stella remarked, when he'd walked away from them in the corridor. 'And he's a brilliant surgeon. So I'm pleased you'll now get a chance to work with him.'

Tess, of course, already knew this – it was one of the many reasons she fell in love with him. He was a very nice man. It was wonderful, though, to hear others say so too. If earlier hadn't happened, Tess could now be enjoying this turn in their relationship and put a lid on that brief unhappiness for always. The very nice man she woke up to this morning was the same nice man she first met, and he didn't deserve this happening. He'd been passionate about this move, and was always passionate about his work. She just hoped she hadn't spoiled it by making him have to mislead Stella. Tess would, of course, take all the blame if or when Stella found out, and Stella would at least remember Mr Myers giving his wife a chance to come clean.

Reminded of how much she cared about him did something to soothe away her worry, and made her think less about what she wanted. She had a husband who wanted to have a large family with her if she let him. She could be a full-time mother bringing up their children and making this home a more solid foundation. She was nearly thirty. She could have a ten-year-old by the time she was forty. It was definitely not too soon to start trying.

Closing the bathroom door and locking it, she put the plug in the bath and turned the taps on full. Her eyes were drawn to the bathroom cabinet, compelled to check how many were left. She opened the mirrored door, took out a large box of tampons and hurriedly emptied the contents into the dry sink. Along with the tampons were the contraceptive pills she had been hiding. She had a few left yet before needing a new prescription. Twenty-one tablets in one blister pack and eleven remaining of the one started. She stared at the tablets intently before putting them away again, having made a decision. She'd finish the started pack so as not to mess up her cycle, then ditch the unopened one and stop taking them all together. In the mirror she stared at her face, ignoring the red blotchiness, concentrating instead on her eyes. They looked more determined to her now. They were eyes she recognised because they were honest again. Happier for having no more lies hidden in them.

Daniel further surprised her when they sat down to eat. Far from telling her to leave her new job, he said the opposite. 'Why don't you see how it goes? Give yourself the rest of the week to think about it. You're not in the department for the next two days as you're on an induction course.'

'But, Daniel, we could only carry on like this for the short-term. We won't get away with it for long.'

He sighed as if a bit baffled, and she felt guilty for putting this on him. 'I'm really sorry,' she said. 'I've put you in an awkward situation.'

He shrugged his shoulders as if it were nothing. 'I'm sure I've faced far worse. And what's the very worst that can happen? We get found out? I don't think being married will get us hanged, drawn and quartered. Especially not me,' he added, with a little smirk on his face. 'They might hang you! But not their brilliant new surgeon!'

She laughed at him as she threw her napkin at him across the table. 'Oh, so you heard what they said?'

A smug look was on his face as he touched hands lightly to his chest, before he spread his arms wide. Then she felt a delicious shiver down her back as he spoke in an arrogant sexy voice. 'What can I say? If you've got it, flaunt it.'

His signature kisses came back. Tess felt the warmth of them to the point where she thought she'd combust. Lying beside him in the dark she could honestly say that being unhappy for that short period was almost worth it, if that's what it took to be feeling this complete happiness. She might not have experienced this otherwise. Losing him for those few days and then finding this wonderfulness made her never want to know him any other way.

They'd had some shaky moments, there was no denying it, which they might not have had if they'd stayed in London. Nothing would have changed for them, apart from them being legally bound as man and wife. Though she did wonder what that would be like for them now if they were still there. Perhaps it wouldn't make her feel as married with everything still the same, with nothing to mark it as a new beginning. Apart, that is, from having to find space to hang her clothes, which she was beginning to see as less appealing now she was getting used to all this space around them.

Working again was the right thing to do. She'd be busy and feeling useful. Being a mother probably gave that same feeling. She'd heard many mothers say time wasn't their own anymore. She would be like that one day and look back at this time and not even remember it. She'd be busy raising a family. But that was the future and this was the now and still *their* time.

They should get out more and explore their surroundings. They'd not had a single day of sightseeing yet, which was deplorable considering where they lived. They should take some evening walks together down Milsom Street to the Abbey, cross Pulteney Bridge and stare down at the weir. Bath was supposedly one of the most romantic cities in the world. They needed some romance in their lives. Seeing him like that at the table tonight, looking carefree for the first time in ages, it was hard to imagine him any other way. She wanted to keep him like that always.

She snuggled into his back contentedly. She felt relieved in some ways that today happened as it did, because it got them to where they were tonight. There was no telling if moving here was the cause of his random behaviour changes, and right now it no longer mattered. Everything was as perfect as it could be. There was nothing now she would want to change.

CHAPTER FOURTEEN

Coming to the end of the second week in her new job, Tess was relieved she hadn't quit after that first day. She attended the induction course and reported back to the department for the two-day orientation. The Thursday and Friday had passed without any awkward situations arising. No one asked about her personal life. Mostly everyone was too busy to notice her, which suited Tess as they weren't being unfriendly, just busy.

She'd been buddied up with a genial Filipino nurse named Peter who'd thrown a fair few questions to help build her knowledge. Did she know how to work the service lift to bring clean instrument trays up to the department? Did she know there was a second service lift near the sluice for the dirty instruments to go back in? Was she aware Sterile Services – the place where all surgical instruments were washed then sterilised and put into sterile tray packs ready for operations – was on the floor below them? Though she wasn't to think the tray packs were all the same, as some types of surgery required different or additional tools. So she would see obs and gynae, orthopaedic, laparoscopic, vascular, ENT and so forth, as well as major general. Peter was being so helpful Tess didn't like to tell him she already knew all of this.

When he saw her on the Monday she was in full theatre gear. Gown tied up at the back over her blues, mask on face, cap on head and double gloved to assist as scrub nurse in a major case. He'd looked askance, ready to intervene until Stella told him Tess used to be a band 6. Tess wished she had told him herself as he was embarrassed and she'd apologised afterwards.

Her first time at the table had been observed by a few of her new colleagues, and there was an element of relief when it was over that she'd passed. The urologist had given her a quiet *well done*, satisfied the removal of his patient's kidney had gone smoothly. She didn't get quite the clap Daniel got, it was more of an air clap, but it was enough to tell her they were confident of having her in their team. She was one of them now. Cameron had watched her too and given her a big thumbs-up. In the staff room afterwards he'd made her a cup of tea, and Stella had stared at him pointedly, probably wondering why he hadn't made her one. At some point Tess was going to have to let him know he was wasting his time. She didn't want it to get to the stage of him asking her out.

As for Daniel, she'd barely seen him in the department. Even though she was now assisting as a scrub nurse every day, she had yet to work with him. They occasionally passed one another in the corridor, but she avoided looking at him, keeping her eyes firmly fixed ahead or down at the ground. Mindful to preserve her job. She already loved being there, not only for the work but feeling she was with him again and seeing the difference this made to them when at home. Their evenings were now more convivial. Sharing the cooking and the chores and decisions together.

Despite the deception she was happy. Her colleagues were getting to know her and she was feeling a part of the group now, having their mobile numbers and sharing in the hospital chats, and while she wouldn't phone or text them she enjoyed relaying the chats back to Daniel in the evenings. His eyes showed he didn't mind her talking about colleagues and he seemed happy to let her carry on.

She now wanted to do something nice for him and let this happiness continue. So after her shift she was going to set up memberships for the hospital gym and tennis courts. The outdoor

pool had closed two days earlier for winter, which was a shame as
the first week of October was predicted to be hot, and it would have
been nice to swim in the open air. Still, she shouldn't grumble; the
outdoor tennis courts were open, and there was a badminton and
squash court for indoors if it rained. It would be good for them,
doing some new things together. Learn something more about
each other. The thought was making her gleeful. He'd shown her
how skilful a golf player he was the one time he'd taken her. Well,
now it was her turn to show him how good she was at tennis. It
was going to be lovely to thrash him in a game.

Tess was in a reverie about her plans as she restocked the
shelves after the morning's four operations so as to be ready for
the afternoon gynae list.

'Tess, would you mind taking your lunch break now so that
you can assist Mr Myers this afternoon? I've had to send Peter
home with toothache. I can have someone else do the gynae list
if you don't mind?'

Tess had her back to Stella and was able to mask her alarm. It
would be her first time working with Daniel.

'Of course, not a problem. What time does Mr Myers' list start?'

'Two o'clock. So you've got plenty of time to get something
to eat first.'

Tess sat in the atrium for her lunch break, having a coffee and
sandwich, preparing herself mentally for the afternoon. Before
leaving the department she'd looked through the surgeons' require-
ments book. Though it wasn't a book but index cards in a plastic
box in alphabetical order of the surgeons who worked there, it
was called The Surgeons' Bible. Each surgeon had their surgical
preferences listed, such as which sutures they liked to use, which
retractors they preferred – useful to know when there were half a
dozen different types. Mr Myers' list was relatively short: Ligaclips
and the complex major surgery tray – basically the kitchen sink
of major surgery instruments.

She had taken a peek at his afternoon theatre list and saw nothing on it to be alarmed about. She'd worked as a theatre nurse for eight years now and knew most procedures, particularly in vascular surgery. She had scrubbed for dozens of emergency operations, where the patients were Cat 1 cases and classed ASA 4 – life-saving and immediate surgery, where the patient is in an extremely poor physical state. If a patient was ASA 5 it meant he or she was moribund, not expected to survive the next twenty-four hours with or without surgery. Tess had been scrub nurse for these patients too.

What was harder to know was how the surgeon worked. A new rhythm and pace and personality had to be learned. Knowing Daniel as a husband didn't mean she knew him as a surgeon. She was blind to his ways the same as any person working with him for the first time. Absorbed in her thoughts, she hardly noticed the chair being pulled out beside her until Cameron spoke.

'You looked miles away. Can I join you?'

She nodded in surprise and watched as he sat down, placing a baguette and a can of Diet Coke on the table.

'Nice to get out of theatre and see the sky for a bit,' he said, looking up at the glass ceiling.

'It is,' she agreed, before carrying on eating.

He sat quietly next to her eating his food, occasionally checking his phone and tapping a quick response to something seen on the screen. He was nice-looking, and not much taller than her, and she wondered if he had a girlfriend or wife, though hoped not if he was a flirt outside of that relationship.

Halfway through the baguette he paused eating to speak again. 'You seem to be settled in?'

'I am.' She smiled. 'I'm loving it here.'

He smiled back, his eyes lingering too long on her face, making her look away.

'So what about your days off? Have you done all the touristy things in Bath yet? Taken a ride on the open-top bus around the city, or had tea in the Pump Rooms? I know a good guide if you're looking for one?'

She didn't wish to offend him, he seemed like a nice man, but now was the time to tell him it could never be him, as a guide or a boyfriend.

'I'm with someone,' she said.

His face fell. 'Oh, I see.' He quickly smiled again to cover any awkwardness. 'Well, as a friend then, if you need any?'

She reached across and lightly patted the back of his hand, looking right at him, chuckling a little. 'Nice try, Blondie, but that won't work as, like I say, I'm with someone.'

He laughed really loud, attracting the attention of the doctor at the table beside them. 'What's so funny, Gouldie-locks?'

'She called me Blondie,' Cameron replied.

The man gave a small shrug and carried on with his meal.

Cameron was still smiling. 'I have two nicknames now.'

Tess was amused, she hadn't meant to call him that, but it slipped out. She supposed the other nickname suited him better, as his surname was Gould. She'd like to have him as a friend she realised, having lost Sara to the other side of the world. Maybe if he stopped fancying her it would be possible.

As if reading her mind, his eyes stopped flirting and his expression turned genuine. 'OK, no more trying it on. I can respect what you've told me, but my offer of being a friend still stands. So, are we?' he asked, holding out his hand to shake.

She sighed, not knowing whether to laugh at him as he waited. Seeing the kindness in his eyes she couldn't refuse without offending him. She wasn't like that, she knew what it felt like to be rejected.

Clasping his hand, she grinned at him. 'Friends,' she stated firmly.

A polite cough interrupted them and Tess turned her head to see Daniel standing almost beside her. His eyes were cool as he stared at her and she wondered how long he'd been there. He directed his attention to Cameron.

'Forgive me disturbing your lunch, Dr Gould. I can see I've interrupted a jolly affair, but as you told me at the start of this attachment that you needed more operative experience, I thought you might care to know I will be starting my fem-pop bypass sooner than two o'clock. I finished the morning list earlier than expected.'

Cameron was already on his feet, discarding the rest of his lunch. 'Absolutely. Not a problem. Thank you for letting me know. I appreciate it.'

'Good,' Daniel replied crisply, before addressing Tess. 'Same goes for you, Nurse Morris. Or do you need more time?'

She shook her head, now also on her feet, feeling like a child at being caught out doing something she shouldn't, and resenting Daniel for making her feel she had.

'Thank you for your consideration, Mr Myers, but my lunch break is over so I'm happy to start earlier.'

'In that case, I'll see you both in theatre shortly,' he announced, before striding away.

Tess wanted to hurry after him, first to tell him she'd done nothing wrong by sitting there with a colleague, and second to ask him not to be so curt in future. She did neither. Instead, she gathered herself calmly and went back to theatre. It would be there that she would show him how to behave. She would conduct herself in a professional manner and give respect to all their colleagues. Remind him what good manners were. That they cost nothing.

CHAPTER FIFTEEN

When Tess finished work she didn't make a detour to the north side of the hospital for membership passes, she went straight home. Fuming.

Everything had gone perfectly fine in theatre. The four operations on the list had been carried out without delays or mishaps. Tess and the circulating nurse had done their jobs well. Daniel's surgical assistant, a female registrar named Suzanne, knew what she was doing and did her job well. Everyone did their job well so there had been no need for Daniel to act like a bastard to Cameron. To pick on him like that.

In theatre as an observer, Daniel had chosen to test Cameron's knowledge in front of the team. He'd answered straight back on most things, until Daniel's questions became more exacting, requiring more effort, more attention, more time. It turned embarrassing for Cameron as the demand for right answers on minor and trivial details caused him to stutter.

What saddened Tess was that Daniel had done it by extending a helpful jolliness to the junior doctor, pointing out how difficult it was to balance one's time while learning and being young. No women, no beer, no social life, he'd informed Cameron. Leaving Cameron to look like he could be better informed, more genned up, if he were to follow the example of his consultant.

Afterwards, when the theatre emptied, Cameron stayed behind while Tess was clearing and cleaning her trolleys. He leaned against the operating table looking like a forlorn figure who had just lost his master's approval.

He laughed a little harshly. 'I don't have time for beer or socialising, and haven't had a girlfriend in nearly a year. I don't understand,' he said. 'I thought I was doing well.'

Tess was left in a fury with Daniel for causing this. He hadn't fooled her with that 'helpful' act. He acted that way because he was jealous of Cameron, because he found her and Cameron talking.

In the kitchen she threw her bag on the table, and yanked out a chair to sit on. She pondered what she would say, what approach she should take. It was doing her head in, this sudden behaviour change again. How could it turn so quickly from one day to the next? Surely he didn't think she had eyes for Cameron? Well, she wasn't going to put up with it. He needed to sort himself out and deal with the issues causing it. They had the whole weekend off together and she was not going to sit there in silence with him brooding. He'd ruined the end to her lovely week, ruined the last two weeks of happiness. Why couldn't he behave consistently without these flare-ups?

To make matters more difficult, Stella informed her poor Peter was going to be off for a week, which could mean Tess would be working with Daniel again. Stella would expect her to be pleased by this because as far she was concerned Mr Myers was a very nice man.

She heard noise in the hallway, the front door closing, and stayed in the chair. She had no intention of jumping up to greet him. She picked up her mobile and pretended to look interested in something on the screen. A moment later his footsteps fell silent and she suspected he'd gone into the study, which he'd claimed as his office when they moved in. Tess stayed silent, not making a sound to let him know she was there. It was up to him to find her. It was up to him to make amends.

It was silent for so long she actually got engrossed in the phone and checked for any messages from Sara. There were none, but she had a new friend request on Facebook. Cameron had sent one, which she accepted without thought. He was a friend after all. The phone pinged back a message straight away. *Hello friend.* She smiled, was still smiling when realising she was not alone in the kitchen. Daniel was staring at her with his arms folded across his chest.

'So you're home,' she said.

He didn't say anything back, just continued to look at her. Tess ignored him by looking back at the small screen. She intended to annoy him by staying busy on her phone. She smiled to herself as she typed back a message to Cameron, aware that Daniel was now coming close to her to see what she was doing. She hoped her behaviour was frustrating him just as his earlier behaviour frustrated her.

The flash of movement to snatch the phone out of her hands left her mouth hanging open and eyes wide. He held it in front of her like a magician.

'Do you think this is some sort of joke?' he quietly asked.

She looked at him briefly, then lowered her eyes trying to calm her nerves. She hadn't expected him to behave like that. If anything, she thought he'd be remorseful. Her mouth went dry, and she determined it would be better to give him her attention.

'That's what this is to you, isn't it?' he said. His quiet tone was making her more nervous. 'You think my career is something you can joke about, something you can sabotage with your pretence of being someone else. Well, that's not going to happen, Tess. You will remember who you are married to when you're in that workplace. You went and got this job behind my back without even telling me. Don't think I haven't thought about that. Then you take advantage of my ignorance by being presented to me as someone else. You have deceived me, Tess. You have deceived Stella

Malloy and my other colleagues, and now you have the audacity to hoodwink Cameron Gould into thinking you're available and unmarried. Well, it stops now – do you hear me? – before you do any further damage to these people. Cameron needs to stay on track and I'm doing my damnedest to help him do that. What he doesn't need is false hope.'

Tess felt herself trembling, in a state of shock at what he said. She felt her face flood with colour, because most of it was true. All of it was true in some way. Cameron did think she was unmarried. May still even think he had a chance with her. As for her deception, while not considered her finest moment, she thought Daniel was okay with it. He'd supported her, teased her. He hadn't made one derogatory comment about any of it. Not even to mention his disappointment when she denied knowing him. Tess really didn't know what to say. She felt as guilty as hell.

'Another thing,' he said.

She closed her eyes in despair. He hadn't finished with her yet.

'I'd ask you to refrain from broadcasting your life across social-media sites. I have no desire to have colleagues know my wife's activity every minute of the day. Even though they don't know you're my wife yet, they might someday.'

Tess clamped her teeth together to stop her jaw tremoring. She was burning with humiliation. That he felt the need to mention the recent occasions he'd seen her on social media highly embarrassed her, because in truth it didn't come naturally to her. She hadn't grown up using Facebook. She hadn't grown up with a mobile in her hand.

The first mobile she owned was a Nokia from Argos. A pay-as-you-go phone that let her send texts and make calls. She bought it at the grand old age of twenty-one. It was really only in the last few years she'd used a smartphone, mostly to make looking-up things on the internet easy. She'd never had a Facebook account before as she hadn't felt the need to connect with people that way.

Not while she and Sara were living together every day and Sara her only friend. It was only in the last two weeks she'd joined Facebook to get to know some of the people she was working with and feel less of an outsider. But again she hadn't thought how her behaviour might affect him.

She opened her eyes and saw his bleak expression, and wished she could go back to the morning and begin the day again so as not to have him look at her this way. He looked so disappointed as if something had been taken from him. Had her behaviour caused this much of a problem?

'Tess, I'm going to ask you something,' he said quietly. 'And I want you to tell me the truth. I don't want you to say something because you think it's kinder.'

She waited anxiously, and wished he'd hurry up so that she could reassure him. He was clearly going to ask if she was happy.

'Do you want to stop trying for a family?'

She shook her head hard, trying not to cry as he looked into her eyes. If he knew she'd deceived him on this as well he'd probably walk out the door.

He sighed heavily, before slowly nodding. 'Well, that's good, then. I don't want to stop either. I want us to have a family.'

She couldn't see his face. Her eyes were swimming. After the last two weeks of feeling him love her in a way she hadn't experienced before, to now feel his disappointment with her was a sharp shock to her senses. How could she have been so flippant in what she was doing? She had spoiled things. Not him. If he set her adrift she wouldn't blame him. She would blame only herself for what she had done.

CHAPTER SIXTEEN

Martha was pleased when Jim left her in the capable hands of the nurse. He'd be back to get her when the scan was over. His mollycoddling was getting on her nerves.

Yesterday he'd come looking for her while she was watching the house. She'd felt like telling him it was not his business what she did in her own time. He was not her minder, or her jailor, come to that. His interference had already cut into her time with these blasted tests and doctor visits, and she was getting sorely fed up with being prodded and probed and endlessly questioned. Especially when she had more important matters to deal with like the whereabouts of the new wife.

Martha hadn't seen her once in the days she'd managed to get out and go watch the house. Jim had said it was nothing to be concerned about. In other words, none of her business to be there looking for this woman. It was all very well for him to say that when he didn't think there was a danger, but she knew differently, and was more than worried to have not had a single sighting of her in so many days. She should be there now searching for her, not wasting time being in hospital.

A woman in a blue-top-and-blue-trousers uniform came into the room with a cheery smile and went to a trolley with a monitor screen next to the examination couch. The pretty nurse standing on the other side of the couch gave Martha's hand a light squeeze, and asked her if she was comfortable. Martha would have liked another pillow, but she'd been told they wanted her flat and her neck arched a bit. The woman doing the scan now spoke to her.

'Just going to put a little cold gel on the sides of your neck, Martha. That's the worst you'll feel.'

Martha stayed quiet and still, quite enjoying the sensation of having her neck stroked with something and hearing the *whoosh whoosh* sounds. When the test was completed the nurse wiped her neck and raised the head of the bed a little.

'I'm not going to sit you up too high after lying flat. We'll give it a few minutes.'

'So is that it?' Martha asked.

'It is.' The nurse smiled.

Martha smiled back, relieved so little time had actually been taken. 'So I can go home now?'

'You can after you've seen the doctor, which shouldn't be too long. By the time you've rested and got dressed he'll probably be ready to see you.'

Martha was doubtful of that. The same thing had been said to her recently while sat waiting to see another doctor. She'd thought she'd have a sore on her bottom after sitting on a hard chair so long. Still, it was nearly over with and then she could get out of this place altogether. Hopefully, before Jim returned to fetch her.

Nearly an hour later, according to Ted's watch on her wrist, she was shown into an office that had a chair on both sides of a desk. Her nurse stayed with her and introduced her to the male nurse already in the room. He picked up a beige file from a row of others neatly laid out on a trolley, and put it on the other side of the desk.

'The doctor won't be long,' he said. 'Just finishing up with the patient next door.'

Her nurse had said this to her before as well, or something similar. She checked down by her feet to make sure she still had her shopping bag, relieved to see it there as she wanted to put her glasses back on to hear the verdict. While fetching them out, the door opened and Martha was aware of man in a suit sitting down opposite her. Settling her glasses on her face she looked across the desk and felt instant fear. Her shaking hand rose of its own accord to cover her open mouth.

'It's you,' she gasped.

'I beg your pardon,' he replied.

Martha was on her feet, her tiny frame rigid with tension, especially in the arm she stretched out to point at him. 'Your new name won't hide you!'

He gave a stiff smile. 'I think you have me confused with someone else. The only name I have is Myers. Why don't you sit down so we can start again?'

Martha stayed on her feet, staring at him hard. 'What have you done with your wife?' she accused angrily.

'Mrs King, I suggest you sit down,' he said calmly. 'You're clearly upset about something.'

Martha felt a rage. How dare he put on this show for the benefit of the two nurses behind her. He had no shame. 'I know what you are,' she snarled. 'You've got rid of her, haven't you? Haven't you?' she hollered as he got up from his chair.

'I really don't know what you're talking about, but I am concerned by your behaviour. So if you'll excuse me, I'll take my presence elsewhere until you've calmed down.'

As he walked past her to get to the door she looked daggers at him. 'I know what you did in that house, Mr so-called Myers. You won't get away with it a second time. Trust me on that.'

She'd only seen him for a few seconds but she was shaken to the core. She sat down, still shaking, and saw the faces of the two nurses staring at her horrified. She pulled her shopping bag up on her lap and hugged it to her chest. They could look at her all they liked, she wasn't sorry for her outburst. They didn't know what she did. Their opinion didn't matter, didn't bother her in the slightest. She turned away from them to compose herself and sat perfectly still, aside from the wobble in her small chin.

At quarter to six that evening, even though it was so early, she told Jim she was going to bed. He didn't try to change her mind, instead encouraging her to have a good sleep. In the bedroom she drew the heavy velvet curtains across the window, shutting out the daylight. The bedside lamps were turned on, making it look cosy.

On the left side of the bed she eased the drawers away from the wall, taking care not to make any noise, to create enough space for her to get behind them. She got down onto her knees and saw the wall needed more light, so reached for the little lamp to shine upon it. She felt her heart settle. They were still there. Kept protected in this space behind the drawers, they hadn't faded away. The paint prints were still white and not yellowed. Martha put out her hand and touched them. She traced her finger around the small one first, before following the outline of the bigger one. She kissed her fingertips twice and placed a separate kiss on each. This was her little shrine: two painted handprints. The palms and the fingers had been painted with the brush Martha had been using to paint the skirting boards white, to bring it up fresh against the new wallpaper. Ted hadn't known it was ever done, that the two handprints were there. It was their secret. She had kept it from him and now it was only hers. Only she knew they were there.

'Goodnight, my loves,' she whispered.

CHAPTER SEVENTEEN

Tess stared at the varied colours of the trees. The sky across the horizon was a blanket of white hazy sunshine. Splodges of copper and gold dropped new colours into the green hills to herald a change of season. She was surrounded by stunning landscape, yet it may as well have been wasteland she stared at from the dullness in her eyes. October had become the month of her cold-feet days. Blunting her emotions. Growing this apathy.

After Daniel said all those things to her, she'd expected a cooling-off period between them, a period of penance for what she had done. What she hadn't expected was for him to be kind to her. Which made her feel worse as it hadn't felt deserved, and it hadn't taken away a certain look in his eyes. When he asked if everything was all right she wanted to ask the same back, but wasn't brave enough in case he answered he'd lost trust. Her worries had dug in firmly.

He had taken to standing at their bedroom window, looking out of it as if looking for answers, while smoothing those stale curtains. She felt she had ruined something between them and didn't know how to make it better.

Yesterday morning he made love to her but it was more of a coupling. He hadn't been rough or hurt her, or forced her like he did that one time. He'd asked first. *Do you mind?* And that politeness felt like she was lying in bed with a stranger.

She'd spent the last two weeks with a great deal of agonising over how she could put things right and the only conclusion she could come to was to quit her job. She'd woken this morning with the idea fixed in her head. At the end of her shift today she was going to hand in her notice to Stella. It was the only sensible action to take if she wanted to save her marriage.

In the early hours, a few nights ago, she'd tried calling Sara for advice, but her number was currently unavailable, and the option to leave a message failed. The number was as good as useless to Tess if Sara had her phone switched off. Tess could honestly say she was missing her friend and could have done with her right now. Sara was noisy, brash and dressed too loudly, but underneath was a sensitive soul who recognised when someone was troubled, and was able to counsel, having been hurt herself. Sara would have been able to fix the problem.

Tess checked her appearance in her compact mirror before she got off the bus. She tried to put on a brighter expression. It was going to be a long day today. She was scrub nurse for Daniel all day.

At the morning brief, held in the anaesthetic room, Tess was conscious of Daniel gazing at her. She chanced a look at him and her breathing stopped at the smile he gave her. There was a warmth in his eyes not seen in a while and she quickly had to lower her own gaze. One smile was all it had taken to loosen the stranglehold on her emotions. Any minute there'd be a puddle of tears on the floor if she wasn't careful. She sniffed and cleared her throat as if she had a bit of a cold.

The assembled team introduced themselves to one another as was protocol before any operating list began. It gave Tess a moment to compose herself and to now focus on the people around her. The registrar assisting was Dr Suzanne Lewis, with her calm clear voice – something Tess wanted when listening out for instructions spoken through masks. She was pleased the runner was Julia. She'd worked with the nurse several times now and found her very competent. She was also pleased they'd been given Lucy, the healthcare assistant supporter. She was always in a good mood, sharing some happy news regarding her two small children.

As the operating surgeon, Daniel gave a rundown of the operations listed on the sheet of paper in his hand. There was only one listed for the morning, but three for the afternoon. 'There are no changes to the order of the list as far I'm concerned unless the anaesthetist says differently. We're starting with seventy-eight-year-old John Backwell. Procedure to carry out: a femoral popliteal bypass to right leg. The vein graft will be taken from the left leg, it has already been mapped out and marked by the vascular studies team yesterday. I will need a sterile doppler and Prolene 4-0 and 5-0 sutures as usual. Can we let the radiographers know we will need the C-arm for completion angiograms, please?'

As he finished speaking, the anaesthetist, Dr Reid, but known as Dr Bob, began his part. 'I'm happy with the patient after seeing him this morning. There are a few concerns to consider: diabetic, peripheral vascular disease, but non-smoker, and BMI twenty-six. I've ordered some blood, should we need it, as his haemoglobin is low. This is going to be an intubation anaesthetic as he has a regurgitation reflux. And we'll put in an arterial line. That's it from me.'

Daniel gave a short nod. 'OK, everyone, thanks for your attendance. Let's get started, so send for the patient as soon as, please.'

The next forty-five minutes went by in a rush. After leaving the briefing, Tess put on a surgical facemask before heading to the scrubbing area, a three-person stainless-steel trough. In readiness she tore open a sterile, singular-use, nailbrush-sponge. She washed her hands and lower arms with liquid soap before beginning in earnest the five-minute hand-wash scrub, nudging the taps with her elbow. Using a nailbrush across her fingernails, she next worked on palms, backs and sides of hands, making her way methodically up her arms to her elbows, before raising her hands for the final rinse. With a sterile towel ready Tess dried her hands and then opened her sterile gown. She pushed her arms through the long sleeves, keeping hands tucked in, while Julia tied her at the back. Then lastly, and very carefully, she worked her fingers into sterile gloves, without touching the outside of them, ensuring they covered not just her hands but sleeve cuffs as well.

Ready, she clasped her hands together in front of her chest, the safest thing to do to keep them sterile, and followed Julia to the layout area, the designated place in the corner of an operating room for the scrub nurse to set up the trolley of surgical instruments.

Julia opened the outer paper cover of a vascular surgical tray, allowing Tess to open the sterilised inner cover. Together they checked the instruments listed were all there. They did swab counts and sharp counts and Julia recorded the count numbers on the theatre whiteboard. At the end of surgery she would confirm the count number used matched. No one wanted a swab or an instrument left inside the patient. They then prepared a second trolley for a complex major general surgery tray.

Tess was now ready and watching the anaesthetist. Dr Bob was telling the patient he was going to be asleep soon, and to have nice dreams. Tess heard the patient chuckle. 'You mean stop jabbering? The wife will be glad if I do that.' And then he was silent. A few minutes later Tess could see that the anaesthetist and his assistant, the operating department practitioner, were nearly done with their checks on their monitors and infusion pumps. All that was waiting was for the surgeons to appear.

A moment later, the doors to the operating room swung open. Tess was surprised to see Cameron walk in. For some reason she hadn't expected to see him working in Daniel's theatre again, which was nonsense, he was an ST1 and needed to learn. Mindful of Daniel's warning, she'd kept conversations between them short since then. In the staff room he'd glanced at her questioningly, but what could she say to him? That her husband thought she was a bad influence on him and didn't want them to be friends?

It was best if she said nothing at all, given that Daniel was his boss, and let him lose interest naturally. After today it would no longer matter anyway. She wasn't going to be there much longer. She was sticking to her decision even though he'd smiled. Their relationship needed more than that to repair it.

Suzanne was next to arrive. Getting the nod from the anaesthetist that the patient was under, she commenced prepping skin with bright pink chlorohexidine solution. Indelible ink marked the operation sites: a black arrow pointing down from the top of the right thigh, black ink following the course of a vein below the left knee. She was placing green drapes across both legs when Daniel made his entrance.

The ODP, whose name Tess forgot, picked up the WHO laminated card to do 'Time Out'. Part of the World Health Organisation surgical safety checklist was a list of questions that had to be read aloud, literally a time out period where everyone stopped what they were doing to check their readiness for the operation.

'Are we ready? Can we do "Time Out" now, please?'

Everybody stopped what they were doing to give their attention.

Tess glanced briefly at Daniel and saw he was looking at her. She gave a small smile and hoped it showed in her eyes, because of course he couldn't see it through her mask.

The first two questions asked the patient's name and the procedure, and checked the name on the patient's wristband matched the name called out.

Daniel answered, 'John Backwell. Femoral popliteal bypass to the right leg. Vein harvest from left leg.'

The anaesthetist confirmed that yes, this was the name on the consent form, and yes, this was the procedure signed for. The ODP then confirmed this was the procedure written on the theatre whiteboard. He directed his next question to Tess.

'Are instruments and equipment ready?'

Tess replied, 'Yes, thank you.'

'Estimation of blood loss?'

'Minimal,' Daniel replied.

The next questions the ODP himself answered. 'Patient's temperature is thirty-seven. Antibiotic prophylaxis has been given.' He then looked to the anaesthetist. 'ASA classification? Any concerns?'

'ASA 3. His diabetes is well controlled. Satisfactory vital signs and observation checks. As stated, low haemoglobin. Bloods on standby if needed. I've booked a HDU bed just in case, given his age.'

The final question was for Daniel. 'Are you happy to start?'

Daniel, seeing everyone was ready, nodded. 'Yes. Ready to start knife to skin.'

Daniel and Suzanne took their positions at the table. Tess would be passing instruments to both of them, as while Daniel located the blocked femoral artery, Suzanne would work on the lower part of the left limb to harvest a good vein that could be used as an anastomosis so blood in the artery had a new channel to flow through, bypassing the blockage. Vascular surgery was not unlike plumbing, Tess thought – replacing and re-joining blockages in pipework. The main difference being, a plumber could cut off the water supply and walk away. A surgeon didn't have that option. The pipework in the human body didn't bleed or block water but *blood*. Blocked blood.

'When you're ready, nurse?'

Tess looked up across the table and saw Daniel waiting with his hand out. Her face warmed as for a moment she'd thought to take hold of it. And how would that have looked if she had? Nurse holds surgeon's hand across the operating table. She almost giggled and had to control herself. She needed to be sensible. This was only her second time as his scrub nurse.

'I'm ready, Mr Myers. What would you like?'

He held her gaze for a few seconds as if to steady her. Then he spoke. 'Knife, please.'

The operation had been ongoing for over three hours and Tess's shoulders were beginning to ache from taking one action after another after another. *Knife, swabs, suction. Knife, swabs, retractor. Suction, sutures, swabs. More light, please. Less noise, please. More suction.* Tess wished for less noise too. Her hearing was getting muffled from the slurping sound of wetness being suctioned through narrow tubes. The annoying buzz the diathermy made cauterising bleeding capillaries. Daniel wasn't talking about those noises, though, when he asked for quiet. It was the talking at the head end of the table between anaesthetist and ODP, the ringing of a mobile phone in someone's pocket, and the singing, or rather the humming, poor Lucy was doing, which stopped immediately.

The long incision made down the inside of the lower left leg had been closed neatly by Suzanne, and a clear-window dressing covered it. They were reaching the last stages of securing the anastomosis graft. The femoral artery had been clamped either side of the blockage. The new vein had been attached to the healthy artery below the blockage and Daniel was now readying to secure the other end above it.

'Prolene 5-0 suture, please.'

Tess picked up a needle holder and clamped the threaded curved needle securely before handing it to him. She was startled when Cameron interrupted them. She'd forgotten he was even there.

'Sorry for interrupting, Mr Myers. I've got surgical assessment unit on the phone and they wonder if they could have a very quick word with Dr Lewis, please?'

Daniel sighed behind his mask, then spoke to Suzanne. 'I'll start attaching so be quick.'

Tess watched the doctor hurry over to a corner of the room to let Cameron carefully hold the phone to her ear, so that she didn't desterilise her hands. When she brought her gaze back to the table she thought she saw Daniel eyeing her a little coolly. *Damn.* He probably thought she was looking at Cameron. He returned his attention to the job and put in his final suture, securing it with a surgeon's knot.

Suzanne's voice was rising a little and she was talking rapidly. Tess stared into the operation field. Daniel was waiting for his assistant. She picked up the suture scissors to have ready. There was only one suture waiting to be cut. The operation would then be over. The clamps on the artery could be removed. The blood could start flowing through the new vessel. She looked at Daniel. He looked at her. Then he nodded. She could see the suture clearly. The tails of the tiny threads were being held by atraumatic forceps. She needed to get the scissors in below the forceps but above the tiny surgeon's knot. Daniel angled the instrument to give her a clear view. She captured the threads in the opened scissors and slid them down the suture. When satisfied with the length left, she cut.

Daniel released the clamps, one at a time, slowly in case of a spurt of blood from where the new vessel was attached. There was a small amount of blood oozing from the suture line, which was to be expected. They paused with a swab over the area for a few minutes. Whilst everyone had visibly relaxed and started talking, he winked at her and said, 'All bleeding stops… eventually.' He then switched back into business mode and asked for pedal pulse check, for a blood pressure check, ensuring the redirected blood flow was passing through the vein graft. He took his time making sure all other checks by both him and the anaesthetist were satisfactory. He could now close up.

Tess felt the tension leave her. It had been a long operation, but Daniel had been easy to work with. Giving clear, precise instructions every time from beginning to end.

When Suzanne came off the phone, Daniel released her to go visit the ward as clearly it was a problem that could not be sorted out over the phone. Sign Out – the protocol checks to be completed at the end of an operation – was directed by Lucy. Again, everyone's attention was required to answer the questions:

Are instruments, swabs, sharps a correct count? Has blood loss been calculated, swabs weighed, suction bottle fluids measured and total added up? Was the patient ready to go to the recovery room?

Yes, everything had gone well, the patient could be taken to recovery.

CHAPTER EIGHTEEN

Tess was ready to eat by the time she got to the atrium café. At the counter she ordered a jacket potato with a tuna top, a large coffee and a can of regular Coke in hopes of reviving her energy. Her seesawing emotions after that smile this morning followed by that long operation had all but drained her. She needed another few hours of concentration before she finished her shift. Before she finished her job?

How she wished she didn't have to – wished she had told Stella at the very beginning who she was, then this decision to leave wouldn't have arisen. Tess was good at her job, she loved it, but come five o'clock it would end, because she loved her husband more.

Loving someone can hurt, Sara said to her after she and Tess moved in together, after her doctor boyfriend broke up with her and married someone else. She was right. Even though she was only twenty-one at the time Sara still carried that hurt eight years later, better hidden but still there. Tess would like to reverse that, because love could also heal. She wanted to heal this rift between them, heal the cause. That smile this morning might not be seen for another while. It could go back to how it was last night, when she caught him staring out the window. A smile that barely raised his lips. In retrospect, regardless of her deception, leaving her job was the right move.

The two o'clock brief, in the same anaesthetic room, hadn't begun yet as they were waiting on the surgeon and the anaesthetist to join them. Suzanne had a copy of the afternoon list and was discussing the three cases while they waited. All were quick procedures that shouldn't tax them. The ODP, whose name Tess now knew to be Oli, was itching to get started. The tall lanky man was setting out infusion trays on the counter, saying he had to get off on time as it was his turn to mind the kids.

Right then the door to the anaesthetic room opened. Daniel quickly stepped into the room and spoke only to Suzanne. 'Sorry, can't stay. Cameron can assist unless you're not happy.'

Suzanne nodded to show she was okay either way.

'Dr Bob will be back any minute. He's just handing over to the anaesthetist in the emergency theatre.'

Suzanne stared at him surprised.

Daniel's expression showed he was too. 'Our patient this morning; he's not doing well.'

Tess looked at the clock on the wall at every passing hour, hoping to hear an update of the Cat1 patient in the emergency theatre, and hoping Daniel was okay and able to sort out the problem that brought the patient back into the operating room. The only thing she'd gleaned was the man never left the recovery room, so while she was having her lunch, Daniel and the anaesthetist must have spent their time there.

Suzanne was finishing up with the last patient on the table, a woman with debilitating veins stripped from her right leg, and was bandaging the limb now with Cameron's help. He had assisted with each case and Suzanne had been full of praise. His eyes smiled at Tess several times, and she was pleased for him. He'd needed that after having his confidence knocked.

At quarter past four the patient was wheeled to the recovery room. The anaesthetist and ODP returned to theatre fairly quickly, the handover of care to the recovery nurse taking little time as it was uncomplicated. The team for the afternoon then set about putting the theatre back straight, snapping off gloves, freeing faces of masks, and finally relaxing. It was the end of another day.

Julia was untying Suzanne's gown when Stella and Daniel made an appearance. Daniel's face looked strained. Stella's serious. Stella spoke first.

'I'm glad you're all still here. As I'm sure you're aware an incident Datix report now has to be completed. If at some time between now and tomorrow you could all write a statement on your actions and observations for the patient operated on this morning, I would be grateful.'

Tess, like her other colleagues, expected a Datix to be completed. The form for reporting any unintended or unexpected incidents leading to harm or a near miss to a patient had to be documented. A patient returning to theatre was an incident, but it was not uncommon. It shouldn't happen, but sometimes it did. What she hadn't expected was for them all to be asked to give a statement. This was only asked for if the situation was being investigated. Her heart fluttered with alarm. Her eyes sought out her husband. Was Stella asking them all to write about him?

Suzanne stepped away from Julia, making her way towards her consultant, who had yet to say a word. Her lovely calm voice spoke only to him.

'What happened? Did he die on the table?'

Daniel shook his head quickly. 'No, he's in ITU.'

'So what happened?' she asked again. 'A bleed?'

He folded his arms against his chest and slowly nodded. 'The anastomosis had dehisced. The whole lot must have burst apart when his blood pressure returned to normal in recovery.'

Suzanne's eyes rounded. 'Surely not. How?' she said, less calm now.

'When we went back in, he was bleeding out from his femoral artery. Once I had proximal control, you could see the suture end was floating in the wound. The final suture must have been cut too short. The scissors... clipped the knot as well.'

Suzanne looked horrified. 'But you wouldn't have...'

He sighed heavily, looking briefly away as if it pained him having to admit this to her. 'I didn't.'

'Well, then who? How? I was on the phone. I don't understand.'

Daniel stared right across the room. He took a couple of steps towards the person he was looking at, his expression regretful. 'I'm sorry, Tess,' he said. 'I know you were only trying to help, and if I'd seen what you were about to do, I would have stopped you. But regrettably you did and unfortunately you cut too short.'

Tess gazed unseeing back at him. Her mind had gone fuzzy. She couldn't feel her legs beneath her, or move her head even. She could feel shock, though. Her heart felt like it was pushing its way up her throat. Her husband had just said the most incredible thing. If she didn't know better she would believe him. She focused her eyes on his face. Waiting for him to take back what he said. But he just stood there. Why didn't he say something? Do something? Didn't he care? She couldn't breathe for looking at him. She couldn't turn or get away.

The room spun. Her eyelids fluttered and she felt herself falling through air.

'Oh Christ,' she heard her husband say. 'Someone help her.'

Tess felt hands touch her as she was lifted and repositioned onto something soft, and then she was able to stare up at their faces as she lay on her back.

'Let me see her,' she heard her husband say. 'She's in shock. Suzanne, get a line in, please. Let's give her some fluids.'

Tess smiled. This was the second time he'd joked about her having fluids. A sharp prick went into the crook of her elbow. She saw Cameron's face above her. He smiled down at her kindly. 'You're okay, Tess,' he said soothingly, stroking her brow.

A minute or two later, Tess wished she couldn't see so clearly the faces of the people standing around her as she lay on the operating table. Stella, Suzanne, Lucy, the nice Dr Bob, Cameron, Julia, Daniel. Stella looked deeply concerned.

'Tess, when you're rested and feel better, I'm going to organise a taxi to take you home.'

'I'll go with her,' Cameron offered. 'She shouldn't be on her own.'

'Good idea,' Stella replied, giving him a grateful look, and a nod to say she wanted a quick word.

'That won't be necessary,' Daniel said quietly, interrupting their plan, causing Stella and Cameron to stare back at him puzzled. 'I will take Tess home,' he said firmly.

'Mr Myers, that won't be necessary,' Stella replied, sounding shocked by the suggestion. 'Cameron is more than capable.'

'As am I, Stella,' he answered wearily, before looking around the table at them all. 'Thank you for your kind offer, Cameron, and thank you everyone for your help, but Tess is my responsibility. As her husband, I will take Tess home.'

Later, Tess will wonder if she only imagined hearing the gasps. What she won't imagine is the hurt in Cameron's eyes or the disappointment in Stella's.

Tess got off the bed. She'd been lying down since they got home, not sleeping, but with her eyes closed. Padding over to the window she drew back the curtains. It was dark outside and she had no idea of the time. Moving over to the tall chest of drawers where she left the things she'd emptied out of her pockets, she couldn't see her phone. Her pens, scissors, tourniquet and lanyard were still there, but no mobile. She'd definitely had it in the pocket of her scrubs, which she was still wearing, but more importantly she definitely brought it home and put it here with her other things.

She went back to the bed and searched under the pillows, in case she'd picked it back up unconsciously and taken it there. But there was no sign of it.

She sat back down on the bed, listening to the silence. She couldn't hear any sounds in the house and wondered if she was home alone. Had he gone back to the hospital after she'd gone to bed? She would go downstairs and make herself a drink. Then have a bath. Then she'd do some washing or ironing or some cleaning. She would put on the garden light and bag up the hedge trimmings. She saw yesterday they were still on the ground from two weeks ago. After cutting back the growth he hadn't cleared up the dropped leaves and branches. She would stay busy. That was the best thing she could do. She was not yet ready to think about her husband. Or say his name. She just had to stay busy.

Quietly entering the kitchen she went stiff with shock when Daniel rose from a chair. She blinked, then carried on moving, reaching for the kettle to turn it on. She took a mug already in the sink and rinsed it with cold water, not bothering to dry it before spooning in coffee. She fetched milk from the fridge and splashed some in, then put it back, before returning to the kettle not yet boiled to stir water into the mug. She drank nearly all of it in one go, taking gulp after gulp, then put the mug back in the sink, before moving on autopilot towards the door.

'Stella said to tell you not to worry over keeping your married name a secret. She said she'd call you tomorrow.'

Tess turned to stare at her husband. 'And what will she ring me on?' she asked in a hollow voice.

He held up her phone. 'I've taken this away from you. I think it best you don't be bothered by people. Best you not contact them and have chats that might upset you. Stella has the landline number. She'll call you on that. She understands how difficult this is for you.'

Tess felt her eyes press with tears. 'I understand why you did it. You needed me to take the fall, but did you have to do it like that in front of everybody? Could you not at least have warned me?' She didn't really want to hear his answer. She hurt too much. She wanted to be on her own curled up in a ball.

'Well, I'm sorry it was done that way, but I had no choice. The shame of it is, it wouldn't have happened if you hadn't been there, if you'd stayed home. I realise that now. It was a mistake I shouldn't have let happen.'

Tess found she couldn't swallow. What did that even mean? Was he saying this was her fault because she'd distracted him? She caused him to make an error?

'Are you blaming me for something you caused? Is this to punish me because I got a job? What actually happened?'

He gave a maddening sigh. 'Look, I've seen it all before. Juniors, who haven't been properly trained to use the tip of the scissors and don't have proper control, commonly cut too short.'

'Why are you saying I did that?'

'I'm just stating a fact.'

The lump in her throat was lodged so hard it was going to suffocate her if it didn't move. His words were killing her. His voice, more so. He could be discussing the weather, not the monumental shock she was suffering!

'I didn't cut short, I saw the knot and cut above it,' she insisted. 'Why don't you admit that. If I'm taking the fall I at least deserve some honesty.'

He stared at her, shaking his head from side to side, his eyes pitying her. 'You see, there's the problem, Tess. I can't help you with that, I'm afraid, if you really believe that. Maybe tomorrow when you've had time to think, you'll remember it better. You've had a shock today. Your mind is still cloudy.'

She stared at him astonished. Was he trying to deceive her or himself? The wheels were already in motion. She was getting the blame regardless, because what else could she do? With no other witnesses it would be his word against hers and his were far stronger. And what of their marriage – was it now over? Should she move out and file for a divorce? Why couldn't he do this one thing and tell her the truth? Could he not trust her enough with it? She was not going to blurt it out. It would be between them and it would help her to at least not feel so alone. 'I didn't cut short,' she said again. 'And my mind is clear.'

'You need some rest, Tess. I'm trying to help you here for both our sakes.'

She fixed her eyes on the black-and-white chequerboard tiles in the hallway. She would wash them tomorrow, get rid of the scuff marks left on the whites from his shoes.

'Try not to dwell on today.' He gave her shoulder a light squeeze as if to add weight to this advice.

'Do you even love me?' she asked quietly.

He tutted mildly. 'Of course I do, you silly thing.' He kissed the top of her head then gave her a light push towards the door. 'You need sleep. You're exhausted.'

On leaden legs, Tess climbed back up the stairs. At the bedroom door she looked for herself in the bed, sure that if she looked hard enough she would see her sleeping form still lying there, tossing and turning in a nightmare. She couldn't be awake because to be awake would make downstairs real. He hadn't given an inch. She was taking the fall, yet he couldn't even acknowledge it. Was the truth really that hard to reveal? Whatever caused the problem was an accident. It was no one's fault so why make it hers? Was he that desperate to save his reputation? She guessed he probably was, which made her feel even sadder. He'd used her to save his career without a second thought.

CHAPTER NINETEEN

Tess didn't know how she got through the night. Probably by keeping her mind blank, by keeping her eyes busy seeing things to dissect, follow, shape. She had traced the hairline cracks crossing the ceiling, turning them to streams following their course to small brown stains that shaped nicely into islands or curved bridges or elephants. Yellowy flakes gave texture to baby hair, desert grass, tiny hairs on a bee. Small stains, small cracks, small blemishes of a ceiling and lights kept on had kept her busy. All the while it was dark outside.

His side of the bed was smooth, the pillow undented. He'd let her sleep on her own and was now at work as she'd heard his car pull off the drive. She pulled back the sheet and got out of the bed. Her legs felt rubbery and had the same feeling in them as after running the London Marathon. Run only once and never again. Her legs had been weakened for days.

The landing floorboards were awash with a golden light from sunlight shining through the window straight ahead. It was a beautiful window without curtains that you immediately saw when you came out of the rooms on this floor. It was her favourite part of the house. She had seen images of her future on this landing. A small boy making *brum brum* sounds as he rolled his cars along its smooth length. A small girl pushing her pushchair with her baby doll or having a large doll's house against one of the walls where she could play with her make-believe families.

Tess walked resolutely ahead. After yesterday, she had no idea about the future anymore.

When ready, her bed made, bathroom tidied and scrubs hidden in the laundry bin, she went down the stairs. The place was quiet except for the tick of the clocks which in the quietness she didn't mind. For now they were soothing. In the kitchen she saw he had left her a note and also a twenty-pound note. *Money to buy something from the butcher. Nothing too fatty. D x*

She stared at the money as if it were alien to her. Why had he left it? She had a bank card to one of his accounts if she wanted anything. She saw her bag on the kitchen table and went over to look inside it. Her purse was at the top, but she normally kept it at the bottom. The pockets of the purse now only held a Sainsbury's Nectar card to collect points and a Costa coffee loyalty card. Her Lloyds debit card was missing. Tess computed this information very quickly.

She had virtually no money of her own. Her Barclays account, the one she'd had for the last ten years, had dwindled away to nothing as she spent the small savings she had getting married. A wedding dress for her, a bridesmaid's dress for Sara, and then a huge list of other things: bouquets, hair, nails, a gift for him, flowers for his mother, shoes, underwear. Added to her last payment of rent on her flat it had taken almost all her cash. She and Sara never got back their deposit, as they hadn't the time to do all the things one was supposed to do when giving up a tenancy – fixing the toilet door handle back on, cleaning the cooker properly. With Tess suddenly moving to Bath, Sara took the option to move in with her parents while waiting for her job in Australia to start. He knew she had no money of her own. So why had he taken away her debit card?

She took the twenty-pound note and put it in a compartment in her purse. She would find something in the freezer to defrost. Whether she cooked it or not was not something she could think of right now. She had things to do. She needed to make some coffee and then be busy. The clock on the kitchen wall read ten past ten. Yesterday, she had been up four hours by now.

As she switched the kettle on she heard the telephone ring. She walked out into the hallway and stared at it as if it were a dangerous animal, before gingerly picking up the receiver.

'Hello.'

She slumped with relief at hearing a man's voice. It wasn't the call from Stella. Her mind elsewhere, she missed the introduction of who he was or why he was ringing and asked him to say it again.

'Sorry,' he said pleasantly. 'It was really Mr Myers I wished to speak to. This is Dobsters Estate Agents in London.'

'I'm Mrs Myers,' she replied.

'Oh, well, that's good. It's about the flat. Very good news indeed I'm happy to say. We've sold it and with no chain either, so we're looking at a very quick move here. So it's really now a matter of the contents. There's a lot of furniture, of course, but also a lot of personal stuff. So perhaps you or Mr Myers could get back to me with a timeframe of when this can be done?'

Tess was still numbed from yesterday so all she could do was parrot back his message and say that she would tell her husband, and of course get back to him.

When the call ended, Tess computed this new information. This house had not been bought with the money her husband got from the sale of his flat in London. He had not yet had that money to buy it. Did this mean he was up to his ears in debt? She went back to the kitchen. She had jobs to do. She finished making the coffee. The sun outside was shining through the kitchen window making her want to feel its warmth. She didn't feel cold, but when she'd touched her skin it was like touching something from the fridge.

The garden was large and square, laid mainly to lawn with a path to a small summer house. The tall hedging wrapped around it looked neater for its trim, the hedge clippings dry on the ground from the sun. She would fetch the garden bin from the garage and collect up what he'd just left dropped there.

The garage was unfamiliar to her. The wide doors were tricky to undo as there were two locks she had to find keys for from the big bunch she had in her hand. She'd taken them from a hook on the wall next to the back door. Once inside the garage she was surprised that it looked smaller, though that was probably because of all the stuff left there. Old kitchen cupboards converted for garage use and metal cabinets used for storing heavy-weight tools. Lawnmowers, three of them, none with electric cables, and an old grass roller made of cast iron. Gripping the handle of the garden bin she wheeled it out of its space and saw a small wooden toddler trike with red handles and red wooden wheels. It had been hidden behind it. The sight of it saddened her. She imagined such a contraption being used by a toddler on the landing floor. The space was long enough and wide enough to have a good ride.

The sound of the phone ringing had her walking at a faster pace than she cared for, as hurrying anything – washing herself or washing a mug, coming to the garage – required energy she didn't have. Breathlessly, as if she'd run at speed to answer it, she said hello.

'Tess,' Stella said. Saying her name made it sound as if Stella was breathless too. Maybe she had run to make this call or else it was the difficulty of making it that caused her to lose breath. 'How are you? Oh, don't answer that. That was a stupid question to even ask. You must be feeling utterly overwhelmed. I'm so sorry about what happened to you yesterday. And I know, of course, you were only trying to help. But God love you, Tess, what on earth possessed you to pick up a pair of scissors and cut a vascular suture? Without permission? Without even having done the course?'

'How is he, Stella?'

Stella inhaled deeply. 'They've still got him on ITU. I don't know any more than that.'

'When do you need my statement by?'

'Today, while it's still fresh in your mind, if possible? I've given Mr Myers a few blank statement sheets for him to take home to you if you're happy to handwrite it. Or you can email it to me and I'll copy and paste it onto one.'

'I'll write it, Stella, it's not a problem. You'll have it back by tomorrow.'

'Tess, I think if I were you, once that is done, contact the union rep. Get their help from the start.'

'I will,' Tess said.

'Well, okay, Tess, that's all I really needed to do today. Touch base. While this is under investigation, you'll be stood down, so to speak. You know how it goes, Tess. You've been a band 6.'

'I do, Stella.'

'And don't you be worrying about that husband of yours. We'll be looking after him too. This has been a terrible shock for him as well. Understandably, he'll be worrying about you. So, we'll keep an eye on him. Tess, I'm going to go now, but please, in the meantime, take care of yourself.'

After the call Tess stood still in the hallway to think about her husband. When they first arrived here, he had carried her into the house and set her down beside this table. She had been so full of hope and naivety then. It was shocking to realise how much blind faith she'd had, how willingly she let herself believe she had a happy future ahead.

She mentally listed all the things she needed to do. Her statement for Stella was first priority. Get that out the way and then she could concentrate on other things. She would not wait until she got the statement sheets. She would write it now on some plain paper from his printer. She had plenty to keep her busy from now until he came home. She wanted to be ready by then.

It was nearing four o'clock when she heard a knock on the front door. Looking out of the dining-room window she could not see his car and breathed more easily. Tess was surprised when she opened the door to see the old lady standing there, looking at Tess as if Tess was not who she was expecting to see. She'd put her hand to her mouth and just stood there considering Tess.

'Are you all right?' Tess asked, and then smiled kindly. 'Have you come to the wrong house again?'

The woman shook her head, taking her hand away from her mouth. 'No, I've come to the right house, my dear. I came to the right house first time.'

Tess stared at her and was now concerned. She'd had a gut feeling that something wasn't quite right with her.

'Is he home?'

'Is who home?' Tess asked.

'Your husband.'

Tess shook her head. 'He's at work.'

The woman nodded, satisfied. 'Then I have something to tell you,' she said. 'Your husband is not who you think he is.'

Tess reared back slightly. Her eyes fixed on the woman's face. 'I don't understand.'

'I know you don't, my dear, which is why I'm here. You need to ask your husband a couple of questions, Mrs Myers. You need to ask him about his first wife and you need to ask him what happened to her.'

Tess's mouth was still hanging open as the woman scurried off up the driveway and away, catching a last glimpse of her fluffy white hair before it disappeared from her view. Was the woman mad? She was certainly eccentric. But was she mad? Was she wrong? She called Tess 'Mrs Myers'. She had not got that wrong. Tess closed the front door and leaned back against it. *Had he been married before? Had he a first wife?* He surely would have told her this if it was true.

Tess curled her hands and pressed her fingernails into her palms to get a hold of herself. Had he really kept this from her? After yesterday she didn't know what was true anymore. Except for the fact that he could lie. That was true. And not little lies either. Monstrous lies at her expense. Nothing about him added up anymore. His odd behaviour and mood swings were part of a background that was blank to her. The call from the estate agent and now this old lady's visit had blindsided her when she was already in the dark.

Was her husband ill or just a liar? She had wanted to heal him, find the cause for his behaviour. She had wanted to uncover more layers to know him better. And now she had. Looking at his behaviour last night she would say he was a narcissist for doing what he did to her. Denying her the truth when she was already in agony.

Had he a wife before?

She needed to keep busy. She had computed this final information. She didn't need to dwell on it now. It was there for her to think about when she was ready. She had to stay focused.

A minute after six the clocks stopped chiming. The house was silent again. Tess sat on the bed waiting. He was late and delaying her now. She didn't want to sit downstairs. She wanted to walk down them when she was ready. She was grateful for the bundle of notes she'd found in one of his drawers and had them stowed safely in her bag. It would be enough to allow her to walk out that door without resorting to sleeping on the streets. Though she would, if she had to.

She looked around the bedroom making sure she had not left anything behind, but couldn't see any of herself remaining there. She had cleared herself from every room. She wanted no part of herself left behind in this house. Everything not herself – the clothes and the perfumes he'd bought – could stay and were his for the keeping now.

She sat up straight as she heard his car in the driveway. He was home at last. Getting up from the bed, she smoothed the covers where she'd sat. Then with head held high and shoulders back she put her bag over one shoulder, and picked up her suitcase. He was on the phone when he walked through the front door, and he hadn't seen her or heard her yet. He was listening to whatever was being said to him and responding accordingly. A moment later she heard his goodbye.

He sensed a presence and looked up the stairs at her. He showed no reaction at seeing her with a suitcase. She had her short speech rehearsed.

'I'm leaving.'

Tess ignored his mild tutting. The pauses in between the tuts sounding like he was giving her a slow handclap. She ignored the sad indulgent smile he gave her. She concentrated instead on reaching the front door. He halted her at the bottom of the stairs by stepping in her way.

'I knew you'd want to run away from this, and I can't say I blame you. It's why I took your bank card.'

'I don't need your money, Daniel. I don't need anything from you except for the truth.'

'And what truth is that?' he asked.

She thought she detected a slight narrowing of his eyes. He was probably assuming she was referring to yesterday. 'I had a visit from an old lady,' she said. 'And she said something very strange about you.'

He raised an eyebrow. 'And did this old lady have a name?'

Tess shook her head, her eyes boring into him. 'She said you're not who I think you are.'

'That's what she said, is it?'

Tess nodded.

His expression showed concern. 'Well, that's all very interesting, but I hope you didn't pander to this poor old lady. I hope you invited her in. She sounds like she needed some help.'

Tess stared at him mutely. Was he stonewalling her? His reaction wasn't giving her an answer. Was he married before? She wished that question didn't hurt so much. It would be easier if she could just hate him and feel anger. Easier if her heart had not been so full of love for him. Because what did she now do with all these mixed-up emotions? How did they empty out of her? And where then did they go? There wasn't a place to put them. Maybe it was better if she didn't know. She was leaving with enough sorrow. She raised her chin determinedly. 'Would you mind stepping out of my way? I'd like to leave, please.'

'You may have to reconsider that after what I have to tell you, Tess,' he said in a soft tone.

She eased back from him, glancing apprehensively at the front door. Was this a trick to make her stay? 'What are you talking about?'

He looked briefly away, before his troubled gaze came back to hers. 'I'm so sorry, Tess, but it's not good news, I'm afraid. I think you're going to need all my help to get you out of this mess. I've just had a call, you see. And I hate to be the bearer of bad news, but I've just been informed the patient is dead.'

His voice was a little more impassioned than the one he used last night. The topic then had been about a live patient. Not doom, with no hope to come. She visibly shuddered.

He drew his finger lightly down her cheek. 'You poor thing,' he said. Then he relieved her of the suitcase and put it down on the floor.

'He'll have a post-mortem,' she said quietly. 'It will prove I didn't do it.'

He pulled a sad face. Slowly shook his head at her. 'It won't. All that will be seen is the new suture I had to put in. That I cut. To replace the one cut too short. It's a documented fact, Tess.'

He sighed as he reached down to take hold of her hand. He raised it to his lips and kissed it lightly. 'We have something to do now, though. I have your statement ready for you to sign. It's already typed so you don't need to worry about it. It just needs a signature.'

Tess allowed herself to steal a look at his face. Seeing his beautiful eyes so matter-of-fact. He was asking her to sign away her life as if it were dispensable. How could he be so unmoved by what he was doing? Was he so desperate to save his own career? Or were layers hiding another reason? Something worse than that?

She needed to be away from him. She needed to breathe a different air. But only a miracle could grant that. With this lie hanging over her head she was trapped.

CHAPTER TWENTY

Tess listened to the silence. The ticks of the clock in the hallway seemed interminably slow in coming, as if deliberately delaying to make the day seem longer. Her suitcase was still in the hallway. It seemed so long ago that she had walked down the stairs carrying it, but it was just last night. She would unpack it and put away her old self again.

She would have to stay now this patient was dead. She had signed a statement admitting to something she had done wrong. It was pointless to say her husband had written a lie, because he hadn't. She had cut the suture.

Under the explicit roles and responsibilities of a scrub nurse she had no permission to do that. She could assist with superficial wound closure. She could cut superficial skin sutures. These were ticked boxes in the list of permissions. Unticked: *cutting deep sutures and ligatures under direct supervision of the operating surgeon.*

The Royal College of Surgeons had introduced the qualification of a surgical first assistant to safeguard both patients and professionals. It took the pressure off the nurse to surgically assist when tasked with the role of being a scrub nurse. Tess had yet to do the course, even though she could have, as the more experienced she got the more she forgot about what she was legally allowed to do. As a qualified SFA she would have had permission to cut deep sutures. This box was ticked.

The responsibility lies with the surgeon doing the case to supervise. But how could he be held responsible if he didn't know what she was about to do? She had caused this death, according to her husband, and would be blamed and the outcome decided by others. She was not expecting any decisions to be made soon, as it would be a protracted process. When you were going to take someone's job away from them you had to make sure it was done by the book, that everything was done fairly. When you were going to stop a person from ever working in their chosen career again, well, then it had to be watertight.

Tess would be struck off the register. Her licence to practise as a nurse would be taken from her. She had not just caused a mishap, she had caused a death. If her act was judged to be negligence, she could even face a criminal charge.

Stella had advised her to contact her union representative, but with her husband as the surgeon saying she cut a suture of her own volition and then cut too short she had no defence. He would not admit to any nod he gave. That truth had been omitted from her statement.

In the rooms on the first floor she put back things she would need to use again. Toiletries to the bathroom, hairbrush to the dressing table, books to bedside drawers, photos of her and Sara to windowsills in other rooms so that she could see her around the place.

In the bedroom she pulled back the curtains and stared at the outside world. She was going to have to accept that her life was now different. She must make this her new normal, with her freedom to do and say what she wanted closed down. She turned away from the window. She had to live inside this house or find a miracle to clear her name. In the meantime she was dependent on the goodwill of her husband and all this help he was going to give. It would help if he gave back her bank card, but somehow she couldn't see that happening. He had taken it to keep her penniless.

When her husband arrived home Tess willed herself to stand still as his arms went around her to hug her hello. 'How has your day been?'

'Fine,' she replied.

He kissed the top of her head. 'I've been thinking about you all day, wondering how you're coping. I never asked how your talk went with Stella yesterday.'

'It was fine,' she replied. 'Stella was very kind.'

'She is, isn't she?' he said, setting her free so that he could make himself a drink. 'She's been very kind to me at work too. Well, everyone has really. Suzanne and Cameron send you their regards.' He placed a cup in the coffee machine, pressed the button then gazed at her concerned. 'That poor man, I think he's more upset than anyone. I saw Stella giving him a hug.'

Tess didn't comment. She let him carry on making his coffee and settle the cup into a saucer. She had been reminded of another phone call.

'I meant to tell you, yesterday the estate agent in London called to say they've sold your flat. They want to know when you'll be able to clear the contents. I said you'd get back to them.'

'I see,' he said, moving to the table to sit down. 'That is good news. I'll have to give it some thought.'

'I could sort it out,' she quickly offered. 'Being off work I could go and sort everything out so that you don't have to worry.'

He was shaking his head at her before she'd even finished. 'No, it would be far too much for you when you have so much to do.' Her eyebrows rose in response to this and he smiled happily. 'Go and have a look in my briefcase. I got you another present.'

Tess set his briefcase on the kitchen table to open it. Her eyes noticed the new perfume first, then a Waterstones bag.

'You can try the perfume later,' he said. 'It's the books I want you to see.'

She picked up the bag and eased the books out onto the table. One was a red hardback notebook. The other had a pale pink cover and was something to read. She kept her eyes lowered at the bold black words jumping out at her. Ladies. Etiquette. Politeness.

'I thought it would be something fun for you to read. To give you some helpful tips.'

'And the other one?' she asked, keeping her eyes glued to the pink cover.

'Ah yes, the other one, well, that's for me really. To help you. I thought we could call it "Improvements". What do you think of that title? I can write a to-do list each day with suggestions and ideas. Plan some weekly routines to help you with the chores and menus. A tidy house is a tidy mind, Tess, and with you not working you mustn't idle your days away and get all depressed. You need something to keep you occupied. Without some structure this house would be very difficult to manage.'

She raised her head and made her mouth form a smile. 'Yes, good idea. Thank you for thinking of it.'

He beamed. 'That's what I'm here for. Righty-ho, shall we say dinner for seven? Would that suit? I'm cooking you something nice.'

She nodded approvingly, hoping she could now leave the kitchen, but he kept her there a few seconds longer by handing her the perfume box.

'Don't forget this,' he said. 'Put some on. This one might be better.'

In the bedroom, Tess took a steadying breath. She was suffocating in a life that was unreal. The book on how to behave, dress, speak was written for the Victorian age and probably *was* a fun read if not for the fact he meant for it to be taken seriously, to improve her and make her into the person he'd like her to be. He'd already corrected her dress sense, her manners, use of Facebook. What more did he want to change? For her to sit straighter, stand taller? Who was this change for? Was it just so he could control her? He was wasting his energy if so. He already controlled her. Or didn't he know that?

Had he let her take the fall to keep her at home? That would be for a worse reason than saving his career.

When she presented herself back in the kitchen he was wiping the counter. He smiled at her pleasantly, making her wish she could read his mind, but he gave nothing away. She knew very little about any of his life. He had skipped through his childhood, giving just scant details. Two parents. No siblings. University. Then a doctor.

When she'd met his parents at the wedding they'd seemed like ordinary people. During the briefest of chats his father said he'd been a plumber, his mother a sales assistant for British Home Stores. Both retired. Tess had only been with them a few minutes and it had seemed rude to have only said hello and goodbye. No wonder his mother hadn't engaged with her more when she'd telephoned. Her daughter-in-law was a stranger to her.

Tess remembered something odd about the seating arrangement for the top table, that she hadn't given much thought to at the time. His parents were not seated beside him, but at another table. At the time he'd said it was because he didn't want her to feel the absence of her own parents. She wondered now if it was for a more personal reason. Perhaps he was ashamed of them, with his father in an ill-fitting suit off the peg, his mother in an everyday floral dress. When his mother came to say goodbye she said it was nice to meet her as if Tess were a stranger, and had not just become part of her family. But maybe Mrs Myers senior had felt it the right way to say goodbye because her son was a stranger to her.

She broached the subject carefully now. 'I wonder whether we should invite your parents over sometime. Invite them for a Sunday lunch perhaps?'

He seemed momentarily at a loss for words. He stared through her, frowning a little, before focusing again. 'They're simple people, Tess. Our lives wouldn't suit them.'

What a sad reply, she thought. 'You're nothing like them, from what little I remember of them,' she commented as he turned away from her to attend to the food he was cooking. 'What were they like as parents? Strict? Or did they spoil you?'

He shrugged. 'One makes do with what one has.'

His reply stunned her, it sounded so unkind. She wondered if this was the cause of his behaviour, if he had a deeply rooted identity problem.

He turned and caught the surprise on her face. 'The trick is to know when to let go of what one doesn't need.'

Tess was struck by the coldness of his words, more so because he was saying it in a tone that was light and matter-of-fact. It made her aware, though, he had no admiration for his parents.

The mushroom risotto he'd made was served in deep white bowls and looked perfect, yet each mouthful was a struggle to get down her tight throat. She had to concentrate hard to swallow and not let her mind wander as she could become immediately overwhelmed if her thoughts didn't lay dormant.

Across the dining table, she noted his amenable manner, as if nothing was changed between them.

'I thought we could go away when all this business is finished with your job,' he said in a pleasant tone, gaining her instant attention. 'Would you like that?'

She smiled and nodded automatically. He made it sound like this business had nothing to do with him. Had he allowed himself to believe that?

'I'm thinking Vienna. Autumn should see it at its best. Fewer tourists.'

'Have you been before?' she asked, knowing she had to respond at some point. She must learn how to cope with conversations like this as he might decide not to help her at all. He was her best bet right now. If she could persuade him to at least admit to that nod it would be something. Even if he were to say he was nodding at something else it would show she had not acted wilfully.

'Yes. And I think you'd like it. I shall take you to the Vienna State Opera House and then maybe dine at the Vestibül. It's rather wonderful.' He smiled. 'Won't that be something nice to look forward to?'

'Yes. Thank you,' she agreed, thinking of the happy holiday they had on their honeymoon. Cornwall in July should have been sunny. For most of the two weeks they were away it was rainy and cold, but she'd been so happy she hadn't cared. She'd frolicked on the sand and gone in up to her thighs in the cold sea. Happy to be loved. She wanted to pinch herself and wake up from this nightmare. How could that happiness have just gone?

He put down his knife and fork, placing them neatly together on the plate. He drained his wine glass, patted his lips and wiped his hands with a linen napkin. 'Now,' he said, standing. 'Let's forget dessert. I think you and I need to do something about this baby-making. What do you say?'

Tears pressed behind her eyes. He was asking her to make love with him, make eye contact with him as if completely infatuated.

Her world had been tipped upside down, pushing her unanchored into darkness, and now this. She smiled, compliant, and rose from her chair.

CHAPTER TWENTY-ONE

In the bathroom she swallowed two paracetamol with a cupped hand of tap water, before seeing a glass she could have used. Her brain was pounding inside her skull. It had been another night without sleep and she was feeling ill from it. Dizzy, disorientated, dulled. She sleepwalked through her chores, struggling to get to this afternoon, unable to sit or relax. Her body wouldn't allow it. She kept feeling the ghost of his hands still touching. It humiliated her to recall how she used to want him, how forward she had been to have him inside her. Last night she thought it would never end and had willed herself to stay in that bed until it was over. Pretended to moan and enjoy, while her insides corroded. He had killed her soul with his lies. He had broken her heart.

She climbed into the bed and buried herself beneath the covers. If she could sleep she could cope. Or at least have the energy to try.

She was drowning. She couldn't breathe. The wet pressure on her face was suffocating and terrifying. She opened her mouth to scream and choked on water pouring down her throat. Her lungs were desperate for air and the added weight on her chest was crushing the life out of her.

The weight on her body suddenly lifted. Something wet was dragged off her face. She raised her head while gagging and spluttering and heaving for air, then opened her eyes. He was standing right beside the bed and was waving something in her face. Her heart skidded to a halt as she saw her pills. *Stupid, stupid her. She forgot about them.*

'I asked for the truth and yet still you lied. You have deceived me again,' he said in a low voice.

On the bedside drawers she saw an empty glass and a sodden flannel. He tapped his finger against the glass.

'Did you think you were drowning? It's shocking how effective a glass of water can be. You've made me do something I'm not proud of, but after seeing you sleeping and seeing tablets left out on the sink... Then the relief when I realised you hadn't taken them all. The relief of putting them safely away, only to be shocked again as my fumbling hands knocked things. Your lies fell out into the sink.'

He stood over her and held the blister pack of contraceptive pills. He shook his head at her sadly and flicked them towards her face slowly, one at a time, while he talked.

'Lies, Tess, have got you to here. Lies even on our honeymoon as you so deviously demonstrated when you spat out that pill.' He let the empty packet drop on her face. 'You've made me not trust you after this,' he said bleakly.

Tess felt her insides buck, forcing her to pitch sideways as more water came up her throat. Coughing, with a heave of breath she spluttered out a *sorry*, desperate for him to go and to leave her alone.

'I won't again,' she wheezed in a high thin tone. 'I'm sorry.'

'Are you?' he said, looking in her eyes. 'I wish I could believe you. After all I'm trying to do for you with this mess you've made at work. Tell me, Tess, do you think that's fair?'

She numbly shook her head.

He stared at her and then at the wet on the bedside drawers, on the pillow and sheet. His eyebrows rose.

'What a mess. What a mess. You'd better clean this bed up. It's not fit to lie in.'

Through stunned eyes, Tess watched him walk towards the door. Too shocked to cry, too drained to find the energy.

He carried on walking to the door, before stopping and turning to look at her. 'You're breaking my heart, Tess.'

Then he closed the door on her.

He was gone when she went down the stairs at five o'clock, and she was surprised it was so early. She'd thought when he woke her in that terrifying way it was evening, that she'd slept for hours, but it was only the middle of the afternoon. He must have left work early to check on her, and having punished her gone out somewhere.

She had been upstairs for what seemed like hours cleaning her mess and didn't hear him leave. She'd dragged herself out of the bed and moved like someone recovering from an operation as she bundled up the linen. Now the bed just needed remaking. She downed a glass of water and climbed wearily back up the stairs.

She was down on her knees by his side of the bed, exhaustedly pushing the overhang of sheet under the heaviest mattress imaginable. She had too much of it over this side and was too tired to get back up and pull more the other way. She wanted to stop having to move altogether and climb into a bath, then into a clean bed.

Making one last effort, she pushed the sheet in further and was surprised when her fingers touched something solid. She groped to get a hold of it and ended up pushing it away. Raising an edge of the mattress she was able to get her head beneath it and hold it up while she pushed her arm in up to her shoulder and stretched her fingers until the palm of her hand landed on it and she pulled it out.

Breathless from exertion, she slumped back against the side of the bed staring down at the small black book in her hand. It had a black ribbon tied around it to keep it closed. She fleetingly wondered if it was his, a notebook bought perhaps at another time then discarded as too small to write down all his lists of 'Improvements'. Tess undid the ribbon and opened it to the first page. The book did not belong to her husband. The three lines of cursive handwriting bore no resemblance to his penmanship whatsoever, which was choppy and hard to decipher most of the time. This handwriting was quite beautiful.

She could see no name written anywhere. Not on the inside of the cover, nor at the back of it. Yet flicking through she saw lots of pages filled with writing. She wanted to get more comfortable, as she was too tired and too achy to sit there slumped. She turned around and got back on her knees. The thought crossed her mind that if he walked in and found her like this he'd think she was kneeling at the bed in prayer. The irony of it was not lost on her – that she would pray when she had no faith in any god anymore.

She shook her head, turning away from her thoughts, and settled the book on the bed. Then, in the surrounding silence, she began to read:

I am writing this in the event that should something happen to me there is a record of what I am enduring. If it is found beneath this mattress then I am lucky as he hasn't found it, and therefore I must be free.

Tess felt her skin crawl with unease.

The book must belong to the woman who once lived here, left beneath the mattress for goodness knows how long. The mattress must have been on this bedstead for years. It was old but not shabby, in fact very comfortable and in pristine condition. But it had a real old-fashioned quality about it. It wouldn't surprise her if she put a slit in its side to find it filled with horsehair. It fitted the bedframe perfectly, which looked antique. Made of solid walnut, it was carved with foliate details, and had a decorative crest on the headboard like a crown on top, its wood having a warm patina with age. It would take fit men to lift the mattress off the bed it was so deep, and probably a small army to lift the bed when it was in place.

How long had the book been lying there? she wondered. How old were the people who lived there? The woman who wrote it? It was hard to judge if the book was old or new. The design of it was hardly different to the one her husband had bought. Maybe what was written inside would give her some clue to its age. She turned the page and read the first line.

This house he calls my home has become my prison.

Tess felt her heart catch in that one sentence. It could have been written for her. This house was now her prison.

These walls I'm sure have eyes. It cannot be just his ability to see through me as he is able to relay back each day my every move. Today I did not wear the brown uniform he provided me with. I scrubbed the front doorstep wearing my ordinary clothes. There is nothing about them to be able to tell him this. And yet he knows. He always knows.

She had to stop reading. She closed the book and closed her eyes. It felt like she had just invaded someone's very private and painful life. The few lines she'd read struck a chord deep within. Someone else had been unhappy in this home. She felt she owed it to this woman to at least read it, but not yet. She wasn't ready to read this secret book while her brain was trying to deal with another shock.

His behaviour. Not accidently or in rage, but deliberately, intentionally, he had done that to her. He had now given her an even deeper reason to fear him. History had taught her that if someone hurt you once and they got away with it, they would do it again. To justify it, they would blame you. *You* made them do it.

She remembered the old lady's words. *You need to ask him what happened to her.*

What did this actually mean? Had he hurt his first wife? If so, how? That's if there was a first wife. She did not want to outright accuse him with everything else going on unless she was a hundred per cent sure. But if it was true... what happened to her?

CHAPTER TWENTY-TWO

Martha stood forlornly in front of the grave. She used her headscarf to give the headstone and surrounds a dusting, trying to make it look shiny again. The flowers from the Co-op she couldn't get to look right as they were too squashed together in the vase. She sighed heavily, and wished she hadn't bothered. The man in the shop hadn't been friendly, eyeing her up and down like an unwanted customer as if he begrudged taking her handful of copper and silver. She should have taken the money out of the jam jar first and put it in her pocket. Which reminded her, where had she put the jar?

She went back to the headstone and smoothed it as if it were a living thing. 'It's all right for you down there, Ted, enjoying your rest. But you should be up here with me, helping me sort out this matter. I'm getting tired, Ted, and I want to come home to you now.'

She was getting maudlin because she would be leaving him soon. It wasn't so much the physical leaving of the grave that hurt but the thought of leaving the man beneath it. She liked talking to him here, felt close to him. On a better day she'd joke with him that he'd better be keeping things tidy down there for when she arrived. Not today, though, not in her present frame of mind. She was too worried by far for any joking. The new wife was still in that house.

Why was she still there? Had she asked him about his first wife? Or worse, not believed what she'd been told. Thinking she was safe and having the same thoughts as Jim: *Poor old fool is losing her mind*. She stroked the headstone one last time before taking her leave. She had to get home now. She had the police coming to see her. The nice man on the phone had said someone would come and talk to her, but next time she rang could she ring 101 and not 999? He'd told her that was the emergency number and she'd told him back that that's why she was calling it. This was an emergency. When she got home she'd tell Jim. Then let the police talk to him so he'd know she was right.

She hurried her footsteps as she headed along the pathway, feeling that it was later than Ted's watch said. It didn't feel like ten past three. It felt later than that. Though that could be from all the trees surrounding her, blocking out the light and making it look dusky. If she had her proper walking shoes on she'd get home a lot faster. How she managed to leave the house in her slippers was anyone's guess, but they were getting ruined from soaking up the damp in the grass. She'd kick them off when she got back before mister-see-it-all saw them. She hoped he had something nice for tea. She'd like a nice piece of haddock if it was their fish and chips night.

She shuffled and shivered a bit as cold air swept in along the path, wishing she hadn't stayed out this long, but not actually knowing how long she had stayed out. It felt like yesterday since she'd last eaten. She was now in the older part of the cemetery, where the graves were very old and caved in and sunken. It was difficult to tell where to walk so as not to step on the consecrated ground. Difficult to identify the graves as lettering had long rubbed off and trees had grown through a few. There were two little graves here somewhere that Father John had shown her. Two little angels.

Martha stopped walking, getting suddenly stressed. Two little graves? She had to think, were they hers? She took a shaky breath and carried on walking. Not hers. It was two little girls. Someone else's loss. A lot of the graves she was passing had their crosses lying down, the stone so old they had fallen. The gothic-looking chapel ahead didn't bother her. There were usually a few old fellers there, down on their luck taking shelter, supping something to keep them warm. Passing under the main archway she saw no one.

A short walk later she stopped again, this time stressed for a different reason. She had passed this great big mausoleum of a grave on her left once already and there it was again. How had she got lost? Jim would start panicking if she got home too late. She'd have to go back to Ted's grave and start again. When she got her bearings she'd be all right. She'd buy Jim some chocolate on the way home for worrying him. As much as she hated to admit it, she'd be lost without him.

It was getting dark, she realised, and the dimly lit pathway was treacherous. She suspected the lightbulb covers needed a clean. Still, she couldn't complain. Who needed lights on at night in a graveyard? She was relieved when she saw the silhouette of someone coming towards her. She could ask for directions now. Then felt a bit unnerved as the person got closer and she saw how tall he was and how dark his hair was. Her instinct was telling her to hide.

She moved off the path and back onto grass further away from the weak white light, to stand close to a tree. She wanted to see his face before she showed herself to ask for his help. The shopping bag in her hand was getting heavy. She should have shaken the dead hydrangea out of the earthenware pot and left the pot there. She was tempted to put it down, but something was telling her not to. She had a feeling she should start walking away from this person, head through the graves if necessary. Or just stay still until he'd passed and was gone.

Her legs suddenly weakened as she recognised the walk and the broad shoulders, and like a child she squeezed her eyes shut so that he couldn't see her. She must have unnerved him with her outburst. His wife may have told him she'd called and now he was going to make sure she didn't say anything ever again. She wished she could shut her ears too. His footsteps were coming slowly, moving the loose gravel along the path, making soft little scrapes of sound, the noise so deafening, so threatening, Martha couldn't help her whimper. Once made, her little noises got louder, until she was crying to God and to all the angels above, and to Michael the Archangel to save her from Satan, and to the Blessed Virgin Mary, the queen of heaven, who had lost her only child. 'Hail Mary, Full of Grace, The Lord is with thee. Blessed art thou among women, and blessed is the fruit of thy womb, Jesus. Holy Mary, Mother of God, pray for us sinners now, and at the hour of our death. Amen. Hail Mary—'

She squealed out in terror at the touch on her shoulder and any remaining strength in her legs failed her. Strong arms enfolded her, a hand stroking over her head. She blocked out the voice calling to her, until she heard another voice she was more used to hearing in the dark, when in private to confess her sins. Martha opened her eyes and saw the tall figure of her parish priest. Father John, looking like Count Dracula in his dark overcoat.

'Is she all right, Jim?' he asked. 'The police have called an ambulance.'

Martha stared at the man holding her and saw Jim's face stark with worry.

'Did I miss my fish and chips?' she asked.

Jim's response was to give her too tight a hug. But she didn't mind. It was Jim and not that demon man.

'Did the police come to the house?' she asked.

He nodded, hard. 'They're here, parked outside the gates.'

'Well, it was good of them to wait. I lost track of time. I lost the jam jar too. Jim, is my bag here?'

He nodded. 'It's right beside you, Martha.'

'Good. I have a dead plant in it.'

'How are your legs, Martha? Do you think you'd be able to stand up?'

'In a moment, I will. I want to ask first, did you see him?'

Jim shook his head, causing Martha to sigh with disappointment. 'No matter,' she said. 'When I've told the police all of it, they'll go see him.'

'Come on, let's get you up. There's an ambulance on its way, and unless you want to spend a night in A & E you'll have to show them you're fighting fit.'

He helped Martha up off the ground and dusted her down, reminding her of her own earlier actions. She felt the top of her head. Her scarf was gone. Hopefully it was in her bag along with the jam jar. She hoped she hadn't lost it. It wasn't a scratchy nylon thing like some of her others. She saw Father John standing on the path; she had forgotten the man was there.

'What are you doing here in the cemetery, Father John?'

'Helping Jim look for you, Martha. You gave us all a bit of a scare. Did you get locked in when the gates shut?'

Her eyes showed her surprise. 'I didn't know they were. What time is it?'

'It's after nine o'clock.'

Martha grabbed hold of Jim's arm, mortified. 'Jim, I'm so, so sorry. And after promising you I'll behave. I'll understand, Jim, if you start looking for new quarters. I won't hold it against you. You've been more than good enough to me.'

Jim tucked his arm beneath hers, to lend her some support, as they walked along the path in the near dark.

'And then who would I have to give me all this trouble? You're all right, Martha. I'll not be leaving. At least not until we've warmed up the cold fish and chips.'

Martha's laughter carried across the cemetery, reaching to the ears of the police, and to the paramedic just getting to the gate. It was a good strong sounding laugh. Reassuring them that someone this old who'd been lost all day – causing mounting worry after a shopkeeper reported his concern at seeing an old lady carrying a jam jar of pennies and wearing her slippers – was found safe and able to make this robust sound. It would have been awful if they'd found her in there dead among the dead.

CHAPTER TWENTY-THREE

Tess ventured out of the bedroom when she heard the front door close. She was desperate for the loo. Treading down the creaky stairs from the top floor she stood still as she reached the landing to listen for any sounds coming from the ground floor. Reassured to hear only the ticking of the clock she hurried to the bathroom, passing their open bedroom door. He'd slept alone in the freshly made bed while she stayed in a single bed in the room above — anxiously, in case he came up to find her.

She winced at the slight sting as she started to pee, she'd held her bladder too long and hadn't drunk enough. In bare feet and wearing only pants and a T-shirt she made her way downstairs, her need for some tea more important than her state of dress.

In the kitchen, evidence of his cooking from last night was left out on the worktops, the remnants of food dried in pans and on plates and vegetable peelings curling on the draining board. He hadn't cared enough to clean up, not even to scrape the food from his plate. He'd left it for her to do.

She drank a full glass of water before switching the kettle on, and started to clear his mess. Working quickly and making a clattering noise in her haste to get done, she scraped dishes and banged pans and then punished them with a scouring pad under a constant flow of water. The room fell silent as she loaded a final pan. She breathed out noisily as she closed the dishwasher door, and then almost jumped out of her skin.

She'd heard sounds coming from the study. He was not at work. But she had heard him go out, heard the front door close. She left the dishcloth in her hand on the worktop and with insides quivering made her way to the study. The door was ajar. He was wearing one of his best suits, a charcoal grey, and was standing looking at the bookcase. She saw his fingers run across manila folders, his hand momentarily resting on an old pale one before he picked up a newer-looking one next to it.

He turned and saw her.

'Did you want something?' he asked bluntly.

She shook her head and moved closer into the room. 'I thought you were at work. I thought I heard the front door close earlier.'

'You did, it closed behind me when I went out to fetch the post.'

'Is there any mail for me?'

'No.'

She fidgeted as she stood there, conscious of what she was wearing, wishing she'd put on more clothes.

'In that case could I have my phone back so I can check to see if Stella has emailed me? The hospital might get in touch with me that way. I'd also like to see if Sara has been in touch.'

'She hasn't,' he replied. 'And nor has Stella. I've been checking for you.'

Her eyes got big. 'How?'

His expression said she should know how. 'Your password was too easy to work out. Using your date of birth is not a sensible thing to do.'

She lowered her eyes, not wanting him to see how this invasion of her privacy affected her.

'Yes, that was rather foolish. It was silly of me to do that.'

He took a step closer at the quiet tone of her voice and studied her.

'You look pale. Are you feeling unwell? You don't look like you have a fever.'

'It's nothing. I might have a water infection. My urine stings a little.'

He looked at her critically. 'Give me a sample and I'll get it tested. I'll bring you home an antibiotic.'

'Don't you think it would be best if I go to my GP?' she suggested, wishing instantly she hadn't been so outspoken or phrased it that way.

He placed the red folder in his open briefcase then locked it shut. He tapped three of his fingers in a slow drum roll on the closed lid.

'No need to do that,' he softly said.

She didn't answer. He stepped around the side of his desk to stand right in front of her, forcing her to look up at him.

'You have me to administer to your needs. If you think you need examining, I'll do it.'

She shuddered at the thought and he put a hand to her forehead. 'Maybe you do have a fever. Stay in bed and rest. There's no need for you to prepare supper tonight. I want you well because we're dining at one of my colleague's homes. The Porters.'

He saw her alarm. 'You'll like them, they're nice. Perhaps you can pop out and get his wife some flowers. She's called Vivien.'

'I don't have any money.'

His eyes settled on her face, as if considering something. He sat on the edge of his desk, letting her wait for his response.

'Shall I not get them?' she asked.

He folded his arms, his manner relaxed. 'You've made things very difficult for us, Tess, and I really hope we can get past it. I've been giving some thought to a few things. One is whether to let you go to London to sort out the flat. The other being, can I trust you?'

Tess held her breath in the hope of a chance to have some freedom. 'You can trust me. I promise.'

A moment later he stood up. 'You don't get back your card or your phone and I'll get your train tickets. I suspect you'll have to make more than one journey.' He pulled his wallet out of his jacket and handed her forty pounds. 'In the meantime, get Vivian some flowers.'

He left ten minutes later, staying long enough for her to pass a urine sample. He told her to be ready by seven when he'd be home to fetch her, and to wear something nice as the Porters were having special guests. He clearly thought it important to attend. She could hear it in his voice.

At the kitchen table she sat down, feeling a little giddy. Her nerves fired with possibilities. She was going to be allowed to go back to his flat in London. Maybe more than once. With a little bit of freedom she would have time to find out the truth about his past. She needed to contain her excitement else he might sense it and change his mind, like the man in that book who saw through the writer. She'd hidden the book somewhere else. Somewhere he wouldn't chance finding it – under the mattress of the bed she had slept in last night. When she'd had some tea and was dressed she'd go and read more of it. She was on two missions now: uncover the mystery of this woman and uncover the mystery of her husband too.

There were two small bedrooms on the top floor of the house but no toilet or washroom facilities. On the first floor there were two bathrooms and five large bedrooms with a further bathroom on the ground floor. Tess had thought the arrangement of rooms could be made better use of and more suitable to a large family. She had imagined some conversions taking place in the future, like having a shower room put in on the top floor, and perhaps an en suite to the master bedroom. That was when she'd been eager to change things and had seen a wonderful future there.

The small bedroom she entered was only small compared to the other bedrooms, as it was larger than the one Tess had at her flat in London. It was not a homely room – it had just a bed, a wardrobe and a chest of drawers. A thin vase of faded fake flowers on the windowsill put her in mind of an old people's home, the pink eiderdown found in the wardrobe and put on the bed making it more so. It would be a good-sized house to turn into one, though she couldn't imagine her husband ever wanting that. He wanted it filled with his children.

She slipped her hand under the mattress and took out the book and then sat sideways on the bed with her back against the wall to carry on reading:

Has he got Mrs Bowden spying on me? She is always kind to me so it is hard to consider that she might do this. Or perhaps Robert has told him, because when I took the car out on Wednesday and put it back exactly as I found it, Robert was in the garden pushing that very heavy grass roller I keep telling him not to, and looking anxious when I returned. He is only a young lad and needs the few pounds he is paid, but if my husband has coerced him into doing this with the threat of him losing his job, I cannot say that I can blame him. I can only blame the person who made him do it.

He knew I took the car that day. Perhaps he is monitoring the mileage. I cannot stay here much longer, but where else will I go where he will not find me? Today I showed my doctor the swelling in my breast, and he avoided looking at me when he gave me some ointment. Nor has he asked me how I came by the bruises which I find rather sad in this day and age. This is not the first time he has seen me with them, and I have to ask myself if this is an old-boy network thing where one professional protects another one's reputation? I think it is. My husband is a very charismatic man, even up close you cannot tell what goes on behind his green eyes.

Tess sat up with a jolt. Then she scanned through all the pages looking for a name, expecting to see *Daniel* written somewhere on a page. After coming up blank, she put the book down and cupped her hands over her mouth and nose to breathe into them. This story could be about him. This could be her husband in this book. It sounded very much like this woman's husband was a doctor too.

This book might belong to his first wife. She breathed in and out, anxiously. She had to find out about her husband's past. She needed to see his parents. Ask them outright if their son had been married before. She needed to figure out the truth about Daniel, if she had any hopes of clearing her name. People might be less inclined to believe his lies if she uncovered a secret wife. And if it was true it would mean Daniel already knew this house. He had lived here before. He was nearly forty years old. Where was he before St Mary's, two years ago? It may account for why he'd not shown her around this city or suggested they explore. He may already know it.

She needed to find this old lady now and when she did she was definitely going to invite her in. She'd ply her with tea, then ask her exactly what she knew about Daniel.

CHAPTER TWENTY-FOUR

He handed her a box of Trimethoprim and told her to take the tablets for the next three days. She was peeing more but with ease now. He didn't say if he'd found anything in her urine sample and she didn't ask. She swallowed the first white tablet in front of him and then followed him out to the waiting taxi. She held the bunch of mixed flowers in her hand and he glanced at them briefly.

'Not much for forty pounds, is it?'

'I should have gone to a different shop,' she replied. 'Not the one on the corner.' She thought it looked a lot of flowers for twenty pounds. The money she'd not spent had been added to her meagre savings.

'I should have got her better ones,' she said.

'Annoying cow probably won't even notice them.'

She looked at him in surprise and saw him grin.

'Dreadful woman doesn't shut up. How Mark puts up with her I don't know.'

'Thank you for reminding me of his name. I would have forgotten to ask.'

In the back of the taxi he felt for her hand and gently pressed it. 'He wasn't as lucky as me, finding someone like you.'

Her insides were doing somersaults. He was behaving like everything was normal between them. He leaned over and gently kissed her on the mouth. 'You do me proud looking like you do. I shall be the envy of every man tonight. I wish we were going somewhere else for dinner. Just the two of us.'

She swallowed hard and tried to relax as he clasped her hand as if they were a normal couple out on a date.

The Porters' home was set on the outskirts of the city, a stone-built house that was once part of a farm, probably at one time the farmer's home. The sky wasn't properly dark yet but full of orange-and-dark-blue clouds over black hilly countryside. It was peaceful, Tess decided, rural, with little traffic to be heard. She could imagine being out here in the winter dressed in wellies and a fisherman-style jumper.

Their hostess was wearing a pink summer cocktail dress, strapless and figure-hugging. Her skin was tanned, probably naturally. Her husband Mark was shorter and rounder than his tall slim wife and more casually dressed in an open-collar pale blue check shirt with sleeves rolled up to the elbows. In a flurry of kissing and handshakes and the pointing out of where the loo was they were brought into a home that had been stripped of its original character. The décor was ultra-modern. Chrome spotlights embedded in a smooth white ceiling – where once would have been exposed beams – shone down on large white floor tiles. A deep-red patterned rug made a walkway between two black leather sofas stacked with stark white feathery cushions. A small glass table bookended each sofa. On two of them were matching red lamps.

Champagne flutes were placed in their hands and the flowers and wine they brought were whisked away.

They were taken into a large conservatory set out as a dining room, and introductions were made to the other couple standing there. Tess smiled and shook hands with the small slim woman as Daniel greeted the man as Professor Ferris. The man waived his title with a warm smile. 'Please, call me Ed. And this is my wife, Anne.'

Tess suspected Ed was the 'someone special' her husband wanted to meet and wondered if he was a doctor in the same field of medicine. They seemed a nice couple, trim and fit-looking, in their early fifties or perhaps older, and more casually dressed than their hostess. Tess felt her choice to wear the simple short-sleeved navy dress again with its Peter Pan collar was suitable after all, having felt underdressed just a moment ago when seeing what their hostess was wearing. She tuned out momentarily as Daniel spoke to Ed and Mark spoke to Anne and was surprised when she felt a kiss on her cheek.

'Thank you, Tess. They're lovely,' Vivien enthused, holding the vase of flowers aloft. 'She's absolutely adorable, Daniel,' she called to him. 'You're a very lucky man indeed.'

Daniel acknowledged this with a smile, while Tess blushed and wondered how well he knew these people. Vivien certainly felt comfortable with him.

'And you look very handsome tonight, Mr Myers,' she added.

'You're looking pretty adorable yourself tonight, Vivien,' he responded.

Vivien laughed. 'Well, one has to make an effort at our age. Can't let it all go to rack and ruin. Though I see you haven't since I last saw you. You've returned to Bath looking even more dashing.'

Tess stood there stunned, but must have hid it well because no one was looking at her oddly. This new city wasn't new to her husband, only to her. She had suspected as much, but now had it confirmed. She felt her eyes prick at the deceit of it all, feeling disconnected to reality. She felt a swirl of anger in her stomach. For a second she imagined taking the vase from Vivien's hand and smashing it over his head. He was the liar. Not her.

She forced herself to smile. Breathe, and let it go. She had to protect her brain, deal it one shock at a time, nice and slowly. Let it process without a rush.

The evening progressed, the food was good, and Vivien delighted in bringing out one course after the other, with an aproned young woman in tow.

'This lovely young woman lives in the village and helps out,' was the only introduction she gave of someone clearly doing most of the work.

'I hear you're a theatre nurse?' Anne now said.

'Yes,' Tess answered quietly, not wishing to draw others into their conversation. Nor tell this woman she might not be one anymore. She had short light-brown hair with a few strands of grey running through, and kind grey eyes that seemed to stare right into Tess.

'And just married?'

Tess nodded. 'Yes, the third of July. Then two weeks honeymoon, and two weeks after that we moved to Bath.'

Anne gave a look of sympathy. 'Crikey, you've been busy!'

Tess smiled as she inhaled. 'Yes. It's hard to believe we'll have been married four months soon. Four months ago we were still living in London. What about you, do you work or have family keeping you busy?' she asked politely.

'Well, we don't have children, but we're fortunate to both have jobs we love. Ed spends a lot of time in the States working with researchers over there; pioneering, I suppose you would call it, developing new methods for less invasive vascular surgery.' The woman gave a rueful smile. 'He'd like us to move there, but my job here as a forensic psychologist is not something I just want to pack up and leave. You sound like you were brave.'

Tess wondered if the sudden zeal of her interest was visible on her face. 'Gosh, they always make that job look so exciting on TV.'

Anne smiled. 'Well I'm no "Fitz" from *Cracker*, if that's what you're imagining, although you're probably a bit young to remember that programme. He was a chain-smoking alcoholic who was also a genius in criminal psychology, which actually focuses more on profiling perpetrators. In my job I focus on the aftermath of a crime and evaluate the mind and behaviour of the criminal, as well as counsel the victims of crime.'

'You must come across some badly hurt people.'

'Sadly I do.'

Tess took sips of air, not realising she'd been holding her breath. This woman dealt with victims who probably had things so bad happen to them they needed her to help.

'Do they ever stop?'

Anne looked at her keenly. 'You mean the person hurting the victim?'

'Yes,' Tess said quietly. 'Do they ever stop?'

Anne slowly shook her head. 'Not always. That's when I get to meet them.'

Tess stared away, then realised a silence had fallen around the table. Her husband's eyes were fixed on her and she hoped she hadn't just lost her trip to London. Vivien broke the spell by entering the room carrying a large chocolate cake with a sparkler on top.

'Dessert is cake, I'm afraid, as it's Mark's birthday.'

Everyone sang 'Happy Birthday'. Soon after eating the cake, Ed and Anne made motions to leave, explaining that even though it was Saturday tomorrow they had work to do. With a fanfare of goodbyes from host and hostess to all their guests, Tess avoided more hugs by stepping out of the front door. Vivien stopped her in her tracks.

'I must give you my number so we can hook up. Have lunch somewhere. Take you to a little place we took Daniel when he stayed with us.' Vivien must have seen surprise in her face because she said, 'Oh, you didn't know Daniel stayed with us when he came for his interview and then again when he was sorting out buying a house?' She gave a small laugh. 'Oh Lord, you must have thought that an odd thing I said earlier then, about him returning.'

Tess masked her surprise. He hadn't lived in their house before, but that didn't mean he hadn't been married before or that the diary she was reading didn't belong to his first wife. She needed the truth to be told. She needed to know what else he had lied about. Because she was damn sure in all of their dates before being married he'd not owned up to having a first wife. Find her and she could prove what he was really like.

Daniel gave Vivien a hug and agreed with her. 'I've got your number. I'll give it to Tess. I doubt it will be next week. My darling wife is heading back to London to sort out the flat.'

'Poor Tess,' she gushed, her eyes flirting with him. 'I hope she's travelling by train, though you should pop her in first class, Daniel. You can hardly ever get a seat crammed in with all those strangers. Dreadful busy things, you don't know who you could be standing next to. Anything could happen to her!'

Tess's eyes darted to Vivien's face for any hidden meaning, but the woman was busy preening herself in front of Daniel as he complimented her on a good night. She finally glanced at Tess. 'Do take care of yourself, Tess, and mind out for any strangers.'

Her words sent a shiver down Tess's spine. The woman had no idea of what was happening in Tess's world, no idea Tess had already met a stranger. She met him after she married him.

CHAPTER TWENTY-FIVE

He didn't say a word in the back of the taxi for the entire journey home, staring mutely ahead and ignoring the taxi driver's attempt at conversation. Tess prayed that whatever was going on in his mind, it had nothing to do with her. She waited as he paid the driver as he had the keys to the house. Inside, she quietly placed her bag on the hall chair and put her shoes away in the cloakroom. He'd gone straight to the drawing room and she could hear the clink of crystal as he fixed himself a drink. Tess hesitated, wondering if she should call out a goodnight. She decided against it, decided it was better to let him be and take the opportunity of slipping off to bed.

She got as far as placing her foot on the first step of the stairs when she was yanked back and then slammed against the hall wall. Her teeth snapped together and bit into her tongue as her head bounced off the wall, filling her mouth with the taste of blood. The cold look in his eyes robbed her breath. He didn't utter a word as he put his hand around her throat, but simply stared right at her and pinned her still. Spittle formed at the corner of his mouth.

Then, abruptly, he let go.

Tess stayed rigid against the wall as he turned off the lights. Then he passed her to climb the stairs and spoke quietly and coldly without looking at her.

'Do not spoil my relationship with Ed Ferris. Do you understand?'

She stayed standing in the dark as she heard the bedroom door shut. The betrayal of fear had weakened her legs, but still she didn't move. She stayed quiet, standing and waiting in the dark, praying for him to come back and finish the job. To put her out of this misery permanently.

When daylight came she stiffly made her way to the downstairs bathroom. She looked at herself in the large mirror on the wall. Slight bruises around her collarbone showed the imprint of his finger and thumb from where he'd held her by the throat. Last night he might have strangled her if she'd struggled. Last night he might have set her free in a way least expected. She could carry on waiting for it to happen or she could find someone who would believe she was innocent of causing this patient's death.

She had no proof that she hadn't caused it. Only her husband knew the truth about that.

Alone in the dark her memory had allowed her to step through all her actions and all of his, and in her mind's eye she kept seeing that moment when he tied and she cut the tiny threads. The site had been dry when he closed. Even after he'd released the clamps to test the anastomosis, there was only a tiny trickle of blood, so what had gone wrong? He'd blamed her by saying she cut too short. Clipped the knot with her scissors? Which might have held for a while, if not completely cut through. That is until the blood pressure increased and the vessel burst apart under the pressure. But she hadn't cut too short. She had seen the length of thread left. So what could have gone wrong?

He had closed up by himself, inserted drains by himself, as Suzanne had gone by then; Tess was only passing instruments automatically, following instructions automatically. The tension had gone as the difficult part was over. Was it possible that in the closing of facia and skin layers, in the removal of retractors, he misjudged a movement of an instrument or his hand, that he accidently caught something, damaged what he had just made perfect?

Or had he caused something more deliberate to make her lose her job to keep her home? It was a heinous idea, but so too were some of his behaviours of late.

She trembled at the thought of only him knowing what happened and only him knowing it wasn't she who caused it. If she went to the police with this – was taken into an interview room and gave a statement – what might happen? Would they investigate? Would her husband be arrested? Doubtful. Even if there was evidence of wrongdoing he'd more likely be questioned and released with no charges against him or against his good character. That would be the reality. It was her word against his, and his was far more powerful, which is probably why he let her take the blame in the first place.

The sad thing was, she might have offered to take the blame if Daniel *was* the cause of it happening. If he did something inadvertently. She would have done it to save his career, to show she loved him, and she would have done it for future patients whose lives he would undoubtedly save. But he hadn't given her that option. He had taken the choice away, thereby destroying her. Letting his lie be her fault. If she hadn't been there it wouldn't have happened, he'd said. He had to have something to blame it on.

She'd nursed a woman once in the emergency theatre who'd been brought in with a fractured jaw after being assaulted by her husband. Tess remembered her blackened swollen eyes and split upper lip, both old and fresh bruising on her thin body, and hearing her crying and saying it was her fault. She was to blame for his behaviour. Believing that after being brainwashed by him.

Do they ever stop? she had asked Anne last night, and Anne had given her an honest answer. *Not always.* What Anne didn't say was how many of the victims survived, or how many of these violent criminals were locked away because they killed their victims.

Her husband was a highly intelligent man. He knew right from wrong. What wasn't clear was whether all of his brain agreed.

Whether one part disagreed and was operating against the good part. Evidence had already shown her that something was wrong with his mind, but the question was, how wrong? Was he feeling guilty after what he'd done? Or was he without a guilty conscience and had no problem committing an immoral act? If that was so there was no hope for him.

She tensed as she came out of the bathroom and heard sounds from the kitchen. He was filling the kettle with water. Settling her hair around her neck to cover the bruising, she joined him. He was dressed and showered, his hair damp, and when he turned and saw her he looked at her with concern.

'You look tired. Did you not go to bed?'

She reached into a cupboard and took out a small teapot, knowing that he liked to see things done properly and would frown at a teabag in a cup.

'I fell asleep on the sofa,' she said softly.

She stiffened when he put a hand on her shoulder and kissed the back of her neck.

'You silly thing. That's how you get unwell. Not sleeping properly in a bed.'

Her throat clogged from the strain of having this conversation. Was he suffering from amnesia or just ignoring what happened last night? His behaviour was unfathomable. Tess wished he'd just leave her be and go play golf, if that's what he was intending. This attempt at showing affection and concern wasn't working. It was shredding her emotions to pieces. She wished she could hate him completely, could forget what she'd loved and lost, after she saw that look of hatred in his eyes.

She had deluded herself that there was love in them when they married. He had just acted as if he loved her so she would fall in love with him, by pretending to be someone he wasn't. His love and kindness had felt so real. Had it all been just a huge pretence, or had his mind unhinged when they moved to this house? Tess didn't have answers. She just knew the man she fell in love with was gone.

She willed herself to stand still as his arms wrapped around her and he hugged her against him.

'You looked stunning last night. Vivien should take lessons from you. She should try fawning less. It's not an attractive quality.' He kissed her cheek, and then, mocking Vivien's high-pitched voice, he said, *'Do take care of yourself, Tess, and mind out for any strangers.'*

When he finally left and the front door closed behind him, Tess wet a teacloth and rubbed her cheek hard. This wasn't living. She was only alive in the sense that her body was breathing and her heart was beating. Supposing she never cleared her name and this life was now forever? Would she really want to carry on, forever thinking about what he had done? She knew already her answer. She would end it. And the only person she would consider would be Sara.

She would do it somewhere private where it would look like an accident. Or else Sara would suffer, forever thinking she should have done more or should have stayed. It would be much better to have her think it was an accident. Much kinder, than to think it planned.

Would he then find another wife who stayed home while he played golf? He may not realise it but it would suit him better if she was gone, because his lies would then be buried.

CHAPTER TWENTY-SIX

Tess woke up to find her husband on top of her. He'd climbed the stairs to find her and hadn't disturbed her coming into the room.

Last night she'd climbed into this bed, leaving him a note to say she was sleeping in the small bedroom again as she didn't feel quite well. She hoped when he got back from being out all day playing golf he wouldn't mind or notice it was the third night in a row she'd not slept in their bed. She heard him grunt as he ejaculated. She kept her face turned to the side as he pulled out of her and stayed quiet as he wiped himself on the top sheet and then got dressed. He zipped up his jeans and pulled his sweatshirt on over his head. Then, leaving the room as if it was empty and she was not lying there, he casually walked out.

She stared up at the ceiling, her eyes dry, relieved she felt nothing. It was over so quick she hadn't gone through the trauma of wishing it to end. She contracted her muscles to expel him from her body and felt the wetness between her legs, praying that none of his seed got left behind. Tomorrow was Monday and with him not at home she would ring the GP surgery and get the morning-after pill. As well as a new prescription.

She swung her legs out of the bed and let gravity finish the work of ridding him from her. In the bath she kneeled in deep water and sluiced herself until the smell of him was gone, and when she was dry she put on clean pants. Downstairs she could hear him in the kitchen sharpening his precious knives. Sharp ringing scrapes of steel against steel hurting her ears.

He was filleting a large fish when she joined him, cutting along the length of its belly. Surrounding him were several shopping bags from Waitrose. She didn't think the shops opened early on a Sunday. She swung her gaze to the kitchen clock and was astonished to see it was nearly noon. She'd been in bed since nine o'clock last night.

He stopped what he was doing and eyed her as if surprised she was home. He gave a rueful smile.

'Short notice I know, but we'll manage. If you're able you can help by laying the table. We have a few hours yet so no rush. That blue dress you wore the other night is nice and she won't judge you wearing it again.'

Tess poured herself a glass of water and drank slowly. 'Who's coming?' she asked, already knowing.

'Ed and Anne. Just the four of us, so it'll be nice and relaxed, no high-octave screeching from you-know-who. Though I feel bad not inviting Mark. He's a nice chap. So tell me,' he asked a moment later. 'What's the sleeping-in-another-bed about?'

Her lips pressed in concentration, her eyes staring into space. 'I didn't want to keep you awake. You know what I'm like when I'm restless. I'd have fidgeted. Got in and out of bed probably, looking for a book to read or fetching a drink. Anyway, I thought it best I slept there.' She paused. 'I wasn't feeling too good and I thought you might need your sleep.'

He was quietly chuckling as she finished speaking, and she turned her head in surprise to find him staring at her. 'It's kind of cute that you do that, but such a giveaway.'

'What is?' she asked hesitantly.

'That you give a long laborious explanation to a simple question. To cover the fact that you're hiding something.' He picked up the fish and held its face close to his own. 'Will she ever learn?' he said in a teasing, chastising tone. He moved the fish's mouth open and closed to show its response, 'Never.' His foolery stopped as he saw her startled eyes. 'Thing is, Tess, I'm not fond of prevarication.'

Tess eyed him carefully. It was more than possible her husband suffered from a personality disorder. His behaviour certainly suggested it. How he'd behaved a half-hour ago showed he was emotionally disconnected and he'd looked at her just minutes ago as if surprised she was there. She wondered if he was aware of it, if there was a catalyst that triggered it. Perhaps his mother's odd reply could have something to do with it – she'd certainly made it sound like that day was significant.

He started humming and Tess gathered her scattered thoughts. She busied herself with collecting cutlery and glasses and new candles even though it sounded like it was going to be a late lunch affair and not an evening meal. She was concerned about Anne Ferris coming, wishing she hadn't been so outspoken. The woman was a forensic psychologist. The keen stare she gave her suggested she had seen through Tess's question. She could be coming here today suspecting Tess of living in an abusive relationship.

She stopped still at the dining table. She couldn't afford to have this woman analysing her. She'd been warned by her husband not to spoil his relationship with Ed Ferris. In order to do that she was going to have to put on a good performance and convince the woman she was in a normal loving relationship with a husband that cared. She'd need some of her husband's acting skills; his were faultless in front of others and left no doubts. Sara had fallen for them hook, line and sinker. She'd thought Tess the luckiest girl in the world. So too would Anne Ferris when she walked out of this house. She would leave believing Tess was happy with her life, and Tess would be better able to cope with Anne not knowing the reality. Tess still needed her husband on board or proof of him being a liar to get out from under the falling axe. Revealing her husband was abusive was no guarantee for a get-out-of-jail-free card. The powers that be might even think she made it up as a defence.

Their guests arrived on the dot of three o'clock and her husband welcomed them into his home effusively. Before their arrival he'd put on some easy-listening music in the background, creating a relaxed mood. Ed handed him a couple of bottles of wine and mentioned that he and Anne had got a taxi, which prompted him to immediately offer them drinks. Tess held back until Ed came forward and gave her a light kiss on the cheek. He smiled at her warmly and then Anne stepped forward to do likewise, handing Tess some mint chocolates. Tess smiled into the woman's eyes and said thank you. It wasn't as difficult as she'd thought it would be to act happy, as it was nice to have some people there, no one ever having visited before.

During the meal Daniel smiled several times across the dining table at her and she smiled warmly back. He rested his hand on the nape of her neck while topping up her glass of wine and she closed her eyes as if enjoying the contact. She flirted and teased and laughed out loud at Ed's jokes and kept direct eye contact with Anne whenever she spoke. She had been gracious and amusing, attentive and listening and spinning a make-believe fairy tale that Ed, for one, was believing.

'So he whisks you away right after you marry and presents you with this wonderful home. And all in secret?' He laughed, clearly delighted. 'My God, Daniel, but you're a romantic. I think it's a delightful story, Tess, and I truly wish both of you many years of happiness here.' His gaze rested fondly on his wife. 'And now, my dear, I think we should leave this relatively newly married couple to enjoy a glass of wine on their own.' He stood up and went over to pull back his wife's chair.

At the door he shook hands with his host warmly and kissed his hostess on the cheek. 'We've had a wonderful afternoon, Tess. Simply wonderful.'

'Yes,' Anne agreed, smiling directly at Tess. 'The ambience could not have been more perfect. I commend you, Tess, on a job well done.'

As Tess stood on the front doorstep waving goodbye, her husband lightly squeezed her shoulder. 'You did a splendid job, Tess. Ed certainly has you up on a pedestal. It was nice how you explained how we came to live here. Anne looked less concerned about you and for that, my sweet, you will be rewarded.'

She closed her eyes in anguish, waiting for him to suggest they go to bed. He bent down and lightly kissed her cheek. 'You can go to London tomorrow.'

Tess inwardly sighed. She'd given a good performance. She had done a splendid job. Now she had to do another splendid job and uncover her husband's past. First stop: London.

CHAPTER TWENTY-SEVEN

The customer at the ticket office counter was holding up the queue, loudly arguing with the man behind the window. 'Too many fucking options,' she shouted. 'Paper, regular, e-tickets. How the fuck was I meant to know I had to print a paper ticket? Gonna miss the fucking train now.'

Tess sympathised. She'd be up on the platform now buying a coffee but for having to queue for this prepaid ticket. There was no queue at the ticket vending machines where she would have bought her ticket if she'd had her debit card. Finally able to get to the counter as the woman flounced off in a huff she gave her address and her husband's name and was handed her seven-day ticket, which she pocketed. She then checked the departure board to find out which platform she needed.

At nine o'clock on a Monday morning the platform wasn't that busy. She supposed the commuters to London caught earlier trains. She could hardly believe she was standing there, that he was letting her make this trip. Or how quickly he sorted everything out. He had managed to book a removal van for the Wednesday and an Oxfam van for the Tuesday. He'd bought her a seven-day train ticket, made lists of what he wanted kept and what could go to charity. He'd worked a small miracle considering only yesterday he said she could go. Making it all very easy. Before leaving for work he'd handed her thirty pounds 'spending money' as if she were a child on a day trip. Which pretty much summed up her new position. She had no access to her own independent income.

Pretty clever of him to have taken her bank card, ensuring her reliance on him.

'Tess!'

She turned and saw an attractive blonde waving at her, walking quickly towards her. A Gucci bag hung over the woman's wrist, her hand free to hold a Starbucks cup.

She forced a smile. 'Hello, Vivien.'

Vivien smiled back. 'So glad I caught you. Daniel rang me last night and said you were going up to London after I rang him yesterday morning to let him know I'd be going. I'd completely forgotten I have a charity meeting there today. That was so sweet of him. Now we can keep each other company, so that will be nice.'

Inwardly, Tess groaned. She would not be able to sit quietly with her thoughts. She would have to listen to this woman babbling for the entire journey. How clever of her husband to ensure she had company. He was getting cleverer by the minute, she was thinking. It felt rather suspicious that Vivien hadn't remembered this on Friday. Had she really rung him? Or had Daniel asked her to make that up? Maybe after enlightening her of Tess's mishap at work? She hoped she wasn't going to be lumbered with her all day. That she did really have a meeting to go to.

Tess smiled as if agreeing. 'Yes, that will be nice. Thank you, by the way, for the lovely evening. We had a lovely time, and it was nice to meet your friends.' She thought it best not to mention that she'd seen them again yesterday.

Vivien pulled a guilty face. 'Mark's idea. I don't know them that well. But he knows Daniel is very keen to get to know Ed better. He thinks Daniel is very interested in the research Ed is doing.'

'Oh right,' she said lamely, while remembering again his dark warning that she was not to spoil his relationship with Ed Ferris. What was her husband after? Was he hoping to work with him?

'You look a little pale. Are you OK?'

Tess decided to test her suspicions. 'Probably just tired from work,' she replied. 'It was a busy week.'

'Work! Of course, you poor darling. My goodness, you put me to shame. Though I have to say I barely have a minute to myself between running our home and my outside interests. Oh, and my charity work, of course. Tess, we could do with someone like you. Especially for the children's charities. They love it when we get a nurse involved in these things. Surely that handsome husband of yours would rather you did something like that in your spare time. Rather than work? How is he? I never got to ask how he's settling in. You must be so proud. I know I would be. Mr Daniel Myers. It has a lovely ring to it, don't you think?'

Tess noticed she placed great emphasis on the word 'mister'. The title reserved for a consultant surgeon. Vivien clearly wanted her own husband to be called a Mr. Tess didn't think it had a lovely ring to it. Mr Daniel Myers had taken advantage of his lofty position and let his wife hang out to dry. She answered with a pleasant lie.

'I suppose it does, and he's settling in well.'

'Well, tell him we must do it again, only next time I intend to sit and chat to him.'

Tess's reply was lost in the noise of the train arriving and she was tempted to let Vivien board the train alone and then find somewhere else to sit, but the woman was waving her to follow and Tess had no chance to disappear. She was ushered into the window seat and was trapped.

Vivien was off again as soon as she sat down beside her. 'I meant to travel first class, but the irritating man at the gate said I couldn't upgrade to first on the train unless I went to the ticket office. Only on weekends, for God's sake. What difference does it make if you upgrade on a weekday, I ask you? They're getting money for it. It's not as if I'm unwilling to pay for the privilege. I do so hate to be hovered over by those left standing.'

Tess closed her eyes and wished the woman would shut up. The ones left standing could hear her.

'You do look tired, a little peaky. Maybe you need a spa day. I go to a fabulous spa and you could come as my guest. It would do you the world of good.'

Tess found she agreed with her husband in wondering how in God's name Mark put up with her. He seemed a quiet, gentle man. Her full face of make-up must have taken hours to put on. And unless she had a hairdresser to hand at some ungodly hour of the day, she must have been one in a previous life to have her curled and swept, pinned and tucked hair so professionally coiffured. She was driving Tess nuts and Tess was pleading for a miracle, an earthquake, anything to make her shut up.

It happened a moment later. A gasp at the sight of brown liquid covering the cream skirt, followed by the yelp as it scalded her skin. Then the shout. 'Oh Christ, not my fucking Chanel suit!'

She was out of her seat in a flash, shoving her way past standees to get to the toilet before Tess could offer her help. She looked around at those standing and saw several holding Starbucks cups but no one staring after Vivien or looking guilty of the deed. Vivien's own Starbucks cup was still sat innocently on the table. Her seat was quickly taken. A young woman in an equally smart suit, but of a more sensible colour, pulled out her laptop, set it on the table and settled herself properly.

'Do you mind?' she asked.

Tess didn't.

CHAPTER TWENTY-EIGHT

From Paddington Station to her husband's flat was less than a ten-minute walk. Tess didn't want to stop and look around at the familiar. The terrace of white houses she was passing was like a slap to her senses. Hyde Park, where they had their first date, was only around the corner. Many of the places they'd gone to were close by. Alexander Fleming Laboratory Museum, Victoria and Albert Museum, Kensington Gardens, St James's Park, and Little Venice with its colourful canal boats where they'd sat and shared a hot chocolate laced with brandy.

She stared at what was once his home, and hers too for those few weeks, and felt the raw emptiness inside her. The ground-floor flat in this large Victorian house was where it all began. Her foolish dream had dared her to believe it was something real. There was nothing she now found pleasing about it. It was a sham. A trick of the worst kind.

Taking the bunch of keys out of her bag she found the one to open the front door. She would spend the day searching every hidey-hole of this flat for evidence of a first wife. She would go through her husband's personal effects like a detective and read everything twice if need be. He'd already shown he was good at hiding things. So she'd have to look extra hard.

The air was stale as she walked through the main living area to the French doors at the back. Using a second key she opened them out onto the courtyard. It was private and sheltered from wind by the backs of houses, the brick walls painted white and the floor paved with large slabs. It was a gem and would fetch its asking price. The bay tree she bought as a kind of moving in present, though grown a little unruly, had survived unattended. The other potted plants had perished. She would leave the tree. It was not on his list.

Walking back indoors she opened the doors of two bedrooms and two bathrooms, and a window in the kitchen.

It surprised her now that he hadn't sorted out the contents before moving. Not even kitchenware or books. Had he thought it would just magic itself away? The burning question was how he afforded it all. He was a successful doctor, yes, but he was not yet forty. He had not worked as a consultant long enough yet to make this sort of money.

Vicious little thoughts kept nipping at her mind. Had he married someone wealthy and this was her money? His new home, was that her money too? Did he become wealthy from a divorce settlement or very rich because she had died?

From her bunch of keys she chose the one to unlock his study and went inside. A large window looked out onto the courtyard and provided light out onto it at night. She realised this was the first time she had been into this room as she'd never had reason to before. At a glance she was disappointed. He had already emptied it of files and office equipment, leaving just his desk, chair, an empty filing cabinet and a wall of built-in open shelves. There was nothing out on the surfaces, and just one framed picture on the wall. She stepped closer for a better look and felt a shock of pain. It was powerfully disturbing. She could not look at it without feeling it. The charcoal drawing was a macabre image of a mother holding her dead child and showing raw grief. The child lay cradled in the mother's lap with eyes closed and looking lifeless. The mother was holding the child in a desperate way, tucking legs and arms around the child and burying her head against the small chest as if every fibre of her being was straining to hold onto life. Tess wished she hadn't looked at it. It would haunt her.

She sprang back startled when the doorbell rang and quickly gathered her wits. It would be the estate agent. Tess showed him into the living room after he introduced himself as Monty. He shook hands and beamed at her. 'Pleasure to meet you, Mrs Myers. I hear you have everything under control and should have this place cleared by Thursday, which is splendid.'

Tess looked around the spacious open-plan dining and living area, at the shelves of books, the collection of music CDs, the lamps, curtains, cushions and mirrors and pictures on the walls, and through an archway into the kitchen that had cupboard doors closed on mountains of stuff.

She smiled. 'Yes, lucky me. My husband has thoughtfully supplied me with two packets of different colour sticky labels. I just have to stick the right colour on everything.'

'Splendid,' he said again, rubbing his hands as if excited they were both going to play a game. 'Well, I'll leave you to it. Just checking we're still on song.'

Tess liked the dapper little man who clearly enjoyed his job.

'We are, Monty. While you're here I just wanted to ask you something. Our new home in Bath, was it you who arranged that for us?'

He shook his head, looking surprised. 'No, I would have if I'd known Mr Myers was buying. What did he buy?'

'A seven-bedroom detached Georgian.'

'In Bath!' He scratched his head looking quite distressed. 'Jeez Louise, that would have cost a pretty penny. What are we looking at? Three mill?'

Tess actually didn't know so she shrugged as if he'd guessed about right.

The man sighed, looking a lot less happy in his job now.

'I'll tell him off when I get back to Bath,' she declared, to show she was on his side. 'Especially after getting him this beautiful place.'

'Do,' he urged. 'I would have loved a visit to Bath.'

'Well, if it's any consolation he loved it here, Monty. As did his first wife.'

He looked at her with a puzzled expression. 'First wife? I don't recall.'

Tess laughed. She'd planned to if she drew a blank. 'Me, of course, silly, unless you know of any other wife. I lived here too for a little while.'

'I see,' he said, laughing politely, his eyes a little over-wide, one foot turning in the direction of the front door. 'I'll get in touch with your husband about keys et cetera, but give me a call if you get any hold-ups.'

Tess would love to see his expression if she told him her phone had been confiscated so she wouldn't be able to call him. She imagined him saying something like, 'Well, that's splendid.'

After seeing him to the door she set about doing the job she was there for. She took from her bag the two separate lists he'd written and a packet of lime green and a packet of shocking pink sticky labels.

The list of things to give away was the much longer list. It even included the linen which was much newer than what they had at the house. He was either being very generous or preferred what they were using now. The king-size mattress on his bed was a luxury Hypnos and though it wouldn't fit their present bed it could have replaced one of the other mattresses in the spare rooms. Not that she should care or let it worry her; these were all his things, the same as back at the house. He'd chosen to have all that stuff there, not her. She'd had no choice in any of it. The only thing she'd ever chosen was the bay tree and that was something he'd chosen not to keep.

She wished she was on the list of 'not to keeps' and stuck a lime-green label on her forehead in the hope she would be collected with all the other things he was parting with. She may get taken to a new home where she was more fitting to her new owner and her clothes and manner perfectly acceptable. She groaned and gave herself a mental shake; she was wasting what little energy she had without dragging her mind lower with silly thoughts.

She sighed and transferred the label from her forehead to a vase. She had a whole day to keep searching. So what if Monty didn't know about a first wife? Why should he? He had sold Daniel the flat not helped him move in. She'd find something. She just had to keep looking.

CHAPTER TWENTY-NINE

Tess settled back in her seat and tried to relax. She had an hour-and-a-half train journey before she reached Bath. She might as well rest. Or she could read? Reaching into her rucksack she pulled out the little black notebook, unsure why she had taken it with her. She didn't know whether to call it a diary or a journal, or what it was: *An Account.* She opened it and started to read.

As I'm writing this my eyes are drawn to the red nail polish staining my fingers. It is a brighter red, like fresh blood, and will stand out against the deeper red in the wallpaper. I have painted the small tear and hope he won't notice the repair. I am running out of platitudes and his moods are less tolerant. He now looks for things he can punish me for as if he needs the daily dose of power. He is home. I have just heard the car so I will stop writing now.

The writing filled only half a page. Tess turned the page to read more.

I should have started this story at the beginning instead of at the end. But I am aware of how quickly things have changed recently and needed to make it known I am in danger. Would he kill me? Possibly. Probably. But it will not look like a death by his hand. He is capable of making it look natural. I should never have married him. I ignored the warnings. My father warned me not to mistake charm for grace. It didn't make sense to me at the time. It's what you do when you're in love. Ignore what you don't want to see.

Tess felt as if her heart had just been squeezed. It's what she had been doing in the run-up to that operation. Trying to ignore the truth about him. Her world had imploded that day. To go from loving someone so deeply to a feeling of abrupt abandonment had destroyed something inside her forever. She would never heal from this.

She saw his car on the drive and her heart sank. He was already home. She had not wanted to face him while feeling this low. She had wanted to sit quietly for a bit to calm her anxiety and disappointment. She had found no evidence of a first wife at the flat. Nothing to prove the old lady was telling the truth. She even quizzed his old neighbours on the off chance that they might know her. But none of them had. None of them had heard any mention of a wife.

Had the old lady just imagined a first wife? She had been fairly certain, though, and used Daniel's name. Strongly hinting that something happened to the woman.

Without proof of her existence Tess was back to square one. Facing something which was rapidly racing towards her. The reality of her future life. A man was dead. Had died in a hospital because of a nurse. Her name would be in the papers. Everyone would know. And there would be nowhere to hide but here.

She felt a knot inside her stomach as she opened the front door.

He was in the kitchen and was fixing himself a coffee from a machine that would more likely be seen in a smart café with all its gadgets for pressing and grinding and frothing drinks.

'Would you like one?' he asked.

'Please,' she said, taking a seat at the table. He set about making a second one and wiped the counter while the cup was filling. The brown marble tops were old and needed professional buffing to bring back their original shine, the shaker style cabinets below and above worn of their cream colour. Everything in the kitchen looked a little shabby and could do with replacing.

He set a cup and saucer down on the table in front of her. The coffee was black, how he liked it. She'd wait a moment before getting up for some milk.

'You met Vivien Porter on the train this morning.' It was a statement, not a question.

'Yes. On the platform actually. She said she was going to London too. I thanked her for a lovely evening.'

'She had an accident and was splashed with boiling coffee.'

'Yes!' she said, looking at him in surprise for knowing this.

'Did you go to her aid?'

Tess's eyes fixed on him like a startled deer. 'She was gone before I could help.'

'You mean, gone off the train?'

'No. I mean, gone to the bathroom.'

'And what did you do? I mean, while our friend was burning and trying to salvage the damage to her clothes?'

'Well, I waited.'

'Ah, I see,' he said quietly, moving towards the table, carefully blowing his black coffee. 'You waited. And then when she returned to her seat, you what? Offered her comfort?'

'Sh-she didn't return,' Tess replied, beginning to stutter. 'Someone else sat in her seat.'

'A rather selfish act, wouldn't you think? To make someone stand after they've been injured?'

'Yes. A woman sat down before I could stop her. I—'

'I'm talking about *you!*' he said, in a honeyed tone. 'You,' he repeated, and without warning tipped his hot coffee straight into her lap.

She screamed in shock and tried to jump up but his hands were on her shoulders. She writhed in pain and gritted her teeth as the liquid burned her thighs.

'Ever,' he whispered unpleasantly in her ear, 'ever embarrass me like that again and I'll bathe you in boiling coffee.'

In the bathroom she soothed the red areas with cold flannels before covering the small blisters with Sudocrem. She didn't want to go back downstairs. She wanted to crawl into bed and hide.

The banging on the bathroom door jolted her. Then his voice shivered her.

'Come on, Tess. It doesn't need a trip to A & E. Splash it with cold water and then come join me in the kitchen. If you're good I'll make you a dessert.'

'I'm coming,' she managed to say. 'Just making myself presentable.'

She heard him walking away and slumped down on the edge of the bath, her skin covered in goosebumps. He was terrorising her as if he had permission to do what he liked now she was under his control. If he yelled or shouted while he was hurting her, she wondered if her fear would be less. His voices – his tones, the timbre, the smallest intake of breath, the half beats measured between words, the utter control he kept when speaking – didn't alert her to his change of mood.

He was a Jekyll and Hyde, but it was only she who saw Hyde. To everyone else he was seen as some sort of god. A very nice man. A brilliant doctor. She'd heard the awe in Vivien's voice, who clearly had told him what had happened. He couldn't have known otherwise, unless he was on the train and saw it happen.

She couldn't go on like this. She just couldn't. She had to know where she stood. She went downstairs to find him. She had to face him and ask him what her future held. Otherwise she would go mad.

He looked up from his newspaper as she came towards him. She had to say what was on her mind before she let him speak.

'Why did you say I cut too short? You know I didn't, so what was the reason for saying that?'

He leaned back in his chair. Then gave a small shrug. 'Are you going to make a fuss about this? You'll get a slap on the wrist and then it will be over.'

She shook her head at him. 'So you're never going to admit to the nod you gave. You're never going to admit I didn't cut short. What future do you see for us, Daniel, after this?'

He stood up. 'I see you happy in this place. Happy to be a wife. Happy to be a mother. All the things you should have wanted to be happy about out if you'd let yourself see that.'

He spread his hands wide. 'I have given you a beautiful home. All you have to do is commit yourself.'

'You mean to you! Don't you? So you can change me into someone who meets your standards.'

A calculating look darkened his eyes. 'You do have other choices. Though what that will be like for you I don't know. Difficulty in getting a new job, I imagine. References, accommodation, money, of course. I believe they hold off doling out benefits if you have a record of gross misconduct. But the door's there if you want it, Tess.'

Tess slowly backed away. This torment was never going to end. He had mapped her future and now she knew what it held. Bleakness.

CHAPTER THIRTY

The train was seventeen minutes late. The passengers standing on the platform had their eyes fixed on the orange writing scrolling on the information board for updates. They stayed still in their places; guarded, aware the platform was becoming increasingly busy with people now arriving for a later service. Anyone newly arrived would be thinking to try and board the earlier train, if it came. Some began positioning themselves where they thought the doors might open, ready to ignore etiquette and just grab a seat, leaving it to the train manager to deal with the arguments over reserved seats. It was going to be a crush on board and the late train was going to leave the platform full and with passengers standing.

Tess gazed at the people around her and saw some edging closer to the yellow line to form a human barrier in an attempt to prevent those arriving after them boarding first.

She felt some relief at standing there able to inhale a different air after breathing in so many lies. *He had never loved her.* He had only pretended. Everything she'd thought real was a lie.

The small relief she felt was in knowing it would soon end. He was not the man she had married, the one who promised to love and cherish her. Without warning he had stopped. Instead he had chosen to *unlove, uncherish,* and do his best to break her into a million pieces…

He could never have loved her.

An announcement coming over the PA system had mobiles leaving the waiting passengers' ears as they raised heads to listen to the rushed and nasally voice of the speaker. 'The train shortly arriving on platform two is the delayed service to London Paddington. Passengers are advised to use all the carriages when boarding and move quickly away from the doors to allow others to board.'

Tess stared to her right and slowly began walking along the platform, her eyes on the horizon. They were stealthy, these great long tubes of steel, coming upon you sometimes before you caught sight of them, before you even heard them.

The crowd towards the end of the platform thinned, leaving it more peaceful away from the crowds and the noise, and she looked along the track to the point where it curved away out of sight, watching for the train's green-and-yellow nose to appear. She imagined the smooth sloping head, with its shiny dark green-and-yellow-coated skin as the sleek head of a mallard duck, swooping in low and fast along the track to take her away. It would be coming very soon. Travelling fast. It would reach this point of the platform still fast enough to do serious damage to anything that got in its way.

She'd heard it wasn't always a sure thing, which was why announcements sometimes said, 'A person had been hit by a train.' The person under the train was still alive, and not a body. If you jumped right into its path you would surely get it right. Maybe those who survived hadn't taken the full brunt of the rushing steel, were the ones who slipped down through the gap and only partially mangled.

She breathed deeply and thought of there being no more tomorrow. No more her. No more thinking of the future. She took a step over the yellow line. It would be quick. And it would be over. The pain merely imagined. She would be dead before her body had the chance to feel it. She would not suffer. Nor know fear anymore.

Her head, the house of her fear, would smash open like a watermelon dropped from high, letting all the locked-in terrors leak away. A soothing river of blood draining away all feeling. The pain would be gone.

She heard an underbelly rumble vibrating in the distance, an enfolding whooshing noise growing stronger, then sweet musical notes trilled in the air; a hiss, a squeal, a wire-drum brush stroking against cymbals – the voices of the train calling. She took another step closer to the edge, breathed air and held the breath as if preparing for a dive into water. Her body tingled in preparation. She pressed her feet on the very edge. She was ready.

The shove that propelled her back came from nowhere. She stumbled and saw bright orange material flash before her eyes, heard a deep warning bellowed in her ear.

'Stand back!'

The dispatcher in hi-vis stared at her with shock in his eyes. 'Not funny, miss. Not funny at all.'

She gazed at him astonished. Betrayed. Shocked. She had lost her chance. She was still standing and now people were pushing past her to get onto the train. She lagged behind until a press of bodies propelled her forward, moving her closer to the steps, and all the while she was waiting to be stopped, expecting a hand to land on her shoulder preventing her leaving, but the platform man was busy boarding others. At the door she stared down at the gap between the train and the platform, imagining seeing her body lying there, but saw only the blackened ballast stones on the track.

She should have been down there mixed with the stones, been blood and bone on the track. Instead, somehow, sometime today, after travelling on this train, she was going to have to return to him.

She collapsed into the first seat she found by a window, trembling with reaction, and in a daze watched commuters get laptops and tablets and smart phones at the ready. Clicking keyboards and multiple voices thrummed in her ears as beginning right then, as if synchronised, they all spoke at once, uncaring of sharing their conversations with people seated beside them because these people, after all, were only strangers.

Tess squeezed her eyelids together to shut out the normality. Only minutes ago she had tried to kill herself, and having failed, now sat there hoping to find sanity.

She felt wetness on her cheeks and wiped away the tears before anyone noticed. She shoved her hands into the deep pockets of her coat and felt relief at finding a pair of sunglasses. Her misty eyes rested on the city she was leaving behind. It reminded her of Rome with its surrounding hills, its Roman Baths and Roman Temple. She had thought this place was her home now forever…

Her chest ached, recalling how ridiculously happy she had been. She held onto the sob rising in her throat and concentrated hard on the scenery passing by her window. She could not break down in front of strangers. She had to hold on until she was alone. They would wonder what she was crying about. Have fleeting thoughts of it being a death, a break-up, a mental health problem, catching sight of her footwear, one black, one navy flat court shoe.

They would never guess at the real reason. That life had dealt a deadly blow. That her husband asked her to sign her name to a truth that hid a lie. A lie she would have to live with her entire life. Confirming she unwittingly killed a man. If these strangers beside her knew this, they would say she had good reason to cry. They might even say she had reason to be afraid. And she would reply that this was not something new. She had been afraid all of her life.

Even when her parents were alive she was afraid to find them dead. Afraid the needles and the special medicines they put into themselves would put them to sleep forever. That she would wake up and find them no longer able to pat her head, break her a piece of chocolate, or pass her some cooling chips. When it eventually did happen, she was five years of age. Alone, without relatives, and afraid of what was to happen.

Not wanted, was what happened. She was neither pleasing nor appealing. *She has a look about her that says junkie child*, she heard someone say. By the time she was seven she knew all the rules of her new home and learned that sometimes a friendly face was hiding a different face for only her to see when alone at night with no other grown-ups around. And she learned the unwritten rule she mustn't break – *never tell.*

By the time she was ten she had built herself a safe wall that made her invisible so fear couldn't find her. When she left the children's home she left her safe wall behind, believing she no longer needed it now that she was an adult… Such foolishness to have believed that. The panther still pounced.

She leaned her head against the window and felt the motion of the train. She let the thought take hold that if tomorrow life was still as unbearable she could try again.

Tess opened her eyes and saw passengers outside her window hurrying by on the platform. The train had stopped, the carriage was emptying fast, and cleaners were on the platform making ready to board and do their job. The London Paddington train was at its destination.

She picked up her purse, to put back in her rucksack, and saw a white card had been placed beside it. It was a business postcard. A small angel or a butterfly was squiggled in blue biro in the top right corner where a stamp would go. Two words centred in capitals read: FOR YOU. Her neighbour was gathering an assortment of objects from the table into a cloth bag and Tess held it out to her.

'Is this yours?'

The large lady smiled, and shook her head. Her floaty kaftan with all the colours of the rainbow billowed out around her as she stood and rooted inside her large bag in search of something.

'No, dear, it's not mine. But thankfully these are,' she said as she held aloft a fan of train tickets.

Tess turned the card over and read a handwritten blue-penned message:

I saw you today standing there. Death nearly took you away. From someone who has seen death you should know there is no coming back from it. Remember, next time you step over the perilous line you may not get a second chance…

She shook the card from her hand fast and it landed on the table. Breath caught in her throat. Someone had seen what she'd tried to do and was letting her know.

'Did you see who put it there?' she asked fretfully.

The woman's dark brown eyes studied her now. 'Seen no one, honey. I slept like you.'

Tess breathed raggedly.

'Hey, you OK?'

Tess stared at the woman's kind face through her sunglasses and saw her deepening concern. She forced herself to nod, and appear less frantic. 'I'm fine. Just wondering if I left an iron on.'

A wrist full of bangles jangled as the woman raised a hand in despair. 'Oh, dear. Ring the neighbour, honey. Get them to check on it.'

Tess nodded and stood up. She picked up the white card, folded it in two and tucked it inside her purse. She hoped the passenger who left it was long gone, not anywhere nearby. The message unnerved her. That something so private had been seen. She felt exposed.

She stared at the people passing by the window. It could be one of them out there who saw her. She felt a tingling brush down her neck as if a pair of eyes was boring into her. She was now eager to get off the train and get away from this message person. They didn't sound normal. A normal person would have spoken to her if they were concerned instead of leaving her a sanctimonious message. Or maybe even a warning. She hurried off the train.

CHAPTER THIRTY-ONE

At just gone nine she entered the flat. Relieved she'd had her rucksack on her back before running from that house, otherwise she'd have been without keys. It had been the sound of the front door closing after him that darted her upstairs to shove on her shoes and have her pelt out the door as if running for her life. Her husband would never know his wife attempted to take her life that morning, would never know she left the house in mismatched shoes. She would put them back in the wardrobe, and put on the red slippers before he got home.

She collapsed into a chair as her legs went weak. Her nerves were twitching from her near encounter with death and from getting that postcard. But for the man pushing her back her husband would have got a call or a visitor to say his wife was dead. His new colleagues would have rallied round quickly, offering him sympathy, offering to help, but not overly surprised. Didn't his poor wife kill a patient? Didn't she pretend she was someone else? The poor woman, the guilt of it must have gone to her head.

He had made her want to kill herself.

She would not forgive him for that.

She forced herself to stand up and go over to the small fridge. She had switched it on yesterday for some milk. She poured a full glass and drank slowly. She would need her strength to cope. Her life had not ended and was not over yet. She may still unearth something she could use against her husband.

The Oxfam van turned up just after twelve. It took until one o'clock for the driver and another man to carry out and load up the stuff they were being given. The flat looked near empty after they'd gone. The removal van booked for the next day wouldn't be taking much back to Bath. A wrought-iron garden bench and table and chairs, a Welsh dresser, a bookcase from one of the bedrooms and his filing cabinet and the picture from his study wall were all that was on the list of items to keep.

With nothing more to do now, Tess decided to leave. Though, she would change out of these clothes first and put on her jeans. She'd brought them with her yesterday to work in, along with a couple of loose tops, and would be more suitable to wear for where she was going. Turning up in the dress she threw on that morning, a bottle green round-neck with white piping on the skirt hem, would have them looking at her in surprise. They might ask her if she was going to an awards ceremony, perhaps, and was she giving out the prizes?

As she walked along the corridor in St Mary's Hospital towards the theatre suite, she hoped this wasn't going to be a wasted detour. Not that it was taking her much out of the way – Paddington Station was right next door. She was banking on Sam still having the same shift pattern and being on duty.

She was in luck, as after enquiring she saw him waving at her and his smiling face as he came out of the theatre doors into the corridor wearing his scrubs. He was on duty but he looked relaxed and not in a rush to get back to work.

His quick lithe walk, black hair and unlined face belied his age. Sam had to be about sixty-five, but she knew he looked after himself with lots of expensive lotions and practised tai chi every morning. She was shocked when he swung her up in the air before plonking her back on her feet again. For a small man he was incredibly strong. He seemed genuinely excited to see her and she felt a pang at not saying a proper goodbye. She thought he only looked upon her as a colleague, yet he was greeting her like she was a friend.

'God, we've missed you,' he said, then startled her more. 'The place is not the same without you. Margie, Brenda – even moaning Molly – we're always talking about you. Brenda was right pissed off you left without a party. She's still got your prezzie we collected for in her locker.'

Tess felt her eyes sting. How, she wondered, had she not noticed or known this before? She had worked in these theatres eight years and thought she was fairly invisible, that it was only Sara who thought of her as a friend. She felt guilty now for not knowing and for thinking she only left colleagues behind, for not getting to know these people better.

'How's my handsome doctor?' He took a step backwards, feigning shock. 'It should have been me!' he whispered dramatically. Then in his normal voice, 'And why do you look like crap?'

Tess blushed. The make-up hadn't quite covered the circles under her eyes.

'She is!' he teased. 'That the reason for the weight loss? Morning sickness maybe?'

Tess shook her head, feeling like crap, wishing she'd stayed with these people.

'Hey, I'm only teasing,' Sam quickly said, seeing her shiny eyes.

She took a calming breath. 'Just a bit overwhelmed to be back, Sam.'

He patted her shoulder. 'Yeah, I can see that. I can see more than that. Is the handsome doctor treating you OK?'

She shrugged. 'Can I ask you something, Sam?'

He looked at her concerned, then ushered her along the corridor to some empty seats against the wall. After he sat down, he said, 'Tell me what you want to ask.'

Tess folded her arms and stared down at the floor. 'Was there ever anything personal you heard about my husband? About his past or what he did before coming here? I know he was here two years, but I don't know anything about him before then or even during the time he was here.'

Sam got back on his feet, and lightly led her to sit down instead. He now folded his arms but he didn't stare at the floor. He looked at her directly.

'Shit. It's not working out, is it?'

She didn't say anything.

'That's a shame, because I can't think of anything. He was at St Thomas's before here, and his reputation has always been sterling.'

'What about other women?'

He gave a tentative shake of his head. 'Well, I'm sure there were. He's bloody handsome, but as for actually knowing.' He frowned. 'There *was* something once. I wasn't paying that much attention. He was scrubbing in beside another doctor. Can't remember who it was, but I remember this other doctor passing a remark about whether this one was for keeps, and your man laughing and saying something like, *for keeps so long as she knows her place*. It was something like that. To be fair, the other doctor didn't laugh back, which is probably why I've remembered it. Chauvinistic crap, of course.'

'Do you think he was talking about me? Can you remember when that was?'

Sam puffed out his cheeks as he exhaled and tried to remember. 'Yeah, I think I do. After my holiday, because when I came back I'd been switched to work in vascular. So that was in May.'

Tess bit her lip and nodded slowly. Around the same time he'd proposed to her, she thought. It was already in his mind then how he wanted her to behave. She stood up and gave Sam a hug. 'Thanks, Sam. Please give my love to the others but don't tell them what I asked.'

'I won't,' he said. 'But you sort it out.'

'Bye, Sam,' she simply said, her eyes taking in one last look at him. Taking one last look at everything she passed. Like the London flat. She wasn't going to find anything here. Apart from finding out her husband planned to keep her in her place.

CHAPTER THIRTY-TWO

Tess stared up at the train timetable information board to see if a platform had been assigned for the Bath train, and felt her chest tighten. 'DELAYED' flashed where the time of departure should be. For a while she willed the word to change, but when it didn't she slumped her shoulders a little, resignedly. If she got home too late he might not let her go tomorrow. Arrange for Monty to be at the flat instead of her, to let the removal men in, which would scupper her plan to visit St Thomas's.

'Always damn late, isn't it?'

She glanced to her side and saw a man pointing his umbrella up at the board. 'Always the same. What is it this time? No fucking train crew?'

He said 'fucking' like he owned the word. His vowels clear and enunciated, the word elongated in a disdainful drawl. Interestingly, he said the word in the same way as Vivien. His wide-striped suit marked him as a barrister, or a would-be barrister, she decided as she stared at his youngish face and newish briefcase. 'If they cancel this train too I'll be fucking livid.'

His words jolted her. 'Was the train before cancelled?' she asked.

He waved his umbrella again. 'Yes. A fucking jumper. Why can't they fucking jump in their own time?'

'Sir, do you mind?'

Tess heard the question and cringed knowing it was directed at the man beside her by the middle-aged man behind them.

The would-be barrister swivelled around to address the speaker. 'Do I mind what? That a selfish bastard has put a stop to the trains? Too damned right I do.'

'You're speaking about someone who just took their life, sir.'

'And don't we all know it,' he replied bluntly, before strutting off and leaving Tess alone with the middle-aged man.

'Some people are truly despicable,' the man said. Then quietly, 'Platform 4 it looks like.'

She stared up at the board and breathed a sigh of relief. It was only six minutes late.

Ten minutes later Tess was settled into a seat with a table, waiting for the train to depart. She looked up as a man took the seat opposite her. His face was familiar and she racked her brain to place him. She was sure she'd met him before. A second man wearing orange hi-vis trousers and jacket with silver fluorescent stripes took the seat beside her, and the remaining seat was taken by a young woman in the same get-up. They were clearly together, chatting to each other. Both wore lanyards showing they worked for the railway.

She glanced back at the man opposite her, still puzzling over where she knew him from.

He said, as if reading her mind, 'You were standing next to that obnoxious man in the pinstripe suit who was giving his opinion on jumpers.'

Her eyes rounded in surprise and she smiled. 'My brain is like a sieve. That was only ten minutes ago. You were telling him off.'

He too smiled. 'I was.'

He had a nice face, hard to tell his age. He could be in his fifties or sixties. She noticed the brown leather *Bradshaw's* book he placed on the table in front of him and pegged him as a train spotter, having seen the same book carried by Michael Portillo in his train travel documentaries.

'You like trains?' she asked, pointing at his book.

He chuckled. 'I do, though this book is more about the history of railway timetables and the towns and villages that once had railway stations.'

'So you're not a train spotter, then?' she joked, feeling strangely relaxed to be talking to a stranger about nothing much at all. Just passing time with easy comments was something she hadn't done in a long while. She'd lost the habit of talking naturally to people since getting married. She could count on one hand the few unguarded chats she'd had. Cameron, Sara, the old lady, and she supposed now this man. She couldn't count chats with people like Stella, Vivien or Anne as unguarded because her focus had been on her husband.

'No, but I do spot a lot of trains,' he replied, smiling. Then, not smiling, 'And sadly hear of too many deaths like this one today.'

Tess lowered her eyes in her shame. She had given no thought to the ripple effects of her actions on others. To the people who witnessed it, the people whose job it was to remove her remains and wash away her blood, to the person driving that train – likely to suffer the most for not being able to stop it – she had given no thought at all. The stranger who witnessed her near death this morning was clearly affected, as they'd been compelled to write to her. No thought to Sara either, even after that chat with herself. Maybe she deserved that postcard for being thoughtless. She would take better care if tempted to do it again to leave no witnesses next time.

More passengers boarded, searching for vacant seats, and he pulled a guilty face as some were left standing. Tess looked around to see if there were any old people or mums with children standing. Seeing no one less able than her, she shrugged her shoulders and stayed put. The *Bradshaw's* book man did likewise.

Tess fetched the notebook from her bag as the *Bradshaw's* book man began reading. She might find more out about the woman.

I have been out of love for too many years and have admitted it to no one. It is my failure, my embarrassment. But it is no longer these things I worry about. It is his paranoia I fear. Last night he locked me in the cloakroom for a 'misdemeanour' – his word for not aligning his suits properly. I think it was just an excuse to punish me because his friend talked to me. He does not want his friends to know what he is like when we are alone.

Tess turned another page.

I met with my friend today. We went to McDonald's, a place he would never step foot in. I've asked her to help me find somewhere to live, but I'm not sure she will. I saw the confusion in her eyes. She cannot understand why I would just walk away. She thinks having money has given me power. How little she knows. Nothing is ever mine.

Tess closed the book. She had read enough for now. It was like reading something familiar yet unknown. She needed facts not feelings. Fact one: this woman had lived in that house. Fact two: she had been married to an abusive man. Fact three: she was trying to run away. Fact four: she feared for her life.

She feared for her life.

Tess felt her blood run cold.

Was she Daniel's first wife?

Had he only pretended to look for a property while staying with Vivien and Mark? Did he already own the house? As how else would the old lady know about him unless he'd lived there before? Tess needed a name. This diary didn't give her one. She would start by looking for it in that house. She had discovered the book there, so how many other discoveries might she find? The library room was full of old books she could flick through. She had dusted and cleaned most of the rooms, but she hadn't put her hands down the backs or sides of sofas and armchairs. She hadn't pulled drawers out from cupboards or taken books off shelves. There could be an old bill left lying around or something that had a name on it. She was sickened by a disquieting thought. Had he killed her?

CHAPTER THIRTY-THREE

Tess was sitting in semi-darkness when she woke. She jumped in fright and gave a little squeal as she saw him sitting in an armchair watching her.

'You frightened me,' she gasped.

His legs and arms were casually crossed, his face inscrutable.

'Who are you seeing?' he asked in a hushed tone.

'What!'

He switched on the lamp beside him. By the side of his chair he picked up her rucksack and placed it on his lap. Her insides quivered. What was he talking about? She'd changed back into her green sensible dress on board the train and wiped her face and mouth clean of make-up and lipstick. And the notebook, thank God, she put in her jacket pocket.

'Clothes, make-up, lipstick,' he said, naming items she knew to be there.

His tone was still soft and she tried to explain. 'I thought it would be easier to sort out the flat in my jeans and a top, and I was going to put on some make-up to… look… pretty.'

'Pretty? For who?' he pressed, his voice ever so slightly changed. 'Who did you want to look pretty for?'

'For myself.'

'Yourself!' he softly exclaimed, before giving her a knowing, amused look. He opened the rucksack and peered inside. A moment later he fetched out a tube of lipstick, uncapped it and twisted it until a pink nub appeared. 'Show me,' he said, and handed her the tube.

She frowned at the thing in her hand. 'It's difficult without a mirror.'

'Try.'

Raising the lipstick to her mouth, she barely touched her lips. 'More.'

This time she pressed firmly, following the outline of her lips and coating them fully. When done, she sat back, trembling, waiting for the verdict. He inspected her slowly and then gently took the lipstick out of her hand and repeated the process. And then again over her lips and around her mouth. And again – only wider, pressing hard beneath her nose and in the centre of her chin.

He recapped the lipstick and studied her face. 'I don't think you look pretty. If I'm honest I think you look…' His expression was regretful as if what he was about to say was something hurtful. 'Like a clown. Yes, a clown.' He sighed and stood up and walked away a little so that he could inspect her from afar. He eyed her for several moments. 'You know, you remind me of when I was a junior doctor. I did a stint in plastic surgery. There was a chap who needed a reconstruction to his lower face. Terrible mess altogether. It looked like it had been hacked with a blunt knife. The operating surgeon called it a Glasgow smile. It's where a person's mouth is cut from corners to ears so that they permanently wear the shape of a smile. Terrible thing to happen, don't you think?'

He passed her leisurely, and at the door he stopped. 'If you're lying, Tess, you will be punished.' Keeping his back towards her, he spoke again. 'By the way, I'm out tonight so you might want to take a look at your "Improvements" book. You're behind on quite a few chores. I've been updating it daily, Tess, but clearly you haven't been checking.'

She sat there trembling, not daring to move. How, she wondered, had she not seen the man she was to marry four months ago? Were all people blind? Were they like her, programmed to believe that someone educated, charming, choosing a helping career, was someone to trust? The woman in the book had been warned of something similar. Her father had warned her not to mistake charm for grace. Tess understood how easy she must have been fooled. Daniel had grace in his movements and his manners, in his performance as a surgeon and as a lover. He had grace flowing out of him. What was not to trust? She hadn't been blind. She had just been unable to see.

When the front door shut an hour later she felt free to finally breathe. It was amazing how tuned her ears were to the closing and opening of that door. It dictated the breath she breathed. Let out trapped air or gasp in needed air. She had a whole evening without him. The atmosphere in the house was lighter, less oppressive. She wanted to fling open all the windows and doors and let its history escape. If she could imagine a perfect life for this house it would be to fill it with the sound of happy children's voices. Laughter would ring out from every room, replacing darkness with light. She hugged the thought of that life. She would take it into her dreams.

Climbing stairs with her tired clown's face, she took off clothes and showered. She spurned the bottles of perfumes and lotions set out for her use, as a rejection of *him*. She dressed in clean jogging bottoms and loose T-shirt in an act of defiance. He was not there to see how she dressed or moved or sat or smiled. He was not there to witness this moment of freedom. She was dressed for action, not to be sat across a dining table. She intended to search this house while she had time alone for this woman's name.

She stilled as she heard the doorbell ring. It was probably a delivery or some such thing. She could ignore it and pretend not to be home. It was after six, a time when most people were busy, having their tea, or bathing children, or just settling in for the evening, so not a convenient time. The bell sounded again and then a voice called out from the other side of the closed door. Tess startled. Her guard instantly went up, never imagining this caller coming to her door.

Anne Ferris smiled at her. 'Impromptu visit, I know, and I would have called first if I had your number. I thought I'd take the opportunity while Ed and Daniel are having a working drink together. They're discussing a difficult case coming up, I believe.'

Tess wondered if the 'working drink' was at Anne's home or somewhere else. She felt sure her husband wouldn't approve of this visit. She'd been surprised at him inviting Ed Ferris for dinner after knowing what his wife did for a living. She could dissect a mind with the same level of skill as he could repair a dissecting aneurysm, and well-qualified to deal with disturbed dark minds. Tess smiled at the woman as she let her into her home. She led the way to the kitchen and automatically switched on the kettle.

'Would you like tea?'

'Yes, please,' Anne answered warmly. 'Builder's tea preferably, but without sugar. Builders all seem to like their sugar. The ones we have do. I have to remember to get it in for them.'

Tess's mouth had gone dry. Why was she visiting? It seemed strange to just turn up like this.

'What work are you having done?'

Anne sighed. 'Endless projects Ed keeps starting and not finishing. We've had them at the house for two weeks now. They're finishing a wall Ed started, a conversion to our front porch because Ed wanted it larger, and a window put in the garage because Ed wanted natural light in there so that he could do more projects.' She laughed. 'The man is endlessly busy and still wants to find time to work on projects. Being a surgeon it seems is not enough.'

'So is he working at the hospital as well as working in the States?'

'Oh yes. As soon as he steps foot on the tarmac he's back to being scrubbed up.' She looked at Tess a little surprised. 'Have you not had the pleasure of working with him yet?'

'No. I'm having a bit of a holiday sorting out this house,' she lied brazenly. She was reassured she hadn't been the topic of gossip at work. The conversations on Sunday had centred on several subjects, interesting ones about plays and places to visit, about food and wine and her wedding, of course. Nothing about the hospital or work had been mentioned. Ed hadn't seemed to know she was off. But she shouldn't be surprised – Stella seemed the type that wouldn't allow it. Possibly only the few who were there that day were aware of why she wasn't working. The few would become most once the outcome was known. Someone being sacked or struck off was harder to keep quiet about. Especially if it went into a newspaper, which it probably would.

She was finding it difficult to think of other things to say.

'I saw Vivien on the train yesterday. That was a lovely dinner party she gave. She's a great hostess, isn't she?'

'Yes, it was a very pleasant evening. Ed and I don't get to socialise much with us both being busy.' She smiled openly and shrugged her shoulders expansively. 'If he's not working on projects, he's sat at his fish pond. Which is another enormous project all of its own entirely. He seems to enjoy watching them. Which is fine, I suppose, as I like to read.'

'Me too,' Tess replied, forcing some energy into her voice. She put a teabag in each mug – *he* wasn't there to see how she made it – and made one stronger than the other. She took out a packet of biscuits. If she was eating she couldn't be talking. She opened them and bit into one. Picking up the mugs she placed them on the kitchen table.

Anne joined her and sat down. 'I hope you don't mind me turning up out of the blue. I enjoyed your company the other night, Tess. I found what you said interesting.'

Tess took a sip of hot tea and swallowed the mouthful of biscuit.

'I found it interesting, *and* a little concerning. Sunday wasn't the right time to talk about it with the men there.'

She wasn't beating about the bush and neither would Tess. 'You mean because I asked if they ever stop?'

'Yes,' Anne said, her eyes showing concern.

'Did you think I was talking about something related to me?'

'Yes.'

Tess quickly weighed up her options. Should she go for the offended look or the surprised look? This woman was shrewd. She went for somewhere in between and shook her head sadly.

'I wasn't talking about me. I was talking about a nurse I worked with at St Mary's. It's quite sad. She said her husband locked her in a cupboard for not aligning his shirts properly. He makes her wear some sort of uniform to do housework. She's been to the doctor with bruises to her breast and the doctor didn't ask how she got them.'

Anne let out a breath. 'So not you, but someone else?'

Tess nodded. 'You do remember I've only been married four months?'

'Yes, I do,' she said, looking Tess in the eye. 'You do know domestic violence can't tell the time? I had a patient once who murdered his wife the day he married her. He told me he was waiting to make her his before he carried out the deed.'

Tess opened her eyes wide as if she'd been shocked. She wasn't. After what he did to her tonight she didn't think much more could shock her. He hadn't hurt her physically. He had stripped her of her humanity. While she sat through his actions it struck a memory from when she was a student nurse of a young psychiatric patient called Wendy. She'd been ungainly, overweight, and slack featured with a heavy jaw and little schooling. She was in love and excited for her new boyfriend's visit. Another trainee nurse offered to make her look pretty. Wendy had wanted to see her face after the make-up was put on, but she forgot after a while, after she was told she looked beautiful. She had smiled at him and danced across the dayroom floor to him, all eyes on her ungainly movements, all mouths open as they laughed and clapped and encouraged her to carry on. It was entertainment. In the toilet Tess had cried. The nurse had made Wendy look like a grotesque clown. White-faced, red-nosed, black-lipped and black eyes stripping her of dignity in front of her new boyfriend.

'Your job must be incredibly challenging,' she said.

'It is, because truth and lies are often told together. The truth to hide the lies and lies to hide the truth.'

'And what advice would you give this nurse, in this relationship?'

Her eyes locked on Tess. 'I'd tell her to get out of it. Today. Tonight. Don't wait and hope he will stop. And I'd tell her to get a new doctor.'

When a short while later Tess waved her goodnight, she was left feeling out of sorts and exposed, as if she'd been talking about herself and not some other woman's account. Recounting back to Anne what she'd read so far in that black book highlighted the things that had been done to her in a much shorter timeframe. He'd poured a cup of boiling coffee into her lap and had then held her down to make it burn more. He had drawn on her face with lipstick, making her look like a clown. He had taken her phone, her bank card, her choice of what she would wear. He had pinned her by the neck against a wall. He had taken her job. He had lied and made her take the fall for a man dying. He had taken, taken, taken.

Anne's response might have been different if she'd told her these things and admitted she was speaking about herself. She might even have called the police. But it wouldn't help Tess's situation go away unless there was evidence. At this moment in time she needed hard facts not counselling. She could get that at a later date. Then take back what he had taken from her. Her life and her soul.

CHAPTER THIRTY-FOUR

The next morning she found a pretty headscarf in the cloakroom. It was square and patterned with swirls of gold on a turquoise background. It felt like silk and looked vintage in style. It wasn't hers so maybe Anne left it behind, and Daniel put it away. She would borrow it to wear on the platform, the last thing she needed was for the platform man to recognise her from yesterday. She'd return it to Anne, if she visited again. Hopefully, next time, she'd give Tess some warning she was coming. Though, without her visit, Tess might not have found what she did. As she would have searched the bedrooms first and not come down the stairs if Anne hadn't rung the bell.

He'd forgotten to lock his office door as he normally did. In a blue-leather phone book left out on his desk she found the telephone number and address of his parents. It was listed under M beside the names: Mother/Father. Not Mum and Dad or Ma and Pa, but Mother and Father. Beneath their title was their address and she couldn't have been more surprised. They lived not too far away, in Bradford-on-Avon. No more than twenty minutes by train. In fact just down the road. Not over a hundred miles away in London like she'd thought, but on their doorstep. Tess was betting it was since Daniel was a child, betting the very small amount of money she had that he was born in the area and this area was his home.

She picked up some envelopes from the mailbox before setting off, in case there was a letter from the hospital. She forgot to check when she got home yesterday. She shoved the mail in her rucksack. She didn't have time to read it now. She wanted to catch the 8.13 so as to be at the flat early again so she could leave early as before.

Of all the people to see at the platform, only seeing Sara would have made her happier. Cameron came right up to her and as if it was the most natural thing in the world gave her a big hug. He then kissed the top of her head and said, 'Hello, friend. Almost didn't recognise you with the scarf on your head. Very Audrey Hepburn.'

Tess smiled, ever so pleased to see him. A second of his company was like a little tonic.

'Hello, Cameron. How are you?' she said.

'I'm off for a day out at John Radcliffe, to go and watch a heart bypass operation. I think it would be good for me to go and see another hospital.' He gave a rueful laugh. 'Before they try and get rid of me.'

She touched his arm. 'You're doing really well. Don't think that.'

He caught her hand and gave it a gentle squeeze. 'Hey, enough about me. More to the point, how are you?'

She scrunched up her nose, and shook her head at him. 'Let's not talk about that.'

He plucked at the collar of the dress she was wearing, the one she'd sworn never to wear, the washed-out lavender granny dress.

'Interesting,' he said politely, pressing his lips and raising his eyebrows.

She elbowed him in the ribs and he looked startled.

'Shut up, I didn't pick it. I just wear it.'

'Phew,' he said. 'I didn't want to say in case you'd been left it in a will by a favourite aunty or something.'

'Funny.' She smiled. 'So are you catching the train to London?'

'Yes, but not all the way. Got to change at Didcot Parkway for Oxford.'

'What time's the operation?'

'Nine thirty.'

Tess stared at him. 'You're not going to make it. It's almost eight now.'

'I'm cutting it fine,' he contradicted. 'I've got a taxi to pick me up at the other end. I'm sure I won't miss anything.' Then sheepishly he added, 'I slept through the alarm. I haven't even had a morning coffee yet.'

'We'll get you one on the train,' she replied, happy to use some of her spending money to buy him a coffee.

'And you? Where are you off to?'

'London. Sorting out the contents of my husband's flat. Today should see the last of it hopefully.'

'Good,' he said more seriously. 'Good that you're keeping busy. I—'

She touched his arm as he looked awkward. 'I'm sorry I didn't tell you. It was difficult.'

He shrugged and then tutted at her mildly. 'Could you not have let me down more lightly and picked someone less tall, less handsome and only half as intelligent?'

She laughed. 'I will next time.'

An hour later she said goodbye to him at Didcot, making no plans to talk to him or see him again. He commented on the journey that she was no longer on Facebook. He didn't pursue the subject when she looked away. And it would have sounded odd if she'd said, 'I didn't know that.' She didn't know that he'd taken something else away, of course. She put Cameron out of her mind. She was at peace now. A brief interlude where she felt they were friends again. It was enough to have that.

Tess felt sick in her stomach. She had just gone through her mail and found an envelope unstamped and unaddressed but with her name on it. Her insides were quivering from recognising the blue handwriting. She had been followed right to her door! By a stranger writing to her. With trembling fingers she tore open the envelope and found a postcard. A plain white business postcard, the same as the one she received yesterday. With a squiggled drawing in the top right corner clearer to see it was an angel not a butterfly.

She read the message on the card.

I have thought about what you tried to do and it has left me feeling somewhat uneasy. I am asking you now to get help. Please don't make me have to do it for you.

She scanned the faces around her to see if anyone was looking at her with an air of ownership, making sure she was behaving herself and not thinking foolish thoughts. Her head swam and she felt woozy and then overwarm. She pulled off the headscarf to let air at her head. She should eat something to settle her nerves before she passed out. She'd not eaten since last night and her blood sugar was probably low. She'd also forgotten to refill her water flask which was now empty in her bag.

Getting shakily to her feet she made her way to the buffet bar and kept a look-out for anyone suspicious, though what the postcard sender looked like was anyone's guess. It could be the man smiling at her now as they carefully passed one another or the man in the wheelchair blocking the vestibule or even the young woman with the toddler on her lap.

She kept her hand firmly over the top of her bag. She was wearing the rucksack front-facing across her chest so as not to be caught unawares if this person tried to slip her another message. Up ahead she saw two British Transport Police and momentarily stilled. They looked tall and imposing with all their equipment padding out their jackets and hanging off their belts. Black was a very imposing colour when worn as a uniform. She flushed as she saw one of them staring at her intently, causing sweat to trickle down her back, especially when he started speaking into his radio. Had the postcard messenger already sought help for her and they were there waiting?

She should be bold and go straight up to them and report the stalker, report that she was receiving unwanted attention in the form of two postcards and it was someone who travelled on trains as she'd received one of them while on board. Would they be interested in helping her once they discovered what she had done? Killing a patient and then attempting to kill herself? They would call this postcard messenger a Samaritan and then have her sectioned before handing her over to paramedics to be carted off somewhere safe.

She let go a sigh of relief. They had turned away from her. She was not someone of interest to them.

At the buffet bar she chose a banana and a bottle of regular Coke. The man behind the counter stared at her with eyes magnified through thick lenses, eyelids seeming puffy and wrinkles exaggerated. Sparse grey hair covered his pale pink scalp. His customer service left a lot to be desired, as he hadn't passed a word to her. She handed over her money and moved away from the counter.

She heard a familiar voice behind her.

'Hello, Bill. Long time no see.' The *Bradshaw's* book man stood next to her at the counter.

The buffet attendant stiffened for a fraction, then cracked a smile at the man. 'Well, I'll be blowed.'

Tess sneaked a glance at the *Bradshaw's* book man and caught the smile he gave to Bill.

'You look like you've seen a ghost, Bill. I'm surprised to see you too. You don't normally do the morning train.'

Bill descended from what must have been a step as he was now much shorter. Shorter than Tess.

'Times change,' he said, folding his arms. 'Nights ain't good for me anymore. Be retiring soon. Can I get you anything from the bar, complimentary of course, seeing as you're a special traveller?'

The man smiled again, but Tess didn't think it looked natural. 'A cup of coffee would be nice.'

'One coming right up,' was the jaunty reply.

Tess peered at Bill. She was intrigued to know what he meant. He'd called the *Bradshaw's* book man a *special traveller*. Was the man a travel writer, maybe like Michael Portillo or another celebrity? He was certainly being treated in a deferential manner.

Bill handed him the lidded coffee. 'You travelling all the way?'

'Only as far as Reading.'

Bill nodded. 'Well, good to see you.'

She saw the man's hand rest on the counter. He tapped it once. 'I haven't forgotten what I saw, Bill, in case you were wondering.'

Tess felt a change in the atmosphere. Bill seemed to shrivel to an even smaller size. 'You got that all wrong about me,' he said in a strained voice.

Stepping around Tess to take a packet of sugar, the man said to her, 'You look pale.'

Tess felt it. The exchange between the two men and the message she got had shaken her. As he walked away she followed and, in the vestibule, he smiled at her kindly.

'Hello, again. Sorry about that. You get them everywhere. Loathsome people.' Leaving Tess to wonder what loathsome Bill had done.

She put a shaky hand to her head and he reached out and steadied her arm.

'Are you OK? You don't look well.'

She felt suddenly tearful and her mouth trembled. He sounded like a father caring about a daughter and for a moment she felt bereft. To have a mother or father she could go to – to have someone she could tell of her unhappiness – would ease her burden.

'Just a headache,' she said.

She watched him out of the window as he got off at Reading, his stride purposeful, and wished she too could just get off. She could disappear right here into another life and not look back.

At two o'clock Tess let herself out the front door of the flat for the last time. She would not be coming back. Tomorrow she would go somewhere new. Though she wasn't going to let her husband know that. He'd given her a seven-day train ticket, well, tomorrow she intended to get a train. She wasn't going to bother with a visit to St Thomas's. Now that she knew where his parents lived.

CHAPTER THIRTY-FIVE

Martha was wearing a proper bib apron with a wide pocket in the skirt. She was in charge of the tea-making. She popped her head out the back door and gazed at the policeman talking to Jim.

'Do you take sugar in your tea?' she asked.

'One, thank you, Mrs King,' the tall man replied. He looked too young to be a policeman. His face didn't look like it had grown any hair. Why Jim had to talk to him out in the garden she didn't know. He'd said so the chap could smoke, but she hadn't seen any evidence of that when looking out of the window. They were just standing there in quite blowy weather and Jim seemed to be doing a lot of the talking.

She'd called the 101 number this time, not wanting to be reprimanded for calling 999 again. When a constable turned up, surprisingly quick, she'd given him a full account of her stolen scarf and where she'd lost it and who had taken it. She then told him she'd seen it with her own eyes that morning on the head of the man's new wife. She was wearing it after he had stolen it.

Jim had come home and found them talking so she'd had to go through it all again. But at least Jim was now taking it seriously. He'd said straight away that he'd like a serious word with the officer about this matter, though she hadn't heard what this serious word was about yet as they'd then gone out to the garden and Jim had put her in charge of making the tea.

She opened the back door again and waved the two men into the kitchen with a tea towel. 'It'll go cold if you don't drink it now.'

The young officer took off his cap and accepted the mug she offered. 'Don't mind if I do.' He sipped it and found it just right. 'Nice cup of tea.'

'If you heat the teapot first you can't go wrong.' She settled down on a small footstool, leaving the two chairs at the kitchen table to the men. 'Sorry I can't offer you a biscuit. I can't find any. I think Jim must eat them all.'

She saw the policeman eyeing a wall cupboard. 'What about in that one?' He smiled and pointed.

Martha saw that he was looking at Jim's label on the cupboard door saying what was inside it. The word 'BISCUITS' was written as large as life and Martha felt foolish for not seeing it. Jim gave the man a bit of a look and saved her further embarrassment.

'They're all gone. Martha's right.'

The young officer stared away awkwardly, before speaking again. 'You have a lovely home, Mrs King.'

'It's been rewired and had a new boiler put in two years ago and, of course, the roof is sound. Ted did it not long ago.' She patted the wall beside her. 'It's been a good solid house, so it has.' She took a hanky from her apron pocket and gave her nose a quick blow. 'So, about this matter. You're going to take it seriously then?'

He shuffled a bit in his seat. 'You could say that. You're absolutely sure though that your scarf isn't somewhere inside your home?'

She shook her head. 'I lost it in the cemetery after he was following me, like I said. I saw him at the hospital and it shook him up to hear me say I knew his real name. That's why he followed me! Not to steal my scarf but to silence me! If not for Jim I'd be dead!'

'Maybe someone picked it up. Someone else, I mean.'

He sipped some more of his tea and she glared at him. She may as well have held her breath for all the notice he was taking. 'I may well be old, Constable, but I'm not blind. His wife was wearing it this morning!'

He placed his mug on the table. 'I'm not saying you are, Mrs King. I'm just making sure you're certain. There are a lot of blue scarves out there.'

'Not like mine,' she cried. 'Someone gave it to me after I nearly did something terrible.'

'I gave it to you, Martha,' Jim said. He smiled at her kindly. 'So as I'd find you more easily. It has a bit of a glow in the dark. Can you remember me giving it to you?'

Her shoulders slumped and her lips trembled badly. She was trying not to cry. 'I don't remember that, Jim. I'm sorry.'

'What did you nearly do?' the officer gently probed.

Jim butted in. 'You don't need to know that, Constable.'

'What's a mortal sin?' she uttered in despair, her voice breaking. 'An act against the will of God. Thou shall not kill thyself. And my maker up there will not have been pleased about it.'

As she cried quietly Jim took hold of her hand and patted it softly. She heard the young policeman call out a goodbye, but she didn't respond. She was busy thinking about what Jim had said. She hadn't known it was him who led her away and brought her home. What she found sadder was that she hadn't remembered him ever giving her the scarf.

'Will you do me a favour, Jim?' she asked.

'Another one?' he replied, teasing her and lightening the mood.

She gave him a teary smile. 'Don't ever treat me like an old fool, will you? I don't mean take me for one. I mean treat me like one.'

'Not ever will I do that,' he said firmly.

'That young officer? He's not going to go looking for my scarf or visit any man, is he? He was just giving me the talk, wasn't he?'

Jim stared at her, and she saw him swallow before he nodded. She lightly gripped his hand. At least she knew. She wouldn't waste time waiting for something to happen. The watching of his house was still in her hands. The safety of his wife was down to her. No one else wanted it. No one believed she was in danger.

She had looked as pretty as picture wearing the scarf. It was the same blue colour as her eyes. Martha would let her keep it. Jim had given it to her to keep her safe. Maybe it would help this young woman. Martha hoped so. She was getting very weary from so much responsibility.

CHAPTER THIRTY-SIX

Tess stepped into her hallway just as the clocks chimed five o'clock. She was surprised to find he was already there. Did the man ever work? She quickly took off her jacket and left it with her rucksack on the hall chair. Out in the open for him to see she had nothing to hide. It was now empty of make-up and the postcard was tucked down the back of her pants for her to hide when she went upstairs.

She was further surprised to find him humming and cooking. He smiled at her warmly.

'I knocked off early. Ed and I got called in yesterday evening for a stabbing. Two sixteen-year-old lads were attacked by a gang. We were meant to be having a drink together to discuss a case I have tomorrow. Good job we didn't as we were needed. Anyway, I didn't get back till late and then was back there again at the crack of dawn.' He grinned. 'Patients are doing well though, so that's something.'

'Well done,' she said, hoping he wouldn't ask her what she did. Or remember the scarf he put away. She didn't want to have to mention Anne's visit.

'He asked after you. Said how much he enjoyed Sunday, how he and his wife thought you were charming, so don't be surprised if we get an invite to their home.'

She gave a sound of approval. 'That was nice of him. They seem like a nice couple. Do you want any help?'

His hands suddenly rested on her shoulders and he gave her a gentle push towards the door. 'Go and have a bath and change. Dinner will be about half an hour.'

Tess made her way slowly up the stairs, feeling a wave of deep depression slam into her like a wall. Why had he had to change from being like this? *This* was how he used to be all the time until they got married. A kind and considerate man. She could, if she was foolish enough, imagine nothing had happened or changed since then, or move forward and forget what followed. Forget her waiting on a verdict. She stopped short at her bedroom door at the sight of the small package on the bed. Her bunched fingers pressed to her mouth to silence her cry. The black-and-white box was tied with a delicate gold ribbon. He'd left her a new perfume to try. His behaviour downstairs was not normal. It was a charade – nothing more. He could play the part of an attentive husband and just as easily switch off the performance. Nothing about him was normal, not these endless gifts of perfume or his humming downstairs.

When she was nearly ready, she heard the landline phone ring, and desperately hoped it was another emergency at the hospital to give her a second evening without him. She came down the stairs as he replaced the receiver. He returned to the kitchen and attended to the pot on the stove. Whatever the call was about he was not hurrying to get ready and leave. She fixed a smile on her face and prepared to help.

'I'll lay the table,' she offered.

'I never asked about your day. How did it go?'

'Good. The removal van collected everything on time. Said they'd be bringing it here Sunday as arranged.'

'Yes, that's right. It needs one of us to be here, and I didn't know how many more days you might need at the flat.'

'I'm giving it a clean tomorrow, and it shouldn't take too long with it empty Thank you, by the way, for the perfume.'

He turned. 'That's OK. Thank you for sorting it out.'

'I've enjoyed the train journeys. I'll probably miss them.'

'At least you won't have to put up with the annoying Vivien beside you again.'

Tess kept quiet. Passing no comment was probably wisest.

'Or crammed in with all those strangers. Dreadful busy things, you don't know who you could be standing next to. Anything could happen to you!' He laughed and surprisingly so did she. It was a near perfect mimicry of Vivien's voice.

'Well, I was lucky. I didn't have to sit next to anyone.'

'Good. It's nice to have a quiet journey.'

He picked up the large pot and drained boiling water into the sink. He stopped humming and was concentrating.

'Does this look cooked to you?' he asked.

She went over to the sink to stand beside him.

'Try a bit,' he asked. Tess carefully took hold of a tendril of spaghetti between finger and thumb to prevent her fingers burning. 'Is it soft?' he asked.

'It's perfect,' she said, though thinking it soggy and overcooked.

'Like you then,' he said softly. He raised her free hand to his mouth and kissed her palm. 'Perfect at lying.'

She tensed as he gripped her wrist. Horrified, she watched in slow motion her hand going into the pot of boiling hot spaghetti.

'Please don't, Daniel!' she begged, feeling the heat against her palm.

'Don't what?' he asked, holding her hand hovering over the steaming food.

'Please, please don't. I beg you.'

'Do this you mean?' he said, keeping a tight grip on her wrist as he submerged her hand in the boiling glutinous spaghetti and forced it down to touch the base of the pot. Her legs buckled as the pain radiating through her entire body folded her to the ground, making him let go. Panting in agony, she climbed to her feet desperate to get her hand under cold running water, feeling the stinging intensify as cold pressure hit burning heat as she thrust her hand under the tap.

He stood to the side watching, wiping his hands on a cloth.

'Stella phoned. She said Cameron called her as he wonders if you've got his mobile. He said he had it with him when you were on the train together. Imagine my surprise at hearing that? Perhaps he left it at the flat. Do you think he might have done that?'

She couldn't speak she was in so much agony. She shook her head.

'I told Stella you couldn't come to the phone right now as I'd just had to put you to bed.' He sighed and tutted. 'I told her how you'd burned your poor hand while cooking. She said you were lucky to have a doctor on hand. That was nice of her, wasn't it?'

As he walked away he resumed humming the tune he hummed earlier. Tess stared after him with pain-filled eyes. He had known what he was going to do to her before he did it. His cruelty was demonic. The heat inside of her was like a furnace as she stood there watching him walk away. He should be put down like a mad dog. Do what would be done to an animal if it behaved this way. Put it out of its misery.

CHAPTER THIRTY-SEVEN

He left her a tube of Flamazine cream and some non-adhesive dressings with a note she didn't find in the least funny: *Doctor's orders.* She spent the night in unbearable pain from the constant throbbing, the paracetamol and ibuprofen giving almost no relief. Only by keeping it submerged in a bowl of cool water was she able to manage. Several blisters had formed under the skin and her entire hand was red and puffy. He must be a sociopath to do something so cold and calculating. He had caused extreme pain just long enough to leave no permanent damage and ensuring it healed quickly with treatment.

She slathered the cream on her hand and was fixing a dressing with a bandage when the phone rang in the hallway. It rang out eight times before the call went to the answer machine. Her mouth dried as she heard Stella's voice.

'Tess, you silly, silly girl. I hope Daniel has made you all better. Cameron has found his phone by the way. It was found on the train and handed in so all good now. Take care and no more burning yourself.'

The words were light and airy as if Stella imagined her at home like a little girl being cossetted and spoiled. Instead, she was punished because he thought she had spent the day at the flat with Cameron. No one would ever believe her if she told them the truth. They would look at him and look at her and they would believe him. Stella, she noted, had called her husband by name. Their relationship must be getting close.

She took two more paracetamol and two more ibuprofen. She needed to be on those trains today. She had her duty as a daughter-in-law.

On the kitchen table she saw the 'Improvements' book standing upright, left like that so she couldn't miss seeing it. She hadn't looked inside its red cover or touched it since the day he bought it. It had been a wonderful gift to receive after him ending her career. What better way to cheer her up than to let her know she was a failure as a housewife? His thoughtful gift had been truly inspiring. The book on etiquette was buried beneath clothing in a drawer upstairs. She didn't ever intend to read it.

Picking *his* book up she opened the hard cover and saw he'd had the gall to write in red and underline the word 'IMPROVE-MENTS'. She saw he'd written on the first page the day of the week he started it: Sunday. Had he done this in the morning or in the evening? After the lovely meal with his guests or after saying she could go to London? When had he bloody well written the damn thing, while in his office sorting out her train ticket? Putting pen to paper knowing that the next day she'd be heading to London to sort out his flat and wouldn't have time to carry out the 'Improvements'.

For Sunday he'd written:

Water in shower is draining slowly. Shower plug hole is full of hair. May I remind you to remove it each time you shower? Use shower cap when not washing hair.

She turned the pages and saw four more entries:

Monday: Have consideration for the bin men. Rinse recycling properly.

Tuesday: Unless you want accidents to happen remove moss between front door steps. A kitchen knife should do it. Then use scrubbing brush to get rid of green.

Wednesday: Read previous entries! Step is getting slippery!
Shower plug hole still full of hair!
      Thursday: I'm eating out tonight. Don't cook for me. Don't
go to London to clean flat. It's unnecessary.

Tess slammed the book down then swept it off the kitchen table to let it fly across the room and land on the floor. She wasn't going to London. She hoped he would slip on the step and crack his skull open. She breathed in deeply and let it go slowly. She needed to preserve her energy for the things she still had to do. *My husband is unwell,* she said in her mind, finding it helped to think of him that way.

A short while later she stepped down the two steps from the front door. They didn't look green or feel in the slightest bit slippery. She heard a buzzing sound coming towards her and saw two wasps flying back into the porch. They were probably attracted to the light that was on during the night. Wasps in October could be aggressive, drunk on ripened fruit and more likely to sting. She craned her neck to look up at the eaves of the roof. The overhang was deep and too high to spot anything but maybe there was a nest up there. She imagined her husband getting up a ladder to deal with it. He'd use long-handled forceps to grip it and pull it out and then be shocked at being attacked by a swarm. Stinging him and stinging him and stinging him. He would know what stinging felt like then. Know it wasn't very pleasant.

At Bradford-on-Avon Tess exited the train station carrying a small bunch of flowers that she'd bought at the flower shop at Bath Station. She saw an old man coming towards her and stopped him to ask directions. It was two minutes before she managed to part company with him as he started to go into the history of the town. Fortunately, he remembered he had a train to catch.

He proved accurate in his timing and descriptions as she reached
a pretty bridge over the town's canal in just under three minutes
and saw what he'd described up on a hill. Old weavers' cottages
near to old textile mills dotted the landscape. If she wasn't there
for the specific reason of finding out if her husband had a first
wife it would have been nice to have listened to the old man. In
another life it was a place she would want to explore. The house
she was looking for was not far from the cottages up on the hill.

Her in-laws' home was a stone-built cottage with a white gate
opening into a well-tended garden with a small vegetable patch
either side of a narrow pathway. Tess walked up it and knocked
on the blue front door. She had racked her brain on the journey
there trying to recall their first names and couldn't. She was not
even sure if she ever heard them mentioned. They were related.
They shared the same surname, yet she did not know their
Christian names.

Mrs Myers' shocked face told that at least she recognised her.

'Tess!' she exclaimed. 'What a surprise to see you. What brings
you here? Is everything all right? Stuart,' she called to the back of
the house. 'Come see who's visited.'

Stuart came out of a room at the end of the hall. He held a
newspaper in his hands and his glasses were pushed up on his
head. He stared at Tess worriedly. 'Everything OK, lass? Nancy,
don't leave her on the doorstep. Bring her in.'

Tess now had both their names. She handed Nancy the flowers.
She looked a little startled and a little flushed. As she entered their
home, she noticed on the walls in the hallway several framed
photographs of Daniel as a boy. Playing in a sandpit at an age of
about four, hanging off a climbing frame as a bigger boy, and then
sat on a bike looking like a young teenager. His face in all of them
was solemn and he was unsmiling.

Nancy ushered her into a small sitting room and invited her
to sit down, offering her tea.

Tess sat in a stripy armchair and curled her hands in her lap. They were both standing there ogling her as if she was from space. Both looked uncomfortable. Nancy had taken off her apron from around her very thin waist and was pushing her straight grey hair behind her ears. Stuart folded his newspaper into a small square as if he was in the process of making something into origami. A pull-along vacuum cleaner sat in the middle of the room and two chairs were standing on a small table. She had been in the middle of her chores, and no doubt would have preferred finishing them before getting this visit. She probably would have liked a bit of notice so that she could change out of her fur-trimmed slippers into some smarter footwear and tell her husband to shave his grey whiskers and put on a shirt over his short-sleeved vest. Tess's well-cut navy dress worn with navy court shoes, matching in colour this time, probably made them both self-conscious.

'No, thank you,' Tess said to the offer of tea. 'I just had a bottle of water.'

They both sat down. 'And what brings you here, my dear?' Nancy asked.

Tess smiled. 'I just thought I should come and get to know you better.'

Nancy frowned. 'Did Daniel ask you to?'

Tess shook her head. 'No. It was my idea. I found your address and thought I'd pay a visit.'

'Why's that, lass?' Stuart asked.

Tess turned worried eyes his way. 'Should I not have come then?'

Stuart replied. 'Well, the thing is, lass, we haven't seen much of Daniel.'

Tess felt herself flushing under his keen gaze. 'He's been very busy since we got married. We moved from London as he got a new job.'

'What I should have said is, Nancy and I don't see a lot of our son at the best of times. Not since he was all grown up. Not since—'

'Since he got busy being a doctor,' Nancy cut in. She smiled at her husband. 'Isn't that right, Stuart?'

Her husband nodded. 'Aye, that's right. Since he got busy being a doctor.'

Tess fidgeted with the folds of her dress. 'So when was the last time before our wedding that you saw him?'

'When he turned twenty-five,' Stuart replied.

Tess stared at him astonished, her eyes open wide.

He could see he'd shocked her. 'Don't be worried, lass. It's just the way he is. He was always independent, needing little of anyone. He was like it as a boy.'

Tess sat silently, thinking fifteen years was too long a gap to simply call it being independent. Something must have caused this absence. This explained why they had not been sat at the top table. It would have been difficult for them after not seeing their son for nearly fifteen years. He'd have been like a stranger to them. She looked at his mother.

'May I ask what you meant when you said on the phone you call him every year?'

Nancy took a tissue from the sleeve of her cardigan. She didn't use it though, just held it in her hand.

'I'm not sure what you mean, Tess.'

Tess chewed her lip. The atmosphere in the room was stilted. It was like getting blood from a stone.

'You made it sound like the date was important.'

Nancy gave a little smile that didn't reach her eyes. 'I think you must have misheard or misunderstood me, my dear. I call my son once a year, every year, to make sure he's well and alive.'

'And do you catch up on everything then?'

'Our conversations are usually short.'

'So you don't know what he's been doing with his life? Don't you miss him?' Tess asked a little exasperatedly.

'As long as he's happy we're satisfied,' she said primly. 'He knows where we are if he needs us.'

Tess calmed herself. She didn't know these people or their circumstances. So she shouldn't judge them. 'I take it this is where Daniel grew up?'

'His bedroom's right up those stairs if you want to see it,' Stuart said, pointing up at the ceiling. 'He went into a big bed when he was three. It looks pretty much the same as it did then. He went to the local schools here, and then he went off to university in London where his new life pretty much started. I don't think Nancy or I were ever bright enough for him, lass. Not that he ever said. It was more that he never looked to us for any of his learning.'

'Never looked to us for any love either,' Nancy said quietly, almost to herself. She looked upset for a moment. 'Are you sure you wouldn't like a cup of tea?' she asked again.

Tess said yes this time, she would have one. Then she asked them if she could have a look at their son's room. Nancy nodded and told her it was at the top of the stairs to the right. While Nancy went to make the tea Tess went to look at her husband's childhood bedroom. There were three rooms off the small landing. A bathroom and a bedroom with doors open. Both looked tidy with loo seat down and double bed neatly made. The second bedroom had its door shut. Tess opened it. Her first impression was it was not unlike the bedroom she'd had as a child.

It was small and rectangular with a window at its far end. A single bed and a chest of drawers sat against one wall, a plain wardrobe and desk on the facing wall. Two pine shelves above the desk held study books. A-Level books on human biology, physiology, chemistry. There were other books on microbiology, pathology and diseases. The rest of the room looked fairly barren with no posters on the walls or left-over toys or games or even reading books. It looked like a room you would rent out to a student only minimally decorated to give it a bit of personality. It was very different to how her husband lived now. Yet, as she thought of the things she packed up from his flat, it was really only the size and space he lived in that was different. He liked quality and he chose carefully but there was nothing personal in those objects. He'd not had among his personal possessions a single photograph of himself or anyone else for that matter. His parents had clearly been out of mind. Tess had a small album of their wedding photographs and one in a frame that he'd put up in the drawing room, but she couldn't recall ever seeing any photos he might have.

She stayed and had tea with them and then a short while later said her goodbyes. She wouldn't be seeing them again. And nor would their son, it would seem. His life was alien to them. She wondered if they liked their son. She had picked up that they were holding things back. Maybe it was their lack of feelings she picked up on. Her impression was of two people heading into old age who were childless. Their behaviour and acceptance hadn't been normal. Where was the natural interest to catch up on the fifteen years of their son's life they had missed out on? They should have been keen to ask her all about him. Questioning her about his welfare, his future plans, not letting her leave until they'd had their fill. Instead, they'd been restrained, guarded when talking about him. Again, she wondered if they liked him. Were they glad not to see him?

As she walked back to the station a realisation came to her. She had sat with them nearly an hour with her hand heavily bandaged in her lap and neither of them had asked what happened to it. Had they guessed it had something to do with their son and therefore wouldn't ask? If that was so then they were guarded because they knew of his dark side and may even have experience of it.

CHAPTER THIRTY-EIGHT

As Tess arrived back in Bath she got off the train feeling sick. The painkillers had worn off and unable to control herself she emitted a low groan and had to stand still, clearly in discomfort.

'Afternoon,' a man's voice said. 'Can I help?'

Tess raised her head and saw a policeman standing in front of her. *Oh God, why couldn't it just be someone ordinary?* She was acutely uncomfortable on this platform after what she'd tried to do.

'Would you like some water?' he offered, sounding concerned.

She tried to summon a smile, but it came out as a grimace.

Blue eyes in a freckled brown face stared at her. 'Let's get you sat down. You're white. There's a bench just behind you.'

'I just need to take some more painkillers.'

'Well, sit down and I'll get you some water.'

Tess watched him disappear into the information office behind her. If the platform wasn't so long she'd get up and leave, but he'd be back before she got halfway. She took from her bag a blister packet of paracetamol. When he returned with a plastic cup of water she was trying to pop one out of the foil one-handed.

'Let me,' he said, taking them from her. 'One or two?'

'Two, please,' she said, breathless, as her energy had been robbed by pain and the effort of the task. She swallowed them quickly, drinking all of the water. 'Thank you.'

'Is it very painful?' he asked.

'Very.'

'They look like they did a good job bandaging it.'

'I did it myself. I'm a nurse.'

'Thought it looked professional. What did you do to it?'

'Burned it draining boiling water.'

'Ouch!'

'My own fault. Too hasty.'

'Less haste more speed my mum always says.'

She managed a weak smile. 'Good advice.'

'You did it yesterday?'

Her eyes met his. 'Yes. Silly me.'

'You travel regularly.'

Her eyes turned guarded. He'd made his remark sound like a statement. Tess caught a flash of orange behind him and saw the platform man standing by the office door watching them.

'I, er—'

She was stuttering and the policeman was looking at her carefully as if sensing something wrong.

'I, um—'

'Tess!' They both turned at the sound of an excited, high-pitched voice further along the platform.

'Tess!'

'I think she's calling you,' he remarked, standing up and edging away as they saw a determined woman waving and making her way towards them.

'Shit,' she whispered, then was aware he was close enough to hear.

Vivien was dressed like she was going to, or had been, somewhere special. Her hairdo and make-up and expensive-looking pale blue suit suggested it might be to a nice restaurant or even a wedding.

'Oh my God, what on earth have you done?' she screeched in alarm at seeing the bandages. 'What happened to your hand?'

'I burned it.'

'You burned it!' the woman repeated like a parrot. 'Good grief! How?'

'Boiling pasta. A whole pot of it.'

'My God! You poor thing. What did you do? Drop it on yourself?'

'I was silly. Poured pasta over my hand instead of into the bowl.'

'Gosh, that must have hurt. So what are you doing here? Surely not going to London?'

Tess stared at her entreatingly. 'No, and Vivien I must ask that you please don't say you saw me. Daniel will be livid if he knows I tried to go. I got as far as here, but I've given up and I'm going home now. So please, don't say you saw me. It would upset him to know I've been this foolish. He left me in bed with strict orders to rest.'

'Of course I won't say anything, my dear. He made enough fuss when he heard I had coffee spilled on me and left you sitting alone. I wish I hadn't mentioned it when he phoned me. Look, I insist upon seeing you home. My meeting isn't important. They can do without me for once.'

'No, Vivien! It isn't necessary. Please don't cancel on my account.'

'Tess, when you get to know me better, you'll know I don't take no for an answer. I'm seeing you home and that's that.'

As Tess walked slowly along the platform she glanced back at the policeman and saw the man in the orange hi-vis walk over to him. They started talking and Tess felt their eyes on her burning as intensely as her hand had burned. She couldn't wait to get off the platform and away from the watchers.

CHAPTER THIRTY-NINE

'Your house is so big, Tess. You could put mine into it twice over and still have room to move,' Vivien declared wistfully.

Tess felt awkward seeing the grandness of it through Vivien's eyes. When she saw the library she climbed the ladder like an excited child. She was finding it surreal having the woman there. The second woman to visit her home in the space of a few days and she knew neither of them very well.

'Your house is lovely. All that beautiful countryside.'

Vivien screwed up her nose. 'I wake up smelling cow manure and go to sleep smelling it. Lovely if you like that sort thing. This house must have cost a fortune?'

Tess feigned getting into a more comfortable position in the chair, wincing with eyes squeezed shut to avoid talking of things she didn't know. Though, in fact, since Vivien gave her some codeine she was nicely floating. The woman carried a pharmacy in her bag, and was leaving Tess with half a pot full.

'We could never afford to move to the city, unless we want to live in a box. Daniel must have been pretty successful, even before his consultant's post.'

'Have you ever worked?' Tess asked, changing the subject. 'I mean, obviously you're working hard in other areas, but I mean for money. You're clearly very capable and driven,' she added in case Vivien had taken offence.

A cat-like quality entered the woman's eyes. She stared at Tess unblinking. 'I was Mark's secretary before I married him, and I worked ad hoc for a long time after that. And then a little miracle happened… we had a baby girl.'

Tess felt her insides still. There was something in Vivien's voice…

'We had her for a long time, so we must count ourselves lucky. And then we didn't have her anymore.'

Tess's eyes pricked and she willed back the tears. This woman did not need to see her cry.

'The only comfort I take is my beautiful girl will always be young. Always.'

'Did you? Could you—'

'I'm forty-five, Tess. I went through the change when I was thirty-six. There is no chance of having another.'

'You look younger,' Tess offered lamely.

'Don't I just?' she said, suddenly twirling and giving a little shake of her shoulders and arms, a determined smile fixed on her face. 'Now, how about I fix you something light to eat? You probably think I can't cook after seeing I had a young woman helping me serve dinner, but let me assure you I can and do. Soft scrambled egg should do the trick and I promise to clean up after myself.'

Bemused, Tess could only sit and watch as Vivien disappeared into the kitchen. Even if she wanted to, she could not have stopped her. Vivien was on a mission. Tess closed her eyes with exhaustion, feeling overwhelmed with what she'd learned. She'd been unkind in her thoughts towards this woman, without really knowing her or knowing of her loss. She was someone to admire, not ridicule. She was living and making her life useful and she made Tess feel ashamed. And very tired as she heard pots and pans clattering in the kitchen.

Vivien was smiling at her kindly when she nudged Tess awake. 'I ate the scrambled egg. You've been asleep for two hours, but I had to wake you, I'm afraid.'

'What is it?' Tess asked sleepily.

Vivien sat down. 'Nothing to be alarmed about I'm sure, but Mark just texted me as he knows I'm here. I sent him a text a few minutes ago and his reply came almost straight back.' She pressed her lips firmly together as if wanting to keep back what she was going to say, before giving an exasperated sigh. 'I'm sure it's nothing. Just Mark being a bit dramatic, I dare say.'

Tess sat up straighter. 'What's happened? What does Mark want?'

She took a deep breath. 'Well, he wants to know where Daniel is. It seems the naughty man is nowhere to be found. They've had to cancel an operation because he didn't turn up. He's gone AWOL, Mark said.'

Tess gazed at her confused. 'Well, where is he?'

Vivien smiled. 'If you don't know then I'm sure I don't. Look, let me quickly reply to Mark and then I'm going to make you a cup of tea.'

Vivien returned with a tray which she set on a table beside Tess. As well as the tea she'd made ham sandwiches cut into triangles and artfully arranged with cut-up cucumber and tomato for garnish.

'You need to eat and not to worry. Your errant husband has at last sent word with an apology.'

Tess felt nauseous and didn't want the sandwiches, but she'd try to eat them seeing the effort gone into making them.

'Thank you, Vivien, and thank you for being so kind.'

Vivien sat down on the sofa. She moved a cushion onto her lap to get more comfortable and then sat back. 'I can't quite fathom you, Tess. I thought most nurses were chatty and confident and a bit bossy. You don't seem any of those things.'

Tess wanted to answer that she was once all those things, but she couldn't. She couldn't be sure anymore of who she had been, or if she'd just been an imitation of how a person should seem.

'How do I seem?' she asked.

'I don't know, Tess. Like a guarded little secret, I think. Holding your true self hidden from all the world. You remind me of my daughter. She had pretty blue eyes like you and I could never fathom what she was thinking.'

Tess wanted to look away. Vivien's eyes had changed. A buried sorrow was showing, and Tess wanted to let her be private, have a moment alone. It passed as Vivien sipped her tea, and then she seemed to shrug it away.

'Come on, eat up. I want you to show me this lovely house of yours. I'm dying to see it properly.'

Tess could have had a friend in this woman, she realised. She sat curled in her armchair watching Vivien's mouth move as she talked and cherished the moment, getting the same feeling of peace she'd had with Cameron. They spent an age in every room as Vivien was fascinated and wanted to ask where everything had come from. She loved the old headboards and abundance of white linen found in blanket boxes at the ends of beds. She was curious about Tess's tastes and wanted to know if she had chosen it all. Tess told her Daniel had, and she hadn't seemed surprised.

'He's a bit old-fashioned, isn't he?' she remarked. 'Mark says he's very conservative. Always sits proper in the dining hall at work.' She wrinkled her nose impishly. 'I think you've got yourself a Mark Darcy there, Tess. Or should I call you Bridget? Does he fold his underpants?'

Tess smiled amiably, but declined to answer. She was becoming fond of this woman and didn't wish to disillusion her.

When the tour was over Vivien buttoned her pale blue jacket and inspected her face and hair in a compact mirror. 'There. Not bad, if I say so myself. It's been a pleasure spending time with you, Tess. Mind to take some more tablets in an hour.' She was halfway out the door when she swung back. 'Almost forgot, this was left on your doorstep while you were sleeping.' She stepped over to a table and picked up a brown envelope to hand her. 'Why they left it there and couldn't post it, I don't know.'

'Did you see who left it?' Tess asked.

'I didn't I'm afraid. I thought I heard a tap at the front door, but that was all that was there when I opened it. Now, I really must be off. So take care and make sure you rest.'

The silence was complete after Vivien closed the front door. Her noise and energy were gone from the room, leaving it suddenly quiet. Tess was holding her breath with fear of opening the envelope in her hand. The postcard sender had got another message to her while she was indoors unaware.

She carried her tray out to the kitchen and rinsed the dishes with her one good hand before placing them in the dishwasher. She checked around the kitchen for evidence of Vivien's visit, then returned to her chair in the drawing room and opened it. Inside was another postcard.

I have learned a few things today that have increased my concern. I am giving this matter some consideration. In the meantime I would advise you to be careful.

Tess breathed out harshly. These messages felt so intrusive, and what did this last one mean? What had this person learned? She stared at the postcard with eyes filled with worry. Who was this person? Why didn't they leave her alone? She had enough going on in her life without having some stranger think they could come and be part of it. Was she to have no control over it?

She needed to resolve the mystery of the journal writer before she was free to leave. She would have to find the courage to stay in order to do that. She'd learned nothing useful from his parents. They hadn't seen him in nearly fifteen years. Hadn't a clue about what he'd been up to during all of that time. He could have been married ten times over and had a dozen kids during that period for all they knew.

She got up out of the chair and went and fetched the black book. She owed it to this woman to at least read it all.

Tess read a dozen or more pages, and the more she read the more the woman's narrative sounded like her own thoughts, how she would write if this were her account. Tess could feel the woman's hope slipping, her panic rising the more she was controlled. What would the police think of this book if they were to read it, Tess wondered? Would they regard it as proof of a first wife or only the words of an unknown author?

She turned another page.

He looks at me as if I'm invisible and yet I know he is watching me more closely than ever. He has locked the garage door so that I can't take the car. Robert has not turned up this week and I am worried as to why. If he gets rid of Mrs Bowden then I will know for sure he is planning something.

If it was not just myself I had to fear for I would run right now with only the clothes on my back, but I can't run with a child. I need somewhere secure to keep us safe and I am hoping this place I have found will be mine in the next week. I have sold my jewellery apart from my wedding ring, which he would notice if gone, and have enough to pay for a month. It will buy me time to think of our future.

Tess sat back in surprise. The woman was a mother. Was Daniel a father? She had not thought to discover this. It made sense of why she would stay. She had put up with it because of her child. The red wooden trike in the garage had probably belonged to the child. She needed the woman's name. It couldn't be that difficult to find out. She could ask the people next door or just ask her husband outright. He must know who he bought this property from. Unless that was a fabrication as she suspected, and already his to own. He would know the name of the woman then as she would have been his wife. She would pick the right moment and ask him. But that might not be this evening after what Vivien had said. It was probably best to wait until tomorrow.

CHAPTER FORTY

Tess jolted awake to the sound of breaking glass. She shot up in the bed and listened intently. It sounded like little explosions of glass and she wondered for a moment if it was the glass shower door smashing to the floor. But that would have been one big noise. The noises continued with one sharp sound after another, and she was sure it was coming from the bathroom. Was he in there wrecking it? She got out of bed and pulled on her dressing gown and slippers. Quietly easing open the bedroom door, the stench of perfume pervading the landing caught the back of her throat. She took one step out of the room and froze. He was holding something large in one hand.

'Where is it?' he asked in a voice that sounded desperate.

'Where's what?' she replied, feeling alarmed at seeing him like this and at a loss to know what he was talking about.

'You know what,' he growled softly. Then he held up something in his hand and sniffed it deeply and Tess saw it was a cushion from off the sofa downstairs. 'You found it, didn't you? You were keeping it from me. Show it to me!'

'I don't know what you're talking about, Daniel!' She gazed at him stupefied, needing some enlightenment.

'Her perfume, damn you! You found it, didn't you?'

Tess's eyes darted from the cushion to his face and it dawned on her he could be smelling Vivien's perfume. Though why that should disturb him to this state she didn't know. He was standing there looking at her with crazed eyes like a rabid dog. Vivien had sat with a cushion on her lap and her scent must have transferred to it.

'It's Vivien's perfume you can smell,' she quickly said. 'She came here to see me. It's hers.'

'Hers? Why would she have it?' he asked suspiciously.

'I don't know, Daniel,' she said, using his name again to get through to him. 'I don't know, but I'll ask her for it. I'll get it for you, I promise. Tomorrow, I'll get it for you.'

He held the cushion to his chest and bowed his head. Then without another word he walked towards their bedroom, and leaving her out in the corridor quietly shut the door. Tess trembled with shock and relief. She waited for more than an hour until she was sure he was asleep, and then carefully and slowly so as not to make a sound, she made her way to the bathroom. Broken glass was everywhere and the room reeked from the wet spillages.

She spent the rest of the night clearing up all the broken bottles of perfume that had been smashed on the bathroom floor. The task was time-consuming as she was doing it all one-handed. She removed towels and flannels and bathroom mats, and repeatedly washed every inch of the bathroom: the walls, the floor, every surface. As if it was a crime scene, she washed away all evidence. Lastly, removing her night clothes and the leather slippers, she put them and the other items on a hot wash. In the downstairs bathroom she showered without soap, removing the bandage from her hand, letting the dressing soak off and fall in the shower tray. She didn't want any scent to linger on her. She didn't want him reminded of it in the morning. The only thing left to wash was the cushion he'd taken to bed.

Tess could not believe the scene she'd witnessed, his frantic behaviour caused by a perfume. She recalled his reaction over the bedroom curtains and her mind couldn't switch off her suspicions. Was it his first wife's perfume he was talking about? He'd called it *her* perfume. Had he been being buying Tess perfume and all the while searching for *her* scent? Was this why he'd married her? Had he been trying to recreate his first wife all along? Had he picked someone like her because he knew she was vulnerable, that she wanted to belong and therefore seen her as malleable? Someone he could train into shape? She needed to find the old lady to get to the truth. She felt sick at the thought of him buying her these perfumes just so he could remember his first wife. She wanted to leave this house today and forever.

In the morning her eyes were gritty and she was careful to stay alert. She was cautious in everything she did or said. She prepared his breakfast and served him carefully. She took care that she was dressed in a skirt and blouse and flat shoes. He was silent and sat at the kitchen table, still and staring at nothing but the wall in front of him, and only the careful sounds Tess made were heard. She wiped and cleared away the used dishes and pans, swept and washed the floor of any crumbs and stickiness, opened and shut cupboard doors, and all with necessary quietness. She was the mouse and he was the cat and she'd rather not let her presence disturb him.

Quietly she opened the 'Improvements' book and took a pen to tick off the shower chore. Remembering the doorstep she ticked that job too. When she stepped back and found him right behind her she couldn't help but breathe fast, and before she knew it she was hyperventilating, unable to get any breath. Her fingers were tingling and dots floated before her eyes. He spoke calmly and told her to take deep breaths, to slow her breathing down, to drop her shoulders and let her arms hang loose, calmly talking to her all the time until her hands un-clenched and she was able to take a breath again properly. Then he kneaded her shoulders lightly and spoke to her in a quiet voice.

'You know you make me not like myself sometimes. You make me do things that I'm not comfortable with. This panic attack made me very uncomfortable. I'm going to work now. I'll see you later.'

After he left she sagged with relief. She needed to be careful every moment now. When she was settled she fetched the cushion from the bed, and then gathered the linen as well, shoving the dark cushion cover in with the whites to wash out the last of the scent. She put the tumble dryer on for the load she washed in the night, throwing the ruined red leather slippers into the bin.

At ten o'clock she went to check for any post and saw two letters for her – one from the hospital and one from the postcard messenger. She ripped open the brown envelope first and had to stem the rise of a second panic attack.

I have a plan to make him stop. I shall be contacting your husband soon.

She fast paced the kitchen floor, fear growing with every thought. Everything was out of control. She felt threatened by the tone of the message. Should she tell her husband about the postcards? She leaned over a kitchen chair and gulped air.

The sound of trains pounded in her head. In her dreams she had seen herself standing at the very edge of a platform right over the yellow line, like an athlete, preparing to run. She'd heard the starter pistol fire and felt herself running through air, taking leaps from soft clouds. On the ground she saw runners passing her, but she didn't mind. She was smiling with arms flung open wide, ready to embrace the smooth green-and-yellow bird flying fast towards her to carry her away.

She was tempted to leave right now and find somewhere. She wanted to… yet she couldn't while there were things left unanswered. She had to finish what she'd started and uncover all his lies. She would not give up and be beaten by this weakness.

She read the postcard again. How did this person even know what was going on? And what did they plan to do? Maim her husband? Warn him? The offer was tempting. She should let someone stop him. To make him aware someone knew what he was doing to her. He should be told about his behaviour. Regardless of her own destiny her husband ought to be stopped before he targeted some other woman.

She sat down at the table to read her other mail. The letter from the hospital was what she'd expected. She was invited to a hearing on Friday November 6 at one o'clock and encouraged to bring a representative with her, where she would be given the opportunity to give her account of what happened that day. A week today, or as good as, her career as a nurse would be over. She shook her head, feeling surprisingly calm, thinking life just didn't get any better.

Or any more strange either, as her eyes followed the fluffy white head passing by the kitchen window. Tess jumped up from her chair, going quickly to the back door and yanking it open. The old lady jumped back in alarm and let go of a cat. Tess regretted frightening her as she saw her inhale sharply and grab onto the wall. What on earth was she doing bringing Tess a cat?

'I've startled you again,' Tess said. 'I'm so sorry. Will you come in and sit down?'

The woman stayed where she was, slowing her breathing, and shook her head.

'I can't step inside this house. Too many memories,' she said breathlessly. 'And I have to get back. Jim thinks I'm having a lie down.' She stared around her at the ground. 'What happened to the little cat? I was bringing it into your garden before it got run over.'

Tess realised the woman, although wearing a coat, had slippers on her feet, and wondered how far she'd walked in them.

'Can I walk you home?' she offered.

'No, Jim will see you and then I'll be in trouble for bothering you.' She pointed at the bandage on Tess's hand. 'Did he do that?'

Tess went to shake her head, but found she couldn't. 'Yes, he burned me.'

The old lady nodded. 'He did that to his first wife. Burned her leg with a poker, accidently on purpose, of course. Why are you still here? You haven't got a bairn to worry about. You should be gone. You're in danger living here.'

The woman turned to leave and Tess stopped her. She had to ask if it was true. If she was absolutely sure Daniel was married before?

'What happened to his first wife and child? Where is she now?'

The woman's tiny form seemed to shrink smaller as she gazed back at Tess. 'They're dead. That's what happened to them, and your husband is free. He murdered them.'

Tess gasped. 'That's not possible. How can that possibly be true? He's a doctor. They wouldn't let him work if what you say is true.'

'I told you,' she said. 'He's not who you think he is. He was a doctor before, but he's changed his name. He wasn't called Daniel Myers then. He was called David Simmonds. Your husband is a murderer, Mrs Myers. Make no mistake about that.'

CHAPTER FORTY-ONE

The front door banged shut and she jumped from her seat. His footsteps tapped hard and quick on the stone tiles in the hallway. He came straight into the drawing room and walked past her fast to get to the drinks cabinet, without acknowledging her. He poured half a tumbler of neat whisky and knocked it straight back and then followed it with another before slamming the glass down and breathing out harshly.

'Bastards! Absolute bastards,' he shouted as he grabbed the glass back up and flung it across the room.

Tess watched it land without breaking and skid along the thin carpet to the wall. She gaped at her husband, alarmed at hearing him shout so loud.

'What's happened?'

'My patient's dead. That's what's happened. And the bastards are holding me accountable!'

He was unravelling, she realised. Something in him was out of control. Last night he'd behaved like a madman over a perfume. Something happened yesterday to make him go AWOL. Something from his past to cause this downward spiral. He wouldn't have forgotten about a serious operation. So why was he not there to do it? 'Why?' she dared to ask.

'Because I delayed his operation by a day. A fucking day and they're blaming the delay for his death. They all have their glass balls out as if they can tell the fucking future. Like a bunch of witches trying to tell me, *tell me,* about my own patient!'

'Jesus,' she whispered under her breath. It was actually the patient from yesterday who died. Not just a patient. She was nervous of his mood, not knowing what to say or do. Where had he been yesterday when he hadn't turned up? What could possibly have been more important to keep him away?

'I need to phone my solicitor. I need to phone some people. This is a fucking nightmare!'

She kept to one side of the room, out of his way, as he paced and ranted and raged, paused to pour himself another drink and then paced more, drank more, stopping once to punch the door. It was like looking at a caged wild animal raging to be free. By eight o'clock he was passed out on the sofa and she covered him with a throw so that he stayed asleep. She hurried as she heard the phone ringing in the hallway, not wanting the sound to disturb him.

'Hello?'

'Tess. It's Ed. How is he?'

Tess sighed hard. 'He's sleeping, Ed.'

'Did he tell you what happened?'

She glanced through the door to the drawing room to ensure he was still sleeping. 'Some. A patient died, and he's being blamed.'

It was Ed's turn to sigh. 'He is, Tess. The surgery was scheduled for yesterday. The team were ready and waiting but regrettably Daniel didn't turn up and nor did he check on the patient during the course of yesterday, despite a dozen calls from his registrar and the ward asking him to come in. Unfortunately, I couldn't step in and do it. I had too many serious cases of my own to deal with. I can't tell you how much of a shock this has been to everyone. To not turn up like that and give no explanation. No warning to at least have given an opportunity to find someone else. The man was forty-seven, for pity's sake. I just don't understand it. How he could have been so reckless. We were only discussing the procedure the other night. He's going to need good representation. There'll be an internal enquiry and we can only hope they'll be fair.'

She gave a small gasp. 'Are you saying—'

'I'm saying he needs someone more than good!' He paused to let that register. 'And you? Are you OK? I feel so bad about this, Tess. We had such a lovely afternoon at yours on Sunday and then this happens…' He hesitated as if about to say something further. 'Tess, if there's anything I can do, please don't hesitate to call.'

'That's very kind of you, Ed.'

'Nonsense, you're a very lovely person, and I fear this is going to be a tough time.'

She smiled at his kindness. 'Thank you. I will call if I need you.'

She replaced the receiver and was filled with a strange kind of relief that she had someone like Ed to call if her husband's behaviour became unmanageable. She felt sure the professor could calm him down.

'Speaking to your lover?'

She spun round to find him standing right behind her, the second time in a day. His shirt was hanging out of his trousers, his tie askew. His face was red from alcohol and sleep, and his mouth curled in a sneer.

'Has he now taken to calling you in our home?' he asked in a voice leaden with quiet menace.

'What are you talking about? That was Ed on the phone. He was calling to see how you are,' she answered firmly, holding his gaze. 'He was concerned for you!' She would not let him see her cower. Nor let him see her afraid. 'He cares about you!'

His sneer stretched wider. He took a step back from her and then proceeded to give a slow hard clap.

'Stop it! Just stop it. The man wants to help you! Though God only knows why!'

Her sudden retaliation seemed to shock him. He took another step back. Tess trembled with relief. She'd stood up to him and he'd backed off! She should have done it before, she—

He raised his hand and curled his forefinger to beckon her. She stood her ground and he let out a puff of air, a sound of resignation. 'Don't make me come over there, Tess,' he said, trapping her with his eyes.

Her body began to shake, hard. He must be able to see how badly her legs were trembling. Her head, her jaw, and her shoulders were juddering, her mouth tremoring, fingertips involuntarily twitching. Her feet the only part of her solid on the ground, because she was struck with fear and couldn't move them, the half-dozen paces between them an impossible quest.

He moved slowly towards her, and then with lightning speed his hand shot out and grasped strongly around the nape of her neck, and he half dragged, half pulled her across the floor. Her feet crisscrossing at the fast pace, the soles of her shoes slipping, until she tripped out of one of them and went down in a tangle of limbs, banging knees, forearms and chin. He yanked her swiftly back to her feet, gripping a handful of hair to keep her upright.

'Oops-a-daisy,' he said lightly, as if she were a fallen child.

She squealed and hit out at his wrists and hands trying to get free, then her legs went from under her a second time as he hoisted her up onto his shoulder, carried her to the drawing room, and threw her face down over the back of the sofa. She seesawed, feet lifted off the ground and hands grappling in mid-air. She had to roll forward to get over it. Roll forward to get away. She screamed as he gripped her hips to keep her from escaping and then screamed louder as he pressed behind her.

'Please no please no please no!' she squealed to make him stop. She felt air against her skin as her trousers and pants were dragged down. 'I'm begging you, I'm begging you!' she pleaded. But instead he pressed his hand against the back of her head, pushing it down and forward until her face squashed in against cushions and her voice muffled. Her cries and desperate pleas were hardly heard as he forced himself on her.

CHAPTER FORTY-TWO

When Tess woke up on Saturday morning she wished the day was already over. How was she meant to carry on? She felt like a tiny mouse living with a very large cat – one wrong move and it would pounce on her. He must not care anymore that she knew his behaviour was not rational. He must think her too insignificant for it to matter that he raped her. He was confident she would never tell, just as he was confident she would take the blame for something she hadn't done. She was putty in his hands as far as he was concerned. She crept downstairs hoping he was still asleep.

He surprised her by being up and dressed in golfing gear, never imagining he'd want to play today.

'Ed says he's rusty and hasn't played in a while. I'll bet he's as adept as he is at wielding a scalpel…' He paused as he stared at her appraisingly. 'And as adept as he is at cosy little chats. I bet he didn't mention he was going to ring me this morning to go for a game? I reckon he's trying to get close to you,' he said in a decisive tone. 'Oh yes, that's what this is all about.'

Her cheeks filled with colour at the implication.

'N-nonsense,' she stuttered. 'He's old enough to be my father. It's you he's interested in!'

He threw her an insincere smile, slowly shaking his head at her.

'He spent five minutes discussing you before getting to the point of his call, wanting to know how you are. The thing is, Tess? Am I going to have to come down hard on you?'

She stared at him in disbelief with her fists bunching and nails clawing into her palms. She wanted to scream at him. As opposed to what? she wanted to yell. What could be harder than being raped and having your life destroyed? Tears blurred her eyes, mucous trickled from her nose and she wiped her face hard with her pyjama sleeve. Special pyjamas from The White Company, hoping to show him she didn't just shop for clothes in places like Asda. She'd put them on for the first time last night after climbing the stairs to bed. Unable to bear having any of her skin exposed to him, she'd taken them out of the bag still new, and taken refuge in the small bedroom again. She would not let him see her cry.

He stared at her critically as if she were a strange object. He tutted as if disappointed.

'Are you going to end up being like her? Sneaking behind my back to see other men?'

Her insides kicked with fear. He was speaking about his first wife. Speaking about her as if it no longer mattered to keep her a secret. His second wife could hear what he had to say.

'She wore this scent,' he murmured, his gaze shifting away from her, his tone soft. 'I can still smell it. I smell it whenever I walk in that room.'

Tess stared at him with anguish. Hating him and yet feeling sorry for him as she heard a longing in his voice. She didn't know the circumstances of his dead wife and child. The old woman had to be wrong about how they died. Surely he couldn't have killed his own child?

'Daniel,' she whimpered, 'maybe we should leave this house. Maybe it's not good for you here.'

He focused on her and she swallowed hard as she waited for him to say something.

The slap knocked her to her knees. She knelt there, swaying, with her eyes and mouth open, unable to breathe or speak. She willed herself to stay on her knees and not sink to the ground.

'You are like her,' he said slowly, in a voice that sounded dazed. His eyes weren't seeing her, even though he appeared to be looking at her. 'Spineless. That's why she left me, because she was spineless.'

Tess got up off the floor and retreated into a corner and watched as he casually made himself coffee.

Then, without warning, she threw up.

Tess rushed to the bathroom and held onto the toilet seat as she vomited again, trying to be as quiet as possible. If he thought she was unwell he might not go out and leave her for the day. He might start thinking she'd go and see a doctor or even think she was...

'*Shit,*' she whispered, as she suddenly remembered what she had forgotten to do. She'd meant to call her GP last Monday and get the morning-after pill. Her stomach clenched in panic. Then she calmed down. It was too soon to have symptoms of nausea. They'd had unprotected sex twice. Last night and last Sunday. She couldn't be having symptoms that soon. Maybe it was a stomach bug or down to nerves. She got up off the floor and turned on the shower. When had he flicked her birth pills in her face? It was over a week ago. She would think about it when he went out. In the meantime she needed to make herself look fresher so *he would* go out, as having him at home all day was more than she could bear.

She stripped off her pyjamas and used the liner from the small pedal bin to cover her bandaged hand to keep it dry while she stood under the water. The heat eased her aches, but not her mind. She was living with someone dangerous. A mad man. The level of his violence was escalating. She had a bruise on the underside of her left forearm that looked like an oil spillage beneath the skin. It was large and black and spread from elbow to wrist, making the other bruises and grazes look insignificant. She now had injuries to both her upper limbs.

She heard tapping on the bathroom door as she dried herself.

'I'm leaving soon, Tess,' he called lightly from behind the closed door.

'OK,' she answered brightly, hoping he hadn't heard her being sick the second time.

He was still standing there, his footsteps not yet moving away from the door, and she wondered if he expected her to come out and give him a farewell kiss. In the bathroom mirror her face gazed back pasty and drawn, her lips bloodless and pale. The imprint of his slap was hardly visible on her cheek, just some faint lines left by his fingers. She didn't often look at herself anymore, not wanting to see the emptiness of her eyes staring back at her from the mirror, not wanting to see what she felt inside. Her chin had a nice blue bruise from where it hit the floor. She would have to cover that.

'I want to see that you're all right before I go,' he called.

'OK. I'll be out soon,' she called, getting back into her pyjamas.

He was waiting in the kitchen staring into space, and she hesitated at the doorway. He turned and she saw his handsome face was haggard. Before she could move he came towards her and wrapped her in his arms, holding her close.

'Try not to worry, my love. This whole mess will soon be sorted. We're both in a bit of a pickle at the moment, I'm afraid.'

His mobile rang and he released her. She moved away and fought to hide her distress. He was behaving like an actor on a stage, acting this climactic moment for an audience holding their breath, hanging on and hoping all would come right for the couple in this drama. She felt giddy from just those few seconds in his company. Giddy, confused, and so very afraid.

He made ready to leave and then said something that appalled her. 'Don't forget to try and get that perfume off Vivien.'

A moment later she heard his footsteps in the hallway, and then the sound of the front door closing. Tess listened to the silence, desperate to know what to do.

He was unhingeing rapidly before her eyes. She was unsure of the direction he was heading. He saw her as spineless because she couldn't stand up to him, blaming her for being like his first wife and yet desperate for Tess to wear the woman's scent. All those perfumes he'd been buying for Tess had been driven by his need to find the scent that his first wife wore. They hadn't been bought for Tess but for his obsession to get back what he'd lost. Or killed?

She took a deep breath, filled not just with air but another wave of nausea too. She splashed her face with cold water at the kitchen sink and leaned over the basin until it settled. It must be nerves. It couldn't be anything else.

The doorbell rang and she instantly tensed. If it was him he would use his key, unless he had forgotten it, along with whatever he was returning for. She just prayed Ed hadn't cancelled. The bell rang again and she hurried to answer it. Vivien was standing on the doorstep. It seemed weeks and not just two days since Tess last saw her. Thursday felt like a lifetime ago. The hours since then had engulfed her in a world of madness. She was pleased to see someone normal.

Vivien looked lovely and fresh and wore a perfume that smelt of summer flowers and fruit. Tess didn't know if this was the perfume her husband smelt but Tess breathed her in regardless. She felt different now about Vivien; she felt safe with this capable woman.

'My darling, you look a wreck if you don't mind me saying. It looks like I arrived just in time.'

Suppressed emotions broke free and Tess let out a strangled laugh, along with a trickle of tears which she quickly wiped away, and which Vivien pretended not to see. Only Vivien could get away with saying something so outrageous.

She tried to look indignant as she responded in a sassy tone, 'I was intending on having a spa day, I'll have you know.'

Vivien looked at her critically. 'I think a spa week might work better. Go and put a bit of slap on while I make us a cup of tea. Go on,' she said, waving the back of her hand at Tess. 'Shoo. I know where everything is. We can't talk with you looking like this.'

Tess grinned a little manically then rushed away to do as she was told. She brushed her dark hair and tied it back in a ponytail, applied a light cover of make-up, dabbing more to the bruise on her chin, but stopped at spraying herself with perfume. She stripped off the pyjamas again and got dressed, choosing a light blue blouse that hid her bruises and brought some life back into her eyes.

In the short time she was away, Vivien had made herself at home. She'd washed up the few dishes, tidied the worktops, made a pot of tea and was waiting at the table with one cup already poured.

She raised her cup at Tess and complimented her. 'Much better, darling. I can see your pretty face now. Come and sit down and I'll pour you some tea and we can have a proper chat.'

Tess wondered how long she intended to stay.

Vivien pulled a face as if she could read Tess's mind. 'Don't worry, half an hour tops. I've got a hair appointment at twelve. Mark dropped me and is picking me up after he's been to Halfords to pick up a new battery. I know Daniel is out because he just told Mark on the phone he was playing a round of golf with Ed. I think Mark was intending to come and have a chat to him. So, I thought, what better time to come see how you are.' She sipped her drink and then asked bluntly, 'So how are things? More to the point, how are you, because in these things it's always the wife that has to bear the brunt of what's going on. Last night must have been terrible for you. So tell. I'm here for you to unload on. Please don't cry, though. I don't do well with tears.'

Tess, incredibly, laughed again, despite having to think of last night. Twice in a short space of time this woman had made her laugh. She was like a breath of fresh air, her energy and vivaciousness contagious. 'I'm not going to cry, Vivien. I promise. Things are a bit... fraught. I'm worried for Daniel, and I think he's worried too.'

Vivien sighed. 'There's no point in worrying. It won't change anything. It will just give you worry lines. You just need to stay strong until it's over. And drink occasionally, because it helps,' she said, matter-of-factly.

Tess reflected on the operation she was being blamed for, and Ed's comments on Daniel's behaviour underlined the seriousness of her own situation. She'd not even contacted the union rep yet. Should she be looking for someone more legal? In both cases a patient was dead. In Tess's case, she'd deviated from accepted practice. She would need her husband's money to appoint someone good, and probably lots of it to appoint someone more than good. 'Do you think Daniel is going to come out of this all right?'

'From what Mark says I think he's going to have a battle on his hands. One he may not win, Tess. And I only tell you this to prepare you. He's caused a bit of a stink with his colleagues, I'm afraid. Not because the patient died, but because he's offered no explanation for not attending, which I don't understand, as he could have just said he was sick.'

Tess nodded to show she understood. She cared not one jot about the outcome for her husband, but she was grateful to Vivien for caring, for taking the time to see if *she* was all right. 'I'll just have to be extra nice to him then,' she said. 'I'll buy him the perfume you're wearing. He seems rather taken with it.'

Vivien looked surprised.

'He could smell it when he came home the other night and asked me to get some.'

Vivien was already reaching into her bag, a bigger bag than her Gucci one but just as smart looking.

'Oh, darling, you can have it. There's hardly any left, but I was getting bored with it. Truly, my dear, I'm embarrassed to even get it out. I'm sure Mark got it second-hand at one of the car boot sales or jumble sales that pop up like clockwork in our village.'

Tess took the tiny bottle handed to her and saw Vivien wasn't exaggerating. There was possibly a millimetre or two left of the yellow perfume. The sage green label was mostly peeled away along with the name.

'I washed it I'm afraid. I'm very particular about germs. I think it was called Gardenia or maybe it was Amelia. But if you take it to a perfume shop I'm sure they'll know.'

'Thank you,' Tess said, sounding a bit emotional.

Vivien eyed her with concern. 'Whatever for? I've just given you an empty bottle of perfume, hardly worth a thank you.'

Tess smiled. 'Well, I am thankful.'

Vivien picked up her phone as it beeped. 'That's him,' she said, standing and picking up her bag, and a few moments later she was gone without even a goodbye.

CHAPTER FORTY-THREE

A pregnancy test sat on the side of the sink. Vivien had returned after only being gone ten minutes with what she'd called 'a second little gift'. Tess had stared inside the paper bag and let out a soft gasp. Vivien hadn't said anything further; she'd just looked Tess in the eye and then given a wave goodbye. Tess used it almost straight away as she needed to pee anyway, and was still staring at it more than an hour later.

Something had shifted in her since finding out, something she thought dead inside. She could feel it carefully unfurling like the tiniest of leaves of a new shoot just germinated. She had no idea how to rationalise what she was feeling, but a wondrous light was drawing her back to something she'd thought gone. Her second little gift had brought back hope. She was holding the most precious of gifts inside of her right now. Her heart raced at the thought. She wasn't even meant to be here, yet fate had given her a second chance and a rush of intense love unfolded inside her for this tiny being.

The nausea had not been down to nerves. She was most definitely pregnant. Remembering having the pills flicked at her face had thrown her earlier. The same way it had thrown her when he waved her pill pack in her face that day. Her brain had not been quick enough to unscramble why she still had them, as the decision she made over a month ago was gone clean from her head. She'd stopped taking the pill while happy and just forgot to throw the rest of the prescription away. They'd had unprotected sex more than twice. While waiting for the result she'd been tracing back to the last time she opened the bathroom cabinet to take out a tampon. She hadn't in a while because she hadn't needed to because her period hadn't happened. She was late and not just by a few days. She was nearly three weeks late which meant she could be as little as three or as much as seven weeks pregnant.

In that instant she knew everything had changed in the way that she thought about her life. She would stop thinking her childhood had dealt her a terrible blow and look at it with more open and honest eyes. There were not enough people out there in the world who wanted to adopt a child, and not enough foster parents either. Some got left behind and she had been just one of them. And there were bad people everywhere – what happened in the children's home could also have happened if her parents had stayed alive because plenty of strangers came to their home for their special medicines. She'd suffered through some hardships, but she'd survived. The same as she would survive this failed marriage.

She could not stay in this house more than another day. She had to carve out a new life where she would be able to live safely. The safety of her child was all that now mattered and raised her awareness of the danger she was in. Another slap, or fall to the floor could end its life instantly. She needed to plan for her departure. The money she'd managed to find from his drawers together with what he'd given her was less than three hundred pounds, but it would be enough for her to get away. Her seven-day train ticket had one last day of travel that she could use if she left tomorrow. She would go to Sam and ask for his help. He worked late shifts on Sundays so he would be there. She was not too proud to ask, either. She was in a desperate situation and would ask for any help she could get. She just had to get through one more night. Until then she would keep busy. She would cook something for his dinner. She would ensure the house was perfect. She would dress and play the part of a dutiful wife one more time and then walk away and not look back. Her fear had not gone, but she could do it. She would walk away from it and leave this life behind. Train in some other career if need be.

What he'd said or what he'd done no longer mattered. She no longer felt empty inside. She was filled to the brim with love and hope and eagerness to start a new life. What he'd taken away had been given back with this precious gift. Her body was no longer without its soul.

Almost eight o'clock and he was still not home. Tess was beginning to wonder if she'd spend her last night in this house alone. She'd taken the small joint of beef out of the oven hours ago, and the vegetables were still waiting to be cooked. Perhaps he was eating out, but had chosen not to let her know about it.

Tess cast her eyes around the bedroom. It didn't look any different to how it was normally. Even if he were to open her wardrobe or look in her drawers they wouldn't look rifled through. She'd packed only some of her old things, some jeans, jumpers and T-shirts, some underwear and a few spare toiletries. Her rucksack and one wheelie suitcase were now hidden in black bin bags inside one of the empty bins by the side of the garage. In the side pocket of the rucksack she'd already put her money and the still-valid train ticket.

The only other item she intended to take was the black book, but she would carry that on her. She was not leaving it behind to get hidden again. She was unsure of what she'd do with it in the long run, but that didn't matter right now. Having it with her seemed to matter, though, as it felt safer somehow than leaving it in this house. She sat down on the bed and opened it. There were only a few pages left unread. She'd read the last page first in case she was interrupted and didn't get time to read it all.

Mrs Bowden hasn't turned up for work today. Friday is her busiest day, her laundry day as she calls it, as she likes to change the beds. I'm suspicious of her not being here, but it will perhaps make leaving easier. If he should ring, she will not be here to answer the phone and tell him I'm not there. I have a feeling she won't be surprised to find me gone. This is the first time she has not come to the house on a Friday so I must take this as a warning and be quick.

He will not miss me, I'm sure, or his child who I love with all my heart. I am sure when I am gone from here he will strike our existence from his memory. He'll probably tell his friends I was unfaithful as the reason for leaving, even though that's not true. If it helps his pride I don't care. I only care to be gone.

Tess read the last words and then hugged the book to her chest as if to comfort the woman. She wanted to believe it happened and that this woman was now safe somewhere. But she couldn't. The woman was dead. She felt it in her bones. She and her child were dead and buried somewhere.

She sighed with emotion and put the book down, then instantly stiffened. The hair rose on the back of her neck and along her arms as she sensed a presence. Then galvanised, she threw the book under the bed. She could hear footsteps on the stairs.

She found the courage to sit still as he walked gracefully towards her. His dark hair looked ruffled and he gave a bleak smile.

'We may have to move back to London if I'm to get out of this situation. It's a mess, to be honest with you.'

She wanted to say it was a mess since coming to this house to live. Both of their lives had changed since then. In his case, though, that may not be true – he may have always been this way.

He took off his jacket and hung it over the bottom of the bed. Then he slowly sat down beside her.

'Did you get it?' he quietly asked.

Her throat closed and she couldn't speak, unable to comprehend how he was asking this after what he'd just told her. The scent mattered more to him than even his career. It was bewildering to imagine what he was hoping to gain. She put her hand in her skirt pocket and fetched out the perfume to hand him.

'It's all she had.'

He let the small bottle rest in the palm of his hand, just staring at it, before carefully untwisting the delicate stopper and raising it almost reverently to his nose.

'It's perfect,' he whispered.

He turned to smile at her and Tess had to close her eyes. She couldn't watch this madness.

Leaving her on the bed he went and turned off the main light before coming back to her and raising her legs off the floor to get her to lie down. He sat beside her as he dabbed the scent behind her ears and then gently down her throat. He then put the stopper back on the bottle and Tess held her breath as he lay beside her and tried not to stiffen as he held her close with his nose pressed in the crook of her neck. He didn't say a word but just held her.

They lay like this all night, him wearing all his clothes and she wearing hers. He had not touched her in any other manner except to hold her and breathe her in. She wondered if he had the memory of his first wife in his arms and was repelled yet saddened by the thought of him having to take comfort in this way.

She would give him this night, wear this scent so that he could bring his first wife back, and then tomorrow Tess would be gone, and she would never have to lie in this bed again.

CHAPTER FORTY-FOUR

As daylight showed through a gap in the curtains Tess carefully peeled herself out of his arms and climbed off the bed. She covered him with a blanket before he noticed the absence of her warmth, then quietly knelt down to retrieve the book from under the bed. She put the book in her jacket pocket on her way through the hallway, and in the downstairs bathroom she quickly washed the scent of the perfume off her skin and out of her hair. She didn't want to wear its fragrance today and have it transfer onto her clothes. She knew its scent by heart and didn't want to be reminded of it again.

Taking the clean underwear, trousers and T-shirt that she'd put ready in the laundry basket yesterday, she hurriedly dressed. She'd like to have had her phone before she left but that wasn't going to happen. If she was lucky he would stay sleeping until she was gone. If he woke she would be delayed until he either went out or got occupied doing something. At least being washed and dressed she'd be ready to take off when the opportunity came.

The clocks chimed seven o'clock as she quietly poured herself some milk. Putting the empty glass silently down on the counter she stepped out into the hallway to get her jacket off the chair, feeling the weight of the book in one of the pockets. She was a hair's breadth away from putting it on when she heard a creak of wood, so she casually carried on the action and put the jacket away in the cloakroom cupboard as if she were tidying.

She feigned surprise at seeing him and gave a tentative smile. He'd not changed out of his clothing from yesterday and looked strangely vulnerable not dressed as his normal immaculate self.

She headed into the kitchen and set about making his breakfast, moving a pot of potatoes and carrots off the stove, part of last night's dinner which never got cooked or eaten. Most of it would be binned, especially the joint of beef sat out all night. In fact, all of it, she decided. She would not be there later to salvage it or add fresh ingredients to revive it. In a dish she cracked two eggs. She would make scrambled eggs as it was quick and easy. She popped two slices of bread in the toaster and switched on the kettle to make green tea, which sometimes he preferred for his first drink.

He was standing silently behind her and she kept deliberately busy, feeling his eyes on the back of her head. *Don't say anything, don't start anything, just stay quiet until I'm gone,* she prayed inwardly, carrying on with what she was doing, hands trembling as she completed each task of buttering toast and cutting it into triangles to serve with the soft scrambled egg. She poured boiling water into a small teapot and her hand shook, conscious that this was the last meal she would ever prepare for him.

She let out a tense breath when he walked out of the kitchen and into the hallway. The light squeak of the cloakroom door opening and the clacking sound of golf clubs reassured her he was putting them away and not opening it to search her jacket. He would eat his breakfast and then probably go and shower. It would not be long now until she never had to see him again.

Nausea suddenly curled her stomach over, and in a panic she ran from the room.

He called out to her as she sped past him to the bathroom, nearly knocking into the golf clubs which he'd not put away. She managed to get out two words that would reassure him she just needed the loo. 'Sorry. Desperate.'

In the bathroom she flushed the toilet as she heaved vomit into the bowl to cover the sounds of her retching. If he suspected she was pregnant he'd hover over her all day. He'd guard her from now until the baby was born, while planning to systematically cut her off from the outside world. He'd never leave her side again.

A moment later she went rigid with shock as the bathroom door banged a staccato outburst of short sharp knocks.

'Can you come out of there, please? I'd like you to come out of there right now!'

She stayed rigid and silent. The 'please' contrasted sharply with the demands of his banging. She wasn't being asked. She was being commanded. She yelped in alarm as a kick to the door shook it. It was followed by another thundering round of hammering as if he were using the side of his fist. The noise was so deafening she shot back fast to the other side of the room. And then she heard him.

'You'd better be listening to me, Tess, because I'm only going to say this once. I'm giving you one last chance to open this door and come out and explain.'

Tess stared at the closed door, petrified. He was enraged. Coming through the quietness in his voice she could hear the fury more powerfully than any loud roar. The quality of this quietness was new and for that reason it felt deadly. Something had switched off his control. She pressed her hand over her mouth to silence her whimper. *Dear God he knew! He knew!* He'd found the book in her jacket, or maybe the suitcase! Either way she was doomed.

He rattled the door handle violently and kicked the wood until it shook again, but the door didn't give way. Then he spoke again.

'When I return from dealing with this interfering little shit, I'll be back to deal with you. You're a whore, Tess, just like she was.' Something in her brain clicked with those words. Something else was wrong.

Tess listened to his footsteps marching away and then a minute later heard the car start. She unlocked the bathroom door and peered out before taking hesitant steps into the hallway. She saw it straight away. There on the floor, like a white chess piece on a black square, was a postcard. She picked it up and read the message.

Daniel, you better come meet me so we can discuss how you treat your wife! Bring your phone so I can text you the address!

She sank to her knees and then down onto her bottom, having no strength to stand. Tears rivered her face as she shuddered with fear. Weeks of pent-up emotion juddered hard out of her shaking frame. She had forgotten about the postcard messenger. In all of yesterday, in all of what she'd learned, she had forgotten about the warning to come. Daniel would hate being sent for with this stark order. And now she didn't know what to do. Run? Or stay? She was trapped by fear.

Daniel could hurt this person badly after getting that message. There was no knowing what he might do in his anger. And then he would come back and hurt her more. If it was made known to him his wife knew prior to him getting this message that a stranger was going to contact him, he could accuse her of laying a trap. He could go to the police and have her arrested. She should have gone yesterday and not waited another day. She was stuck in limbo now, facing the unknown, fearing at every passing minute his coming home.

CHAPTER FORTY-FIVE

Tess's heart had been thumping all day. She would give herself a heart attack if she didn't calm down. It was four o'clock and he'd still not returned. The only phone call she had all day was from the removal company to say they were on the way. She'd let them carry the table and bench to the garden and plonk the rest of the furniture in the hallway as she wanted them gone quickly in case he came back.

She had prepared what she'd say to him hours ago. She'd deny knowledge of the postcard, convince him that she had been equally as surprised at seeing it. Suggest that perhaps he should go to the police to report it. But he wasn't back for her to say any of that and she was growing more frantic in this silence. If only she could speak to Sara and let it all out she'd feel better.

She stopped pacing as she saw the door to his study ajar. It had been like it all day and only now had it registered with her that the door was open. She could have been in there all of this time and searched it for her phone.

Not wasting another second she went into the room and straight to his desk to check the drawers, but it wasn't in any of them. Nor was it on the shelves of his sideboard, which held nothing but piles of medical papers and office stationery. The bookshelf might be more promising. He might have perched it on top of one of the volumes of books on surgery and medicine or tucked it in between the red and blue folders. Then she noticed one that stood out because it was beige and more worn than the others, the card softened as if from much handling.

She slipped her hand in to feel by the side of it and then shifted her fingers to the back of it and felt her hope rise as she touched something smooth and hard. She took hold of it but all she pulled out from the hiding place was a small toy car. She was about to put it back when she shot her hand forward to stop what was happening, but it was already too late. The pale beige folder toppled to the floor and opened with its contents sliding out.

Working furiously she gathered the scattered papers and put them on the desk so she could put them tidily back into the folder. Her hands stopped as she saw a black-and-white photograph of the house. The photo looked old but the house looked just the same. She turned it over to see if there was any writing on the back but found nothing. She placed it to the side with some papers that looked like certificates and land registry maps and picked up a yellowing folded newspaper clipping. She should really just get the contents back in the folder and back on the shelf. It was going to be tricky already to restore it exactly as it was without being caught red-handed.

Her hands nonetheless unfolded it and the headline almost had her fingers ripping through the paper in shock as she saw the words: DOCTOR ACCUSED OF KILLING WIFE AND LEAVING CHILD FOR DEAD FOUND GUILTY.

She sank down on his chair. Her mouth went dry and she was overcome with a sense of foreboding for what she was about to read, sure this headline, this story, had something to do with her husband.

The secret life of one of Bath's best-known doctors, an Oxford graduate and renowned heart specialist, was laid bare at Bristol Crown Court yesterday as David Simmonds was found guilty of the murder of his wife, Rachel Simmonds, and for the attempted murder of his three-year-old son, Daniel. In a trial that lasted just three weeks, all 12 jurors reached a unanimous

*guilty verdict. Simmonds, aged 40, showed no remorse upon
hearing the verdict.*

*In a case which has shocked colleagues and patients,
Simmonds was accused of bludgeoning his wife to death and
leaving his three-year-old son, Daniel, for dead. The boy, who
was initially thought dead at the scene, was covered in blood.
Paramedic Scott Kelly told the jury that when he found Daniel
Simmonds he thought the child was covered in his own blood.
On closer examination he discovered the blood was in fact
from the dead woman, Rachel Simmonds, and that the child
was mercifully sleeping as he lay huddled beside the body of his
mother. Daniel Simmonds was taken to the children's hospital
in Bristol where he spent three days before being placed in the
care of social services.*

*The body of Rachel Simmonds, 28, was discovered in her
home in her bedroom by the couple's housekeeper, Ellen Bowden.
It is thought the body lay there for three days before the gruesome
discovery on September 12.*

*A bloodied meat mallet was found wrapped in a surgical
glove in the boot of Simmonds's car. Simmonds told police he
had used it to put a cat out of its misery after knocking one
down in the road. Examination of the mallet found considerable
microscopic characteristics of human blood. Two hairs collected
from the metal teeth of the mallet were analysed and confirmed
to be human hair. More damning was the discovery of rows
of pyramid-shaped indents found on the victim's skin during
the post-mortem.*

*In his closing speech, prosecutor Robert Whitwell said: 'The
Crown's position is that he bludgeoned to death his wife, Rachel
Simmonds, and attempted to murder his three-year-old son,
Daniel, with a significant blow to the boy's head which caused
a fractured skull. He then left the scene of the crime believing
that life was extinct for both his victims. We have heard that*

Daniel Simmonds, the child, lay huddled beside the body of his dead mother for three days. Simmonds carried on about his life as normal for three days until the discovery of his wife's body by their housekeeper Ellen Bowden on September 12. For three days his child lay in a pool of blood and not once during that time did Simmonds raise the alarm. In a statement to the police he stated he had not stepped foot inside his home during that time as he found it painful to be at the family home because he believed his wife had taken their child to be with her lover. Simmonds cannot account for where he was during that time. If it is the case that he was in fact in the family home during that time we can only wonder if he heard anything. Did he hear his child cry, hear him still alive and choose to ignore it?'

Tess was shivering all over by the time she read the last word. There was no first wife. The date at the top of the paper put Daniel at only three when this happened. The old lady had got it wrong. She'd been talking about Daniel's mother. His father's wife. This story was about his father. The three-year-old boy named Daniel Simmonds was their son. The parents she went to see were not his birth parents, her impression of them being childless was more true than she knew. This house had been Daniel's first home. This is where he had lived with his mother until she was murdered. It was her scent that haunted him. She was the woman he spoke so vilely about. Hers the book found under that mattress. Mrs Bowden was Ellen Bowden, and the poor woman had found her.

Holding her hand to her mouth Tess managed to get up from the chair and rush to the kitchen sink to spew out brown fluid from a stomach that had only tea inside it all day. She scooped a handful of water to rinse out her mouth and then sank to the floor a shivering wreck.

Her husband's father was a murderer, his blood running through the veins of the man she married. Why had he brought her to this house? Why had he ever come back to it? Was it any wonder he changed almost the day he stepped inside. He had known what had taken place inside these walls, known what happened to him. What could have possibly motivated him to come back to the home where his mother was murdered and then to sleep in her bed? Had he thought he could handle it only to find himself tormented by the memory of a scent? Or had he gone mad because he had real memories of what happened here? The newspaper said he lay beside the body of his mother for three days – was he awake for any of that time?

Tess didn't know how to respond to what she had learned. What happened to him had shaped him. There was no doubting it. She would hold that small boy in her arms if she could and make what happened go away. Stuart Myers said he went into a big bed when he was three. *Three.* Her throat closed over and the lower part of her face ached. *Why hadn't he told her?* She drew up her knees and folded her arms around them. *If he had only told her.* She closed her eyes and tucked her head down.

Before he made her afraid. She breathed raggedly, trying to work out what it was she now felt about him. Saddened, depressed, joyless, heartsick, heartache. *Heartbroken.*

And then it struck her with how else she felt and she cried out sharply. *Paralysed.* He'd paralysed her joy, gaiety, spontaneity, dreams, happiness. All the good feelings that made you want to stay with someone forever.

Why hadn't he told her before it was too late? Making it impossible for them to have a future. She could never now stay. This house had broken them. She was not strong enough to live in a marriage without love. In a house that wasn't a home. He had made it impossible when he made her afraid.

CHAPTER FORTY-SIX

At six o'clock her husband still wasn't home. She'd rung the hospital on the off chance and was told by the operator Mr Myers wasn't there. She went back to his study and picked up his address book and took it into the hallway. Her husband was thorough – he would have made a hard copy of his contacts in the old-fashioned way. Under P she saw Porter. Mark was the natural choice to try first. Her husband had been missing all day and Tess's biggest fear was that he was either dead at the hands of a stranger who had obviously been watching them or he killed this person and was now on his way home to deal with her.

She gathered herself and when she was ready she dialled the number. It was Vivien who answered on the third ring.

'Vivien, has Mark heard from Daniel today?'

Vivien sounded surprised. 'I don't know, Tess. Hang on and I'll ask him.' A moment later she came back on the phone. 'No, Tess, he actually rang him earlier seeing as he didn't get to talk to him yesterday. He left him a message but he's heard nothing back.'

'Oh God, Vivien, I'm now starting to worry. He's been gone all day and I haven't heard from him at all. I just hope nothing's happened.'

'Hey, calm down. Tell me what's going on.'

'When I got up this morning his golf clubs were out ready. I thought at first he must be playing golf again today and had popped out for a newspaper or to the shop for something, but they're still there. I've wasted a whole day waiting for him to come home and now I'm not even sure what time he went out. I've phoned and left messages but he's not returning my calls. I called the hospital to see if he was there, but he isn't. I don't know where he is.'

'Hey, calm down, calm down. Have you tried Ed?'

'No, I was going to do that next.'

'OK, well, do that now, and ring us back and let us know.'

'Vivien, do you think…? You don't think…?'

'Stop it, Tess,' Vivien said sharply. 'There'll be a good reason he's not calling back. It's only just gone six, for heaven's sake. He's probably in a pub somewhere.'

Tess heaved a sigh. 'You're right. I'm being silly. You're right. I'll call Ed now. He might know.'

Tess disconnected the call and heaved a genuine sigh of alarm. With trembling fingers she dialled Ed's number. Anne answered in a warm voice.

'Anne Ferris speaking.'

'Anne, it's Tess.'

'Tess! Hello.'

'Hello, Anne, I'm sorry to bother you, but is Ed at home?'

'Well, yes. He's out at his pond. Do you want to speak to him?'

'I um… well, maybe. Or maybe you could just ask him if he's seen or spoken with Daniel today.'

'Daniel?' Her voice turned concerned as she picked up on the worry in Tess's voice. 'Let me fetch him, Tess. Hold on.'

A minute passed before Ed came on the phone. 'Tess, how can I help?'

Tears glazed Tess's eyes. Ed was such a kind man. 'Have you heard from Daniel, Ed?'

'I haven't, my dear,' he replied quickly.

'Do you know if he had any plans to play golf again today?'

'I'm afraid I don't. Look, it's not a bother – would you like us to pop over?'

Tess inhaled a shaky breath. 'No, that won't be necessary, Ed. He probably just needs a bit of time on his own. It's been a bit of a strain for him...'

'Yes, Tess, I imagine it has. Look, I'll ring round too. Call a few of our colleagues. He may be at the hospital.'

'I've tried there.'

'Well, I can try again. He's not rostered to be on call this weekend so if it's only switchboard you called they'll automatically tell you he's not there.'

Tess let out a sigh. 'Thank you, Ed. I didn't think of that.'

'OK, dear girl, I'll be in touch as soon as I hear anything. Go and make yourself a cup of tea and try not to worry. Daniel will be home before you know it.'

Tess did as she was told and made herself some tea. The house was in complete silence. She was keeping noise down to a minimum so that she would not miss hearing the call to say her husband had been found. If she didn't hear from anyone by midnight she would call the police and report her husband missing.

She shivered with trepidation. She must carry on playing the part of his wife until she knew one way or another where he was or if anything had happened to him. She had to press on and get rid of those postcards. If her husband had been killed she could be accused of being an accomplice.

CHAPTER FORTY-SEVEN

Since six o'clock she received two more calls from Ed and three from Vivien, both asking the same question. Had she heard from him? At ten o'clock Ed sounded more concerned, but pointed out the pubs were still open. He'd checked with colleagues at the hospital and there had been no sign of Daniel. Off his own back and because of his position he'd contacted A & E in both Bath and Bristol and enquired if they'd had any admissions fitting Daniel's description. He'd assured her they hadn't so she could put from her mind any fear of an accident.

At one minute past eleven Tess used the landline to call the police. A caring female voice identified herself as Teresa. Tess continued the lie as she talked her through the timeline since last seeing her husband, which she said was yesterday when he went off to play golf. She assumed he must have come home last night as his golf clubs were in the hallway this morning. She heard the tapping of a keyboard as Teresa took down the details.

'And you've not seen or heard from him all day?' Teresa asked.

'No one has,' Tess replied in a tremulous voice. 'I've tried everyone, and they've tried others.'

'Tess? Can I call you Tess? Or would you prefer Mrs Myers?'

'No, Tess, please.'

'OK, Tess, I need to ask you some simple straightforward questions. Is that OK?'

'Of course.'

'Is it normal for you not to hear from your husband?'

'No.'

'Would you say this is out of character?'

'Yes.'

'Has he ever disappeared for a few hours or days before without letting anyone know where he is?'

Tess hesitated. 'Well, once, but that was work-related.'

'Does he have any medical conditions we should be aware of?'

'No.'

'Any history of depression or other mental health illnesses?'

'No.'

'Any alcohol or drug dependencies we should be aware of?'

'No.'

'Thank you, Tess. We just need to know these facts to establish his state of mind and health. Can I now ask you if anything recently has upset him? Anything that may have caused him to take off without an explanation?'

Tess went silent and Teresa prompted her. 'Tess, if we have all the facts we can establish the level of concern for him being missing. I'm—'

'He's in trouble at work,' she said in a rush.

'OK, can you expand on that?'

'He's um… he's a surgeon. Look, I don't know if I can talk about this as it's confidential. I don't want to cause him a problem.'

'Tess, it would help if we know why he may be missing.'

'A patient died and my husband is being held accountable.'

Tess heard Teresa inhale a little louder. It was probably rare for the call handler to hear something like this as the reason for someone going missing. 'OK, Tess, what's going to happen now is an officer will attend your home. If you can find a photograph of your husband to have ready to give to the officer, that would be helpful. I'm just going to repeat back to you the details of your husband and then that should do for now. Is that OK?'

'Yes.'

A few minutes later Tess was alone with just the silence of the house. The call had set the wheels in motion to find her missing husband. There was no turning back now. She could only go forward until either her husband was located alive or his body was found. They would need a photograph to find him and then to identify him. In the sitting room she took the silver photo frame off the wall. It was the only one she'd had framed of them on their wedding day. They were smiling and clearly in love. They looked like a couple who had everything to live for.

Tess lay on her side of the bed, alert so that she would hear the smallest sound outside the room. She had left the door wide open so she would hear any phone calls from the landline or any knocking at the front door. She had been lying there since the departure of the two uniformed officers who'd arrived shortly before midnight, and who insisted on searching the house and garden. The female officer was a similar age to Tess and couldn't hide her surprise at the grandeur of the place, probably assuming – rightly so – that the wealth was her husband's.

Tomorrow, if it had not already happened, they would find him. They were searching for him right now. It would only be a matter of time before they contacted her.

CHAPTER FORTY-EIGHT

On Monday morning when the doorbell rang Tess opened the front door with red-rimmed eyes and stared at the two returning police officers on the doorstep.

The female officer quickly spoke first. 'We have no news on your husband's whereabouts, Mrs Myers, but we do need to come in and talk with you.'

Tess let them into the hallway and shut the front door, where she then let out a shuddering breath. 'So he's not dead.'

The male officer who looked more in charge, only because of being older, gave an odd shake of his head. 'Your husband's car was found around five o'clock this morning by a local farmer with the keys still in the ignition.'

'So he might have broken down. Or run out of petrol,' she suggested.

'Mrs Myers, we are extremely concerned for his wellbeing. The location of your husband's car was found close to a railway track.' His eyes turned meaningful. 'Given where it was found, a place not easy to get to, we think it unlikely he got there by accident. Given also the circumstances you reported to the police it's possible your husband chose to go there.'

Her legs turned to jelly and she held onto the door. 'So if he's there why haven't you found him?'

Her question caused his expression to change slightly. He looked a little uneasy. 'It's not always as straightforward as that on a railway track, I'm sorry to say. Trains are powerful things.

At present British Transport Police are searching that line and location. We will be speaking to friends and family, checking with known associates for anything that might assist in tracing his whereabouts. His photograph has been widely circulated and the police are on the alert for any sightings of him. We will be doing everything we can to find him as quickly as possible, but in the meantime can you think of anywhere he might be, anyone he might have gone to? Do you have a second vehicle he may be using or a second home he may have gone to?'

Tess's stomach somersaulted. They were thinking he committed suicide. While her own thoughts were going a hundred miles an hour in a different direction. Was he dead for another reason? Was he injured? Or lost? Or confused? A head injury? Or unconscious? Was he on the run? Was there a body? His or the postcard person's somewhere on the track? Or was he in a different kind of danger from the person he met? Taken? Imprisoned? Unable to escape?

He would not have killed himself.

She was withholding important information. Something that may have put her husband in danger. Be the reason why he was missing. Be the only reason he was missing. He had gone to meet a stranger and she couldn't tell them that.

She gestured to the furniture in the hallway. 'Only my husband has a car. This furniture is from his flat in London. He's just sold it, but I imagine he still has access as I still have the keys in my bag.'

'Why don't we sit down somewhere and then we can take a full statement?' the policewoman now said. 'You've had a shock and could probably do with sitting.'

Tess sat in a daze. Her husband was still missing with no reports of anyone seeing him or speaking with him since after his game of golf on Saturday with Ed. Tess stuck to the same story in her statement. She'd not seen him Saturday evening as she'd gone to bed, but assumed he slept at home because his golf clubs were there in the morning. She'd not seen him Sunday morning and thought initially he'd popped out to the shop. Then after still not seeing him she thought he might be at work. It was only when after not hearing from him all day she started to worry. She didn't tell them, of course, about the slap she got, about the perfume she was made to wear, about her plan to run away, about his rage when he stormed out. She didn't tell them about the postcard.

According to the police his phone was switched off. But she rang it anyway. Again and again and again.

Vivien was keeping her company while she waited for news, but Tess was unable to talk. Too afraid to say or hear or think the worst. The police came and questioned her as to whether a letter or note had been found. Vivien quietly told them she'd been tidying around the house all day and hadn't come across anything like that.

It was now ten o'clock and she told Vivien she should go home and rest. Vivien stopped buffing the silver picture frame she was working on and set it down on the polished table. 'I can stay, Tess. There's plenty of beds for me to sleep in.'

Tess appreciated the kind offer, but she wanted to be on her own. 'Vivien, it might be another long day tomorrow. I'd rather you got a good night's sleep in your own bed and come back fresh tomorrow. That's if you're not too busy, I mean. I'm fine on my own, I promise, so please don't feel you have to.'

Vivien gave her a motherly stare. 'I'll leave on one condition. You do the same and go straight to bed.'

Tess nodded that she would, and meant it as well. She was going straight to bed.

CHAPTER FORTY-NINE

She had thought never to lie in this bed again, but last night when it came to choosing somewhere else to sleep she found she couldn't. It felt strangely wrong somehow, even cruel, as though she were abandoning the woman after being allowed to read her story.

She was trying not to think of what happened in this room or go down the path of 'if only'. *If only they hadn't come to this house* wasn't going to change the damage done. He had once been perfect to her, and maybe that was the only positive thing to hang on to.

As her eyes drifted closed she dreamed she was at the seaside. The sea was gently dragging at the pebbles on the shoreline. The rhythmic scraping of pebbles sliding against grit gave a whooshing sound as gentle waves rolled over them again and again... Whoosh... Scratch... Whoosh... Scratch...

Her eyes pinged open. A fist of fear punched straight through her chest. It was not waves or the scraping of pebbles she could hear.

In bare feet she crept along the landing and carefully trod on wooden stairs, making her way down them on tiptoes, keeping close to the wall, pressing her palm against it for balance to lessen any noise. The harsh scratching from the kitchen, steel against steel, set her teeth on edge. Daniel was sharpening his knives. She didn't want to go in there. She wanted to get past it as fast as she could. At the bottom of the stairs she stopped still, standing in the spot where he'd pinned her up against the wall. Her eyes fastened on the front door. She could get to it in a flash. Turn the latch to the right and press the handle down. Then pull. She readied to make the dash, eyes sweeping the area to make sure nothing was in her way or easy to knock against. She just had to get to the door. Her heart slammed to a halt as her eyes fixed on the bolt at the top of the door. It was locked. Small intakes of breath quickened the rise and fall of her chest. She couldn't reach it. And now she was panicking because he would hear her soon. She needed to calm down, find another way out. With the noise he was making in the kitchen she could probably climb out of a window unheard, or try the back door. If she acted quickly she could escape without him being any the wiser.

She put one foot forward, one hand sliding over the wall to steady herself. She raised the heel of her other foot and then he spoke.

'I know you're there.'

Tess froze. Every muscle in her body paralysed in fear.

'I know what you did, Tess,' he called in a sing-song voice. 'Clever deceitful Tess found someone to send me a postcard, didn't she? Went crying to someone and shared our private matters. Had someone try blackmailing me. Naughty deceitful Tess ought to say sorry, wouldn't you agree?'

She remained silent and he called again. 'Are you going to stand out there for ever?'

Strength was coming back to her limbs, the paralysis turning to hard shakes. She scanned the hallway in desperate search of a weapon. If he had a knife in his hand she wanted something in hers. His golf bag stood near the cloakroom cupboard. Without thought she ran fast towards it and carefully extracted a smooth polished club. Holding the shaft behind her back she stepped slowly towards the kitchen.

He was standing at the counter. Each of the knives lay shiny and sharp. He had the longest in his hand and slowly drew the blade down the length of the sharpening rod.

'You've been clever, Tess. More clever than my mother. You got someone on side to do your dirty work. Who is he? Your lover?

I hope you've told him about the patient you killed. He may not want to stay around when he knows about that. Though thinking about it now, it may well help my case in this other matter,' he said in a pondering tone. 'Surgeon misses vital operation due to caring for suicidal wife. Followed by this headline: Surgeon's wife takes her own life after causing the death of one of his patients? Two birds with one stone, so to speak.'

Tess stared at her husband. His eyes were lowered so she couldn't see the madness in them. To think the way that he was thinking was neither sane nor rational. Would he seriously plan to kill her and say it was suicide?

'I don't know who sent you that postcard, Daniel. I haven't told anyone about us. Where have you been? I thought you were dead! The police have been looking for you since last night. Did you stay away to punish me? Do you hate me that much?'

His head rose swiftly at that, and his eyes showed his shock. 'Why would you ever say that? Why would you think I hate you?' In the soft light of the kitchen his eyes found hers. 'I love you,' he said softly. He tried smiling, raising the corners of his mouth, but the effort along with the smile slid away as sadness appeared on his face. 'But you don't love me anymore, do you, Tess?'

Her eyes filled with tears. How did he manage to do this to her? After everything he'd done he could still make her feel she could love him. 'I know what happened to you here in this house,' she said softly. 'I know what your father did to you and your mother. You should have told me, Daniel. I could have helped you. Instead you set out to destroy us. Why did you do that to us, Daniel?' She started to cry, gazing at him beseechingly.

He stayed where he was, and answered in a listless voice. 'I went to see my father the other day. He wanted to tell me his important news that he'd be getting out soon.' He pulled a wry face. 'I missed an important operation to hear that. Went to see him instead. I wrecked my career. And for what? All the years I've been visiting him. All the chats about music and medicine and art. A while ago I bought him a copy of this drawing he liked. For him to have for when he got out, because he told me it reminded him of losing me. Ironically, it's a drawing of a mother losing a child. Not a father. At the end of the visit I walked away not sure anymore if he'd ever loved me.' He smiled bleakly. 'It was hard, Tess, to walk away and feel that.'

She hid her shock at hearing that his father was still alive and that Daniel went to visit him. Though was less surprised to learn that the drawing she found in his flat in London was his father's choice of art.

'We can leave here, Daniel. Start again. You can put the past behind you. You don't ever have to think of him again.'

He shook his head, looking at her sadly. 'You think it's that easy. My mother ruined my life. She broke our family with her infidelities. She was going to leave me,' he whispered.

Tess saw the grief he'd been hiding for so long and her heart went out to him. 'That's your father's version, what he tells you, not what really happened. Your mother wasn't unfaithful. She was afraid for her life. She was running away with you! It's in her diary, Daniel!' He stepped back startled and she nodded her head affirmatively. 'I have your mother's account, Daniel. She wrote it in a book. And she loved you more than anything. Your father was the one who destroyed your life.'

His eyes shot open. 'Don't say that, Tess. He was a brilliant surgeon. He should have carried on being a brilliant surgeon. She robbed him of his life's work!'

'He was a monster,' she declared emphatically, trying to drive home the truth.

'Not a monster, Tess. Don't say that.' His green eyes implored her.

'A monster, who was able to leave his three-year-old son to die.'

'Not true,' he denied in a husky voice. His expression looked as though she'd betrayed him. 'He thought I was dead.'

She made a sound of disgust.

'Why do you find that so hard to believe?' he asked wearily.

'Because it's a lie, Daniel. Your father didn't think you were dead. He was a heart doctor. He would know if a heart had stopped. Your father knew you were alive. He ignored the cries of his child for three days. Ignored a child who lay huddled against his dead mother. Your father did that to you for three days. He didn't think you were dead. He left you for dead, Daniel!'

'Shut up. Shut up, I say. He never left me! He was my father!' he cried as if desperate to hear it said. His eyes darkened in despair and he breathed slowly in and out of his mouth. 'He was my father,' he repeated softly. 'He would never have left me for dead!'

It stopped her saying any more. She was losing conviction, her energy fading. She was fighting a losing battle. He had chosen to take the side of his father. She was tired of this toxic hold over him, tired from loving and hating him and trying to love him again. She had nothing more to try.

'I'm leaving you, Daniel,' she quietly said.

His head shot up and he took an intake of breath.

'Don't!' he said, and her heart sank as she heard the desolate tone.

'I have to, Daniel. I have nothing left to give.'

'Please don't,' he uttered again, coming away from the counter and towards her. The point of the knife was coming her way. 'Please don't leave me here alone again.'

Her eyes darted from the knife to his face.

'Put down the knife, Daniel.'

'Please don't leave me like she did. Don't make me do this to you!'

'Daniel,' she said, when only inches separated them. 'Put down the knife! PLEASE!'

A flash of movement cut through the air and she managed to turn sideways at the very last second. He smiled goofily as if sorry for making her jump. Then he turned so swiftly her body failed to react and she fell flat on her back. His eyes found her on the floor and Tess watched him come closer, bending and arching right over her, his wide shoulders blocking out light, except the shine of his eyes, and the glint of the blade. His voice floated near her face.

'Tess,' he whispered like a soft caress. 'You should have stayed.'

She got ready. Her arms bent back, elbows tucked tight against the sides of her head, her hands under her neck pulling swiftly at what lay hidden beneath her, working it through her fingers trying to judge length enough to grip. She sensed him ready, her body tingling in anticipation. She could hear his breathing keeping time with hers... in... out... in... out... As he reared back she rolled a little to release the golf club and raised it up off the floor, vertically, looking straight up at its ceramic head. Her hands gripped tight as she swung it backwards first and then forwards as hard as she could. A wheezy sound came from his throat as he sucked air. Confusion filled his eyes as he gazed at splashes of blood falling on her face. Then suddenly, but not from high, she felt his weight against her.

His eyes had closed and his body was still and she knew it was over. This house with all its secrets had witnessed its second unnatural death. First his mother – now her son.

She heaved silent sobs, her mind racked with guilt and anguish and wretchedness for the hopelessness of knowing it was not all a lie. Not always. He had tried to love her. She kissed his temple and rocked him gently. Her tears mixed with his blood on her face. Tears and blood. The battle of love. Ended.

CHAPTER FIFTY

Tess dragged herself off the bed at the sound of knocking on the front door. Daylight. *They had come for her.* She saw out of the window their vehicle and knew soon she would be sat in the back of it. She could not run from this. She breathed and then opened the door. Dumbstruck, she stared at the two police officers on the doorstep. She put out a hand as if to ward them off but they stepped closer and then stepped over the threshold of her house.

She stared in confusion at the older one, thinking she must be dreaming. Her anxiety had dreamed him up. It was not possible that he was here in her home wearing a uniform. That he was a policeman. She had thought he was just a man on a train with his *Bradshaw's* book. Tess was too shocked to speak.

She had to be dreaming.

His face told her he was there on serious business. She could see it in his eyes, in his careful manner as he hovered close.

'He's dead,' she said. Then stared at her hands.

They guided her to the drawing room and helped her to sit in a chair. The older one sat with her while the other went to make tea. Her eyes rested on the three stripes sewn onto the shoulder of his uniform. Her *Bradshaw's* book man was a sergeant.

'Mrs Myers, we're from British Transport Police. I'm very sorry to have to inform you but a body was found this morning at around six o'clock. A driving licence bearing the name Daniel Myers was found in some clothing. Along with some credit cards with this name.'

She gazed at him white-faced.

'From a photograph given to us by Avon and Somerset Police we've identified a wedding ring worn. Regrettably, a positive identification of the body requires the request of dental records, previous blood tests and obtaining fingerprint information. Under such circumstances viewing the body might cause considerable distress.'

She covered her mouth as she gagged. She had nothing in her to vomit out. The sergeant called out to the other police officer to bring some water. A moment later Tess was given a glass and she swallowed the contents in gulps as if dying of thirst.

'Easy does it, you don't want to be sick,' the sergeant gently advised.

The younger officer carried a tray with three cups of tea, no saucers, and an open bag of sugar with a teaspoon poking out of the top. He placed the tray on a low table and brought it over to where she was sitting. He hunched down and asked if she took sugar. She shook her head. His cap was off and she saw his hair was a warm ginger. She guessed that when he was a boy it was brighter and he was probably teased.

'We've met before,' she softly announced. 'On the platform. You gave me water to take some tablets. And here you are in my home bringing me more water, and tea.'

The red-haired officer smiled at her kindly. 'You'd burned your hand.'

'Yes, I'd burned my hand. Daniel made it better.' She held it up to show him a smaller dressing. 'Did you see him?' she asked.

He gave a hesitant shake of his head. 'You mean Daniel?'

'Yes,' she whispered. 'Did you see him in the kitchen?'

He looked to the senior officer with concern showing in his eyes and was given a discreet nod to continue. He budged a little closer and rested his hand on the arm of her chair, his movements slow as if anticipating a reaction. He lowered his voice and spoke clearly to answer her question. 'No. He's not in the kitchen. He's not at home, Mrs Myers. He was found by the side of a railway track. He was hit and killed by a train.'

She inhaled sharply. Then stared at her hands again. Where was the blood? The small dressing was clean. Where was all the blood?

Three hours later Tess sat in a daze. He had been identified by his fingerprints. Finger marks, the constable said, from off his laptop and his computer and from diary pages, and from inside his locker at work. She could have told them she could identify him from looking at his hand. It had been uncovered and down by his side. Instantly recognisable from its shape and length and straight-cut fingernails. She had been to see her husband for the last time. The wedding ring on his finger was still new, but she'd not been allowed to touch it. Or touch him. The constable had advised her that he was not medically trained but that injuries to his head and torso were catastrophic, which was why the rest of him was covered in this way.

Vivien hadn't known when she knocked on the door at eleven o'clock that Tess had already had a busy morning or that she would have an update to give. Vivien took charge immediately and also took ownership of Daniel's address book, for which Tess was grateful as she hadn't any energy to give anyone this news.

She could not stop staring at the kitchen floor.

Every time someone crossed it footprints of blood appeared. She was amazed no one else was seeing this. They were getting it on their shoes and tracking his blood all over the room. Leaving pools of red blood in their wake that none of them seemed aware of.

The kitchen had been busy nonstop since Vivien arrived and was filled with the constant sound of the kettle boiling as more people descended and either Vivien or Anne made more tea while their husbands were sent on errands to buy more milk and cake and biscuits to have ready just in case...

Nancy and Stuart Myers had visited without warning but only stayed long enough for Vivien to feed them cake and make them tea, and to tell Tess that Daniel was their adopted son and that he'd inherited a great deal of money from his grandfather when he was twenty-five. When Nancy squeezed her hand goodbye, her eyes had shown sadness at the loss of her son but not raw grief, and Tess knew intuitively it must not have been easy for them to have been his parents.

A pretty policewoman in plain clothes, from British Transport Police, turned up some time after noon and was offered tea by Vivien as soon as the front door opened to her. She'd accepted and then spent half an hour explaining her role to Tess and telling her what to expect. Investigative officers would probably visit and want to talk through the circumstances again. They may request to take away certain items that would help them in their investigation. They may take away a toothbrush or hairbrush. Someone from the coroner's office would contact her as unexplained deaths were reported to the coroner. They would speak to her about what would happen next, let her know if they were deciding to investigate, and how to go about making funeral arrangements. The woman was a detective constable, and also a trained FLO, Family Liaison Officer, someone for Tess to have direct contact with so that anything not understood could be explained. She left Tess her business card and a pre-emptive booklet to read. *Help is at Hand: Support after someone may have died by suicide.*

On one of the pages there was a list of organisations she may wish to notify of her husband's death: Bank, Building Society, Mortgage Provider, Car Insurance, Dentist, Solicitor, Library, and many, many more. After reading them, Tess was left bewildered by all there was to do. Dying meant telling everyone.

At the beginning of the booklet there were paragraphs on what she may be feeling: Despair, Disbelief, Depression, Guilt, Numbness, Pining, Sadness, and Relief...

She read the words under the heading of Relief, and one sentence stood out, which was intended to give comfort to those who felt relief at the ending of their loved one's suffering: *Relief is a natural response after a period of tension and stress…*

Fear… is what she felt. Stark fear thrashing at her breast. Anne was watching her too closely, analysing her every expression. Was she behaving as Anne would expect of someone who'd just lost their husband? Was Anne able to see inside her mind? See her husband's body on the kitchen floor?

'Tess, can I make you something to eat?' Vivien asked gently. 'Maybe some scrambled egg, like I did before, only this time you get to eat it?' she added with a smile.

Tess rose from the chair, but her legs gave way.

'Tess, it would be better if you lie down. Let me help you upstairs,' Vivien said.

Tess saw the imprint of her head on the pillow. His pillow was smooth. He would never lay his head on it again.

'I don't want to lie on this bed,' she said as she lay down.

On the bedside drawers Vivien placed a glass of water. Then she sat down on the edge of the bed.

'At first I couldn't bear to leave my daughter's room. I wanted to be surrounded by the smell of her,' she said sadly. 'I didn't want to be anywhere else in that house but her room. It took months for Mark to persuade me to move back into our bed, and then I changed the whole house round. I stripped it of warmth, I now think.' She soothed Tess's brow. 'It takes time to get over the loss, and the anger, too. I was angry for a long time.'

'Why anger?' she asked tearfully, feeling Vivien's pain.

'Because I never spotted it until it showed its true face. The cancer had spread throughout her abdomen before I realised it wasn't just stomach pains or period pains. I was her mother. I should have known it was something more.'

Tess grabbed Vivien's hand and kissed it. 'Not your fault,' she whispered, meaning it. It wasn't always there to see. Some cancers were buried so deep there was no spotting them or stopping them once they spread. She'd only seen Daniel's malignant growth when it overtook him and eradicated his goodness. Leaving nothing of him she could heal, as all of him was gone.

CHAPTER FIFTY-ONE

The next day her home was just as busy. Mark, Ed and Anne must have taken time off from their jobs as they had been in Tess's home along with Vivien for most of the day, letting in police officers to take Daniel's laptop and computer away or answering the phone or making tea. Tess listened to Ed talking to Stuart Myers on the phone about funeral arrangements even though the body had yet to be released and Ed relayed to her that they would like to help organise it when the time was right, if that was OK with her. Tess gave her agreement and Ed got back on the phone to the man.

To get away from the noise she went out into the garden to breathe some air. She noticed the black bin by the garage had been moved from its spot. She realised why when she went over to look inside. It was Tuesday yesterday. The bin men had been and collected the rubbish. Her clothes, the money and the train ticket were gone.

Tess listened to the silence. The constant talking had ceased. The constant boiling of the kettle had stopped. She had insisted she was all right to be left alone and, without wishing to offend anyone, would prefer it that way. Daniel's mobile had been staring at her from beside his kitchen knives for the last hour. Anne and Ed, Vivien and Mark had been there all day yesterday and all day today and not noticed it. She was desperate to hide it and too terrified to turn it on in case it rang with a call from the postcard messenger.

Daniel met a man. But that's all she knew. He hadn't said where he'd been for all those hours he was missing or how long he was with them. Had this person now gone away? She'd checked the post box after her visitors left, fearful of finding a new message. This person and now this phone were a constant threat to her peace of mind. She would leave this house as soon as she could. She would go back to London, go back to her maiden name so that this person could never contact her again.

When someone knocked on her door at nearly seven, an uneasy feeling began in her stomach. The red-haired officer was back in her house again, along with the pretty female officer. Tess was worried about him being there. She hadn't forgotten his probing eyes following her on the platform that day.

She led them into the kitchen and invited them to sit down at the table.

She automatically turned on the kettle and then faced them.

'I'm sorry,' she said, sounding as exhausted as she looked. 'I remember your faces from yesterday, but I can't remember your names.'

'Pippa,' the woman announced. 'And this is Phil Ross.'

Tess gave a slow nod. 'I'll remember them now. And I'm Tess.'

Pippa took the lead. 'Yes, I know,' she acknowledged with a kind smile. 'Yesterday was a long and very difficult day for you, which is why I'm here now to talk about anything you wish to have explained again.'

'The booklet was helpful,' Tess murmured. 'I take it my husband will have a post-mortem?'

'Most likely.' Pippa nodded. 'The coroner will decide on the type of examination or whether an inquest needs to be held. The coroner's office will contact you if it's decided that your husband's death needs to be investigated.'

'You mean if they think it's not suicide?' she asked in a quiet tone, fearing the reply.

'That's right,' Pippa replied. 'When a body is found in such circumstances we have to determine if death is suspicious, unexplained or suicide. In the absence of witnesses we look for things like a letter or his state of mind during that period. We've spoken with the medical director of the hospital and understand your husband failed to turn up for an operation which subsequently resulted in a patient dying. With this being recent it sounds as if your husband was under a great deal of pressure. This may have caused him to be unable to cope. It will be for the coroner to determine that. This may take several days or even weeks, I'm afraid, but it is important to establish beyond reasonable doubt how the person came to their death.'

Tess gazed at them blankly and Pippa rose from the table. 'Why don't you sit down? Let me make the tea.'

Tess gave a harsh laugh. 'That's what we do, isn't it? Make tea for people when they've lost someone. I've done it. Made tea for others. Even for parents who have lost children. We make them tea.'

Tess sat down and saw the other officer looking at her. He had kind eyes and she was briefly reminded of Cameron. 'Thank you for yesterday and for that day on the platform. You were very kind.'

He gave a polite nod and then got to the point of why he was there. 'As Pippa has said, we are looking into the circumstances leading up to this sad event. May I ask if you've found a letter from your husband? I'm sorry to have to ask, but some people don't like to say as they feel it's private. Which of course it is, but it does help for the police to know.'

'No,' she replied tremulously. 'I've already been asked that yesterday.'

'What about his mobile?'

Her insides stilled as he held her gaze. 'I was told it was switched off.'

'We haven't found one, I'm afraid. And it is switched off. But we've been able to download his data and know when and where it was last used.'

Tess kept her eyes fixed on his face. He was going to tell her it was in her pocket and then tell her about the text message. The one Daniel received to give him the location of where to meet the person who sent the postcard.

'The last time it was used was Saturday at the golf club. Is it possible he left it here?'

'I don't know,' she said, feeling like she was walking into a trap. *Where was the message he would have got?* 'I haven't seen it.'

'Would you mind if I look for it?'

'What difference does it make if you can download his data?' she asked, beginning to get distressed.

'Perhaps none.' He gave a small shrug. 'But I'd still like to try and find it.'

She made to stand, thankful this was over, but he was not finished talking with her yet. His face showed he felt awkward about asking something.

'What is it?' she asked frankly.

His gaze shifted away for a second as if finding this moment difficult. Then he looked straight at her. 'Forgive me asking, but was anything else concerning your husband, other than this incident at work?' She went to speak but his hand rose to stop her. 'I ask because when I saw you that day I noticed the story you told me of how you got burned didn't quite tally with the one you told your friend. It may be that you told it in a different way because you were in a great deal of pain, so it's easily done. But then I heard something afterwards and that *did* cause me concern. For you,' he softly added.

Tess felt the blood drain from her face. *He knew.* He knew what she'd tried to do. Her lips began to quiver and her chin started to wobble. She could not move her mouth properly to talk.

'Take your time and take it easy,' he said. 'There's no rush.'

Tess now understood why he was *really* there. He wanted to know why she had been standing on the very edge of that platform. They were concerned her husband hadn't left a letter. They were concerned at not finding his mobile. Was his death connected to his wife's unhappiness? Had his wife told them the entire truth? Tess would tell them what she believed to be the truth, she would, but not about the postcards and not precisely in the correct order of events.

She was afraid. What she said now could bring an end to her new-found freedom – the end of any point to her life. She'd thought yesterday she'd be arrested, but she'd been given a reprieve because they still didn't know what she had done. Her unborn baby would never know its mother and she would never know her child. If she got this wrong, she would lose everything. And then she would want nothing more than to be back on that platform edge.

'He told you what I tried to do?' she whispered tremulously. 'The platform man?'

Phil nodded. 'Yes, he spoke to me after he recognised you. Said that it was an extremely close call which is why he remembered your face so well.'

She slumped forward to bury her face in her hands.

'When you're ready and when you're able,' he said quietly. 'Just tell us what you can.'

She raised her head, her face stamped with pain. They were waiting for her to speak. She had one chance to get it right. Slowly, she began.

'The day that happened I had just discovered my husband had never loved me. We had only just got married and I was no longer loved.' Tess felt the impact of saying those words out loud and breathed out hard. 'He was unable to love anyone – including me. That was the message he gave me. Then he told me why. He'd kept a terrible secret from me, one that no one should have to bear. My husband was adopted. I don't know at what age he discovered this or when he found out the reason. But what I do know is my husband was suffering a personal agony long before this situation at the hospital happened. Having failed to take my life that day I went back home and I witnessed it. My husband was tormented every day of his life.' Her voice was raw and she needed to pause.

The two officers sat in complete silence as they waited for her to continue.

'When you leave here today there is a file you may want to take with you. It shows the history of what happened to my husband when he was three years old.' Tess felt her throat swell as she imagined that three-year-old boy and placed her hand where her baby would grow. Her eyes blurred as she imagined the same fate for her own child.

'My husband's father was a murderer. He murdered his wife and attempted to murder his son. Daniel was three years of age. It took three days before his mother's body was discovered, and for all of that time he lay beside her in her blood. And it happened in this house.'

Through tear-drenched eyes she gazed at them hard. 'My husband was a brilliant surgeon. If his life ended it is because of what happened to him here, in this house, not because he failed a patient. He was not that kind of man. He would have found a way back from that. His name and reputation is tarnished, please don't let it be tarnished further by what I give you. It would be unforgiveable. I don't want his child growing up knowing his father's history. I want his child only to know the name that will be on the birth certificate. Nothing more. Do you understand?'

Tess could see she had shocked them. Pippa's eyes were stretched as if keeping her emotions in check. Phil had his eyes locked on her face and he visibly swallowed. He then got up from his chair and said he'd have a look for the phone.

Tess felt her hand taken. Pippa was holding it to offer her comfort.

'I'm so sorry,' she said. And then, 'How far gone are you?'

Tess smiled at her tiredly. 'I've only just found out. And I'm so glad I did. I now have something to live for.'

When the two officers left with her husband's file, Tess held in her hand what Phil had found. Not her husband's mobile, but her own from the bookcase in her husband's study on a shelf below the manila files. Which is where, she told him, she had left it.

CHAPTER FIFTY-TWO

In the kitchen she pressed the power button on the side of her phone and saw it come to life with a full battery. She entered her password and was relieved to see he'd not changed it. She'd received eighteen messages. She opened them and was grieved to see Sara's name repeated down the screen. Every single one was hers. She must be thinking Tess didn't care. She would be hurting from getting no reply. Tess clicked on the last message sent four days ago.

Tess, bloody well reply. I know you're in love, but I'm getting worried not hearing from you! X

Tess stretched her eyes wide to hold back tears. Daniel had lied, and denied her this contact with her closest friend. She composed a message to send back.

I'm so sorry to have alarmed you. I'm well, but please don't call as not up to talking yet. Have both sad and good news to tell. Daniel took his own life. Really not up to talking about it yet. I'll contact you when I am. And I'm having a baby, Sara. I'm pregnant. Just knowing you'll be there when I'm ready gives me comfort. All my love, Tess.

The phone pinged a minute later.

Oh God, I'm so shocked I don't know what to say. I'm so sorry, Tess. Please ring me as soon as you can. I'll be waiting. Love you, Sara. X

Tess curled her hand around the mobile. He had taken it as part of his plan to control her. No doubt thinking Sara would eventually give up on waiting to hear from her. She would never tell Sara what he did or allow it to define her future. She was going to leave sadness in the past where it belonged.

When the phone in the hallway rang Tess was tempted not to answer it, but it might be the police wanting to ask something else. She was surprised to hear Stella's voice, having forgotten about the outside world for a while. Stella sounded like she had a heavy cold as her voice sounded clogged.

'Tess, I've got some rather startling news to tell you. The police asked to see inside Daniel's locker and there was a letter in it addressed to me. The police now have it, but I can tell you what was in it as I have a copy. Tess, I'm so sorry. This letter was written three days after John Backwell's operation. Tess, have you got somewhere you can sit down?'

Tess felt her heartbeat in alarm. What had her husband written?

'I'm okay, Stella. Just tell me.'

'Are you sure, my dear, this might distress you?'

'Stella, just read whatever it is, I'll be fine.'

Stella cleared her throat before she began. '"Dear Stella, I did something which has now badly backfired. My patient John Backwell has died. I cast the blame onto my wife, Tess Myers, as you well know, but this is an inaccuracy in my report. It is a lie. Tess cut a suture at my instructions and cut it at the perfect length. The post-op bleed was not caused by her actions. I was aware of a problem during the first operation. I knew I had put my proximal clamp too high and had mistakenly avulsed a vessel on the back of the artery. I used surgical packing which had stopped the bleeding at the time. I thought I would get away with it, and did not want to admit I had made a basic error in front of my wife and team. I should have taken the time to locate the vessel and do a proper repair or make sure it had been ligated.

"'On return to theatre there was torrential bleeding but I was able to maintain proximal control and prevent further loss. I suspect post-mortem findings will prove this tragic event more likely to have been caused by the vessel bleed that I had failed to ligate properly prior to performing the anastomosis. Needless to say my behaviour in all of this has been contemptible. For which I expect no forgiveness. Sincerely yours, Daniel Myers.'"

Tess made no response, prompting Stella to ask if she was all right.

'I'm due to attend my hearing on Friday,' was all she could think to say.

Stella let out a soft moan. 'We're not expecting you to attend that, Tess. This letter will, of course, be put before the board.' The woman paused and then sighed. 'I'm so sorry that he didn't make this known sooner, but I can only imagine he hasn't been in the right state of mind. Tess, I'm here for you if you need me. Please call any time.'

When the call ended Tess finally got to sit in silence. He had caused it. Not deliberately, but accidently. Then blamed her, perhaps thinking the patient wouldn't die. Had he done this solely to save his career or also to stop her working? To mould her into becoming more like his mother and treat her in the same way his father treated his own wife? Tess would need a psychiatrist to answer that. Her husband had been on a journey of conflict from the moment he was left for dead by a father who didn't care.

The day had turned into a day of revelations. His letter being the biggest one of all. He had told the truth even if it was only in secret. Just knowing that gave her some courage for the days ahead. She would now be in a period of waiting. Waiting for the coroner's verdict to come back and waiting to bury her husband. And in that waiting she feared only one thing – the police finding out the truth. The postcard messenger was still out there and so was the man who took her husband's body away.

CHAPTER FIFTY-THREE

In the hallway Tess shivered from the coldness blasting in through the open front door. The weather over the last five weeks had gradually turned colder and colder. The bookies were predicting a white Christmas and they could be right if it dropped a degree or two. Parked between the gate posts and taking up nearly the entire length of the drive, a large removal van sat with doors wide open. It had taken hours to pack by the two men working hard, and was almost full. There was only space left for smaller items.

The men's footsteps echoed loudly from the stone floor of the hallway, louder now than when they first arrived some hours ago. The house, empty now of nearly all of its furniture, was making a great deal of noise. She kept back just a few items, a bed and some chairs, especially a Queen Anne chair which her daily visitor liked to sit in, and a cot she'd found in the attic. Large rectangular patches of wall marked out the spots where paintings had hung. She'd been given back her wedding photograph after the inquest, but had chosen not to put it back on the wall. Eventually, such personal items would disappear altogether. She needed no other reminders of her past life apart from her growing bump.

At the inquest an open verdict was reached by the coroner's jury because intent of suicide could not be proven. The train that hit him had not been identified. No reports had come to light of bumps felt or damage found from any driver. For which Tess had been thankful, not wishing to have on her conscience someone out there thinking they'd killed a man. It was explained freight trains more often travel at night. Sometimes even when something is felt if nothing obvious is seen trains just carry on. It was something she could live with at least. Ed and Mark and Vivien rarely referred to it, but she knew they all thought the same, that it was the state of his mind that brought him to that railway track. Whether to intentionally kill himself or just to get away for a while, he had not been thinking straight.

If Anne thought differently, she kept it to herself and Tess was grateful. That chapter was closed. Nancy and Stuart Myers never spoke about the circumstances of their adopted son – and the newspapers so far had not revealed the identity of his real father. Tess suspected it was the coroner who decided to keep that information under wraps, maybe out of respect for the Myers. They had, after all, been his parents – the ones who had raised him. His real father was in hospital and she'd been asked if she could visit. Something she was not looking forward to.

Her eyes fixed on the golf bag, pondering what to do with it. A knock on the sitting room door made her turn. The older chap stood in the doorway. She imagined the two men were father and son. 'We're all done, Mrs Myers.'

'Thank you,' she said. The van full of furniture would soon be heading to an auction room. The money she made would go to good use. She'd decided not to run away back to London but to stay and turn the house into a children's home. It was still only at the pipe-dream stage, but she would pursue it once she was sure of staying free. There had been no more postcards but it didn't stop her being afraid. Keeping her baby was all she cared about. She hadn't known how far gone she was five weeks ago and had feared miscarrying due to stress, but she had reached the end of the first trimester as her scan yesterday put her at twelve weeks. It was safe. They were both safe.

The man's eyes gleamed as they rested on the golf bag. 'That's a beautiful set.'

'Do you play golf?' she asked.

He nodded. 'I do. We both do.'

'Take them. They're yours.'

He protested until he realised she was being genuine, and a short while later she waved them off happy with their gift. They might not mind too much that one golf club was missing. As the vehicle exited out onto the road she caught sight of a man standing at the gate and felt her insides flutter. She placed her hands across her stomach. It was five weeks since Daniel's death and she hadn't seen him for all that time. Had he now reflected on what they did and decided it to be too big a secret?

Tess held onto the front door. She could scarcely breathe as she let the *Bradshaw's* book man back into her home.

'I knew you would come,' she said.

He closed the front door. 'I thought you might want to chat about that night.'

She stared around the hallway at all the open doors. She didn't want to take him into any of the rooms. He gestured to the stairs and obediently she sat at the bottom of them. Unable to look at him yet she gazed at the wallpaper and saw the shiny patch where a small tear had been painted over with red nail polish. She had forgotten to ever look for it. She felt it now with her fingertips and then turned haunted eyes to look at him remembering back to that night five weeks earlier.

'I didn't intend to. I didn't plan to... it just happened. He was going to kill me,' she whispered. 'Then afterwards I saw you standing there in my kitchen and I thought I was hallucinating. I couldn't make sense of anything or work out how you were there. He had locked me in. Bolted the front door.'

He nodded and sat down on the floor, leaning against the wall.

His voice was calm. 'I came in through the back. It wasn't locked. When I saw him on top of you I thought at first it was you who was dead. The knife in his hand... all the blood on the floor.

I thought it was yours. Then you blinked and I realised it was his. I made the decision then to just take him away. Take his body to a place where his death could be explained. His body would be…'

'Destroyed,' she uttered in a distraught voice. 'But why would you do that? You cleaned a crime scene. You put me in a bath, though I don't remember it much, but it had to have been you because no one else was there.'

'It had to be done. I knew the police would come knocking on your door as soon as he was found.'

'Only you never warned me it would be *you*!'

'Again, it had to be done. You needed to register shock in view of what we were coming to tell you.'

'That my husband was dead when I already knew?' she asked.

'Exactly.'

'But I still don't understand why. You're a policeman.'

'What I did, I'd do again,' he said simply. 'I have never broken a single law in all of my life, but that night I felt I had to. Too many people have suffered already. You included. And it might not have ended well for you.' He looked straight at her. 'It might have been argued that he held a knife to defend himself. A weapon that was readily available to hand. Whereas a weapon brought into that room might have been seen as intent to do harm.' He gestured towards her bump, starting to show. 'It wouldn't benefit anyone to let it be known you killed him. You don't want your unborn child to carry that stigma their whole life.'

'You couldn't have known then I was pregnant. You didn't know.'

He shrugged. 'True, I didn't. But I knew you weren't guilty of murder, either.'

'How could you have known from just meeting me on a train what I was like, what I was capable of?'

'As soon as I knew who your husband was I knew it was self-defence. You were a type a man like him would pick.' He shook his head slowly and released a long drawn-in breath. 'You were just like another young woman who once lived here. A woman who married for love, who was gentle and kind, whose life was brutally ended by a man who only ever wanted to control her. Her father warned her against marrying him. Her mother grieved for her for half her life. The housekeeper found this young woman and her child covered in blood. She called the police, but it was the woman's mother who came first. And she discovered something that destroyed her. She knew the man who killed her daughter was in this house after it happened. Though her daughter didn't tell her she was running away she'd seen packed suitcases hidden under the bed a few days before.' He paused and stared around at the empty hallway as if only realising all the furniture was gone.

Then he looked back at her. 'There were no packed suitcases found. He'd unpacked them. The prosecutor tried to prove he was in this house after he murdered his wife and therefore would have known his child was still alive, but it wasn't backed up with sufficient evidence. And that's when things got sadly mixed-up in the mother's mind. She thought this man had got away with it. She thought her grandchild was dead. She lost a hold on reality, lost sight of the living, of the people who loved her who were lost from her mind.

'Then one day she surfaced. One day she went out and her husband had to go looking for her. He found her here watching this house. For years she watched it. Terrified that something bad would happen in it again. She knew somehow someday that he could come back. And in her mind he did. The day her grandson came back from the dead.'

'Daniel,' she whispered.

He nodded. 'And she was right. Something bad did happen again. Something bad enough to make you want to jump in front of a train.'

Her eyes stretched wide in her shocked face. 'It was you!' she whispered almost to herself. 'You wrote the postcards! You wrote to Daniel!'

He nodded. 'And I'm glad I did otherwise history may have been repeated in this house. When I met him that morning I warned him his family secret would become public if he continued with his current behaviour. He was fuming that I dared to say such a thing, but not in the least deterred. I followed him not knowing quite what else to do. He drove to a few places, got out at two of them for a drink. And that's when I lost him. I spent the next few hours watching your house. Then as you know the next morning his car was found. I got a shock when I heard where. He'd returned to the spot where he and I met and left it there. I got an uneasy feeling straight away so I drove back here fast and parked up the road and waited. I waited all day. He didn't turn up until dark. I saw your friend leave and then thirty minutes later he showed up on foot.' He shook his head at her. 'He left his car there for a reason. He didn't want it to be seen. I don't know if he intended to disappear afterwards and let everyone think he was dead. He didn't come back here that night to play happy families. He came back to kill you.'

Tess felt she was walking through a maze with no exit. His explanation shed no light on why he was involved in her life in the first place. How he knew who Daniel was? How he knew who his real father was?

Her eyes turned anxious. 'I have to visit his father tomorrow, and I don't want to.'

He leaned his head back and looked up the stairwell and pointed to the chandelier.

'How on earth do you change the lightbulbs in that thing?'

Tess stared up at it, realising she still didn't know. A ladder, she supposed.

His eyes were on her when she looked back at him.

'There's something that I need to tell you, but perhaps it would be better to wait until after your visit. Why don't I come back the day after tomorrow?'

Tess found herself nodding. This man knew her darkest secret yet she wasn't afraid. He wasn't there to harm her or turn her in. She put her hand in her pocket and pulled out Daniel's mobile.

'I found it two days after he was dead by his kitchen knives. I was too scared to give it to the police as it would have a text message from the person who sent him the postcard. The postcard said he'd be sent an address of where he was to meet the person. Only now I know you didn't send him a text as they didn't find a message. So how did he know where to meet you?'

He half smiled. 'I'm a policeman. I wasn't going to leave a message on his phone. I left directions on a piece of paper under his windscreen wiper instead.'

'I didn't know what to do so I hid it in his golf bag.'

He took it from her hand. 'It's gone,' he said. 'It was never here.'

CHAPTER FIFTY-FOUR

Tess delayed going straight to the ward. It had taken three hours and three train rides to get to the hospital to visit this man, yet all she wanted to do was walk back out the door and head home. She would never be ready for this visit. This man had destroyed his son. She wondered how Daniel discovered his real father. Had Nancy and Stuart told him he was adopted? Or had David Simmonds been the one to contact him? The Myers lost contact with Daniel when he turned twenty-five. Was it from then David Simmonds started poisoning his son's mind? It would mean Daniel had been coming to see him for fifteen years. Fifteen years of believing in a man who left him for dead and only on his last visit he understood the father he really had.

David Simmonds could die for all she cared. He had no part in her future, and if she could help it, she would never think of him again. She was here now so she would see him but only this once.

On the ward a nurse asked her to wait before visiting as the doctor would like to speak to her. A short while later a harried-looking man introduced himself as Dr Newman.

'We've been trying to get hold of you for a number of weeks, and have left several messages on your phone.'

Tess stared at him nonplussed. She never checked the house phone now she had her own phone again. It was only by chance she'd answered the call yesterday morning.

'I'm the doctor looking after your father-in-law.'

Tess cut him off before he said anything further. 'David Simmonds is not my father-in-law,' she stated firmly.

The doctor turned visibly flustered, and immediately apologised. 'I do beg your pardon. Your late husband is down as next of kin, and I just assumed.'

'Well, then don't. My husband was adopted after what his father did, and I am only here because I was asked to come.'

'I see,' he said, gaining back some composure. 'So I don't suppose you want to hear about his condition.'

'No, I don't, but I'll see him,' she said.

Tess kept her coat buttoned-up as she made her way to the bed. She didn't want the man to notice her condition. She could see he was tall like his son, even lying down under the covers, and his thick grey hair still had some dark strands showing through. It was his eyes, though, that held her. They were Daniel's eyes, the same dark green. An interest flickered in them as she stood near the bed.

He took his time to speak, and then a small sneer moved his mouth. 'You're like his mother. Dark hair and small. I thought he would have chosen better.'

She felt her face go warm, but she made herself stand there and not turn away.

'He loved his mother,' she answered back.

He harrumphed. 'I dare say he did. So is that all you came to tell me?' he asked.

'Yes,' she said simply. 'That's all.'

Then Tess walked away without looking back.

CHAPTER FIFTY-FIVE

Tess walked up the tree-lined road towards the burial chapel, feeling finally free. The call from Dr Newman last night to tell her David Simmonds had died had shocked her a little. She hadn't realised until that moment that he'd had a hold on her while he was alive. She supposed it was only natural to feel freer with him gone and consigned to the past. Her child need never know about his biological grandfather.

Pushing her face into the wind she walked faster and took the path to the left. Further into the cemetery the grounds became utterly peaceful. The graves dotted on the sloping hills lay in dark grass and plenty of small trees guarded over them. Tess made her way down the westward incline and came to a halt as she saw the fluffy white hair.

She joined Martha at the grave and fixed her eyes on the name on the headstone. Rachel Simmonds. The surrounds would be put back when the mound of earth was settled, and eventually Daniel's name would be added to the headstone below his mother's.

Father John at the church had helped make this happen after Tess first made enquiries about a burial service. She sat with the priest and told him about her husband and he had then introduced her to someone she already knew. Martha. Her daughter Rachel was buried here, and Rachel's father Edward King, 'Ted', was buried in the grave next to her.

Martha had shown her photographs of David Simmonds and Tess had been shaken by the striking likeness of father and son.

Apart from a moustache, Daniel was the image of his father and poor Martha had thought Daniel was her dead daughter's husband. Martha had not connected the dots yet and realised that Daniel had only recently died, she knew it was her grandson buried here and was just relieved he was now with his mother. She might question his age when the date of his death was inscribed on the headstone and that's when Tess would help her understand. But that conversation was not for today. Not when Tess had a visitor coming to the house.

Martha inspected her quizzically. 'That's my scarf you're wearing. He stole it from me from right here in this cemetery. He knew I knew his real name when he saw me as a patient. Shook him up it did. Caught him a few times staring out of the window looking for me.'

Tess felt a shiver run down her spine. She was remembering the times she caught him looking out of the window, and she now knew it wasn't Anne's scarf as she'd asked her. She hoped if he had done such a thing it was because he realised who Martha was and wanted to introduce himself. But if it was to do something bad...

'Then God forgive you, Daniel,' she whispered under her breath.

She squeezed Martha's hand and suggested they go back for some tea as it was too cold to stand there. Martha picked up her large shopping bag, her tiny frame already moving past Tess to get back onto the path. Tess smiled. Martha loved having tea at the house.

Martha came down the stairs and Tess could see her brimming with happiness. She'd just been up to look at the cot. She was lost in the past but living it as if it was the present. A week after Daniel's funeral Tess opened the front door to her. She'd come to offer her condolences. She entered the house cautiously and then a moment later it was as if she'd sensed the darkness was gone as she went and sat in the Queen Anne chair. From then onwards she'd been a daily visitor, happily following Tess around the rooms and Tess loved having her there. She knew sometimes Martha got muddled and regarded her as her lost daughter. Tess didn't mind if it helped erase bad memories. After all, Martha was family. She was going to be her baby's great-grandmother one day.

The *Bradshaw's* book man smiled kindly at Martha as he poured her tea. They had been talking generally on topics Martha picked. Tess sensed he was a considerate man and was curious about him.

'Is that how you met Martha? Did you find her watching the house?' she asked him, quietly.

He glanced across and asked her to hold that thought. Then asked her if she was aware they'd never been formally introduced.

Mild surprise filled her eyes as she realised they hadn't. 'I only think of you as the *Bradshaw's* book man.'

'My favourite book,' he said, deadpan. 'Especially when I'm undercover.'

Tess appraised him more seriously, curious to get to know him. 'Well, I'm pleased to meet you. Tess Myers,' she said.

'James King,' he replied. 'Though Martha prefers to call me Jim.'

'That's right,' Martha said, coming back into the conversation. 'He's always been called Jim. Ted said it suited him better. James, he reckoned, was too big a name for a little boy.'

Tess stared at the two of them, her mind slowly adding it all up until her mouth dropped open. He was one of the people Martha lost sight of, one of the people who loved her who were lost from her mind.

'But you call her Martha.'

Emotion briefly flickered in his eyes. 'I think it made it easier for us both. When she lost Rachel that day I think the trauma made her think she lost me too, as she got confused about who Rachel's little boy was. Martha had a breakdown and when she came out of hospital Daniel was already gone from our life. I was eighteen at the time and had just joined the police. When Martha came home and saw me in her house she smiled at me sweetly and told me her name was Martha.'

Martha took hold of his hand and traced his palm with her finger then she held it against her cheek. 'I had to hide yours and Rachel's handprints from your father.'

Jim had a glimmer of tears in his eyes, but no embarrassment on his face.

'That's right, Martha,' he said. 'Rachel's and mine. She painted our hands and we left prints on the wall. We helped you move the bed and the drawers to cover them.' Then he looked at Tess. 'Martha is my mother. My incredibly brave mother. And Rachel was my incredibly brave older sister.'

Tess stared at the two of them and felt quite stunned. All the time she'd been surrounded and watched over by Daniel's grandmother and his uncle. She didn't realise she was crying until Martha handed her a clean hankie.

'It's just hormones, dear. I was exactly the same when I was expecting.'

Jim patted his mother's hand gently.

'That's right, Martha. She'll be fine in a minute. It's a lot to take in all in one day. A lot for anyone to take in,' he said, looking at Martha and then at Tess. 'But you'll get there. You'll see. You're not alone. You have family now.'

A LETTER FROM LIZ LAWLER

Dear reader,

I want to say a huge thank you for choosing to read *The Next Wife*. If you did enjoy it, and want to keep up to date with all my latest releases, just sign up at the following link. Your email address will never be shared and you can unsubscribe at any time.

www.bookouture.com/liz-lawler

I hope you loved *The Next Wife* and if you did I would be very grateful if you could write a review. I'd love to hear what you think. I was inspired to write this story from working in a railway station and seeing all the people taking the train. Going to work. Going on holiday. Or shopping or visiting family or friends. It's incredibly sad sometimes to meet people who don't know where they're going. They're not lost because they don't know where they are. They're lost because of unhappiness. When I wrote this story I found myself remembering them and hoping that they found a new journey. We never know who we will meet, but I'm always mindful of that person stood beside me on a platform, they may not always have a journey to make.

I love hearing from my readers – you can get in touch on my Facebook page, through Twitter, Goodreads. If I'm late in responding please never think it's because I don't care or that

I've ignored your name, it's only because I'm absent for a little while writing.

Thanks,
Liz Lawler

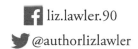 liz.lawler.90
@authorlizlawler

ACKNOWLEDGEMENTS

So many amazing people have been with me on this journey who I wish to thank. So casting all barriers aside I'm just going jump right in and say this from the heart.

I'm indebted to my agent, Rory Scarfe, for being by my side and believing in me. Only seventeen more books to go before we say goodbye.

I would like to thank my editor, Cara Chimirri, for her unwavering support and amazing insight at seeing a better way for me to tell this story. It has a been complete pleasure to work with you.

I'm extremely thankful to the brilliant Bookouture team for all their hard work and creativity that went into the making of this book and am thrilled it was given such a showstopping cover!

I would like to give a very special thank you to Miss Samantha Williams BSc MBBS FRCS (Gen Surg) Oncoplastic Breast Surgeon for sharing her awesome expertise and for showing these characters in this story how it's really done! And for going to ingenious lengths to deliver me a perfect letter.

All mistakes are of course mine.

Thank you to Theatre Sister Alena Studentova and Registered General Nurse Mr Srinivas Bailoor Pai for letting me walk in your shoes and stand at the operating table. Your help was invaluable.

I wish to extend my sincere gratitude to Inspector Shawn Taylor for tirelessly answering all my questions in such a generous manner and for allowing me to shadow the officers. Thank you to PCSO

James Turner for your kindness for explaining so many details I didn't understand.

Closer to home, my husband Mike. Thank you for putting up with a pyjama-clad wife for half a year and for not minding too much that I thought we were in September when we were only in March. I couldn't have done it without you!

My thanks to Martyn Folkes for keeping it honest. My brother-in-law Kevin Stephenson and sister Bee Mundy for reading all of first and second drafts! Bradley Gould for dropping everything and sorting out my lost files and for lending me his name also. Michael Knight, my son-in-law, for knowing about trains. Harriet, my daughter-in law, for forcing me to take breaks and watching out for me! To my brothers and sisters for being there when I finished.

To the loves of my life Lorcan, Katie, Alex. Thank you for letting me spend a crazy amount of time away from you without once asking if I'm nearly finished. Alex, thanks for sharing lockdown with me and putting up with my habit of mumbling to myself as I write.

To Darcie, Dolly and Arthur the lights of my life always.

To the incredible frontline workers. You inspire me every day.

To the amazing GWR team at Bath Spa railway station. This story started there. From wondering about all the people who start their journey by getting on a train. To wondering where their journeys end.

Finally, for Mum. Hope you like Martha…